Silent Thunder

Archie Macpherson

Ringwood Publishing

Glasgow

First published in Great Britain in 2014 by
Ringwood Publishing
7 Kirklee Quadrant, Glasgow G12 0TS
www.ringwoodpublishing.com
e-mail   mail@ringwoodpublishing.com

ISBN 978-1-901514-11-7

British Library Cataloguing-in Publication Data
A catalogue record for this book is available from the British
Library

Typeset in Times New Roman 10
Printed and bound in the UK
by Lonsdale Direct Solutions

About the Author

Archie Macpherson was born in Shettleston in the east end of Glasgow and began his professional life as a teacher in Lanarkshire. He started writing fiction in his early teaching career before coming Headmaster of Swinton School in 1965. His first short story appeared in the Glasgow Evening Times, followed by stories for the BBC Morning Short Story series.

This all preceded his career in sports broadcasting which began fully professionally in 1969 with BBC Sport where he went on to be the principal presenter of *Sportscene* and broadcast as a commentator in six World Cup Finals and four Olympic Games. He then became a regular broadcaster for Scottish Television.

He has written several biographies including the best-selling and critically acclaimed *Jock Stein: The Definitive Biography*.

Upon moving on from full time broadcasting, he has returned to his first love, fiction.

Silent Thunder is his first novel. He is currently working on the second of a series of adventure stories.

Acknowledgements

It seems like it is always my first act to thank Pat Woods, who has researched six books already for me and who for this work made the transition from biography to fiction with enthusiasm and relevant advice.   Tom Brown, former assistant editor of the *Daily Record*, cast a professionally stringent eye over the text which was of great value.   Hugh Macdonald of the *Herald* lent me the confidence to seek publication and Paul Brennan, a good friend, was always on hand for a chat on the issues within.   The information from the Crail Museum and Heritage Centre added impetus to the narrative as did the invaluable assistance of Laura Adamson and Jill Dryburgh of the Scottish Seabird Centre at North Berwick.

I am indebted to Sandy Jamieson at *Ringwood Publishing* for eagerly accepting the novel, and to my editors, Isobel Freeman and Amy Glasgow, for their hard work and charitable forbearance.

My wife, Jess, has always inspired me simply by always being nearby, enduring the many hours of solitude imposed on her by my writing periods with inestimable tolerance, and making even the occasional decaffeinated tea she serves seem like the elixir of life.

Dedication.

To Jess with love.

Chapter 1

Telling the truth, the whole truth and nothing but the truth was not an option for him. Tam had started that morning with deception, and it had to continue that way. They had asked him to empty his pockets since they must have been suspecting possession of drugs. All he had on him was some small change and the envelope with the photograph inside. When they had asked him who the man in the photograph was, he had simply said, 'Brother-in-law.' From then on he was anchored to that deception, little realising then how long it was to last.

Now he was in Jane Street police station for the first time, although he had passed it often before and heard many stories about it; the stuff of rumour that gave credence to the notion of 'them and us'. Cell beatings, brown envelopes being passed, and those not exhibiting Glasgow pallor being suspected of illegal entry into the country, were regularly trotted out by those who nurtured local cynicism. Nobody he knew bothered to dispel the turgid rumours except the Duchess, who as usual went against the flow and who had once said that the sight of a police-station in the community was like knowing you had a winter-coat you can reach out for when the frost sets in. Protection against the cold was not what was coming to his mind now. The sun was blazing outside, after all, and his sister Sarah had been griping that very morning about having to be on her anti-histamine tablets for hay fever, even though there was not a blade of grass within several miles of the flat. She blamed the neighbourhood cats for her condition. Tam blamed her excessive make-up which to him at times looked like the product of an infant's finger-painting session. The current weather, which was hot enough to make mascara run, was certainly freakish for the city. So the winter coat idea, from where he was, seemed even more far-fetched than when he first heard it. It seemed suffocatingly warm inside there; a feeling exacerbated by the dull throbbing in his head, as a reminder of the attack that morning, and the growing feeling that he was being allowed to sit there like he was lost property waiting to be picked up by somebody.

He had heard his father say that the police had to contend with too much paperwork now. He felt he was beginning to sense the reality of that around him as they moved here and there around the office with barely a glance in his direction.

Nothing seemed threatening. That's what was galling. And for all that some folk talked about this institution like they were talking about a Stalag, this lot around him looked as if they couldn't cuff a sozzled lollipop man. They had brought him there in the police car because '....there are some things we want you to see,' the young constable in the car explained. 'You can help us with our inquiries.' Maybe being a rookie cop he shouldn't have been talking to him the way he did, but he had made out that Tam's presence at the station was crucial. Crucial? So this is what being crucial is like? Then it changed.

'All right, son. In here.'

The voice broke the boredom siege, and a plainclothes officer stood in front of him carrying papers in his hand. Tam followed him into a small room which was bare of decoration, and of a two-way mirror there was certainly no evidence. That disappointed him. A table and two chairs, the furniture of inquisition, reminded him that he had made a monumental blunder and that acting the Good Samaritan, as he thought he had, was a story the Good Book could have done without. The starkness of the room was intimidating. For the first time he did really feel his nerves twitching. And, he now felt like being clamped into a situation he was beginning to dislike intensely.

'So, sit ye down there, son,' the man said pleasantly enough.

He did as he was told and gripped the sides of his chair, to try to squeeze out some of the tension he was now feeling, like he would an orange for juice. The grey-haired man sitting opposite him had a slight paunch and was showing greasy-looking stain marks on the loosened tie lying on his chest, which suggested sloppiness. However, Tam felt a slight degree of comfort in being faced by just an ordinary bloke who might like to down a few pints of an evening, followed by a curry madras spilling over his tie, and not a smarmy Glasgow cop. On the other hand he might be the kind of bumbling officer he had read about who could take clear DNA evidence and turn it into a pig's breakfast.

'So you're Thomas Brownlie. According to your statement you're 17, live in flat 16a in the Douglas block in Ballater Street and you had an eventful morning. Ok? Eventful indeed,' the man

mumbled to himself. 'Involved in incident....blah, blah, blah...' The
voice tailed off and he looked up at Tam with a mildly suppressed
smile on his face. He was taken aback, for the man suddenly seemed
like he wanted to be seen as a benefactor, exuding a gentle
disposition that would not have been out of place coming from
within an ice-cream vendor's van out on the street.

'Waited long?'

'Ay, is it Christmas yet?' Tam replied, looking through the
window at the late July sun basting Glasgow with uncharacteristic
generosity. He said that without belligerence, more a declaration of
obvious boredom.

'It's like that, eh?' the officer replied. 'We're snowed under at
the moment. Lots on. It just goes from bad to worse at times.'

What are you moaning about? Tam thought. If no crime, then no
job. No job, then scrap-heap. Think yourself lucky.

'Are you in the crime squad?' he asked instead.

'Kind of. Special duties and all that. By the way, why are you
wearing a Barcelona jacket?' he asked Tam suddenly. 'I thought you
might be into Rangers or Celtic.'

'The Old Firm don't have a Lionel Messi,' he replied simply.
'And my ma thinks it's safer anyway.'

The Barca top was almost welded to his body, except on school
days. His mother said the scarlet and blue only made him look pale.
Then she would wonder, aloud, if it was down to the fact that he had
grown so quickly inside a year and was now just over six feet, and
that with his mousey brown hair now cut close to his head, by his

4

own choice, it perhaps accentuated his pale complexion which in itself drew attention to his deep blue irises.

'Bit o' common sense in that, eh?' the detective replied. 'Have you ever been in the Nou Camp?'

'Camp Nou,' Tam replied, being rigorously pedantic about his Catalan loyalty. 'Maybe one day. If we win the lottery.'

'I've been in the Camp Nou,' said the detective, corrected. 'It's like being in the Grand Canyon. Honestly. You feel as if you could get the whole of Spain in there. So you're a television Barca fan then?

'I suppose so. When I get the chance. My uncle has Sky Sports. I go round tae him sometimes.'

'You don't have it at home?'

This all seemed so contrived. But, artificial or not, it was clear he was trying to bond with Tam. He slightly bridled at that last comment, as if the man was pretending he didn't know why he couldn't watch it at home. But he made him aware of it nonetheless.

'We cannae afford it,' he said, looking the man straight in the eye. In truth his mother also hated football and his father hated Sky because he thought their money only encouraged rich, layabout players, and fat slobs called agents. 'The Mafia are intae it,' his father would say, not being prone to sitting on the fence on issues. At that moment he detected a slight change in the body language of the detective; a straightening of his posture on the seat, a more pensive look at the notebook in front of him. And a slight pause before continuing.

'You smoke?'

'Naw. Well, to be honest I've tried it a bit. It was on a school trip to the Lake District. About two years ago,' Tam replied.

'You smoke fags on school trips?'

'It was up one of these hills when nobody was lookin'. We did in a packet between ten of us. I didn't like the taste. I never went back to it. I train hard. We run a football team.'

'Got a future in that, professional like?'

'Naw. I'm no' that good.'

'Drink a lot?'

'A few beers now and again. I never get tae the pukin' stage though. I think I know my limits.'

'Drugs?' the detective added almost nonchalantly.

'What d'you mean?' Tam asked, his voice rising above a mutter for the first time.

'Ever got into them at any time? Any kind? Or been around anybody who deals in them or buys them? Know anybody you hear rumours about? They're not heroes you know.'

Of course he knew about drugs and some of the faces around his neighbourhood associated with them, who wouldn't? You'd have to be deaf and blind not to. But it gave him the opportunity to be frank and honest.

'I've never touched drugs. I don't know anythin' about them. I wouldn't know one from the other. Why are you askin' me this? What's that got to do with why I'm here?' Tam nipped at him, sitting as bolt upright in his seat as he could to indicate indignation. The detective cupped his two hands together and balanced his chin on them. He ignored Tam's reply.

'I've seen so many lives ruined by drugs,' the man said.

'So have I,' Tam snapped quickly wanting to take the wind out of the man's sail. Did the man think he was a mug, a silly boy who didn't know something about what could happen out there in the streets?

'Then you might be able to help us.'

He opened his bundle and produced four photographs, mug shots. Tam looked at the four men and wondered if what he had in his pocket, the photograph he had taken from the scene, without anybody knowing about it, had any connection with what he was now being asked to inspect.

'Any of these ring a bell?'

Tam took time.

'Naw. At least I don't think so.'

'What do you mean?'

'The men I had the fight with wore sunglasses and their dark-hair was glossy and shedded, like they looked after themselves and were into designer stuff and all that. When I think about it I could have been wrestlin' with Armani. And the funny thing is that durin' the fight their sunglasses never came off. Not once. No, these four here are like tramps compared to the two I mixed with. They were swank.'

The officer was obviously disappointed.

'But they looked foreign? Skin colour?'

'White. Dark haired. Like waiters in Benidorm.'

'And the lady? You knew her?'

'Never set eyes on her before.'

The man's tone then changed.

'If you don't mind me saying so this doesn't seem to add up.'

'What doesnae?' Tam asked.

'Everything seems so normal. Everything,' he said. 'Minding your own business, as you told the officers at the time. Going off to visit your grandmother as you insist you were about to do. It's like something out of Red Riding Hood. So let's cut to the chase. I'm genuinely puzzled. Why did you put yourself into a situation where you could have ended up in a slab in the morgue?'

***

Tell me about it, he thought. There were some things you couldn't possibly explain to anybody. Even if his life depended on it, he couldn't actually speak with conviction about what rushed through his mind at the time. There he had been, on that gloriously sunny July morning, setting out for his weekly joust with the Duchess, as the family respectfully called his grannie; a title tinged with discretely-hushed mockery. She was waiting for him, ready to pounce. He had warned his closest mate, Frankie, never even to murmur a word about his weekly visits to the Duchess, for fear of being ridiculed by those who wouldn't know a chess-set from a chest of drawers. They simply wouldn't understand. ' I swear to God, and may my toenails be ripped out wi' bloody pliers if ever I tell anybody that every week you go to play chess with your grannie...and every week you get skinned,' Frankie once promised him. Too true. Tam felt he had been up against it again in his last incomplete session with her when they had sat so long pondering the potential for stale mate, and had agreed for more analysing before the next move. After which, overnight, he had worked out a move he felt exposed a weakness in her pawn defence. *Bishop to Knight 3*. It would work. It was one thing for him to feel that it was bad enough being beaten remorselessly at chess by a woman; but an eighty year old woman at that. She let him away with nothing and had complained about his Barca jacket, because of its association with a city where her grandfather had been killed in its defence against the 'fascist hordes', as she put it, in the Spanish Civil war in the thirties. It still pained her, apparently, especially as the Duchess was still a very political animal despite her age. He had been advised never to mention the name 'Maggie Thatcher' in her presence, and worse, mention 'Tony Blair' and the foundations of the building would be at risk. It made him completely fascinated by her. She was different from others. So it wasn't just about chess. It was about hoping that some of her worldliness would rub off on him, being a wise old bird and still interested in national events around her. Try explaining that to his mates or especially this man with the notebook. No chance.

The detective had been right though. Everything had appeared normal. He had another three weeks off before he went back to his studies and since he hadn't been able to get much part-time work he had the luxury of reading more about physics in a more relaxed frame of mind, and study some of the great chess games, especially the famous Fischer-Spassky encounter in Reykjavik. And he had plenty time to organise his football. So he had been taking his usual short-cut to the bus which would take him to the north of the city. He went past the greystone Evangelical church with another of its catchy slogans on a display-board, *Free Trip To Heaven. Details Inside,* turned into the lane, at the corner of which there was the boarded-up Chinese restaurant whose wholly unfounded reputation for the culinary delights deriving from the canine population had helped towards its demise. Admittedly, he could have walked all the way to Maryhill north of the river, but he was holding himself in store for the five-a-sides later that night. The lane itself was about a hundred yards long. Parked at its entrance was a black Lexus, as if it were deliberately acting as a barrier, for some odd reason. It was empty. So, as he slipped round past the boot, he put his forefinger on the gilt emblem and traced the L, as if it could give him a feel of the luxury the car embodied.

On one side of the lane were the back entrances to shops and small businesses facing the main street. On the other was a bleak row of tenements, boarded up and due for demolition, from which, once upon a time, he developed part of his athleticism by running up and down the stairs kicking people's doors and running, just for hell of it. KDRF they called it. The RF, run-fast bit, was what made it athletic. It had stopped when an ex-para was waiting behind a door one night and caught one of his mates and carried him all the way to the Jane

Street police, under his arm. But these were the good days when they would play twenty-a-side games in the backcourts, on ground which resembled at times pictures he had seen of the battlefield at Paschendaele in the First World War. It had toughened him and given him a certain idea of what the difference was between right and wrong. Kicking or not kicking people can help with that. Now the whole place was a dump, and sadly many of his old friends were scattered to the winds.

The lane was never a busy thoroughfare, and Tam surmised that was because of the emptiness of the tenements and the rumours of druggies or drinkers frequenting that area. But in daylight it was certainly a convenient passage. That is why, at first, he paid little attention to the figures half-way down the lane, in deep conversation.

He kicked at the stones with his trainers, scoring plenty goals along the way against imaginary opposition, until he suddenly sensed something different.

Tam heard what he thought was a quick "No!" barked out. It made him look up. He was about twenty yards from three figures; two men hemming in a girl, mid-twenties perhaps, who had her back to a graffiti-splattered wall and a finger being pointed straight into her nose like it was about to impale her. But he could tell she was angry, her lips firmly pursed and her chin thrust out at them. There was no sign of terror about her. Defiance, that's what it was. She was holding on to what appeared to be a shoulder bag with a long strap and, as they tried to drag it away from her, it was like an unfair tug o' war.

Get outta here, the safety voice inside cried. But that voice got weaker as something was aroused in Tam that was elevated way above thinking of his own safety. That feeling was beginning to take command. They were now trying to drag her towards a door in the wall which separated the lane from the shops. There were grunts and groans, and the muffled sounds of what he considered were threats from the two men, who were dressed nattily in black suits, white shirts and wore shades, very dark shades. The Men in Black came to mind, from the images he recalled from the film.

The girl was making it difficult for them. Wriggling, straightening her arms and bending them, to resist the pull they were exerting on her. As she got to the open door she suddenly put one foot against the wall and pushed. It supplied a totally different leverage to the struggle and it surprised the men. She fell on her back and although she had instant release, her position on the ground just made her more vulnerable again and this time she kicked out with her flat shoes. The kick caught one of the men on the shin and he yelled in anger, grabbing her round the neck and pulling her up, as the other pulled at another leg and dragged her towards the door. Some of the contents of the bag had spilled out on to the ground and he could see this enraged her. She hadn't screamed though. This was certainly not feminine surrender. One of them put his arm round her neck like they might have been in a wrestling ring and squeezed. Her face seemed to change colour. Purplish-pink it may have been but there was no sign of submission about her.

That same man was unprepared for what hit him seconds later. It was Tam's right-foot. He lashed out at the small of the back, using the right edge of the sports shoe, with a sharp push of the thigh, an Eric Cantona-like kick once delivered to an idiot in the crowd. The man knew this was no peace offering and, although he staggered, delivered Tam a short right-hook that caught him on the side of the head and made him feel like his brain was coming out the other side.

His knees buckled slightly. As he had always believed of himself, he was no coward. On the other hand he knew that to survive in this area you had to try to avoid dumb acts that would lead to self-destruction. Translated another way, it meant pick fights you think you can win. But, as he saw the man turning back towards him, and the other clenching his fists and glowering in astonishment at him, he knew he had probably perpetrated the truly classic dumb act to end all dumb acts.

What then followed was a rising anger that he could not restrain, and a mix of flailing arms, kicks, and body thrusts, as the four figures, if seen from above, would have resembled ants fighting over a crumb of bread. No screams, not even curses. Just a grunting mess which was eventually broken up when the girl, falling back, hit her head against the wall, stunning her, and as she did so a voice screamed out from above them.

'I've phoned for the polis. I've phoned for the polis, leave that lassie alane.'

He had quick glimpse of a woman hanging out of a window above the back of one of the shops. The contents of the girl's bag were strewn around the lane now and as he moved towards her, one of the men swung another punch which struck him on the side of the neck this time, compounding the dizziness and making him first slump, then collapse, on his back, his disorientation making the sky above seem watery and about to pour on him, cloudless though it was. He could sense the agitation of the two men as they seemed to be collecting the contents of the bag, scurrying around him, as if they were no longer interested in pursuing any more violence. Then he heard the sound of their feet running, and something being shouted, in what was definitely a foreign tongue.

Tam gritted his teeth and turned to watch the Men in Black head towards the Lexus at the end of the lane. His vision was fuzzy now, but he was able to see they were getting into the car. Astonishingly the sunglasses had remained on their heads as if they were welded there. There was a screech and they were away.

He lay back again, his chest rising and falling erratically, his mind jammed with incoherent thoughts. What was he doing there? How could he get out of the corner he was in with the Duchess who had taken his two knights and a castle in their last session. Would Barca ever sell Messi? How many muggings had he seen? The odd jumble of disconnected thoughts rambled through his brain, defying sense. That tangled thinking was starting to sort itself out when he heard a woman's voice.

'Oh, my God! Are you alright? I saw everythin'. I've called for the polis.'

He managed to look up to see a plump woman in a shop-apron leaning over the girl.

'I was in the upstairs back-shop lookin' for things and happened to look out. My God, what's the world coming tae? I ask you, is anybody safe nowadays. My God! I phoned for the polis. They said they'd be here in five minutes. How are you, dear?' she asked the girl.

Tam's eyes were clearing and he could concentrate on the girl. She was breathing deeply and her eyes had opened. She put her hand behind her head to feel it and grimaced, and then, blinking, she cast her eyes on him. There was firstly a look of bewilderment on her face, dissolving into a calmer appearance as her thoughts obviously re-interpreted what had occurred. The boy had come to her aid. She could clearly get that bit. There was only the slightest pause before she started to get to her feet.

'My bag. Where is it?' she asked falteringly. She looked around the lane, quickly realising it had gone. Then she cupped two hands over her face, as if to weep, but almost immediately pulled them away with a snap of self-assertion, her face now contorted with rage and determination. For a brief moment she did not look like a victim, but, strangely, a victor. Tam slid backwards and sat up against the wall. The sound of a police siren wailed somewhere in the not too far distance, getting closer.

'I'm sorry,' she said, softly.

Her long fair hair had been mauled in the tussle, but she was running her hands through it, and shaping it round her head, as she moved towards him. Even in the confused state he was in, he was surprised at how quickly she had recovered her composure. Indeed, it was as if she was taking stock, coolly appraising the situation and even trying to fend off the overwhelming advances of the woman who had phoned for the police; almost ignoring her, as if she didn't need any sympathy or assistance.

And immediately he knew she was making an impact on him which was as real as the punch he had taken from one of the men. She was pretty. Fair, slender, no make-up, bright eyes. Even in that briefest of encounters he found himself running down the scale of girls he normally fancied, placing her in a kind of ranking. She was certainly well up that ranking. Older than him, of course. But not too much older he reckoned. He simply couldn't help himself from making those judgements, even with his head throbbing with pain.

'I can't thank you enough,' she said. 'I'm not going to hang around. I'll be all right. I'll be safe now. For the time being.....' Her voice tailed off as if she implied something more sinister. 'I don't know what I would have done without you. Please, I'm so sorry. You should get to a doctor. Please leave, when you can, for your own good. They are angry and dangerous men, believe you me. They won't forget you. Please understand that.' The voice, soft but determined, chimed with him in a strange way, like he was not hearing it for the first time; that it had a strange familiarity. Not that anything else was making sense. He was still stunned. The vital part of his body though, his legs, seemed fine. It consoled him that he would still be able to play in the fives later. He hated leg injuries.

They sidelined him and made him feel old. It was then he heard a police siren blaring away, coming up the main street.

'I must go,' she went on. 'Please, believe me. I'm very grateful. I can't wait,' she said, this time with a note of anxiety in her voice. 'I'm deeply, deeply sorry about all this. Thank you.'

Was it his disorientation that was making him believe that he had heard that voice somewhere before? Scottish, yes. But there were certain cadences to it which reminded him of another country, the USA, unerringly so, for some reason.

'C'mon,' the woman from the shop said, 'You need a cup of tea, dear. It'll settle you'

But, as if the very thought of police approaching formed another inexplicable threat, the girl turned and went back through the door in the wall, towards the back of the shops, the shop-woman charging after her like she was an unrepentant do-gooder. The disorientation of it all now began to numb Tam, as he tried to absorb it all, sitting there with his back against the wall. The police siren was now a loud blast, close-by, and he heard a screech of tyres coming down the lane. As he had lain there he had felt a large stone pressing on his back. He put his hand behind him to feel for it, as it was pressing now against his right buttock. He felt more than the stone though. Something like paper. He drew it round to look. Although it was slightly crumpled and there was dirt on the surface he could plainly see it was a manila envelope, slightly bigger than the size of a man's hand, and slightly protruding from it was the edge of a photograph. He slipped it out and saw it was a man standing looking upwards towards the camera. He looked at it for a moment, rose unsteadily to his feet, and was about to make off after her, when he heard a gruff police voice saying, 'Hey, you! Stay where you are!' Tam slipped the photograph into the envelope and back into his inside pocket, without the policeman seeing the furtive action; although it wasn't until much later he realised that that simple act of deception would thrust him into a world where roamed wild animals, purporting to be human.

Chapter 2

Bishop to Knight 3 would have to wait. The girl was his preoccupation now; the violent encounter, her strange warning and a photograph that seemed to stare back at him with the demand, 'Who am I?' as he gazed at it outside the station, completely blotted out the possibility of a routine day. They had quizzed him about the girl, as if they still felt he was not telling them the whole truth. There was nothing he could tell them more. The man, in the snapshot, was maybe late twenties, as he reckoned, wearing a dark pullover, hands in pockets, casual, at ease, cool-looking. The camera angle made him look upwards as if it had been taken from a window on the other side of a street from him. It was at the edge of a cobbled pavement. Nothing more than that.

Then on the back he noticed the faint, spidery writing of a telephone number, a mobile. Hers? He took out his and dialled the number, hoping. The voice that answered was male, clipped, brief.

'Nicholas Carson here. Try me again later or leave a message.'

The voice was very proper. He imagined a business man or something like that. Somebody who probably could afford a centre-stand season ticket. He tried the number several times, as he walked homewards, thinking that he did not feel like uttering a word about this to anybody. If you can't explain events to yourself, what is the point of trying it on others? 'Call me,' he said into his phone.

It was mid-afternoon now. Tam walked back to the lane. He wanted to find the woman who had called the police, to find out if the girl had taken tea with her or said anything. His restlessness had replaced any anger he felt and he had to look for even any slender connection with the girl. In the lane he spotted the window the kindly shop-assistant had come from, then went into the street at the front and judged it to be a shop selling greeting cards, and what looked to him like an assortment of junk. Inside, there were two customers who were prowling around the shelves, watched carefully from the back of the shop by a thin woman sitting in a light-blue overall. He could not forget that kindly face.

'Oh, it's you, son,' she said. 'How are you feelin'? Wasn't that just awful? This place is gettin' worse by the day.....'

'The girl, did she have a cuppa wi'you?' Tam butted in, but phrased himself politely wondering if she had hung around to have the police catch up with her.

'No, no. She got off her mark quick. She was well gone before the polis came round to see me. You see I live above the shop and went to make tea when I saw you from the window. You were lucky I'm a tea-jenny. But I called the police again.'

'When? Why?'

'I was having my lunch upstairs and I saw this big black car comin' down the lane and the same two men got out. I swear to that. They were lookin' for something I think. They gave up and left. But I phoned the police again about them. They still haven't come back to me.'

He knew what they had come back for.

'The girl. Did she say anythin' to you? Anythin' at all. What she was? Where she was goin'? Anythin?'

20

'No. Barely anythin'. Short of words because of what she had been through I suppose. But I would say this to you, son. What was a well-spoken lady like that doin' in that back lane there with these two men wearin' sunglasses? I mean, who wears sunglasses around here. You've got to find that a wee bit peculiar. You'd have to ask a few questions about her.'

If only he could, Tam thought. He left the shop bereft of ideas. The city of Glasgow stretched away in front of him in a series of layers of buildings whose diverse shapes and sloped roofs made him think of mountainous terrain within which any fugitive could easily be hidden. That was what she was to him now, a fugitive. Who was she? Where had she gone? Why the fight in the lane? Was the photograph of her boyfriend? And the Men in Black, how did they keep their sunglasses stuck to their faces while throwing their bodies about?

The street was showing signs of the build up to the rush hour with buses jamming the width of it. Between a gap in two of them he looked across to *The Elgin* pub on the other side. The smokers were outside. Some were leaning against the wall, their banishment from the interior making them look as if they were begging for pity. Two were on seats. He recognised one of them. Dave Wallace was old, or looked older than his years because he always had a fag in his mouth and a pint at his elbow. He was a friend of his father, although with a different outlook on the world. Dave had wanted Baghdad carpet-bombed, whereas his father was part of the Stop The War Coalition on Iraq, and had marched in the streets for it. But at heart they were

21

pals from the 'hauf-and-hauf-pint' bonding. He appeared to sit dead still, talking to nobody, but even when he was speaking he was the kind of drinker who soaked up more than booze when he stared out at his street. He was nosey. It was worth a try.

Tam strolled over until he stood in front of the old man. The eyes rose towards him.

'Your sister Sarah got a job yit?' Dave said, still with his fag perched on the side of his mouth.

'Naw. She keeps trying though," Tam replied. 'It's no' easy, as you can imagine. I just wish she wouldn't take it out on me.'

'Whit d'you mean?' the old man asked, this time reaching forward to lift his beer-glass to take such a minute sip of it, a pigeon could had downed more. He knew how to use his pennies. 'Whit's it got to do wi' you?'

'She's a moanin' git at times, to be honest,' Tam went on. 'She thinks I'm being molly-coddled, being allowed to stay on at school next year and all that. She thinks I should get out and look for a job like the rest of my pals. What jobs are there? She doesnae seem to understand that I get good marks. The teachers want me back.'

'They should never have banned the belt,' Dave said abruptly, as if it was a favourite gripe of his, brought up at the least opportunity. 'A good hammering off a teacher never did me any harm.'

Tam looking down at the beer, the fag, and listening to the wheezing coming from the chest, felt Dave's personal advocacy of the belt would barely stand up in court.

22

'There's something I wanted to ask you,' Tam asked instead. 'You been here long?'

'As always. Since about mid-morning, when the pub opened.'

'Did you hear the police sirens this morning?'

'Ay, in fact I saw their car racing down towards the end of the street there.'

'They'd be turning into the lane. There was a bit of a disturbance there this morning. Did you see anythin' else unusual after that? Like anybody coming out of the close over there?' he said nodding in that direction. 'That close is really only used by the ironmonger. Anybody else might have caught your eye?'

Tam hoped his voice was revealing no hint of his desperation for information. He was trying to remain cool. The old man shrugged his shoulders. Speeding police cars? There were plenty, all the time.

Dave took the tiny stub of fag out of his mouth and rubbed a stubbled chin with the free hand. 'Maybe......'

'Well?' Tam encouraged.

'Could've been.'

'Could've been what?' Tam prompted.

'A girl was over there on her mobile. I remember that. Ay, she might have come outta that close. Dark blue jacket. She started to kinda half-run towards the *Arrow* taxi-office down there.'

He was pointing to a large Nissen hut that looked unique amidst the surrounding buildings. Tam had passed it often. It was set back from the street, in what had been waste ground after the first tranche of tenements had been demolished. It had looked like something temporary at first, but had been there for years now.

'Tell me this, Tam. Do you fancy this bird?'

But all that Dave was left looking at was Tam's back as he jinked across the road to avoid the traffic, heading for the taxi office. When he reached it, he didn't stand on ceremony but pulled its front door open so violently it almost came off its hinges. He found himself staring into the face of a lady whose skin suggested she had fallen into a vat full of oranges. He knew other sun-bed addicts but this was definitely the Orange Queen. She was staring at him, eating a sandwich. A crackling noise was coming from the large battery of equipment to one side of her, behind the counter. A voice was heard, from one of the drivers out on the road.

'Did you say Rambling Road, or Rampton Road?' was the ethereal request.

She put down her sandwich coolly, bent towards a microphone, made her last chew, swallowed and then spoke.

'Ramp-ton....as in Trump-ton,' she spoke with great and perhaps over-theatrical emphasis. 'Did your weans never watch Trump-ton, on the telly, Alex?'

'I only ever let them watch serial-killer films. You know me!' replied the voice from somewhere.

'Oh, I do indeed. How many kids have you run over today?' she asked with a sigh and went back to her sandwich again, as if Tam simply wasn't there.

'Can I help you?' The voice came from behind him and with it he heard the running of a toilet having been flushed. A woman had emerged from what he supposed was the office washroom. She was slightly stooped and there was an aroma of tobacco about her.

'I hope you can,' Tam replied. 'I'm lookin' for somebody. She left somethin' behind. Did a girl come in here lookin' for a cab about eleven or eleven-thirty this morning? I don't know where she was headin'. Would you have anything about her in your records, by any chance?'

'We don't give out any information about our clients,' she said. 'You could be a stalker or something like that.'

'Do I look like a stalker?'

'Nothing would surprise me nowadays? Swat up on the privacy laws, son,' she said as if she was attending night-school for them.

The woman with the microphone then turned to him and stared, a look of recognition spreading over her face.

'Hey, you're Tom Brownlie's son, right? I recognise you now. You're at school with our Betty, right? You know the one that plays the guitar, right?'

'Right,' he replied.

'Of course, of course I know who you are. Now we have to be careful about what we can say about our hires, but seeing it's you.......Anyway what are you after her for? Now that I think about it, isn't she a wee bit out of your age group, right?'

'It's not like that. She left something behind her and I want to return it.'

The other woman was looking as if she was not wholly in agreement with this and walked in semi-circles, back and forward, behind them. The orange-faced lady was speaking into the mike.

'Pat...Pat Murphy. D' you hear me?'

A crackling response came.

'Ay. I'm heading back from the airport....'

'I think you picked up that girl just outside of the office here this morning, right? Well, where did you drop her off, what address?'

'It wasn't an actual address.'

'Be specific, right?'

'It was at the front of Kingslie Industrial Estate, right at the entrance.'

'She say where she was goin' from there?'

'She never spoke a word.'

The woman turned and looked at Tam, wishing to be appreciated for what she had done.

'Kingslie Industrial Estate. Never been there,' he said, trying to display some kind of gratitude even though what had been revealed had a vagueness to it. 'I suppose it's vast, right?'

'Better than nothing, right?' she said.

'Right,' he replied and thanking her he took his leave hoping that she would take to the bottle for her skin colour, not the sunbed. Then his phone rang. It was a mate, his voice like a fire-alarm.

'Jesus Christ, where have you been?' Frankie Anderson rattled out to him. He was the kind of person who liked to know that the whole of humanity had to be within arm's reach of him constantly, and that the phone system was entirely his alone. 'I was expectin' the usual call from you. We're one bloody player short for the fives tonight. We could be in deep shit. You might think the Tradeston team are a bunch of poofs. But we're minus big Eck and you know how bad that can be for us since he could put the fear o' death into Dracula. So where the fuck have you been?'

'If I told you, you would never believe it,' Tam replied.

'Try me!' Frankie replied.

Chapter 3

Ten minutes later they were together, sitting in a corner of the *Khyber,* or as they always called it, Gabby's Place; a cross between a cafe, a fast-food shop and a newsagents. There was never any bevy in there. It was taboo. They got their fill of that in other places. Despite his initial reluctance to tell anybody anything, Tam wanted to unburden himself now, in this congenial atmosphere letting it all spill out, even though it made little sense to himself.

'The Kingslie Industrial Estate? Are you kiddin'?' Frankie said on hearing the conclusion. 'It's like a wee town.'

Tam and his mate were gazing occasionally at the photograph of the man which lay on the bench between them. The mobile was burning a hole in his pocket. There was nothing worse than waiting for a possible call.

'Let's face it, pal,' Frankie said, 'You hivnae a clue *who* he is, and you don't have an earthly *where* she is. In fact you know bugger all about what this is about. And maybe you'll never clap eyes on her again. Apart from that, things are looking up for you.'

'The only thing I can go on is that phone number on the back. It's at least somethin'. These men came back looking for this. That's for sure. But they couldnae find it. That's obvious,' Tam said looking down at the photograph.

He had told the story in graphic detail, with little need for exaggeration, to the slightly beefy Frankie who was wearing a white teeshirt bearing the emblem 'The Smithsonian Institute', the acquisition of which was still a mystery, to even his nearest and dearest, as he had never been further west than Greenock. The knees of his blue jeans were almost white and probably they were hand-downs from his two older brothers. Frankie was not the sort who could morph into anonymity, even if he had wanted to. He had a mop of red hair, which was largely unkempt; had a long loping stride which always conjured up an image for Tam, of a clansman off to fight at Bannockburn, or, as in the case of Frankie, who moaned constantly about life not doing him any favours, Flodden. The blue jeans, which were slightly short for him, exposing red stockings encasing large feet in black trainers, did not disturb that image. Not that his friend was fully conscious of this, as he exuded the impression to his friends of a self-image based on an elegant D'Artagnan, handy with a rapier. His ambition in life of becoming a chef was based on the glamour which television had attached to those countless kitchen programmes on the schedules. He could rave about the uses of a Kenwood Chef mixer as if it were a magical tool straight out of the Hogwarts School of Witchcraft and Wizardry.

Tam could hardly deny what his pal had just said though. He felt lost. He just went along with Frankie's obvious suggestion.

'You're right. The Kingslie Estate is no' much to go on. But I'm going to get a list of the firms there. That'll be a start.'

'Why don't you just chuck the photograph in the nearest bin? It's not as if it's a string o' valuable pearls, is it?'

'Because there's more to it than just a photograph. Or else there wouldn't have been a fight.'

'Look,' Frankie said, putting down his can on the seat beside him, as a calculated warning that he was about to offer Tam some sound advice. Frankie had a disarming modesty about his intelligence or lack of it. He had a habit of declaiming, 'Alright, I know I'm as thick as shite, but......' before going on to dazzle folk with the wisdom of the under-appreciated. He didn't bother with that introduction for Tam. 'All this happened about six hours ago or so. Right? Are you tryin' to tell me that after that short space of time you've decided you're gonnae spend the rest of your life chasin' after a bird who got you into trouble, whose name you don't know, who probably doesnae want to know you, who would get you into more trouble if you ever found her by the looks of things, and I'm supposed to sit here and listen to this crap. Get a life, man!'

Tam was hardly taken aback, as he had expected this. Now, he assumed, would come the theorising. It did.

'As I see it, here is this posh bird, comes down into where she hears she can pick up drugs,' Frankie continued. 'She's probably one of these ones who think we're all muggers and dealers and hoodies here and doped up to our fuckin' eyeballs and all that. She probably plays tennis, for God's sake. You know the kind. Anyway there is an argument about price. She doesn't want to fork up. They are no' havin' any. So they bash her about. You arrive on the scene, there's this right barney, and she gets off her mark when the polis arrive because she doesn't want her pals in the tennis club in Newton Mearns to hear she's been nicked for trying to get wee white packets. Tell me I'm wrong!'

Tam registered neither approval nor disapproval but simply surveyed the sweating Gabby handing out food to the occasional customer and stuffing money into the cash-register. He had thoughts racing through his head, and questions he had been asking himself ever since the girl had left. He had held them in store in his mind until he could try to make some sense of it all. Now was time to air them.

'In the whole of the city of Glasgow, why that place?' he muttered almost to himself. 'I don't think it was drugs, like you say. It just doesnae seem right. We know the people who push drugs around here, or think we do. The two men didn't belong to this area. I know that. So why were they there in that spot? Now if they didn't belong to the area but obviously knew about a quiet lane, then somethin' or somebody must have directed them there.'

'The girl herself?' Frankie interrupted. 'She would want somewhere private, in case somebody might recognise her. Then she could do the business with the drugs.'

'I don't buy that. Naw, it was another reason. I don't know what, but I just feel something different. They could have had a thousand other places to meet if it was for drugs. No. Something else brought them there. I don't believe they got their heads together over a street map of the city and decided on that place. It doesnae wash. I don't believe the police would think that either.'

'But do they believe *your* story?' Frankie asked. 'You know what the polis are like. They'll follow any lead, any hint, any sniff, any suggestion. They're after the dealers and if they think you've been doing some runnin' for them, then they'll keep their eye on you. Nae apologies for tellin' it straight. They followed my cousin Davie all the way to London just because they thought he had been linked with a dealer from Shettleston in the east-end. They nabbed him at Euston station when he was handin' over a parcel to his contact. It was a cake my aunt had baked. A present for her sister he was going to visit. They never even apologised. The point is they don't let up when they think drugs are involved. Now you got yourself into this and I find it hard to accept you just waded into two men to help a girl you'd never set eyes on before. Great! But how stupid can you get? You pay the price. The polis will be keepin' their eye on you now, pal!'

'Give me a bloody break,' Tam responded. 'It was a one-off fight, that's all.'

'But the girl got off her mark. That's what'll make them suspicious.'

Tam looked out to the street and had a quick look in either direction, as far as he could from a seated position. It was a knee-jerk reaction which immediately he regretted. He certainly did not want to stand up and peer out of the window in response to what had just been said to him, although if he was being perfectly honest with himself, that is what he felt like doing. An old woman shuffling along in what looked like carpet-slippers, and carrying a bag full of groceries, passed in front of the window.

'Look at her,' Frankie said dryly. 'She could be Special Branch for all you know. They could be on to you now.'

They certainly knew of stern plainclothes police who had come to quiz people in the neighbourhood at the height of the Irish troubles. Some of them had looked like they were just dossers. You could tell they meant business though. But Tam knew there was little he could now do to stop the avalanche of ridicule he would now have to sustain.

'They'll be watchin' you when you don't expect it,' Frankie went on. 'And just think of these two men you banjoed. They might be looking for you as well. Ever seen that movie *The Fugitive*? Get a DVD of it and learn how to duck and dive. I don't think I should be seen near you for the next few months! You could be in deep, deep shit, right enough.'

But then he put his arm round his friend shoulders and, as if Tam had not to take it so seriously, added, 'Ach, you've faced up tae worst. Like when I was sent off in the final last year. You understood why I kicked the bugger in the balls. Remember he called me a 'fuckin retard'. And you made that wee speech at the end o' the game to the rest of the lads that I had....what was it?'

'Meted out justice,' Tam slipped in.

'Ay, and even supposin' some of them didnae have a clue what that meant you did make them believe, well, up to a point, that I hadn't let the side down even though we got hammered 6-1. It must have hurt that. Now I don't forget these things.'

'Hey, what are you two cookin' up,' Gabby shouted from behind the counter. 'Can you not spend a bit more money in here? Two Irn Brus in about an hour. I have mouths to feed and taxes to pay and the likes of you two are doing me no good whatsoever. You hurt me more than Tendulkar!' The fact that the genial Gabby had brought up the subject of India's greatest batsman, who had put Pakistan to the sword on so many occasions, meant that the owner wanted a knockabout argument where they would pit their wits against him. But neither of them were now in the mood for that. They were sitting on benches that were there for people who wanted to eat on the premises and not takeaway. They had come in once with cans of beer and Gabby gave them the full blast of someone who still sought redress from the days of the Raj. They had to make do with that fizzy stuff that was supposed to be made from girders. On one side of the shop was the fast-food counter serving all the delicacies, and certainly the crudities, of sub-continental cuisine, from chapatis to khatchapuri, pakoras of many varieties, samosas and their favourite, eggrolls. On the other side was the other world, the conventional counter, selling newspapers, cigarettes and soft drinks, presided over by Gabby's Glasgow-born wife Mira who would scold Gabby like he was just out of nursery school.

A journalist, who had stumbled on the place once, wrote in a magazine that it was a model for multi-culturalism. Bullshit to that, they had all agreed. Gabby was just a good-natured simple fella from the Punjab who had acquired a Glasgow accent, on top of his own fluent sing-song command of English: the effect being like a flute sounding above a full orchestra. He was a business man, with the street market know-how of how to sell new ideas to old prejudices. He had bought a failing boutique and proceeded to split it into those two unified outlets for healthy commercial reasons. They had long since forgotten what his real name was, and had always called him Gabby because of the rate at which he spoke, and the sometimes impossible task they faced of trying to shut him up.

Tam and Frankie would sit there, sometimes for a whole evening, or afternoon, depending on the weather, and try to make sense of life. Gabby's inputs were essential. He claimed an honours degree from Bahria University, Islamabad, and who were they to question why a man with such a learned background could ultimately end up selling chapatis in Glasgow?

'Money is not necessarily the root of all evil,' he once told them in discussion about entrepreneurship. Although it was clear from his sponsorships of various events that he was loaded. They hung onto much of what he said to them, and he welcomed them for many reasons, not the least of which that they spent a few bob in the place and encouraged their friends to visit as well. They could tell that day that he was not in his usual ebullient mood. They had just heard that Pakistan had been bowled out for 85 against Sri Lanka. Gabby loved cricket and intoned about it with the grave authority of a man who would brook no dissent from his opinion. Neither Tam nor Frankie had the slightest interest in, nor knowledge of, cricket and simply nodded assent to his comments, not wishing to offend him.

Sometimes when it was quiet he would sit down with them and talk about 'tragic and beautiful Kashmir.' They knew even less about Kashmir than they did about cricket and consoled him with their support over his obvious distress caused by human-rights issues, whatever they were, in those far-off valleys.

'You two down in the dumps?' he asked wiping a large fleshy hand over his thinning damp scalp, like a window cleaner with a squeegee. 'Is it about girls?'

'Fitba',' Tam said quickly. 'We cannae get a side together for tonight.'

'Hasn't Glasgow already proved that football is a sport for hooligans? You have your priorities all wrong.'

They were not going to rise to that bait though.

'Bat and ball and a firm wicket. That is what you call civilised recreation. I have seen your knees when you come off that all-weather thing you play on and they look as if they have been treated by a paint stripper. Why would you want to do that to yourselves? Anyway footballers don't entertain you, they rob you. Look at what they're paid for running about for ninety minutes. Fortunes. It is obscene.'

'Money isn't necessarily the root of all evil,' Frankie quoted back at him.

'For kicking a ball, and people, it is.'

Tam could not raise a word. The shopkeeper sensed this morose mood.

'Hey, what is the matter with you Tam? Really, what is the matter? I've never seen you looking as if the world was coming to an end. You short of a few bob? You in love? Anybody bothering you?'

That last question was at least pertinent. One of the principal reasons for their respect for Gabby was that everyone had known that he had stood up to a local gang who had been seeking protection money. He had effectively told them to take a hike. Then the leader of that gang was thrown off Dalmarnock Road bridge into the river Clyde, by three masked men, according to on-lookers; suggesting that Gabby had powerful street friends. Nobody threatened him after that. He was no patsy.

Tam decided it was time to speak up and clarify at least a little of what had gone on that day.

'This is just between you, me and Frankie. OK Gabby?' He had to add that rider before he said anything else, for if he didn't, and said anything out of turn, then before midnight the entire Pakistani community in the city would hear about it, not to say a few in the far-off Hindu Kush. But Gabby was, despite his garrulity, as he had proved on so many occasions, a man whose word could be trusted, and who, despite his efforts to portray himself as a lightweight joker, was the man who could summon up masked-men to throw people off bridges.

'I found this photograph in the Fairwell Lane this morning. I was involved in a punch-up with some bampots who were attacking a girl.'

'Ah, bampots,' Gabby sighed. 'Where else other than Glasgow could crooks and villains have such a description that reminds me somehow of my childhood and the pots we used to dispose of human waste when nothing else was to hand. Brilliant. Couldn't think of better myself.'

'This came from her bag I think,'Tam went on as if he hadn't been interrupted. 'I'll say no more than that. I have to find her and give it back. And I don't know where she is. She just disappeared.'

He handed the photograph to the shop-owner who cradled it in the palms of his hands as if he did not want to deposit any grease on it and sniffed.

'You fancy the girl?'

'It's nothin' like that.'

'You want to find her with no ulterior motive, other than to give her back a photograph of a man looking up to the sky at something?' Gabby went on. 'That's all? Nah, I think you must fancy her.'

'Please. For a start she's older than me. As for the fella in the photograph, I don't know anything about him. She obviously thinks these men wanted it. I have a feeling that this is what all the trouble was about in the lane. I just don't know. I'm guessin'. I've got to find the girl. She's owes me an explanation.'

'You said you had a punch-up,' Gabby said, still peering at the photograph as if he were perusing a menu. 'You know who they were?'

'Never seen them before.'

'You know that if you are in any trouble you must let me know. I think you are perfectly aware that I can help.'

As he said that Gabby's eyes narrowed and his voice lost its sing-song tone and became deeper and more deliberate, to add significance to what he was saying. He was talking to ready believers. Then he stroked his chin, looked again at the photograph and asked almost to himself,

'Why would a photograph be all that important? Nostalgia? Romance? Holiday memories? Maybe all three!' Then he added more philosophically, 'No, it is not a holiday snap. It's.......' He paused, ruminating. 'It is a record. There is nothing amusing or attractive about it because it is only about a man. A man in a specific place. Standing on cobblestones. Where do you get cobblestones now? It does not tell us too much.'

'The woman who called the polis told me these same men came back to the lane to look for somethin'. I think it was this. It was the only thing left after the fight.'

They stood up on either side of him looking down at the photograph trying to see it in the same context as the shopkeeper. It looked back stubbornly and silently at them. It merely conjured up more images of the girl in Tam's head. He thought of how quickly composed she had become after the incident. There were no hysterics, no emotions of any kind other than steeliness set in her face. She was one tough cookie.

'Snap out of it,' Frankie barked. 'She's given you a dizzy. You'll never hear from her again. C'mon, we've got the fives to think about. It's gettin' on. We've one hour left. I've made the calls and we'll just have to wait to see who turns up.'

Gabby walked away to tend more customers and made the parting comment.

'All social problems to be solved on a football pitch? Huh! What a forlorn philosophy.'

Tam slid the photograph inside the envelope again, carefully, like it was part of a treasure trove. As he did so he felt a slight vibration passing through his body as if it had found a nerve ending, followed by a ring tone and to which he responded as if he had been touched by a cattle prod. His phone had come alive. Tam walked quickly out of the shop to get away from the others, ramming the phone to his ear.

'Hi,' he said expectantly. It seemed to be an eternity before the voice at last replied.

'Good afternoon,' it said. He recognised the man's voice right away.

'Nicholas Carson?' Tam asked, recalling the recorded name.

'I think you may have called me earlier in the day. Who are you? Your number is unknown to me.'

'My name is immaterial. What matters is that I have a photograph wi' your phone number on the back. It would be simple enough but for the fact that I got involved in a fight wi' a girl to save her from bein' battered by a couple of men and by pure chance I ended up wi' this. Plus a few bruises.'

'I see.'

'And I want to know just what this is all about?'

'The photo. You still have it?'

'You bet.'

'I think I know what you are talking about. Of course I am interested in acquiring it.'

The voice was soft and extremely polite, 'toff speech' the Duchess called it, particularly blaming it on most folk from Edinburgh.

'But I want to return it to the girl. It's hers. It came out of her bag. That's the first step.'

'Please, don't be hasty. There could be some value in it for you. If you knew the full story you would realise that I would have first claim on it.'

'How long would the full story take to tell me?'

'Till your bedtime. It is too complicated to explain over the phone. We would have to meet.'

'I want to meet the girl. Nothin' else will do.'

There and then the realisation was growing on him that although getting the photograph to her was the basic transaction of this whole business, their encounter had been so brief, it was almost as if it hadn't happened at all. He felt the uneasiness of something inexplicably gripping him, like a feeling of imminent entrapment.

'H'mm,' was all that came through the phone to him, in a tone of almost dignified exasperation. Then after a slight pause came the response to Tam's obvious growing frustration.

'I have to be very frank with you. Think of what you experienced this morning. It might just be enough to make you realise that she, and I, are not playing games with you. We are dealing with some very dangerous people, very dangerous. Even as I speak to you it is

41

entirely possible they have their eyes on you already, for they are not without resources to do just that. I hasten to add I am not being alarmist. I am being a realist. As they don't have the photograph, then it follows that they would conclude, without greatly exercising their mental faculties, that either she would still have it, or if not her, then, just possibly you. Have you worked that out? You might now be a direct target.'

'So what?' Tam replied, with just the appropriate tone of bravado.

'That is a very commendable spirit you're showing, young man,' the voice said. 'But I have to say it sounds as if you could be too headstrong for your own good, as witness your intervention this morning. If your path is crossed again by the same sort of people you might not be so lucky. Get that photograph out of your hands for your own safety. I want you to do the following....'

'I want to meet her. And I mean that!' Tam blurted. 'No messin' about. Got that!'

'Let me put it another way,' the man said slowly, and with emphasis.

'Ay, do!' Tam retorted.

'There's one hundred pounds in it for you if you just hand over the photograph to me. '

A sum of money like that being handed to him, for whatever transaction, was beyond his immediate comprehension. Money surely could not be made that easily, he thought. He had been in the local bookies often and had seen such sums passing hands. But that

42

wasn't easy. His father had lost enough in there to prove that. Those sums seemed unattainable, foreign, not part of his own tuppenny world. He wondered what his nagging sister would think of him earning one hundred pounds just for passing on a photograph, as she ploughed on trying to get herself a job that would make her life much more worthwhile, moaning git that she could be. She'd think he had mugged an old lady for it. He would give her a tenner just to shut her up. His mother could get herself some perfume. If he gave it to his father he would send it on to Oxfam, now that he had kicked the gambling habit. One hundred smackers. And what for himself? Dismiss it lightly? Stick to his principles, mainly being that he must meet the girl? As his trade unionist father would say, 'Everything is negotiable.'

'Are you still there?' asked the crisp voice from the other end of the line.

'Yes, what do you have in mind?'

Chapter 4

When Tam returned he decided not to say too much about what had transpired during the call. But he did admit that somebody was interested in the photograph and he did mention the money. Gabby fired the first volley after hearing that.

'I would have stuck out for five hundred,' he had said, his wide eyes pleading with Tam to understand the wiles of commercial transaction. 'If somebody wants something badly enough he is in a weak bargaining position. You can dictate the value. From the evidence I have of you so far Tam, you are not going to be the next Bill Gates.'

'Gabby, do me a favour,' Tam asked.

'Name it.'

'Keep this in a safe place for me.'

He took out the envelope and handed it across to Gabby. He wasn't going to carry something, now valued at a hundred pounds, around with him any longer.

'You sure?' the man asked, slightly puzzled.

'I'll feel better if I don't have it on me but I know where it is.'

'H'mm. Maybe there is some potential as a hedge-fund manager in you after all,' Gabby replied. 'I'll put it in my safe here. Nobody gets into that, not even my dear wife,' he added, looking across at her with a smile as she served cigarettes to an emaciated-looking man with a cough. Frankie wore his, 'Ah-cannae-believe-this,' look on his face which came with an open mouth that looked as if it would never shut again.

'You haven't told us all that much,' Frankie said. 'Negotiate? Who with? Where? When? What did he tell you? Out with it.'

'I've to go to meet him tomorrow.'

'Where?'

'Don't worry I've chosen it. I know my way about. Although he did suggest I was being watched.'

'Told you,' Frankie asserted. 'Didn't I say? You're a marked man.'

'I don't feel 'marked'. I don't feel scared. I don't feel as if I'm going to lose sleep over it so just keep your cool and that will be all the help I need.'

'You're kiddin' yourself. You're trying to imagine nothing much happened to you today. I get the feeling you were lucky and that they could have given you a right doin'.'

'I can look after myself.'

'Oh, dear,' Gabby interrupted. 'Where have I heard that before? Do you know what the word 'chutzpah' means?'

'Sounds like something from a cookery book I read once. Somethin' to do with German sausages? ' Frankie suggested. Gabby blinked in a show of minor horror.

'No. Not exactly. It's a word that does not derive from my culture, but it is nevertheless a word you should get to know. It describes what it means to be almost stupidly, outrageously brave. Showing plenty guts, but with unsure outcomes. In other words you might do something which we could all applaud, but only when we sit at your bed-side in an Emergency Ward feeding you grapes and chocolates because you have tried to be a hero. Beware the chutzpah mood. In short you must listen to friends and, perhaps, above all, that inner voice, which all of us have, warning us about what might lie round the next corner. Does your inner voice tell you nothing at the moment?'

Suddenly a silence fell over the three of them as if they were listening stupidly for that inner voice to pipe up like a chipmunk. Tam went for reassurance.

'Ma inner voice tells me that I'm goin' to play in our fives game tonight and win. I'm up for that. Nothin' is gonnae change till the mornin'. Time to be cool.'

'But if they're watchin' you, you never know what's going to happen,' Frankie said.

'I think it was somethin' personal between the men and the girl and I've nothin' to worry about,' Tam said, at the same time indicating that he would argue no further on the matter.

Gabby sighed. He lifted the photograph on high, as if he were putting a five pound note to the light to determine authenticity, and gave it a long look before turning on his heel and making for the back of the shop where he had a small cubicle which he amusingly called his office. They followed him through the shabby curtain which separated it from the shop. The room was a Fingal's Cave of Indo-Pak goodies; supplies stored up in columns and rows, which, from the look of it would have served a multitude in minutes. A small desk was squeezed into the middle of this space. On it sat an Acer laptop, in sleep mode. There were pictures of relatives propped up on cartons, all looking like they had been taken on the sub-continent; sunny, cheery pictures, which Tam had seen before, of course, and felt that for Gabby they were windows on the past, and on a valley that circumstances had forced him to desert but which he would never forget.

'Supposing you are wrong,' Gabby suggested solemnly. 'Supposing that there are people who value this more than you think. Supposing they see it, for whatever reasons, as a jewel worth possessing. You cannot predict what value people place on things. One man's shrine is another man's target. You may be handling something that is bigger than you think. Remember, if there is trouble, you must let me know.'

He put the envelope into a tiny safe in the corner of the office.

Tam was beginning to accept that events might not run as smoothly as he would like. He put that behind him as they both stepped outside with a completely different sense of purpose. At this time of day, with a game of football beckoning, the world was beginning to slip into its natural format and nothing could replace their urge to get out there and display their talents with a bit of showboating thrown in. Normal service was resuming.

When Tam returned to the flat for his sports gear he was fortunate. It was empty. In the hall he stood and took pause, relishing the silence of a house which most times sounded like the percussion section of an orchestra. He found himself deep-breathing, almost unable to move, as if he had reached sanctuary. Normally he paid little attention to the two photographs on either side of the living room door, but now they were taking on a new significance as they brought to his mind his father and the great sense of stability he always felt when the big man was around. He savoured that moment. For these were two portraits of the people for whom his father had deep affection. On the one side the Nasmyth portrait of Robert Burns, the Bard's eyes which sank a thousand women, as his father would say, staring past him with an elegance that Tam could never associate with ploughing the soil in Ayrshire. On the other, was a large framed photograph of his father's mother, the Duchess. These eyes stared, not past him, but straight at him with a slight upwards tilt of the chin as if she was trying to tell the photographer, whoever the poor soul had been, that she wouldn't tolerate sitting around too much and get it right first time or else she was outta there. It had been on her sixtieth birthday.

His father would certainly want to know why he hadn't put in an appearance for the chess duel since it meant so much to the old lady. He was relieved he wouldn't have to face up to that at the moment. It would give him time to think, to ponder, to make up something that sounded credible, because there was no way he was going to mention the police, a strange girl and an even stranger photograph to any of his kin. Not at this stage anyway. He was fortunate that like many other people Tam saw Thomas Brownlie as a rational man; certainly big, certainly with a dominating personality when he was on his soap-box, as he often was; certainly too heavy now since he had given up on the booze a lot, but ate too much instead; and he certainly never seemed to convert his undoubted passion about injustices in society into rabble-rousing anger. In fact Tam loved listening to him talk about some of his political engagements, particularly of that period when he was a flying-picket during the miners' strike, running away from police surges - whether the tales were embellished or not - and getting a chronic knee problem as a result, 'And bloody worth it' he had apparently told his surgeon who put him under the knife but without permanent cure; the click from his knee and his grimace when he rose from a seat always announcing that. 'There were values to be defended,' he would tell people. Value was a much used word in his vocabulary. The word clung to Tam from the many times listening to his father bring it up on politics, religion, football and even about who should command the television remote control. 'Listen, son,' he once said to him. 'If you don't have principles what's the point of fightin' for anythin'. Hold fast to what you believe in. Too many bloody politicians are pragmatists. That's jist another way of sayin' they're guardin' their own backsides.'

It was a belief that stemmed from a man who claimed he had learned more from reading in the public library than he ever had in school. He wasn't slow to tell anybody who cared to listen that he had read '*War And Peace*' from cover to cover, like a runner boasting he had completed the London Marathon. In that mode Tam always felt his father was trying to reveal something of a regret about his life; that he had been an under-achiever; that there was a lot more to him than that stereotype of the shop-steward which he had nevertheless been proud to be. That narrative was part of Tam's own academic motivation.

As was his relationship with the Duchess who stared back fiercely at him from the wall. '*Bishop to Knight 3*. Wouldn't you like to know?' he asked the portrait with an impudence he couldn't match face to face with her. The chess challenge had come out of the blue two years ago. She had seen an obviously much used chess-set with tiny chips out of some of the pieces, at a church jumble sale one day. The pieces supposedly represented the opposing armies at Waterloo. That attracted her. She fell in love with the armies. It seemed to rouse that militant spirit that had obviously resided in her all her days. She bought the set, then invited Tam to tell her how to play the game which he himself had learned from his maths teacher at school. He did, little realising that he would eventually be taking on a cunning reincarnation of Napoleon, the master of strategy, on the other side of the board. So increasingly the commands came for his regular presence at the chess-board backed up by his family who thought her very resilience and longevity gave her unchallengeable authority. That was something she certainly exploited at the family get-togethers, where they paid court to her as she narrated her life story. Over and over again. It wasn't a rag to riches story. More a colourful tale of hardship and endurance, but she could make it sound like she had inherited the earth and belonged to a kind of aristocracy of the underprivileged. Crisp haughtiness was her style and with a penchant for the lurid. One night at the dinner table she described how his father had come into the world through a breach-birth, with such eloquent detail that Tam discovered that listening to gynaecological minutiae made the stovies he was trying eat seem like entrails and he had to make a mad dash from the table.

All this obeisance was accepted with coolness by his mother, a diminutive, cheerily-rotund woman who when beside her huge husband seemed reminiscent of a Russian matryoschka doll, which deceived people into thinking she didn't have a mind of her own. But it was she who had christened her mother-in-law the Duchess, deciding that the least she could do was to give her a rank that fitted her imperious nature. His father, for the sake of peace within the four walls, did not really want to know what lay behind his wife's motive and for the sake of the family treated that as simply a display of affection that would, in any case, never reach his mother's ears.

'*Bishop to Knight 3.*' he whispered again to the portrait before grabbing his bag in his room and leaving. Down the stairs he went three at a time, as was his wont, and almost collided with a figure heading upstairs humming tunelessly. Bloody hell! Sarah! His sister was the last person he wanted to see now. There was no avoiding it. She had her earplugs in, listening to something that made her humming seem like grunts from an outdated plumbing system. Her head was festooned with curlers, obviously having been at her pal's flat for a makeover of some kind. A hen night was obviously on the near horizon.

'Why don't you just put a Batman outfit on and have done wi' it,' she hissed at him stepping back startled and whipping her earplugs off.

'I'm in a hurry,' he snapped back trying to move round her.

'Fitba' I suppose,' she said with disdain. 'Along wi' Forest Gump nae doubt.'

'Maybe you badmouth my mate because he's never given you a second look.'

'Thank God, say I. I can live wi' that.'

He tried to move round her but she grabbed his arm.

'Haud on!' she said deliberately.

Her grip was surprisingly powerful.

'What's this I've been hearin' about you?'

Tam backed away but certainly didn't like the knowing smile that had broken out on her face.

'About me?'

'Aye,' she said with a suddenly developing smugness on her face. 'So spill it out'.

'What are you on about?' he asked.

'That girl you were chasin' this mornin'.'

'What girl?'

'Don't give me that. I bumped into auld Dave Wallace. He said you were runnin' like the clappers after some girl opposite the pub this mornin'. He said you looked demented. Don't deny it!'

'He's gettin' it a' wrong. For God's sake, he's twisted what he saw.'

'Now I know he's gettin' on a bit. But he's all there, old Dave, and since it was early this mornin', it's not the bevy that was talkin'.' So who is she?'

'I don't even know what you're talkin about.'

'He gave me a description o' her. A good lookin' blonde wearin' a blue jacket. Was Dave imaginin' that? Was he makin' it up when he said you took off like a wee dug on heat when he told you?'

This wasn't just sisterly curiosity, it was also a taunting as Sarah saw him incorrigibly and crudely as the macho man who might wake up some day realising there was more to life than worrying about football results. He could sense her eagerness to seize this as a possible chink in that armour. Was this a Tam she had never seen before?

He glared back at her. She was thin. Certainly not from a tendency to anorexia because she could put away the side of a cow and not put on an ounce. Despite falling well short of voluptuousness Tam had to admit she could attract men. It was difficult for him to fathom why. But she got them all right and they passed through the house week after week looking to Tam like vagrants seeking domestic asylum. In seeking Mr Right she could have built a turnstile in her room as they came and went, and charged admission. It seemingly would not have turned them off. Apparently she made men feel pleased with themselves and at ease when they were with her. He did know all about what she was up to but had kept his powder dry in a family circle that tended to be prudish. Sometimes he wondered why he never cast things up to her. Whatever she did with them it was her change of personality that irked him. With her various boyfriends she was all innocent, eyes-a-flutter Little Bo

Peep. As soon as they were out of the house and the door was shut, she would turn back into Cruella de Vil again.

'I suppose you'll be blabbin' this about the place?' he said.

'Whatever gave you that idea?' she said, smirking. 'We'd all like to meet your bird.'

So would I, he felt like saying.

'But it's no' the right technique to be rushin' about after her. Is she playing hard to get? Be cool. Make her come tae you,' she said patronisingly. 'You're a simpleton when it comes tae that.'

She was off and running now. There would be no holding her back. There was little point in trying to explain. Just ride with the wave he thought. Let her think what she likes. What harm will that do? That would be simpler.

'Own up! Who is she? I mean if you brought her to the house Ma would hang out the buntin'. She'd bake her scones, for God's sake. She's been waitin' for somethin' like this for a long time, I'll have you know. She's never seen you bring one solitary lassie into the house. Maybe they were gettin' strange ideas about you. You just cannae tell by appearances nowadays, can you?'

'Are you suggestin' what I think you're suggestin'?'

'I'm just sayin' that we have to be tolerant these days about people's choices about who they pair wi'. That's all I'm sayin'.'

By that Tam had decided she had crossed over a red line. Enough was enough.

'You're so wrapped up in studyin' and fitba' and bevvyin' wi' that galoot of a pal that you don't understand what Ma would really like you to be. So it would be a red-letter day if you walked in the door wi' that girl,' she said haughtily.

Sarah's weird slant on the information that Dave had given her had taken on a bizarre quality that was simply aggravating the sense of loss he felt at having the girl out there somewhere beyond his immediate reach. If the girl was Sarah's fantasy, then he worried that she was becoming his as well.

'You know what ma will shout when she hears this?' she bawled as he fled downstairs.

'What?'

'Hallelujah!'

Tam was at that moment thinking of a reprisal. There would be many ways of describing it but by any account he knew it was about time to play the blackmail card.

***

The sight of Frankie waiting for him outside brought him to his senses. He had one immediate question to ask him.

'Have you still got those pictures on your phone?' he asked.

'What pictures?'

'You know. Sarah in action.'

'You bet!'

'Don't think of deletin' it'

'Give us a break. Whit chance is there of that?'

'I might still need it.'

'What for?'

He didn't bother to reply because he was beginning to smell football again.

'Time to get goin',' he said and strode off.

'Hey, don't forget the warnings you got this morning,' Frankie said trying to catch up from a slow start. 'This is how we'll play it,' he instructed. 'I'll follow on close behind. Kinda out of sight. Trust me. It'll be better if we don't walk together because it means I can protect your arse and see what's happenin' where you cannae see. I'll hang back about twenty yards or so, keepin' my eye on that Barca jacket, not lettin' it out of my sight and at the same time lookin' for anythin' fishy. I'll always be in touch, watchin'. Any funny business and I'll be there, make no mistake. Make sure your phone is on.'

'Are you fuckin'serious?'

'Of course I'm serious! You were warned weren't you? Somebody could be watchin' you. When you get out into the street it'll look like you're on your own. If we were a pair they could jump us without warnin'. You see? I'll be your second pair of eyes. They won't know. That's the beauty of it.'

'Who won't know? You're goin' over the top. I told you, you go to too many movies. Give me a break.'

'Did you imagine you'd be in a punch-up in the lane this morning? Could you have predicted you'd end up fallin' for a bird you've only seen for ten minutes, top whack? This is a whole new ball game for us now.'

'Us?'

'Ay. Us! I'm in it as much as you now. You wouldn't have it any other way, would you?'

Tam looked at his mate and couldn't fail to notice the quivering arousal that seemed to have taken grip of his friend. He was relishing all of this. And there was no way he was going to change Frankie's odd strategy.

'Ok. If that's what you want. Ta. I appreciate it. Let's get goin'.'

They could have taken the route to the fives blindfold. They always walked. It was part of their warm-up. Their way would be along Crown Street with the Nautical College on their left, over Albert Bridge, along the Saltmarket until Glasgow Cross, up the High Street, pass the solid, dour Royal Infirmary and into the maze of streets around the Kennedy Street area where the all-weather pitches were situated. The early evening felt cooler. There would be many people moving into the city for their Saturday evening out. It could make spotting anything unusual more difficult. As his mate walked breezily forward Frankie suddenly began to appreciate again how firm their relationship was. Tam did trust him. He appreciated that in many ways there were as unlike as a plough-horse would be with Kauto Star. He the plodder, particularly at school; Tam, the thoroughbred, who could jump exam hurdles with an ease that was beyond Frankie's comprehension. They had known each other for years, since they were toddlers in fact, aware of each other's presence in the general melee of growing up. But it wasn't until they were in the first year at their secondary school that the relationship was cemented. Frankie remembered it as a day when the rain was lashing the window panes outside and another kind of lashing was taking place in the class-room. Miss Mitchell, their English teacher, had ridiculed a boy for an essay he had been forced to write about his family. Essay writing was not a favoured pastime in that neighbourhood. It was the perfect stage for the sadistically sarcastic teacher to mercilessly rib the boy to the point where the class was in uproar as the poor target visibly wilted. But as an astounded Frankie looked around his hysterically laughing classmates he noticed one face on the other side of the room which was stonily contemptuous of what was going on. Tam was simmering with anger. He looked over. Their glances met. Frankie, mouthed silently over towards him, 'She's -an-arsehole!' Tam nodded back in agreement. That was it.

The resulting gravitational pull saw them grow through puberty in a mutually protective way. There were drugs about a-plenty and they had some great sessions with their six-packs but, somehow, without any profound discussions, they skirted round the temptations on hand in the need to keep fit for the remorseless football which dominated much of their lives.

They both knew in their different ways without ever daring to speak it aloud that they were destined to branch off in different directions in a future life; Tam propelled by his ambition to study physics at the highest level; Frankie bolstered by his belief that he could eventually concoct a dish fit for kings in a five-star kitchen. Like Tam's sister he was desperately job-seeking, but perhaps too fussy for his own good. Tam could never see the attraction anyway of working over a hot-plate for a living. 'It's just a sweat factory you'll be in, feeding fat toffs who wouldnae let you over their doorstep,' he once tried to remonstrate with his mate. And Frankie could never understand why a boy who could pass exams as easy as unzipping a banana could have such a passion for a wee foreign footballer who off the field was probably only skilled at adding up his cash. 'Why would you no' put a poster of Einstein up on your bedroom?' he once asked him. All this was beyond cynicism though. The mutual slagging was the simple tool to remind them of their instinctive bonding despite everything. And despite their startlingly obvious differences they were on the same wave length when it came to picking out the bampots of this world.

Bampots are certainly on Frankie's mind as they cross the river. Just over the other side he is on high alert with more people around. Suddenly two men emerge from a close-mouth. They wheel on to the pavement and appear to be about to block Tam's walk. They are in black suits with startlingly white shirts and black ties. Frankie's heart starts to pump furiously. Isn't that THE description? The Men in Black? He moves into a slight jog. Is this it? But Tam seems unconcerned as the men stop and the one with a satchel under his arm (Could it contain a weapon? Frankie thinks) with a broad smile on his face seems to say something to Tam that looks innocuous enough. As Frankie approaches, the three are conversing, and Tam is pointing back towards the bridge as if giving directions, and suddenly it dawns. They are Mormons. As lethal as a pair of turtle-doves. Again Frankie relaxes and again he has to reassure himself that he is right to be jumpy about anybody. He looks back down the Saltmarket which is now even busier. Nobody seems threatening, but anybody could be. Men in particular worry him. He tries to associate in his mind the kind of person likely to be pursuing Tam. He has an image of two swarthy individuals, with thick foreign accents, but that seems to come from his reservoir of villains he has seen on film or TV. He knows that is a prejudice that might not square with reality. Perhaps he has watched too many *Die Hard* movies, he admits to himself.

They are approaching the very heart of the city, Glasgow Cross, and that sturdy structure, the Tollbooth Steeple, where once his uncle had almost bored Frankie to death by lecturing him, like a tour guide, about the great days of the Tolbooth in the 18th century when the wealthy tobacco barons would come out in their red cloaks and gold –topped canes, to strut their wealth, just as the convicts inside the jail in that same building were allowed to create their own rules of imprisonment and in their own way lived like lords themselves. It had been no torture chamber. He cranes his neck to look up at the large clock, seven stories high, and as he lowers his gaze to the level of the street he senses something is not right. They have dug up part of the Trongate, the broad street which passes on either side of the steeple, running parallel to the river. There are phased traffic lights in operation guiding the east-west traffic into a single lane. There is a cacophony of car horns blasting into the sky because one car at the head of the traffic, at the temporary lights, seems stuck. Tam is moving towards it, still looking casual and relaxed. Frankie is not. A

Lexus is trying to move round the Tolbooth in direct contravention of the emergency traffic arrangements, as if it hadn't been fully aware they existed there. It is being hampered by other cars moving in the opposite and correct direction.

A coincidence? Coincidences in these situations simply do not exist, Frankie decides, as he starts to run. As he runs, he shouts to Tam and points toward the car in particular. Because of the din it is clearly impossible for him to be heard, and as his mate is not in the same state of alertness to potential danger, as he is, there is not the slightest indication of concern from him. Frankie knows then that he is taking a gamble and that this could be another piece of fantasy that will end up in ridicule. Suddenly, from the opposite side of the steeple a white van sweeps round towards the Tolbooth, as if it had sprung from a parked position. Again, astonishingly, it is going against the grain of the traffic, but this time on the opposite side of the Tolbooth. Horns are blaring as the traffic is beginning to congeal. But the white van makes straight for Tam. Frankie feels as if a lead weight is holding him back, as his legs are not functioning as quickly as he thought they should. The white van mounts the pavement just underneath the steeple right in front of Tam, who almost instantaneously freezes in shock, but only for a fraction of a second, for the side door opens and two men, big, burly, but nimble are throwing themselves at his mate who does the quick body-swerve so often employed on the football field, and makes an audacious leap across the front of the van, throwing his sports bag away, spinning in the air like a clay-pigeon. As he does so one of the men, not as badly wrong-footed as the other, leaps to the side and trips him. Tam lands with a vicious slap on the pavement.

It is then Frankie arrives. He arrives with a screaming yell like he has come straight from the bowels of hell. It is the blood-curling screech of a newborn urban warrior. His body action is like that of a runaway combined harvester, his legs and arms flailing wildly in lethal uncoordination. The men react like a bolt of lightning has struck between them, for they are now faced by the wholly unexpected, in the shape of a red-haired tornado who appears not to wish to take prisoners.

Frankie throws a large right foot in the direction of the backside of the man holding Tam's leg now, which, given his size elevens and a thigh muscle which is like a bull's, causes the man to emit a high-pitched squeal like a punctured balloon. It means Tam is free, just for that vital second, enabling him to scramble up and away from the grasp, even though the second man tries to throw himself after him. There is that moment of uncertainty between the two men as to who should now do what. Which one chases? Which one deals with the red-haired madman now in their midst? It is enough for Tam to disappear on the other side of the van and Frankie is now sure that his mate's legs will now be in top gear, pounding the street in front of him.

'Run! Run like hell!' Frankie bawls at his mate.

It is his last thought for some time, as something hits the side of his head which, to him, is like dark shutters suddenly being brought down on a sunlit room.

Chapter 5

The shock of the attack produced a jittery, jangling, breathless feeling inside Tam. From it came an overwhelming surge. He cut left towards the Merchant City. His feet seemed hardly to touch the street at all as he raced away. When he reached the narrow pot-holed Tontine Lane across the street from the Trongate, he turned quickly to see if he could catch sight of Frankie. All he witnessed was the van slewed across the pavement and a large man with a closely-shaven head running round the end of it heading in his direction. He turned and ran along the lane, appreciating that its very narrowness and the fact that scaffolding was clinging to the buildings there, all around, meant that it was unlikely the van could get along it. He also hoped that if they did not know the area well they might try, get stuck, have to reverse and that would give him more time. For he wanted to move into this old part of the city which had now been gentrified into one of the city centre's focal social points. There were plenty outlets for a good night-out, amongst the plethora of pubs, restaurants, small wine bars and tiny cafes; an eclectic mix which made an effort to remind people of their holidays abroad in different parts of the continent. He knew on a Saturday evening, particularly in this good weather, that it would be crowded.

When he turned right sharply into one of the streets running at right-angles to the High Street he had just left, his guess was correct. There were hordes of people around, spilling out on to the streets, or sitting at pavement tables, ample bottles of wine and pints of beer decorating the tables. He wanted to disappear among them somehow.

He made straight for O'Neill's Bar, which looked as if it were under siege by people. He knew he could pass through there to the inner expansive courtyard, the Merchant Market. He pushed his way through the throng and entered the Market area, which housed several bars and restaurants under the same canopied roof.

It was mobbed. There was a party going on in the middle of this 'piazza', with balloons and streamers floating around, in the middle of which was a large lady, surrounded by about twenty or so other even larger ladies, all doing the hokey-cokey, and, from looking at their sizes, lending the impression that this dance was their first exercise in some years; the glasses in their hands suggested to Tam they were also well-pissed. He skirted them carefully, but quickly, reached the other side of the court where a door led out on to the next street, hoping that in the confusion of crowds he had become 'lost'. Then as he stood just outside, hiding partly behind a door column he had now the presence of mind to discard the distinctive, easily identifiable Barca jacket, which he tied now round his waist. His football gear must still have been lying somewhere back at the Trongate. He could still see the door on the other side of the court at O'Neill's and it was there he saw the bulky man from the van entering, slowly, surveying the throng inside with a clearly bemused expression. He had obviously spied Tam entering, but his body language seemed to suggest that he didn't really know his bearings around this area and that he had been taken aback by the size of the crowd in front of him.

Tam gained a reassurance from this uncertainty. This was his territory, not theirs, whoever they were. He knew this whole area like he knew the contours of his own family flat. So that immediate, almost panicky, scary feel, he had felt at the Trongate was giving way to an almost audacious urge to take them on, to lead them a merry dance. Then that cautionary word of Gabby's came to mind. *Chutzpah.* This was no game. Firstly, from that morning he had the image of the black Lexus on his mind. Now a white van had suddenly emerged on to the scene as a threat. He was being seriously hunted. You can't toy with people like that. That was the more rational thought now uppermost in his mind.

The man had taken his phone out and was chattering into it now as he slowly advanced towards the very fat women carousing in the middle of the hall, looking all around him, and from the vivid reactions to what was being said to him on the phone he looked decidedly uncomfortable. Tam waited to see what the man's next move would be. It was then he suddenly became aware of the white shape out of the corner of his eye. It was the van, slowly cruising past the outside of the court and he could quite clearly identify the man in the passenger seat leaning forward, looking left and right and speaking into his own phone, obviously to the pursuer inside the Market. The van stopped at the corner of the street allowing it a view in all directions. They weren't going to give up easily. They would spy him immediately if he stepped out right on to the street. So he eased himself into the doorway, away from the possible view from the van, but at the same time aware that he might be exposing himself to the other threat.

From time to time he lost sight of the man behind him, as the large figures in their rollicking merriment inside were obscuring his view. It was then he was seized by the idea that perhaps he could risk moving back in, behind the partying women, obscuring himself behind their generous girths. It was also an admission to himself that he did basically want to take these people on, that he did want to show that he had had enough of the cat-and-mouse, that he did want to flaunt himself, and to let them realise he was not easy game. Somehow taking the risk of being spotted excited him. Chutzpah or no Chutzpah, this was the way he was going to do it.

He slipped back into the courtyard, crouching. In that position he felt it would be impossible for the man to see him behind those acres of flesh. But he had to move quickly. He slipped round the figures, spiderishly, clockwise, noticing the man's legs moving in the other direction. It was possible he could reroute himself without being seen, and go out the way he came in, thus upstaging them. It seemed credible and it seemed as if it was working as he edged further and further around the group. Then, as the noise, trapped under the Market roof, seemed to increase in intensity, one of the women, stumbling backwards on her precarious stiletto heels, bumped against Tam, shrieking with laughter and as, inevitably, she fell on top of him, Tam felt like he was being hit by the collapse of a condemned building. The group exploded in hysterics, wholly enjoying this spectacle, and completely unaware that the boy squirming underneath this unexpected avalanche was beginning to think the hokey-cokey was about to endanger his life, in more ways than one.

He heaved at the woman, who in her relaxed and merry state obviously thought this was a great wheeze and grabbed Tam round the neck, followed by an enormous hug the likes of which he had never experienced since a large aunt of his had almost suffocated him one Christmas after giving him a present of a toy Rolls Royce. He tried to extricate himself and realised quickly that she would have been better off being a participant in Cumberland wrestling, so firm was her grip. He did manage to squint up and see the man still engaged in phone chatter but who still, fortunately, had not noticed the merry fracas. Please, don't look this way, he thought. Suddenly the others crowded round offering ribald comments to the woman and starting to chant and clap their hands. As hands started to reach out and haul at the woman to get her to her feet, Tam saw the man turn and look straight at him. For a moment he stopped screeching into his phone and looked in some amazement at the scene unfolding before him, and at the figure of the boy he was hunting, trying to extricate himself from the figure on top of him, which was looking more like a beached whale by the second. He seemed to freeze for a moment then erupted into life, screaming into his phone, undoubtedly to communicate his find to the others, then leapt across the court floor towards the group.

As fate would have it, one of the large women backing away in joyful hysterics about the plight of her friend quite accidentally cut across the man's path. Tam watched their spectacular collision with something approaching the relish of a physicist observing particles smashing into each other. This was the Merchant City's equivalent of the Big Bang model and Tam felt as if the entire Market shuddered. The mountainous woman was pole-axed and the man seemed to loop-the-loop before crashing to the floor, losing his grip on his phone which Tam saw sliding across the floor of the Market towards him like a miniature curling stone.

Until that moment he had felt he was in a human vice, the arm round his neck mistakenly thinking it was providing some pleasure. He had heard that professional escapologists knew the secret of relaxing, making the body seem like nothing more than a piece of string, which was the secret of wriggling free from any contortion. He tried that, as the woman in her disorientated state seemed to want to cling on. But, what suddenly helped him was that the mood of the group was changing, rapidly. The woman, who had collided with the man, sat on the floor with a stunned expression and it was clear she was hurt. The laughing was switching into sounds of concern for her. The woman's grip loosened. Tam prised himself free, at last, reached out for the man's phone, grabbed it, shoved it in his pocket, then launched himself to his feet.

His first intention was to make for the O'Neill's entrance until he recognised the other second man pushing his way through the crowd from exactly that direction. There was no mistaking him. For a moment he felt cornered and the sight of the other pursuer beginning to struggle to his feet searching around, to see where his phone had gone, and looking like he was about to burst a blood vessel, his face a mix of bewilderment and anger, did not allay Tam's anxiety. His thinking time was minimal. His legs did it for him. He found himself leaping past the knot of fat ladies, now huddled around their stricken companion, and making for a swing-door which showed the sign Exit. For a moment it did not matter where it led, the word Exit itself seemed like seeing Sanctuary writ large. He pushed his way through the door, ran down a short corridor, turned a corner to the left and came out on a double door leading certainly to one of the streets outside. They were the kind with horizontal bars, above which read, Push To Open. Even before he touched them something told him that that they wouldn't. Sure enough, they didn't, no matter how hard he pushed. For a moment he felt he had simply entered a sealed chamber and then heard the door, through which he had come, being kicked open.

To his back, there was a flight of stairs. There was no other option. He leapt at them, sweeping up three steps at a time. He came out eventually on a small balcony which looked down on the courtyard, the sounds of revelry from all quarters, down there, in stark contrast to his darkening mood as he realised he had come to a dead end, no way out. Then he noticed the banner which was strung from the balcony to the roof of an adjacent restaurant. He assumed it was an advertisement for something. He noticed it was attached to the balcony railing by a chain. It was obvious. It had to be a space walk. Would the chain support him? There was little option but to try it, as he heard the footsteps proclaiming the presence of his pursuers behind him. He threw one leg over the railing, then the other, and gingerly pressed down on the banner with two hands. It gave a little, but not sufficiently to put him off. He took a deep breath, then slid into a crouched position before grabbing the top of the banner, then lowering himself into a position where he could allow his body to drop into space. There was a violent sag, and his heart seemed to pass through his body and end up beating somewhere near the top of his cranium. The internal lurch seemed to match the external lurch of the chain. He felt it would buckle any second, but did not stop him from trying to edge along it, his legs dangling and his hands clenched around the top of the banner and shuttling, one after the other, even though he felt he would not make it to the roof on the other side. It did not matter. He was there. He had to get on with it especially as he caught a glimpse of the two men reaching the balcony, and could tell that they were trying to loosen the knot there. It was his body weight which decided the issue. Suddenly he felt the chain giving way and away he swept.

Curiously it was not an Icarus plummet downwards. He had managed to inch along to an extent that the shorter segment of the chain, which he was now gripping, seemed to swing him more in a pendulum-like arc that, bolstered by the strength of his grip, aimed him as much sideways as downwards. But he could see his plight coming and could do nothing about it. It took the form of a waiter. He was heading for the tables with a broad Italian smile on his face, carrying a large tray on which there were steaming piles of food of some sort. It was not until Tam had swung straight into him like

70

Robin Hood, from the branch of a tree, dislodging one of the Sheriff of Nottingham's henchmen from his horse, that this momentum meant something. With the astonished man seeing his tray flying into the air like a stringless kite, and much of the food landing on the side of Tam's face in a dripping mass, and his tongue automatically licking at the liquidy mess, it meant that somebody was not going to get the Spaghetti Bolognaise they had ordered. Nor was it likely that the white-aproned Italian was likely to forget this moment, as his face had drained of colour, as ashen as those of his ancient countrymen in Pompeii who had been taken by surprise by Mount Vesuvius. There was no time to apologise though. At the very least Tam knew the collision had not been fatal and in any case the Bolognaise sauce was quite tasty, although he instantly wiped at the mess on his face to get rid of it as he climbed to his feet, feeling, luckily, only slightly winded. And the din from the surrounding areas was so loud that hardly anybody had noticed the latest fracas except those in the restaurant nearest the incident. But, by the look of some of the patrons sitting at the tables, they seemed to be absorbing this incident like it was just part of Saturday evening's normal rough and tumble and that in any case what else would you expect in a busy Italian restaurant?

Tam looked upwards at the balcony only in time to see the two heads there disappearing. He moved, rapidly, only casting the briefest glance at the hokey-cokeyers, who were now grouped around the ailing woman who had inadvertently acted like a picador to his matador in the bull-ring for him. No time for sympathy for her

71

either, as he took off the way he had come, realising that the parked white-van would be at the other end of the building and could not possibly see him disappearing towards Glasgow's High Street, leaving behind him mayhem in the Merchant Square. He knew he had just enough leeway to get in the clear and leave them wondering what direction he had then taken. A bus was sliding to a halt at a stop just round the corner from Merchant City. One man was in front of him. Tam leaped aboard behind him, looked back to see if he was indeed in the clear, paid his fare and then sat on the right hand side of the bus as it trundled up the hill away from Merchant City. It was giving him at least temporary clearance. But he felt less than relaxed though. He busied himself first of all with the pursuers phone that he had come by, something that he had to with a fumbling urgency, but with the presence of mind to transfer the man's sim card's details to his own phone, before it would be cancelled by the supplier. Then he slipped it down on the floor, to leave it behind, satisfied at what he had accomplished. It was when they were in sight of the elegant baronial-style grey-stoned Provand's Lordship, standing as a 15th century reproof of the ugly Victorian edifice of the Royal Infirmary that Tam's own phone rang.

The screen said 'Frankie'. But the voice was not his.

***

The inside of the van was dimly lit, with an insipid light clutching the interior roof. Frankie had slowly revived. They had come to a stop somewhere. He lay there thinking of himself as a

72

failure. Inspector Clouseau could not have done worse. On the other hand perhaps he had set the bar too high for himself. The task was perhaps beyond him, right from the outset. Still, no time for regrets. Who were these bampots? Whatever happened to the black Lexus? Where did that go to? Was this a co-ordinated strike? This was gang stuff; a professional gang that knew how to do these things. It had to be. Why? For a photograph? Give me a break, he thought. People just don't do that for photographs. Must be drugs, Frankie thought. They don't go to all of this trouble for something that didn't look any more interesting than some of his old family-album snaps that you looked at once and then never again.

He felt for his phone and then realised they had taken it from him. It was then he put his hand to the side of his head and realised it was cut. The blood had congealed to an extent, but there was still a feeling of wetness as he touched it there. As he did so the van came to a halt. Frankie could hear the sounds of people, lots of them, and music like a street party was underway. He guessed from that, and the short time the van had been on the move, that they were still in the Merchant City. If the crowds were still there, then he had a chance. He slipped on to his back again, reached out with his legs and began to batter the side of the van, making it shake violently. He bawled at the top of his voice, 'Help, get me outta here!' over and over again. His efforts did not last long, for suddenly the back-door of the van was abruptly opened and as a shaft of light penetrated the interior, a shape launched itself in beside him and Frankie felt a sharp kick on the ribs which took the breath from him, his plea for help subsiding into a gurgling moan. Then he was pushed on his back again and the door slammed shut. Pained though he was, at the very least he now had company, for the man simply crouched opposite him, and even in the dimly lit interior he could see the stern outline of a face which was not made for cracking jokes. The man made no sound but simply stared at him like a hypnotist. Frankie propped himself up again and moaned, his ribcage having borne the brunt of the kick. This was no lightweight he was up against and knew he would have to control himself to a degree. Although he was desperate to expose his plight to anybody outside, he guessed that the street noise was so loud that the banging on the side of the van and the shouting would probably pass unnoticed anyway. His voice was all that was left to him.

'Thanks for the lift, pal.' Frankie said calmly to the man. 'Now if you would just let me outta here, I'll be gettin' on my way. Ma team will be waitin' for me. Playmaker, you see. Can't do without me. So, I'm off.' He made to rise from his position even though he knew there would be a reaction. There was. A large hand reached out and shoved him abruptly back, the van rocking again.

'Hey!' Frankie snapped at him. 'Manners, please. What have I done to you? The only thing I did wrong was get out my bed this mornin'. Seems like it wasnae the cleverest thing I've ever done. I should have stayed put. I haven't a clue why I'm here and don't deserve to be treated like I was rag-doll. Who are you? What are you doin' here? What's this all about? Say somethin'!'

Silence. The man was like stone, unflinching. Frankie could now make out sharp features, a large sharply ridged nose, with dark, liquidy eyes and a mouth slightly open as if he was deliberately avoiding looking intelligent, but be clearly seen as the purveyor of brute force. Take him at face value, Frankie thought, and then it occurred to him that maybe the lack of understanding was simply language.

'You don't understand me, do you?'

Silence. Test him again, he thought, this time spacing out the language slowly, like feeding a kid his rusks.

'What.... are.... you... lot... after? I... have.... nothin'.... that.... would.... interest... you. No... money. Nothin'..... Skint....Search....me...if...you...like!'

The man let the words simply waft past him. This time Frankie felt he had to really test him.

'I...will...tell....you....everything....you....want......to....know.....ab out....the......other....boy....and...lead...you...straight...to...him. Straight....to....him. Because.... he has.... got me....right... into.... this... deep.... shit...and.... deserves... everything......comin'...to...him. Say...the ....word...and I...will...lead.... you....straight... to.... him.

Tam, he knew, would have approved of the subterfuge. An offer they could hardly refuse. But the gamble looked as if it was paying off. For from the man came only a tiny furrowing of the brow as if he meant to reveal incomprehension this time. Now was the time to push the boat out then.

'So...I....have...to....call....you....the....Silent...One..then...eh? I..could...call...you...worse...for..you..have..the...face..of..a....baboon after...being....head-butted...by...an...orang-utang.'

These words of endearment provoked nothing more than an almost imperceptible narrowing of the eyes. English was well beyond him, Frankie had proved. So he decided he was good for one more insult for good measure, and to give vent to some anger that so far he had kept well in check, the sort of thing he would loved to have done with some of his elders but hadn't the courage for it.

' You.... smell....like....you....sleep.....in....a....piggery!'

'What wis that?' came a sharp response from the front of the van in a voice that had a distinct Glaswegian twang to it. Tam suddenly felt cold. He saw a shape moving into the driver's seat, and, as he did so, the door at the back of the van opened and another three men pushed their way in, brusquely treating him like a doormat as they then crouched just behind the two front seats. The van's engine sparked into life and they began to move.

'Keep that big mouth quiet in the back there,' said that same distinctive local voice in a manner that made Frankie aware that controlling his tongue now would be a health benefit. Two in the front, three in the back beside him, and at least one who understood the language. Perhaps insults were not appropriate now. But how about a threat? Try it, he thought.

'Any of you lot feelin' bad Karma, because believe you me you've picked the wrong boy. I've got pals who can sort out folk like you. Take it as read they'll be wonderin' what's happened to me and there'll be no place in this city you can go, no hidin' place, they'll get to you and sort you out....'

'He said to keep your mouth shut,' said one of the men who had just joined them. It was perfect English. Too perfect in a way, devoid of any local inflexion. Like he was a reader of news bulletins at the BBC. As he did so he leant over and shoved a very strong finger into Frankie's chest and poked him, like he had been hit by a spear.

'The mouth remains very shut, or else' the sort of BBC voice said. 'My Karma happens to carry a large punch. Got it?'

Frankie looked round them slowly. They stared back at him as if they required just the merest excuse to lash out. He was now beginning to feel he was in a kind of mobile dungeon as the van began to bump along, turning occasionally in such a way that they almost collapsed against each other in the back. This brought a loud protest from the one with the broadcasting voice.

'For God's sake, go easy. The last thing we want to do is crash this thing.' Then he added a name which Frankie couldn't hear distinctly but which sounded like Puss, or Noose, or Moose, or Goose.

The driver replied only with a snort.

He was a Glaswegian, that was for sure. But against the light shining through the windshield and into the back he was merely a black shape. In trying, too conspicuously, to look at the driver, the Silent One leant across, alerted to Frankie's inquisitiveness, pushed him back against the van wall and then forced his head down until it was practically between his knees.

'Here,' he heard another other voice say. 'Put this round his head.'

Frankie couldn't tell exactly what it was but in a few seconds he had been pushed further downwards with a rough cloth wrapped round his eyes to blindfold him. It smelled of oil. Then they pulled him upright, giving him immense relief, as he had begun to feel his stomach was cramping.

'Don't even think of putting your hands on that cloth or you'll regret it,' said the very proper voice. 'We have your phone. It should help us with communication and make your friend see sense.'

Frankie received that last piece of information with mixed emotions. Firstly, he had always hated the idea of 'losing' his phone, which now effectively he had, to their obvious advantage. Then, more importantly, it verified his lingering feeling, since the others had joined him in the van, that they had failed to get their hands on Tam. He felt so uplifted by that thought that he felt it almost as news of a victory. So much so that he had to say something, anything, despite the warning about keeping quiet.

'If you are gonnae torture me, please don't tickle my feet. I cannae stand that!'

Chapter 6

The strange voice on the phone was not aggressive. It was like it was reading from a script, precisely.

'We have your friend. Consider that carefully. You have something we want. No harm will come to him if you remain sensible....' the voice said from Frankie's phone. Tam let it go no further, but butted in 'See that red-head of his, if you so much as touch a single hair of it, I'll put a match to what I've got. You'll never see it again! Is that clear enough!' And shut off the call.

The bus took Tam well away from the Trongate and up the winding slope past the Royal Infirmary and then turned towards the city centre, where he felt it was safe enough to slip off, given that he had kept his eye on the road behind and nothing resembling a black car or a white van could be seen. He was sure he was in the clear now. The phone call about Frankie certainly disturbed him. But there was also consolation in an afterthought. He had the photograph. Would Frankie understand, pursued and harried though both may have been, that he had the upperhand? He still hadn't a clue to its significance to anybody, but it was his for the moment. That trumped everything else.

As he was crossing back over the river, this time by the Millenium Bridge leading to the Glasgow Science Centre, the dusk light made the river seem black and lifeless. He had deliberately made this long, wide detour, twisting his way through various streets, the balls of his feet ready to erupt and dash at the slightest indication of threat. For the first time in his life, though, he felt the entire city was an encroaching threat. It was certainly the long way round to get back to the south bank but he did not need to worry about the time, as he was aiming for Gabby's. The shop kept going well beyond midnight, the man slaving like his very existence depended on it, a workaholic who at the same time was blessed by making it look like it was a form of relaxation. And indeed, when Tam arrived there, about half an hour later, he could see there was a small queue inside waiting to be served. That was normal. He stood on the other side of the street, looking up and down to determine if there was anybody hovering there, or if there was any sign of a white van or a black Lexus. He neither saw nor felt anything immediately suspicious.

He crossed over, turning occasionally to look behind him, then moved into the shop with its steamy mix of spicy aromas and body-sweat. Gabby did not notice him at first, but was bobbing up and down behind the counter like a pigeon picking at crumbs from a window ledge. Tam walked straight through to the office, the movement of which clearly demonstrating to the shopkeeper that something was amiss. Fit though he was, Tam suddenly felt drained and was glad to sit on a stool in the corner. He sat there patiently eyeing his phone lying on the desk. At last a sweating Gabby silently entered, sat down on a seat behind the desk and asked the simple question, 'So what's up?'

'They've got Frankie!'

'Who's got Frankie?'

It did not take him long to recount the incidents to Gabby, who, because of his interest in all things culinary, managed a smile, as Tam detailed the fate of a certain plate of Spaghetti Bolognaise. But only a brief smile. Other than that the man rested his chin on cupped hands on the desk and looked at Tam with the intensity of a doctor listening to a patient revealing serious symptoms. When Tam finished speaking Gabby reached over the table and gripped him by the shoulder, to which he applied a gentle supportive shake.

'Please, don't be blaming yourself. I think you did right in what you said to them on the phone. This is a form of naked bullying which nobody can ever overcome by being faint-hearted. I know from bitter experience you have to stand up to bullies. Easier said than done you might think. Of course. But sometimes it just happens and you find the courage from somewhere deep inside and when it lets itself out, you feel great relief. I know you are still concerned about Frankie but you are also correct. They want this badly.....'

He reached into the side pocket of his white overall and produced a key, pushed it into a desk- drawer opened it and then drew out the photograph. He put it down flat on the table between them and looked over at Tam as if to suggest it was hard to credit that this flimsy photograph could provoke such interest and drive men to violence.

'I took it out of the safe over the last few hours and came in here deliberately to study it now and again, and I must admit it is having a hypnotic effect on me. I look for signs, anything. Am I missing something? Something so obvious that by its very nature we are stupidly blind to it? There is nothing on the surface, back or front. Except that phone number. No signs or messages. You messed it up a bit of course when you sat on it. But apart from the slight diagonal crack nothing on the surface is telling me anything. Yet Frankie ends up in the clutches of what appear to be desperate men. All because of this!'

The last sentence came with a snort of disgust.

'Just think how I feel then,' Tam said in a consolatory way. 'I wanted to talk to you first though before I did anything else. I might not be able to take this on all on my own.'

'I told you before that I could have ways of helping. Contacts, you know. So do not feel like that.'

This was the very sentiment Tam wanted to hear and which helped to dispel the increasing feeling of alienation he had felt as he had walked back through the city. The weight on his shoulders seemed to lighten and sparked him into activity. He lifted his mobile and speed-dialled Frankie's number. Gabby smiled, a relaxed understanding smile as if he could read Tam's mind. The phone kept ringing. Tam held it steadfastly to his ear. He tried to conjure up an image of Frankie amongst them. He knew he was someone who was not easily cowed by anybody even to the extent of being foolhardy. But Frankie's head was screwed on the right way. He was street-wise. Tam knew they would have to reply. Then, eventually, they responded.

'Yes?' the voice said on Frankie's phone.

'I want to speak to my mate.'

'He is eating,' replied the very polite voice.

'He's eating?'

'Correct. A very large pizza.'

Tam was slightly taken aback by this. He knew Frankie could gorge pizzas like a whale swallowing a school of tuna fish, but it did not exactly fit the image of the emergency they were in.

'I want to speak to him, like fuckin' pronto!'

'Were you not brought up to believe that you must never speak with your mouth full? At the moment his mouth is very full.'

'Get him to the phone, smart-arse!'

Gabby reprimanded him for that remark with a frown and a slight shake of the head.

'My, my!' the voice said. 'Patience, please. We must all be very calm about this. What purpose is served by losing our cool? Please, tell me.'

'Is that the instruction you gave the bampots who treated me like a punch-bag today?'

'Bampots? What are they?'

'You and the rest are bampots. Scumbags, crooks, shite. Take your pick. '

'It is you who is picking up wrongly on this. I can assure you. We had nothing to do with what happened to you in the lane. So it is time to be calmer and sensible or else....'

'Or else what? And what do you mean that you'd nothin' to do wi' what happened in the lane?'

'I mean exactly what I said. We do know about it, because one of my friends was near the scene, observing. But it was not us.'

This didn't make sense at that moment and he had another purpose in mind anyway. He would leave that puzzle out, at the moment.

'Get Frankie to the phone,..... or else!'

'Ah, so that's his name. He told us it was William Wallace.'

'I don't care what you or I call him, get him to the fuckin' phone. No speak, no deal.'

He could tell from the brief silence which followed that the man was trying to think of how to comply without wishing to appear to lose his apparent dominant position.

'To show you how reasonable we propose to be, of course we will let him speak. There is no real problem. Wait!'

He did not appreciate how long he did wait, but it was annoyingly protracted. Then he heard Frankie's voice.

'Hi, mate. How's it goin?'

'You're eatin' pizza?' Tam asked with a degree of incredulity.

'Ay, pineapple and ham. Smashin'. Not my choice, right enough, since as you know I like the chorizo to add some edge to the taste........'

'Belt up! How could you be sitting there eating pizza with a bunch of bampots who could still slit your throat?'

'Hunger. Nature talks. And my stomach's on good terms with nature.'

'What about the rest of you? Are you hurt?'

'They clunked me at first and I've had a few bruises from being pushed about their van. My head's cut a bit. Apart from that I'll survive.'

'Where do you think you are?'

'I'm in the van. We could be at Loch Lomond by now. I just don't know.'

'Listen, I'll contact your ma and tell her you're stayin' over with me. That'll cover us for a while. Now can you tell me anythin' about them? Anythin'. What have they said that might give me a clue to what to do next?'

'Nothin' much. It's definitely the photo they're after though.'

Frankie paused.

'I've already warned them that they won't get their hands on anything if they harm you. That photograph is our ace.' Tam said.

'You know up till now that photograph has been as useful to me as a hole in a bloody parachute. And now you ask me to place my faith in it? My faith is in you, mate. I know you. I wouldn't trust anybody else in this situation other than you.'

And, before Tam's throat could choke with emotion at such a touching sentiment, Frankie changed the tone again.

'By the way, I think only one or two of them speak English. Certainly the driver's from Glasgow. They call him. Puss or Noose or Moose or Goose. I couldn't quite make out what it was. He went for the pizzas I believe. He thinks he's a bit of a hard man, gruntin' and snarlin' and all that....

Then it sounded as if he was being interrupted. The other voice came on.

'I think that's enough. This is to show you that your friend is hale and hearty and that we have nothing against him, or indeed yourself. Now what do you have in mind to settle this matter?'

'What I have in mind is for you to let him go,' Tam replied sternly.

'Cut to the chase. Give me the grounds on which we should. You have something which does not belong to you, but does, most emphatically, belong to us.'

'I'll give you the grounds when I'm good and ready,' Tam replied and hoped that the man at the other end did not detect, from the slight artificiality of his rather high-handed response, that he was simply playing for some time to think.

'Please yourself.' And then he added almost pompously. 'You cannot expect me to wait until hell freezes over, as a man once famously said. I would think you should be able to reach us by the morning with a solution. We look forward to hearing from you.'

He disconnected. Tam put down his phone and took a deep breath. They won't wait until hell freezes over, he thought. So who did say that? The man was being a smart arse. And at a time like this. Gabby reached over and gave him that supportive grip on his shoulder again.

'You handled that well. You might end up as a hostage negotiator someday,' he said with a beaming smile, in an attempt to radiate some cheer on to what seemed an intractable situation.

'What have you learned about them? Did he say anything that might give us some sense of direction on this,' Gabby asked. 'Any slight clue?'

'What did I learn? I learned that Frankie could eat a pineapple and ham pizza if he was in a snake-pit. I learned that the man leading them sounds like a real smoothie and is probably a ruthless scumbag. I learned that they have a driver called by a nickname. Puss, Noose, Goose, Moose, he didn't quite make it out. That's your lot. In short, we're up shit-creek.'

Gabby was pensive, like he was already into forward thinking.

'He said he wasn't goin' to wait until hell freezes over,' Tam went on, 'Big deal.'

'Hell freezes over,' Gabby repeated screwing up his face. 'Hell freezes over. Why does that stick in my mind? There is an echo of something in there. Where have I heard that before? Something stirs.'

Gabby stood up from the table and stretched himself, puzzling over that reference. He stroked his chin and walked round the tiny space, fidgeting with various items like he was tidying but clearly giving him time to mull over these words for some reason; then he sat down with a thump on the tiny chair, as if in defeat. He remained like that for a moment and, just as Tam was about to break into conversation again, Gabby reached out for his computer and started to play with the keys. From the other side Tam could see he was googling. It didn't take him long. He looked over the screen at Tam and announced a find.

'I just inserted words about hell freezing over and up it came. It was Adlai Stevenson, USA ambassador to the United Nations during the Cuban missile crisis of October 1962. Addressing the Soviet Union ambassador, and wanting an answer to his demand, he stated, 'I am prepared to wait for my answer *until hell freezes over.*'

'So?' Tam muttered. 'You live and learn.'

But he could also tell that Gabby was pondering this carefully. He snapped the lid of the computer shut and looked at Tam intently.

'What does that tell us?' he asked, rhetorically.

'Fuck all, to be honest.'

'That depends on interpretation. It suggests something to me. It suggests that this man is well-educated, well-read, who takes some interest in history, perhaps of modern history in particular. It tells me also that such an anecdote would stick in the mind of someone who was politically minded, someone with a particular view on life. He might not be able to say who won Wimbledon in the year 1962, but he can recall a statement made in the heat of debate about the possibility of Armageddon, the ultimate nuclear disaster. That suggests to me he is no ordinary thug. Yes, it might seem flimsy to go on. And it may make me sound like the resident of Baker Street. But we need to look for openings, ever so slight perhaps, even if it only sheds a tiny light into the darkness of confusion. Sometimes you have to let your instinct dictate to you and it seems to be suggesting something most strongly to me. And that instinct seems to be telling me that you are probably right.'

'About what?'

'That all this trouble has probably nothing to do with drugs.'

Chapter 7

Frankie could hear the heavens opening. Thunder blasted the city. It had been humid and unusually hot and now the area was paying the price. He did not know where he was but they were in conference outside, even in the pouring rain, discussing him, or whatever their next move was to be. He thumped the back door.

'I need a pee!' he shouted. There was no reply. He hammered the door again.

'You hear me? It's either out there or in here. It's up to you. And when I pee I don't pee Brut For Men. Got it?'

Then he pulled himself back a bit. Can you actually deliver ultimatums to a bunch of bampots in a situation like this he wondered? It was his bladder that was doing the talking though.

'Cannae hold out much longer!'

The door opened and two pairs of hands dragged him out, the rain, cascading down, simply welcoming him back to the real world again. They had pulled the van into a small road beside which there was a broad grass verge and bushes. They pushed him there, his feet sinking into marshy ground, his trainers almost sticking in gluey stuff. When he was finished, the hands gripping him pulled him back to the van past a huddle going on amongst the group, with two of them on their mobiles. They almost threw him inside where he landed on his back. To get upright again he pushed one foot strongly against the wall of the van and levered himself up. He was only in there a couple of minutes when the door reopened and they piled in beside him again.

They took off his blindfold. He beheld a motley crew. Not a pretty sight. The leader of the group, who had used his phone for the contact with Tam, was dressed in a school-masterly kind of way; properly suited, with a clean white shirt and a dark tie bearing some sort of emblem on it, his nose thin and long. He had more hair than the rest of the group put together, who had obviously been working overtime with their razors, using them like locusts to a harvest, their shaven heads glistening even in the dim light. They wore a varied collection of t-shirts, sweaters, shirts and jeans. Then there was the first man he had spoken to with nil response, The Silent One. Frankie had actually begun to think he was in fact a highly developed robot. But he had also observed him, earlier, putting a finger into an ear, and wiggling it as if he was suffering an itch there. Robots don't itch.

When the leader had been speaking on the phone to Tam he had sounded very proper, like listening to an answering machine. He turned and stepped towards Frankie again.

'Blood,' the leader said without any emotion, peering at the side of Frankie's head. He produced a small handkerchief and handed it to Frankie. 'Put that on it.'

'Blood,' he repeated. 'The very last thing we wanted spilled. I hate the sight of blood, believe you me. That is why I try so hard to avoid it being shed. The trouble with spilling blood is that it can become very contagious. One drop leads to another...and another. Once the genie is out of the bottle there is no telling where it all stops. What a pity!'

Phoney, Frankie thought. Playing to the gallery. Trying to show the other bampots that he was kind-hearted and all that. The van was on the move again.

'I want that blood cleared up and have you examined properly. We wish you no more harm. As you will see when we get there.'

Where? Frankie thought. The first stage, though, was to rid himself of the thought that he was in an impossible situation. That was going to be tough. The Silent One's stony demeanour only suggested that he was capable of strangling a babe. Better to think of him that way. A lot of the hard men he had heard about in Glasgow were renowned not for oratory but for action; the kind that had its own effective grammar. It looked like it wasn't confined to Frankie's native city.

'You need some attention for that self-inflicted wound. We take no responsibility for that. We want you to be untarnished when it comes to negotiation. Your wound will be treated and you will be in more comfortable surroundings.'

'The Hilton?' Frankie asked. 'My uncle tells me they've got flat-screen tellys in all rooms and Wifi....'

'I do apologise. It is beyond our budget. We do not like living beyond our means. You will be accompanied of course. You will stay there until your friend sees sense.'

Puss, or Noose, or Moose, or Cruise, whatever his name was, kept throwing the van about, making him feel as if they were in a rodeo simulation machine. His head pounded. He took a quick look at the blood-soaked handkerchief and put his bare finger to the wound to test if there was still a flow. It was sticky. Also his head ached now, like the pain was spreading. But he didn't feel faint or weak overall. He started to sing 'O, Flower of Scotland' and rocked himself side to side, only interrupting the verse with a 'Come on, join in!' to the others. By the time he had reached the last line, 'To send him homewards, tae think again,' they were looking at him like men who had just discovered a species yet unknown to anthropologists.

'Comes from the heart,' he explained to even more intense black expressions. 'Sounds better at Hampden, or in a busy pub.'

The Silent One and another stony-faced captor instantly decided to show they were less than understanding of Scottish patriotism by reaching out, pulling Frankie forwards and between them taking a large rag and gagging him. Thus silenced, soon after that, they arrived at their destination.

Frankie smelled newly cut-grass as soon as he stepped out, suggesting they had perhaps reached a suburb. The driver remained in the van as the other two released the gag, at the same time as the Silent One wagged another admonitory finger at him to suggest that if he tried to warble again they might garrotte him. Frankie, paining, was in no mood to contest this. He tried a quick sweeping look around him and could see street lights, the black shapes of what appeared to be mansions with driveways and walls and hedges. It was all of a blur because of the way they hustled him out of the van and up towards the house they were heading to, the crunching sound of driveway granite chips underfoot, scarring the night's tranquillity.

Just before they reached the house he could see a figure silhouetted in the doorway, a hallway light shining strongly from within. It was like looking at a tall block of ebony. It wasn't until he was pushed up the steps that he could see it was a woman.

'Good evening,' she said, coolly. Then she issued a barked command to the others, in another language; a couple of them offering tugged forelocks, like peasants. The way they shuffled around her, as they did, was almost as if they were now in the presence of some goddess. She was about the same height as Frankie but clearly many kilos heavier, with broad shoulders which lent the clear impression of a solid body, encased as it was in a dark-blue dressing-gown, secured by a gold cord with tassels tied round her waist. She barely looked at Frankie but turned and snapped, 'Follow me, please.' He wondered if he was about to experience the same phoney courtesy the leader had shown. They made their way along a vast hall and then up a broad staircase, his guardians following close behind. His head was throbbing incessantly now.

He followed the woman into a large room with tall, heavily curtained windows, a long bookcase at one side, a huge leather sofa with matching chairs and a wide desk on which sat a computer and lamps and untidy piles of paper. But, what caught his attention, above all, was a narrow bed, the kind which can be raised or lowered to provide back support, covered with a white gauze sheet like he had seen before when he had been in hospital being examined for badly sprained ankle ligaments. The fact that he also sensed in his nostrils that hint of the distinctive aroma of disinfectant made it clear that whatever else the woman was, she was certainly into medicine of some kind.

As he looked at the sheet he asked politely, 'Do you give massages?'

'Let me see your wound,' she said as if he had not spoken at all and ushered him into one of the leather chairs.

'Are you NHS?' Frankie asked her as he took the blood-soaked handkerchief away from his head. 'You know ma mother's been waitin' six months for a hip replacement. You think that's fair? Do you do hips? Private or NHS?'

She ignored this and he felt something like cotton wool being put against his head.

'Anyway, why are you botherin' with the state I'm in? You're goin' to get nothin' out of me. So I think you might be wasting your time.'

'Have you heard of the Hippocratic Oath?' she answered dabbing at his neck.

'Naw. But I could repeat a few oaths from round my neighbourhood, if you're in the mood.'

She stopped dabbing for a moment and looked at the two others as if she could not believe what had been said to her.

'I tend to the sick and to the maimed because it is my duty and moral obligation to do so, even to those who indulge in self-immolation and who stubbornly refuse to see sense. Now, hold this to your wound and come with me.'

He did as he was told and walked behind her through a door which led into a darkened area, but when she turned the light on he could see they were in a small room whose walls were covered in glass cabinets, filled with tiny boxes and cartons like you would see in a pharmacy. The antiseptic atmosphere was like he was being cleansed, simply by entering. There was a large wash-hand basin with a mirror above. She led him to it, got him to bend down and proceeded to mop his head with hot water and a swab of some kind after which she applied something which stung sharply.

'Hold that in place. I am going to insert a stitch or two.'

She turned away from him and went to one of the cabinets and started to fuss with material from it. Frankie looked into the mirror, delighted to know that his dishevelled self had altered little after all the activity of the last few hours. He turned sideways to have a look at his head and took the gauze away from it. There was a red welt there. Not very pretty. But in the mirror something else suddenly caught his attention. At the other side of the room he could see a small notice-board, appended to which were various papers, and in the middle of which were separate photographs of six men. He turned and looked past the woman who was busying herself preparing for the stitching. He moved closer. Then he realised why his skin was beginning to creep. It was from recognition. Of the six photographs he had noticed, five had large red stickers attached to one of their corners. The one without, could not be missed.

It was the man from Tam's photograph. No mistake. Perhaps the head shot revealed him as cleaner, smarter in appearance, and wrapped up this time in winter clothing; there was snow in the background. But the same man, nonetheless. Even then, on that spot, he couldn't help but think that these bampots were just waiting to put a red sticker on that remaining face.

* **

Gabby was on his own in the shop. He had to make a quick inventory before he visited the cash and carry the following morning. His wife had long gone and although he liked to get back to his kids as soon as possible because of the incredible hours he worked, he could not avoid the drudgery of taking stock. It meant money after all. But even as he painstakingly went through the usual routine of checking the shelves, the last conversation with Tam was intruding on his thinking. It was no use. He wasn't applying himself to the task properly as the freezing over of hell comment had sucked him into deeper thinking of the matter. He had not taken their plight lightly of course but on the other hand he had stayed his hand, requiring to know what might have lain at the root of all this. He couldn't resist. He left his clipboard on a shelf and unlocked the drawer; then placed the photograph in front of him on the table.

'What can you tell me?' he whispered. 'What terrible things are you doing to these two boys? Who are you strange man?'

He liked the two lads immensely. They were genuine. The generational difference was not only of no consequence, it also accentuated the enjoyment of dealing with boys who could stimulate him with their lively discourses on life that caused him so often to reminisce about his own adolescence, in an entirely different culture, but which led him to understand perfectly a phrase that someone had told him at a Burns Supper he had been invited to, that 'We're all Jock Tamson's bairns.' There was never any suggestion that they would caricature him behind his back. Far too many people patronised him and his family. And he could tell which ones would behind his back most likely use the word Paki, which although it might not always have a sinister meaning was nevertheless hardly a term of endearment. So he could recognise such phoniness immediately. And had done so since he had first arrived in Glasgow almost two decades previously where he had a share in the family cash and carry business. This gave him time to adapt to the strange ways of the city and because of his bubbling demeanour and getting around the nooks and crannies of the shopping world he became well-known to a variety of folk. Although he was doing well during the first decade he always felt the need to go independent. He wanted to be his own master without having to conform to the consensus within the family.

His firm had sponsored a boxing night at a large Glasgow hotel on one occasion and thereafter he became a regular at the monthly shows. Because of the generous nature of that sponsorship he developed solid contacts in the boxing world and those people associated with it. Not all of them he would have brought home for a meal. There was always a feeling that some figures came from the darker side of life. He listened avidly to rumours about them. Many of them were around him on those evenings and it is clear that whatever their reputations, they had taken a fancy to him. He took it all in his stride. And he became popular. He felt confident in their company no matter their reputation. He was being accepted by a wide variety of people. This made him commercially viable. It also encouraged him to break out on his own with the blessing of the family and established his shop with the kind of collateral that he hoped would ultimately spawn a chain of cafes. That was his aim. What he had now had succeeded beyond his wildest imagination even though at first it was small fry compared to the cash and carry he had left behind. But he was his own master now. Through hard work and a geniality which rarely let him down, he had amassed a network of associates through his various sponsorships that he could turn to in times of trouble. Now two of his favourite customers were in deep shit and there was no way he could sit back and let them down.

He touched the photograph with a forefinger as if there were a tactile clue to its origin. A good-looking man of maybe about thirty looked at ease as he stood on the cobblestones and the silence in the room mixed with the exasperating minimal information that he beheld compelled him to action. It was time to call in a favour. He lifted the office phone, punched in a number that he knew by heart and when there came an answer all he said was, 'Tell him I need his help.'

***

The bells reminded Tam it was a Sunday morning. At least that was normal. When he had got home late the previous night he could hear a family discussion going on in the living room. Sarah's voice was the loudest as usual. They were talking money. Something about benefits. Spare me that, he thought. So he slipped to his room and within five minutes had tanked out, his body feeling he had been through some threshing machine. He did have a sensation that somebody had come to his room much later, but only subliminally. When he awakened there was silence. Perhaps their discussion had gone on late into the night. When he got up and dressed there was still no arousal of the rest of the family. So he hurriedly took a glass of milk, a roll with some cheese, then beat a retreat before he could waken anybody. All he wanted then was to get out and walk, anywhere. Then his phone went. The voice was Gabby's telling him that there was something he needed to talk to him about. The walk became a jog. He was breathing deeply when he arrived at the shop.

'No news is good news, you might say,' Gabby said to him, opening both palms of his hands to the ceiling and shrugging his shoulders; his body language assisting him to stress that point. 'They haven't been in touch?' he asked Tam. 'No, of course not. They want to dangle you for a while. But today is a key day though. We mustn't allow things to drag on in their terms. I know you are very concerned. So am I. But we must remain calm. I am leaving my wife in charge this morning for we have a journey to undertake. Come with me.'

Gabby treated his large dark-green Mercedes as if he were a potentate from the days of the Raj. It gleamed with constant, affectionate attention. When they drove out from the shop the driver's window was down and the shopkeeper stuck out a waving gesticulating hand as if he were semaphoring to the public in the street a translation of the monologue he was conducting inside, his other hand controlling the steering wheel, sometimes with just the tips of his fingers, in a display of almost artistic nonchalance. Occasionally he would wave at someone he recognised. He claimed he never forgot a face. But it did not interfere with the talk which was about the nature and character of his adopted city, Glasgow. It was incessant. Then he mentioned the man they were going to meet.

'He knows this city like he built it. He knows people, all kinds of people. From the top to the bottom. None of the so-called hard men would dare cross him, you take it from me. He knows some of the richest business men in this city as well. You know why? Respect. They can talk to him. He makes them feel.....significant. There is little that happens on the streets without him hearing about it. He is the man who helped me with my little problems some time ago. And when I told him everything I knew about what happened to you, and what Frankie said on the phone to you, every little detail, something clicked with him. He spotted something, something that made him more than interested in all of this.'

'Like what?'

'Just you wait and see.'

They were travelling east. Tam mentally switched off eventually from the cascade of talk at his elbow. It was a part of the city Tam had never warmed to, largely because he did not know it so well. He could see, way to his left, just over some of the lower buildings, the bulky ramparts of Celtic Park and the white shell of the newly-built Commonwealth Games velodrome. Gabby took a bewildering route of one-ways, sudden twists and turns, one-handed, that by the time they had arrived at his destination Tam felt quite disorientated. They turned sharply off the main road eventually, and slid into a yard, at the back of which was a low-set building with a large board on its roof proclaiming, 'Sammy's Gym'. As they stepped out of the car they could hear pounding sounds coming from within. Tam followed Gabby inside, quite unsure of what to expect and why they had come in the first place.

The sight of the full-size boxing ring, in the middle of the large room they had entered, almost overwhelmed Tam. He had only ever seen one on television. Inside the ropes were two lads, with headguards on, who were probably not much older than himself, circling and dabbing at one another, sparring like they had been told to, but with little conviction, until there was a sudden eruption, resulting in a flurry of punches that ended with them becoming entangled and a voice from one of the men surrounding the ring bawling 'Break! Break!' When they still remained in the clinch the man doing the shouting pulled himself up on to the ring, on the outside of the ropes and screamed, 'Willie, Hughie! When I say break I mean it. Got it!' He was annoyed, and since he dwarfed them, they got the message and broke. The noise from around was incessant, bags being punched, lads skipping, and through a door on the other side of the ring Tam could see into another gym where there were various clattering exercise machines being used by both men and women.

'This way,' Gabby said, moving round the ring to the other side of the room. There was a small man sitting at a table sipping from a cup, but with his eyes darting about, to the rhythm of what was happening inside the ropes.

Gabby addressed him. 'Sammy, how are you, my amigo?'

'Got a new drug for my arthritis,' the little man replied, putting down the cup, but without taking his eyes off the ring. 'It's workin' a treat....so far. Might put on the gloves again, eh?'

That was said with a lilt in his voice. As he then turned his attention to them, Tam saw plentiful silver-hair, a face dabbed with cherry-red cheeks, a nose that seemed slightly squashed and bent to one side, and very prominent and obvious pearly-white false teeth, which on every smile seemed like a portcullis.

'Tam, meet the former fly-weight champion of Europe, Sammy Paterson.'

As Sammy clasped his hand firmly in the shake of welcome, he looked Tam up and down like he was a future prospect for the ring. Perhaps he did that with everybody instinctively.

'Fancy puttin' the gloves on young fella,' Sammy asked him.

Tam shrugged, to give the impression of being non-committal, but in fact it had never been one of his burning ambitions in life, and which the closeness to the ring was now confirming.

'Just ask Gabby here,' he said, 'He'll let me know if ye fancy it any time. Great man. Great for the club here. D'ye know he sponsors a lot of the events we have in here for young promising boxers. We couldnae have them without his cash.'

They could hardly stop him after that, as he heaped praise on Gabby and went through many of the events he had supported and the number of young boxers he had helped stay on in the sport. Eventually the shopkeeper had to interrupt him.

'Sammy, this is the boy I told you about on the phone. He's in a bit of bother. I tried to explain. Can we go somewhere quieter?'

The little man rose and perkily, with a pronounced shoulder swagger, led them into an office with a widescreen television showing ESPN boxing, like there was no escape from the man's continuing passion. There they sat in deep leather couches.

'I've heard every detail of your story from Gabby. So I start off by sayin', "Never throw in the towel",' the little man said, his cheery, squashed face beaming out at both of them. 'In all the time I fought in the ring, none of my seconds ever threw in the towel. And I took some beatings in my day, particularly in my later days. I remember fightin' in Italy defending my European title. Now you need to knock your opponent unconscious in the first round in Italy just to get a draw. You see, the referees and the judges were all bent in Italy, every last one of them on the take. Bribery and corruption was second nature to them. I knew I was on a hidin' to nothin' but I didn't give in. I lost my title that night. But I went out with my head held high.'

No matter how much he was appreciating just what this little man had achieved in the sport, Tam was beginning to prepare for the long session of nostalgia which he suspected Sammy normally dished out to newcomers. Then the former champion stopped and you could see he was sifting through in his mind what had just been told him. Then he spoke.

'Gabby said that there was a Glasgow man there and he got a name. The driver, right?'

'Frankie couldn't hear it clearly enough. He wasn't sure what it was,' Tam replied.

'If it was Moose, then we're going places.' Sammy said, and threw a quick right hook at an invisible opponent.

Chapter 8

At least there was a degree of comfort where they had now put Frankie. He was in a tiny attic room with a bookcase, some framed photographs, a small table with a jug in the middle and a divan couch which as the lady doctor had explained briefly could be converted to a bed. That information hardly exhilarated Frankie as it inferred a longer occupancy than he had in mind.

'If you're keepin' me to Christmas, I have to tell you I don't like turkey. Cannae stand it. A curry carry-out would do me. I can even recommend a place. I could phone them just now if you're a bit peckish.....'

The doctor had the disconcerting manner of seeming not to hear a word he spoke. She maintained a derisory silence that was different from the Silent One who clearly could not speak a word of English. It seemed a neutral stance, as if she did not really want to have anything to do with him, even though she was clearly a significant part of whatever kind of operation this was, and that she would simply have to put up with him. Bit of a snob, he supposed. She certainly had done a quick, effective job on his head which he had politely thanked her for, although it was clear he really disturbed her when she had finished, as he pointed towards the photographs on the board and asked, 'Who's that geezer? The one second from the right. The one without the red sticker on him. '

She gripped his shoulders firmly and turned him towards the door.

'Come,' she softly. 'You will rest now. We will give you plenty water to drink.'

That was all, until she had led him upstairs, briefly explained the couch situation and then left him. The Silent One followed behind, but only to look around the attic which seemed to satisfy him that it was secure, as the tiny window on the slope of the roof might have proved difficult even for the exit of a cat. Then he was left on his own, where he lapsed eventually into sleep, wakening with a start, the light flooding in, and immediately wondering where Tam might have got to. No watch, and no clock in the room meant he was in a time warp.

It didn't stop him from thinking about the photographs he had seen in the tiny surgery. What was so special about the one Tam had found? It irritated him increasingly that there was no sensible answer he could provide for himself and nobody around here was likely to be forthcoming about it. To release some of the tension of frustration that he was clearly feeling, every time he tried to tackle that conundrum, he started to prowl around the small room looking at the pictures and the bookcase. There was a whole variety there. Many of them were medical books but some were about travel and then one with a colourful jacket caught the eye. He pulled it out. *Stalingrad* by Anthony Beevor. It looked promising with its red and black jacket portraying men with bayonets charging. It would be a better read than its neighbour on the bookshelf, *Haematology-Practical Notebook*. He settled down and within minutes was engrossed in the Second World War. Then he heard the door behind him being opened. It was the Silent One carrying a tray on which there was a mug of tea, some toast, and a large jaffa orange. Breakfast was being served.

'I suppose French toast was out of the question?' Frankie said pulling a face at the sight of the orange. So they were not only a bunch of bampots, but health freaks into the bargain. What a combination, he thought. But he could not just sit there passively munching their hospitality. He had to do something. The small austere attic and its minimal furniture offered no solace to one brewing the thoughts of escape. The tools simply were not there. Or were they? Perhaps it was contemplating that bleak outlook for some considerable time that led him to a kind of reverse view to what seemed the logical objective, to get out of there. The tiny window meant there was no way OUT. And the door was the only way IN. So?

Even though the desire for freedom was at its acutest now, he began to feel a change of mood. More like the cold hand of realism stroking him. All he had left was to allow his natural temperament take over. He could resist. Outright defiance. Blatant, perhaps even reckless or ridiculous defiance. But show it. Don't just sit and take it all. He thought about the first few pages of the book he had been reading. It had stirred him and now it introduced the germ of a notion.

Frankie rose from the couch and surveyed it closely. He went to one end of it and started to push it towards the door. Not surprisingly it felt like he was pushing against a car with its brake on. Fortunately the carpet on the floor was one of those plain, thickly woven ones which prevented the sound of scraping. But, even so, he pushed in small movements and quickly began to sweat with the effort of manoeuvring it into the position he wanted, which was at right angles to the door. When he satisfied himself with that, he had to face possibly the worst part, which was to lift one end until it was propped against the door, and to do so with the minimum of noise. He had heard a story once of how a woman had lifted a car with her own two hands to save her child trapped underneath and the very necessity of doing so produced the miraculous strength to achieve that. Saving your own skin, he was now discovering, was as powerful an incentive as that. He heaved at it, and then managed to prop his back underneath the end he had elevated and, in a shuffling motion, he gently rested the sofa against the door until it was forming a wedge directly against the handle.

Next he turned to the small bookcase, and with quick flipping motions divested it of the books and magazines there, before turning it on end and 'walking' it towards the couch. He had judged by eye that it might be the right length to jam between the couch and the wall against which it had been standing. He laid it flat down. It was slightly too long to fit that space. That was an advantage. It meant he had to force it against the wall, causing a scraping down the paintwork, until it was securely jammed, and as he did so he could feel the tension stretching from the wall, through the two pieces of furniture to the door, which shook slightly when he had finally secured that improvised buttress. When he looked at the door itself he could see that the pressure exerted on it, by the end of the couch, had made a dent in the wooden panel. The door was secure. If he couldn't get out, they couldn't get in.

He had to test that though. He started to jump up and down on the floor, so that if they were around they would have heard this. They did. He heard the steps approaching and then the key being tried, the door handle turned and an attempt to gain entry. The wedge stood firm. The movements on the other side became increasingly frantic until he could tell that someone was shouldering the door heavily. It quivered slightly, but nothing more. It was all holding firm. He guessed it must have been the Silent One at the other side, for no commands had been issued, no questions, only grunts.

Then there was silence for a while. Frankie picked up his Stalingrad book then squeezed himself under the angle of the couch and propped his feet firmly against the door to add more resistance if needed, his knees bent almost to his chin, preparing for any reaction, but now with time on his hands. He started to read the blurbs on the cover, telling of how a city bravely survived. Then he heard voices speaking in that gruff language and suddenly there were quite plainly two enormous kicks on the door, followed by a loud shriek of protest. Foreign language or not, he could tell that was the woman doctor's voice and it sounded like an objection, as if she wanted no damage to her property. There were more heaves and shoves and pushes but no kicks. The door stood firm. Frankie's legs on the wooden panels, crouched underneath, felt the trembles run down them, and felt reassurance from that, for nothing was budging. He was secure. Then she spoke.

'I must look at your head. I don't want anything septic arising. And we want to provide you with a lunch, since it is not our intention, really, to hurt you. Can you hear me?'

Frankie remained silent.

'I don't know what you have done in there and what purpose this serves. '

That was the first payback. He had annoyed her.

'It does not make sense. What kind of game do you think you are playing?'

'Sieges!' Frankie replied, turning to the opening chapter of his book on Stalingrad.

***

'Once upon a time there was a professional driver we knew called Moose,' Sammy told him. 'A rogue. Started off as a taxi driver, then got big in the head. Would do anythin' for a bob, including getaway stuff for some of the gangs. Good at the business. That's why he got a lot of work. Then he boobed.'

Gabby and Tam were hanging on every word.

'Drove a car for a robbery on a bank on the south side. Unfortunately for him he turned down a road which had been dug up just hours before. He was obviously goin' so fast he missed the signs and ran it through a barrier and straight into a six-foot trench and they and the money all got trapped there. The polis could have taken their time to get there in rickshaws if they had wanted. He was a laughin' stock. Gettin' nabbed like that did nothing for his so-called 'hard man' image and I don't think his social life in jail could have been up to much after that. That was years ago and I hadn't heard about him until now.'

'Funny name, as well, I thought,' the shopkeeper added.

'Sure,' Sammy said. 'Not too many people around with a moniker like that. Can only be the one person. 'Moose Malloy. That would be his full name. I never did find out what his Christian name really was. Not that I was really interested. Nicknames stick to folk. There's a lot of them round here. I knew a man once, called 'Pigeon' Mulgrew. Never knew how he got it, but it stuck to his dying days. 'Pigeon' was on his gravestone. They didn't lay flowers down there. Instead they scattered the grave wi' bird seed.'

He cackled and slapped a thigh in merriment.

'Gabby is a name my mother would not like,' the shopkeeper said dolefully, but with gracious acceptance.

'So he's driving them is he?' Sammy went on. 'You say there are probably foreigners among them. They won't know the city all that well then. They probably needed somebody who knows every district, every nook and cranny. They probably learned about him from some of the low life around here. Moose, would you believe! Help ma Boab!'

That last expression he had heard often on the lips of his grandfather, culled from the famous comic strip *Oor Wullie*. They were words of comical horror, but not to be dismissed lightly.

'Look, Mr Paterson,' he began.

'Sammy, please. Just Sammy. Like everybody else.'

'Sammy, maybe you think I'm being cool. Too cool. I'm no' really. Believe me I'm scared stiff at times. Especially about my mate. I just don't know what's happened to him. He sounded all right on the phone last night but I'm no' sure how to play this. If I phone them and try to suggest a way out, they might think it's a sign of weakness. And waiting to hear from them is torture, honestly I'm round the fucking bend.'

'Ok. There's a way out of this. Give them the photograph. That's what they want. They get it. You get your mate back. Simple.'

That certainly was no fighting talk. He couldn't find the words to react properly without perhaps causing offence. He looked sideways at Gabby who was staring straight ahead, avoiding a facial judgement on what had just been said.

'You see, son,' the little man went on, 'I'm no' throwin' the towel in for you. But I'm tellin' you there's no shame in thinkin' of your own skin. What does it matter if that gang comes and goes? Life'll go on for you, as it will for that lassie you helped yesterday. Tomorrow you could be back to normal, all forgotten. Think o' that! Don't dig a grave for yourself when there's nae need to. That's the alternative.'

'I'm going to get that photograph back to the girl. That'll be the end of it for me. I don't want to give in to them. I don't like bein' pushed around. Would you? '

Sammy stood, in response to that, stretching himself, hands above his head as if he wished to lend the impression of height and strength to his diminutive frame. Then he reached out and offered his hand for a shake with Tam, who, slightly hesitantly, reached out as well, and then felt such a hard clamp on it, as to remind him he was being held by a fist that had fought to the top in Europe, and had apparently relinquished nothing of its potency.

'You've got spunk, lad. I like that in folk. I just wanted to see what you're made of. So I might be of some help. Some of my boys know who Moose is all right,' he said quietly.

He rose and led the way out of the office into the activity outside.

'Donald! Craig!' he shouted at two men pounding on punch-bags. 'Find Moose. And quick.'

They were highly muscled. Their bodies glistened with sweat and the intensity of their attack on the large bags suggested that they were a kind of human insurance policy for Sammy. As they moved away from the bags, Tam could sense they were relishing this request. He had been invited to linger awhile but the Frankie situation was continually biting at him. He was feeling steadier though, impressed by the authority the little former champion obviously and easily exerted.

There was no way Tam was returning home just yet, though. When Gabby drove him back to the neighbourhood he walked down towards the very spot he had first encountered the girl in trouble in the lane; drawn to it, as if it had yet to tell him something. There were marks still to be seen on the earth where the scuffle had taken place, but they offered nothing other than a sense of regret that it revealed nothing to him, but certainly heightened his sense of frustration. He had left his phone alone, since the last call to Frankie, looking at it from time to time as if it was toying with him, holding off telling him something vital, something to change events. He had not even bothered to look at the numbers he had copied to his phone from the sim card of the man from Market Place in the Merchant City, so engrossed had he been in Frankie's absence. But now it was time to contact the bampots. He dialled the number.

It rang out and continued to do so until he received the answering machine. He tried again, to the same response. This time he left a message. 'You'd better reply to this if you are still interested in getting that photograph.' Within a couple of minutes came the response.

'Are you beginning to see reason?' the voice simply said without introduction.

'I want to speak to my mate.'

'I think he talked enough to you the other night. We don't want to protract this. We are being quite firm. You will not be able to speak to your friend until you have offered something tangible to us. So what do you have in mind?'

Tam hesitated.

'The photograph is in a safe place,' he replied. 'Very safe. Maybe we should meet to talk about a swap.'

'That is possible. Where?'

'I'll think about that. Somewhere your mob won't be able to touch me. You'll come on your own.'

'Of course, that's understandable. Now you seem to be talking some sense. I appreciate that.'

'I'll get back to you and let you know.'

With that Tam clicked off. Stalling, that's all it was. He still hadn't an idea of how to go about this. He sensed that, at this stage anyway, they wouldn't harm Frankie. He turned on his phone and tapped the sequence to bring up basics of the mobile and the sim card details he had copied. He tapped into the registration and saw the name there. Vasil Kisel. Next he went for the contacts. He began to spin through them. There was a wide variety of numbers and names. Some of them were obviously foreign. The code for one country in particular kept recurring. He didn't want to run up an unnecessary charge on his phone by contacting a foreign number direct even though the temptation to do so was strong. Instead he phoned the operator to check which country the digits identified. She sounded as if she had enjoyed a late Saturday night, her voice drowsy and adenoidal. Nevertheless it did not take her long.

'Belarus,' she said.

If somebody had offered him a tenner, to pick that place out on a map, he wouldn't have been able. That was the truth of it. There were other contact names on the phone. Lots of them. Tam spun

116

through some of them and picked one at random. It was a London number. Another was Birmingham which he recognised from having several times phoned an aunt who lived there. Then there were a few Glasgow contacts with numbers. One of them had the same local code as their own house phone. The name was simply MacPhail. He let the cursor hover over the name, trying to convince himself that it must be a number very close to where he was sitting against the wall in the lane, but still unsure how to handle it. He decided he had to try that local number. Tam pressed it. He did not have to wait long. The answer came.

'Agnes MacPhail.'

The voice sounded prim.

'Hello,' Tam said hoping that his voice did not reveal the slight nervousness he felt. 'I'm phoning on behalf of Vasil Kisel. He's had an unfortunate accident in his car. He was involved in a collision...'

'Oh, dear! How serious?'

'Broke his jaw in the process. Can hardly speak. So he asked me to call.'

'That's dreadful. Is that why he missed his appointment? You know I was so much looking forward to it. His voice alone told me so much about him. Foreign, isn't he? Eastern Europe? Am I right?'

Tam ignored that.

'The point is that he lost your address.'

'He told me that he got my address from some girl or other. That was the only reference. But, of course, if he wants another appointment then I would be delighted to oblige, so long as he lets me know in advance if he can't make it again.'

'I'll remind him, of course. But knowing him he'll probably have forgotten what you said. Could you explain a bit more? Had he to bring something with him? And of course he forgot your address. It would be a help if you could remind me of it.'

'16a Cochrane Terrace, and I would have thought that......'

Then there was silence at the other end as if she had realised she had gone too far with this anonymous person. No sound at all. She was suspicious. He felt it coming through strongly to him.

'Hello,' he said. A second later the phone was put down on him.

At least he had the address. And she had mentioned a girl. Could it be the same girl? But the sense of that achievement quickly wore thin as he realised that the girl was still so distant from the reality surrounding him, that he was starting to think she was merely a figment of his imagination.

Chapter 9

The knock on the door was almost polite. Frankie, feeling a bout of cramp coming on, had eased himself out of the doubled-up figure he represented, knees almost tucked up to the chin, large feet on the door, giving added support to the long wedge which was buttressing the room against entry. There had been solid kicks aimed in various ways at the panelling, but it was clear that the doctor's view had held sway and there was no way she was going to allow her property to be wilfully damaged, even by those obviously part of her tribe. As well as that, the bumping and heaving against it had long since ceased. Frankie responded to the polite knock by sitting up, slightly tensing again, although realising that they would have to take a pickaxe to get to him.

'We have some food for you.' It was the first time he had heard the voice of the leader since he had put up his barricade. Frankie guessed he must just have arrived.

'It is outside the door here. You eat or you don't. It's your choice and I don't see how it makes much difference to what eventually is going to happen to you. I will be in touch with your friend to let him know that our patience is not unlimited. Meanwhile, I suggest you open up and eat.'

Frankie did not reply but stretched himself, feeling just a tad superior now.

'Do you hear me?' the voice asked. 'Food. Just outside the door. We have no need to manhandle you. And the food is right up your street I would imagine. It's from McDonalds. It is a beef patty with carmelised onions, lettuce, tomato, bacon, in a seasoned, smoky tomato sauce, all inside a sesame seeded bun.'

Frankie felt it sounded like he was reading from a McDonald's handout. Nevertheless, on hearing that, despite his determination to maintain his fortress, he did feel a slight wilting of the spirit, and his taste buds seemed to salivate with the strength of geysers. He rose to his feet to try to fend off that possible erosion of his fortitude. He doubted if the doctor would have had a hand in changing the diet, from fruit to a calorie time-bomb.

'My uncle says that McDonald's contribute a great deal to global warmin',' Frankie decided to reply. 'They are the biggest producers of beef in the world. Can you think of all that cattle fartin' all over the place, sending the gases into the atmosphere and meltin' icebergs in the Arctic. That's what he says. And I believe him. For it was him that told me that if you put old coins into lemon water and let them soak for a minute or two, and then put them on a piece of paper, they will look like they were brand new. Chemical reaction. Take it from me, he knows a thing or two about science. Like my mate Tam. So where will all the Eskimos end up livin' if we keep eatin' all that beef and the North Pole ends up wi' palm trees?'

From the other side of the door there was a long silence as if they were trying to digest the significance of the scientific analysis which they probably had not been expecting. Or perhaps it was just incredulity. The environment was clearly not on their agenda. Then came a reply, based clearly on sarcasm.

'Would sir prefer muesli in skimmed milk with a scattering of raspberries on top? That, I take it, would help the survival of the Arctic ice-packs, yes?'

He did not reply to that as, simultaneous with the question, there was a sound of scraping and bumping above his head and then the sliding sound of something running down the roof, like a slate coming loose. Frankie looked up to the small dormer window and could see a shadow flitting across the glass, then a shape, then something more discernable, a face staring down at him. It was the Silent One, looking as if he had triumphantly climbed the north face of the Eiger, but at the same time breathing heavily with relief that he had not followed the slate downwards. In effect all he could do was look down at Frankie, since there was no way he could slip through the small window. And in any case it was locked. Lying alongside the skirting-board beneath the window was a long wooden pole obviously there to allow those folk who could not reach the lock, secure it with the cleat at the end of it. Frankie lifted it and showed it to the Silent One; but not as a domestic aid, more as a potential weapon, like if he dared push himself through that window, by any miraculous means, he would end up impaled on the kind of weapon that he loved seeing used on *Game of Thrones*. On the other hand Frankie began to ascertain that the Silent One was only there to spy, and keep the others informed, in case he was going to turn into an arsonist and take the extreme route out. He turned to the door.

'Tell you friend on the roof no' to go near the pigeons. My uncle says there is bird flu on the go again.'

The response to that was of a dramatically different tone. It was as if they were now beginning to run out of patience.

'If you think you can hold out until you are rescued, then you are utterly mistaken. You have no idea where we are. Nor do any of your friends. Not one clue. We can wait. The McDonalds meal will not go to waste. That has been your choice. So be it.'

On hearing the last remark Frankie did feel a pang of open rebellion starting in his stomach, but with stoic determination he looked upwards and gave the Silent One a thumbs up.

***

It was half-past twelve. Tam had not forgotten the arrangement he had worked out privately with this Nicholas Carson, to meet at one o'clock, but the time had crept up on him. Nobody knew where he was heading. He had mentioned it to Frankie but so much had happened since then. It took him only a ten minute walk to where he had personally chosen. He was ready to bolt if he became suspicious of anybody and kept swivelling to look behind. If anybody had really been looking closely they might have thought that he was a squaddie reconnoitring a street in Helmand province, like they saw nightly on news reports. There were several cars parked in the large crescent at the edge of the river Clyde. That is where Tam had told the man to park. As he walked towards the cars he could see framed in the background the royal blue struts of the narrow St Andrews Bridge which led pedestrians across the Clyde into Glasgow Green, that vast acreage of recreation where he had played much of his football. Or just fooled around in the park with his pals, being chased by authority when they got rowdy or spent many a time throwing stones into the river from behind the protective railings, when no one was looking. The locale was convenient for him, just in case he was leading himself into a situation that would prove dangerous. He knew the area like the back of his hand. It was the best he could think of for both privacy and providing space for an emergency exit, if needed.

That side of the river was certainly not green. It was a veritable building site. Flats were just being completed and there was a huge structure being erected around the large crescent where the car was parked, which Tam guessed might eventually turn out to be a hotel. Even on a Sunday there was still work going on around the crescent. There were the shouts of kids on the other side of the river cavorting about on the grassy banks there. A few people were slowly strolling over the bridge in harmony with the idyllic setting on this bend of the river, a stark contrast to the surrounding commercial grimness which lay just beyond the park's trees. To him it was the ideal place to negotiate about the photograph, although, if a barrier was going to be imposed on him meeting the girl, there would be precious little negotiation.

There were half a dozen cars parked there but all unoccupied. No sign of anybody. Tam looked behind him towards the main road and then towards the river. All he could see were families and couples, gently meandering along the paths like pieces of driftwood, heading nowhere in particular. Kids were rolling down the grassy banks. Prams were being pushed. Old men were sitting on benches either staring ahead, or reading their Sunday papers. The meeting place he had chosen was hidden from any passers-by.

Tam strolled towards the bridge. To his right was the old red-bricked boathouse which looked to have seen better times, strapped up as it was with wooden beams, perhaps to prevent the imminence of a collapse down the bank and into the river. That was the chosen spot though. He strolled towards it almost as if he were feeling his way in the dark. The uncertainty of the situation seemed to cloud everything around him. Then he saw a man in a light-coloured summery jacket, sitting on the grass, a mobile clearly in his hand, playing with his car keys nervously in the other. Beside him on the grass was a yellow folder. Tam halted and gave the man a concentrated look to announce his presence, and in the hope that he had got it right. The man rose, small, dark of hair and with a tiny ribbon of a moustache, looked Tam up and down, then started to walk up a small hillock towards some bushes. Tam followed.

'Your directions were spot on,' Nicholas Carson said, without any formalities and clearly sensing that Tam was the boy had had spoken to on the phone. 'But do you think anyone followed you?'

'Nobody followed me,' he said.

He could tell the man was not at all sure about that. They stood under a tree, the dark waters flowing past only yards away.

'Good. My name is Nicholas Carson. I'm a lawyer. Now do you have the photograph?'

'No. I'll hand it back to the girl and only her. And I asked you for an explanation. I expect that. A lot has happened since we talked last.'

Tam took a few minutes to detail action of the past couple of days and then asked abruptly, 'What does Belarus have to do with it?'

'Belarus?'

'You know what I'm talkin' about. Belarus.'

The man looked at him, as if Tam had matured in front of his eyes, a more profound look on his face as recognition of that.

'What put that into your head?'

'Phone numbers,' Tam replied. 'Plenty o' them. Belarus numbers. People can get careless wi' their mobiles.'

'I see,' was the reply and he noticed the increased rate of the swivelling of the car-keys around the man's forefinger, as if reflecting a tension. On the lapel of the man's jacket there was a little silvery badge. It was of a knight, on horseback, charging, with a sword in hand.

'There is nothing much I can tell you about that except to say that nostalgia for Belarus is very strong among certain people. Some people can no longer return there without great risk to their lives. Nostalgia is about as much as they have. The men you came into contact with know that only too well.'

'Who are these bampots and what are they doing here anyway? Are they terrorists?'

'Not in the customary sense of the word.'

'What other senses are there?'

'There are some natives of this very city you might define as terrorists in that they can intimidate, bully, cajole without needing to lift a little finger. As a lawyer I can vouch for that.'

'C'mon. You know what I mean, explosives, bombs and the likes. Are they set up for that?'

'Not that it lessens their menace, but at a guess they are an assassination squad, more likely. Or perhaps here to abduct. But, now that I see how involved you have become, I think you need to have one or two things explained to you, if it makes the transaction of the photograph any easier. Here, look at this folder.'

He handed it to Tam. A name had been scrawled on the outside flap by black felt-tip pen. *Andrej.* When he opened that flap he could see it was bulging with sheets of paper.

'I knew a Mrs Rybak, a delicate but highly intelligent old lady who spent her last days in a private care home just outside the city. I had represented her on several matters. My grandfather was born in Belarus and Mrs Rybak's husband had been a career diplomat out of that country, although she herself is Scottish. She said she had contacted a young lady to tell her about her roots in Eastern Europe and about the thriving community spirit that existed amongst those who hailed from those regions, but now domiciled in Scotland. She did not tell me too much about what they discussed but certainly she implied that there was more to this young lady than met the eye. Sometimes Mrs Rybak could be damnably secretive about herself.'

Tam was listening carefully but also taking out different sheets and scraps of paper which were covered in spidery writing or printing.

'In any case I visited her several times and was fascinated by the games she played with the other residents, word games of a sort. You see some examples there. Some residents regarded her as a kind of quizmaster or a master of ceremonies. She seemed to rule the place and had them all involved in these word games. She said this young lady had been impressed by what she was doing. And she did tell me she had been visited by a man, a distant relative of some sort, who had encouraged her to keep those games going, since it would help keep her mind active. Not that she needed much telling, because I think she realised the benefit of that herself. She showed me a photograph of this relative, but said nothing more about him other than that the photograph had been taken close to where he worked. That's all she had been prepared to divulge. Then she put it in alongside all her papers she had in that yellow folder, that very day I was there.'

Tam was looking at one sheet which had shakily written letters printed on it, a long list of them, which made no particular sense. At the head of the list was MMTADRROY. What did that mean?

'Sadly she passed away and when I was asked by the home to pick up her belongings, which didn't amount to all that much, I picked up that folder, but the photograph was missing and nobody at the home knew anything about it.

'So, who could've taken it?'

'I think this mysterious girl. I did get one call from her. A brief call, asking if I knew anything about this man. Even had I known I wouldn't have told her. She was phoning from a hotel, she said, so I couldn't really get any personal trace on her. At some point in her visits she could simply have walked out with it and left the rest of the folder there. Although the old lady, as I've said, was as bright as a button and wouldn't be taken in easily by anybody.'

Tam was now distracted by MMTADRROY. The letters were trying to unscramble themselves in his mind.

'But that is really no concern of yours. I have been absolutely honest with you and told you things that perhaps my colleagues would think go too far. But if I am being fair and open then perhaps you can reciprocate. This is a very simple transaction, hand the photograph over and you go off considerably richer. Why should there be any complications about that?'

Tam was increasingly feeling he had the upper hand. But how to play it? That was another thing altogether. Perhaps there was a deal he could strike with the pair of them, hand over the photograph and get the money at the same time, if ever he was to find the girl and bring them both together. It was not easy to think on his feet, there and then, with the thought of a hundred pounds in his possession affecting his thinking. But he then realised that that was far-fetched. From even the brief explanation he had heard from the lawyer, the girl was a rival, not an associate. Fuck it, he thought. He's no lead to the girl after all. Tam tried to stall, to winkle out anything else he could from the man.

128

'Why do you want it so much?' he asked.

'Because you have confirmed, by what you have told me, that this man could be in some danger. And I want to get all this material and pass it on to reliable ex-patriates from Belarus, who will keep it within their community. They treated Mrs Rybak like she was a saint.'

'Sorry. I have to talk to the girl. I can wait. I have to find her. Even more so because of what you've told me.'

The man sighed.

'What I have told you is as much as I know about the man in the photograph. So I think in all fairness we should just wrap this up and transact our business. It has nothing to do with you. It is a matter for those who understand it to deal with.'

'Tell me what you know about the two bampots in the dark suits and glasses that I got involved wi',' as if to deny the lawyer's attempt at some kind of closure on it all.

The lawyer turned away, moving a few steps down towards the river, as if to collect his thoughts, now that Tam had slightly derailed him with his mention of Belarus. What happened next, even within a millisecond, Tam knew would stay stored in his mind for the rest of his life. One second a man, of obviously some standing in life, was speaking under a tree, in a park, in a sylvan setting, that normally would induce nothing more than idleness for anyone. The next he was dead.

That fractional moment consisted of a gush of blood suddenly issuing from the side of his head, like it had been desperately waiting to be tapped by some force. Where that force had come from he was not sure, but it came with merely a sound like a twig snapping and nothing much more than that. Tam watched as the man collapsed forward on the slope, squirmed just for a moment and then lay still. It was not a case of Tam daring not to move. He found he couldn't move. Blood was pouring from the man's head and it appeared now as if the whole of that side of his face had been blown away, with the grass beside him now looking as if dark varnish had been spilled from a can. How long he stood there trying to make sense of this he could not recall. At least the bushes and trees shrouded him with protection. Gradually, the paralysis receded. He knelt and then crawled forward, making sure he did not intrude on the newly-formed marsh of blood on the grass. He bent even lower and peered across the river. He could see no one. There was not the slightest quiver coming from the body near him. He had only seen dead relatives in coffins before. This was a new kind of death, so foreign to his idea of how someone could die, that it took him a bit longer to realise he had just witnessed a murder, by gunshot. The open-eyed stare of the man chilled him to the bone. Tam lifted the yellow folder.

He wanted to bolt, but since somebody had either tracked him or the lawyer, then he surely could still be in their sights. This clamped him to the spot. He was crouching, the yellow folder clutched to his chest, almost as if his body was instinctively suggesting it could offer protection. That bodily supposition did not last long. He crept backwards towards thicker bushes. Looking at the man, and at the

130

red blancmange which was now the side of his face, he reckoned that the shot had definitely come from across the other side of the river. That would give him some leeway. He would have to move back into the park, where he stood a chance of making his way to another exit to the main road. There was no alternative. There was this sharp grassy hillock in front of him. He felt as if he had a strange wind now assisting him because he took the hill with a speed that astonished him. First there had been the petrifaction of the nearness to death, now it seemed to be electrifying him. There was exhilaration in the escape from it as he sped down the hill now with the park spread out in front of him.

There seemed to be some brass-band competition on, with a swathe of seats filled with people in front of a bandstand, with the various participants tuning up around the vicinity, as if they were awaiting their turn to perform. It produced a cacophony of sound, but comforting nevertheless to Tam, feeling that having just witnessed the brutal denial of life he was in the midst of some sort of celebration of it. Crowds were gathering. He walked quickly into their midst. He went against the tide of those coming into the event, as he made for an exit. The image of death hit him again though, in an after-shock that welled up and made him feel sick. Now he wanted away from the crowd, in case he was going to throw up. He managed to get himself out on to the street and seeing a gap in the traffic made across the road where there was a small cafe. It would have a toilet. He walked in and, without asking, followed the signs and got to the loo. There, he brought up much of what he had eaten in the last twenty-four hours, then sat shivering on the seat, thankful for this unusual solitude.

He was not sure how long he sat there, but when he felt his self-control returning, he lifted up the yellow folder, and out of curiosity again, picked out that sheet of paper. He looked at MMTADRROY for a while. Word games, eh? Of course. It was an anagram. Of what though? He had no pencil or pen with him and could only try unscramble it in his mind's eye. It was when his head was bowed on that matter that his phone went again.

It was Gabby.

'They've tracked Moose. Where are you?'

Chapter 10

They were waiting for him at Gabby's. He virtually staggered in, sat on the bench in the front shop and after an effort described to them what had occurred. They were silent for a spell. Gabby reached out and gripped his shoulder, squeezing it in sympathy. Sammy looked at the two muscular brothers beside him, Donald and Craig, who had pummelled punch-bags like they took demolition very seriously indeed, and shrugged.

'Sure he was dead?' he asked.

Tam could barely take the question in, but tried.

'I'm no expert but if you saw the hole just above his ear with blood gushing out of it like a fountain, what would you think?'

'Curtains!' Sammy replied. 'Sorry you had to see somethin'' like that. I hate guns.'

'It'll be better if you don't sit around moping about this,' Gabby said. 'There's plenty for us to do which might be greatly to your benefit.'

'Took us only a couple of hours on the phones to track Moose down,' Sammy said with obvious satisfaction. 'If you have a reputation like his then you know what kind of level of person to contact, down near the gutter, to be brutally honest. We have one of the lads watchin'' him, at this very moment, in case he moves off.'

The former European boxing champion was relishing this; self-consciously aware of being some kind of vigilante generalissimo. 'The brothers here are ex-paras,' Sammy explained, as if to account for the lack of shock about Tam's experience that morning. 'Been in

Afghanistan. Fought there. Survived, eh lads?' he went on, as if he wanted to inform Tam, in only a few words, that they were the right stuff, and that a sniper loose in the city did not greatly excite them.

'Tae be honest I puked,' Tam admitted.

'Son,' Sammy said. 'We know what you're going through. I think you might just have grown up a bit in the last couple of days.'

Gabby took the yellow folder from him and deposited it in the small safe, without questioning him about its origins or its contents. In Sammy's Land Rover they headed towards the north of the city. They did not need the sat nav. There was little conversation. Tam felt he was with very determined men, although uncertain about what they would have in mind, once they reached their destination. Twenty-minutes later they were there.

Moose's legs were sticking out from under the rear of his white van. A small radio, lying on the ground, was blaring out music. They were standing outside one of the arches of an old viaduct, which had been converted into workshops for small businesses. Around the van, inside the workshop, they could see car-parts and an assortment of tools, with a narrow work-bench to one side, on which were spanners and a small vice. There was a huge colourful poster of Rio de Janeiro on a side wall, lit by a spotlight on the roof. The van had been cranked up for some sort of work to be undertaken underneath, which seemed to entail hammering. It was clear that Moose was wholly immersed in this, and, consequently, he would not have expected what was about to happen.

He was pulled from under the car with the speed of a cork blasting from the neck of a bottle of champagne. Strong hands had grabbed his legs, and his body, supported by a small trolley underneath, shot out. He looked small but burly, the biceps like large speed-bumps and streaked with writhing tattoos of indeterminate design. The look on his face as he found himself staring upwards at the four around him was like that of man facing his final judgement, and not really up to it. His large lips and bushy eyebrows moved in synchronised panic, his eyes widening and his voice rising to a yell that almost scared Tam. He tried to scramble to his feet, but a large foot was placed on his chest, and one of the spanners, which had been lying handily nearby, was thrust close to his nose, like a welding tool.

'Afternoon.'

It was the former European fly-weight champion who spoke first. Just behind Sammy was Tam. On either side were the brothers. Craig held the spanner. Donald had his foot on Moose's chest. The other man was keeping watch, his back to the action.

'How are tricks?' Sammy asked like they were in the throes of a pleasant reunion. 'An old friend of yours told us where you'd be. You certainly mix with real gems, real honeys. I see you like Rio. Better check if Brazil has changed its extradition arrangements with the UK. Don't think they want another Ronnie Biggs, if that's what you've got in mind. Still in the trade I see, still muckin' about with vans and cars. Done any getaways recently? Or are you leaving that to a younger generation? Career change now? Like takin' up abduction in your old age?'

'I don't know what you're talkin' about,' Moose snapped, but wise enough to keep still on the ground with his eyes wandering round the four of them. 'Where have you come from? What's this all about?'

'Don't tell me you don't know,' Sammy went on. 'Don't waste our time. '

'I'm mindin' my own business, that's what I'm doin'. What are you tryin' to prove? I've done nothin' against you and your boys, Sammy. So what's with the fucking heavy stuff? You know I would never do anything against you, Sammy. I've got a lot of respect for you.'

'I'll sleep better tonight thinkin' of that. The problem is you've upset a few of my friends and it seems you haven't chucked some of your bad habits. Seems like you've been hired to do some nasty stuff, like driving around a gang of thugs who don't mind takin' young lads off the street and using them as hostages for some reason. And there was I thinkin' that a stretch in Shotts prison would have been like a visit to a health farm for you. What a pity!'

'You're haverin',' Moose spat at him again. 'I don't know anythin' about any gang. Somebody has made that up. I've got a reputation, I know that, and all I need to do is to drive down the street and folk will be sayin' I'm off tae rob a bank. I can't help what people say about me. Go on, who's been sellin' you this lie?'

'Tam?' Sammy said, and with a hand gesture, like a waiter showing a client a table, invited him to walk to the front and say his piece.

Tam looked down on the sturdy body, clamped to the ground by two brothers, whose utter stillness of frame, and silence, put definite shape to the overall brooding menace that hung in the air, almost neutralising the smell of diesel.

'My friend.....that is, Frankie....well, he was wi' me.....and....'

He was stammering slightly, the atmosphere of imminent violence, getting through to him.

'That is, well, what I mean to say is that my friend Frankie was hustled into a van and he heard the driver's name being mentioned. He told me on the phone what it sounded like. It was like Moose, or something like that. The name of the driver I mean and ....'

He was interrupted by a loud burst of laughter from the body on the floor. It was almost like hysterical screaming. Then it stopped as quickly as it had started, turning to a snarl.

'Just listen to that, Sammy!' Moose spouted, this time attempting to lift his head, which went promptly back, as Craig pushed the spanner to his nose again. 'A boy talks to another boy over the phone and tells him he heard a name being mentioned. Would you believe that? You've come all this way to hold me down, and give me a doin', over what one boy told another boy over the fuckin' phone! He must have misheard it. It could be another name that sounds like it. I know nothing about this. I swear it.'

137

'You're a driver. That's your speciality. You've got the van. Coincidence?' Sammy asked calmly.

'I can prove where I've been over the last few days. Every minute I can account for. And you know there are thousands of drivers with vans around here. You're goin' on a conversation on a phone about a name. That's all. It was misheard, that is bloody obvious. You're a fair man, Sammy. Everybody knows that. Tell me what proof have you? Go on, show me.'

Such was the conviction of his defence that Tam began to panic slightly. Could Frankie have got the name wrong? He had to say something.

'Where's ma mate?' Tam interjected. 'I want to know where he is?'

Moose ignored that.

'Do you think somebody like me who served with the SAS in Bosnia would do what you're suggestin'?' he gasped.

'If you served in the SAS then I'm Mohammed Ali,' Sammy replied. 'Give me a break. You'll be tellin' me next that you helped bring down Gaddafi. '

'I can make a few phone calls. People will back me up. They'll clear me. I know nothin' about this. You're doin' all this because somebody misheard a name? Boys,' he added appealing to the brothers, 'do you really swallow this? I'm not even sayin' the boy is makin' this up. I'm just sayin' it's a case of a misheard name. I don't know anything about his pal.'

Moose was now the pleader, with a voice of such innocence that even Tam, who thought he was a barefaced liar, was impressed. But, worryingly, he wondered if the two brothers were affected by that. They did seem to be looking less assertive in the way they were now positioned above him. He turned to Sammy who, from looking like he was enjoying this, now looked almost expressionless. Was Moose actually getting through to them, putting doubts in their heads?

'He's lyin' through his teeth,' Tam said. 'I know Frankie wasn't exactly sure about the name. But his name and his driving and his record, it all adds up. He's makin' all this up to cover himself.'

'Could be,' Sammy said thoughtfully. 'On the other hand he is right when he says I'm a fair man. All our boys are. If we've to help people in trouble like Gabby, then we like to make sure that we get all the facts right. We might have to get some other assurance on this.'

'We don't have the time,' Tam pleaded. 'I don't know what could be happening to Frankie right now and I'm up against the clock. If I don't get to him soon I'll go round the bend. I don't know what you're going to do to him, but Moose has got tae talk. It's the only way.'

As soon as he had said that it gripped him that this was almost inciting violence. But, equally, that thought was no deterrent. Yes, he knew this was desperation. Yes, it was ugly to contemplate. But it was his closest friend, after all, and it was him who had got Frankie into this mess. He knew he had come this far and there was no way back. He had listened, sympathetically, to his father railing against

139

rendition and waterboarding by the CIA, and yet, here was his offspring countenancing the possibility of some sort of punishment, perhaps even torture. Was it enough to tell himself that he was not particularly proud of that? Probably not. But it might work. That, sadly, is what mattered to him now.

'He's a bloody liar,' he said, almost in despair.

'We can check him out,' Sammy said. 'It might take a bit longer and I'm not stupid. Knowin' some of the people he pals up with, I know they would give him an alibi even if he had been seen walking live into the Crimewatch studio and pinchin' the presenter's chair. But......but....we have to be sure. Don't we, Tam?'

He was swinging the onus back to him. Of course they had to be sure. The whole initiative was based solely on a name, an odd name certainly, but just the name. But if Moose was able to wriggle out of this somehow, what then? Nothing. Frankie would still be out there and his own neck would be on the line. And time was pressing. It was now six o'clock.

'By the way, my young pal here is puzzled as to how you came by that name. And, to be honest after all these years it's time I knew myself. Was it something to do with the beast with the antlers?'

Moose did not react immediately. It was almost as if it was something he wanted to conceal. Then he spoke.

'My real name is John. My da called me Moose. It stuck. It was never anythin' else. Don't know why. But it's no' the name that boy heard, believe you me.'

'Get him on his feet and put him in the corner there,' Sammy commanded the brothers. Moose rose, stiffly, off his back and backed away towards the corner behind the van with the brothers holding an arm each.

'Leave us with him. We'll check his tale out on our phones,' Sammy said.

'You cannae let him go. He's the only connection. Sammy, he was involved,' Tam pleaded.

'Facts. We need some.'

Tam's despondency intensified. He was beginning to feel that perhaps Sammy wanted off the hook on this matter now, and that the link of the name seemed perhaps too feeble to go on, (even though it had come from him in the first place) after having listened to Moose's pleas. He stood at the open rear door of the van and watched them walk into the far corner of the lock-up, Moose continually mumbling his innocence. Tam looked straight into the van. The lamp, which was illuminating the Rio poster, was also beaming reflected light into the interior of the van and revealing that it looked scruffy and unclean, like it needed a comprehensive valet service. Tam heard the lowered voices in the background, his fears increasing that this man might get off the hook. The small radio, lying just inside the interior on the seat, still had not been turned off. It was beginning to annoy him. He climbed into the van, picked the radio up, switched it off and placed it against the side of the van. He smelled something. Pineapple? And that mustiness of dough. Pizza smell. That's it. This stirred him to advance further in. As he did so his eye was caught by a mark on the opposite side; a footmark, a muddied print. He leant forward, the distinct mark seeming to jump out at him, explaining itself. For a moment he was like a reconnaissance expert looking at photographic evidence and trying to determine a cowshed from a missile site. For this was no ordinary print. The distinctly patterned print had been left by somebody wearing the same trainers as himself, the ones Gabby had provided for the rest of the team as their sponsor. And, from the recognition of the size of the print, Tam felt the elation of one who has just come across a dinosaur fossil in New Mexico. Frankie had left that mark.

He looked long and hard at it, trying to visualise how a print had got there in the first place. But after taking his own trainer off and carefully scrutinising it, to make doubly sure, he knew he had struck rich. The pattern was clear-cut and exact. Whatever reservations Tam himself had begun to harbour over the name issue, there was now no doubt that Frankie had been in the van and somehow his big foot had been up there.

He tried hard not to sound too jubilant. He had no way of telling how Sammy would react.

'Sammy!' he shouted. 'Come and see this.'

The little man walked jauntily round the van again.

'There's a footprint in here. It's on the side opposite the seat. Look at it.'

Sammy climbed in and bent forward to examine it.

'Well?' he asked.

'It's the same footprint as mine. Have a look at my sole,' Tam said.

Sammy took the trainer and started to make the comparison.

'Gabby bought the trainers for the team to help us practise. They're Gel Kayanos. They've a distinct pattern on the sole. And look at the size of the print. It's about a size twelve. Frankie's got the feet of a rhino.'

He turned and looked Sammy straight in the face.

'Frankie was in this van,' Tam said softly. 'And so was a ham and pineapple pizza. Nothin' surer.'

Sammy mused over that last sentence for a moment, then shouted.

'Moose, you'd better come here. Somethin' to show you!'

A head appeared round the side of the van with the brothers at each side. They pushed him into the van and held him in front of the footprint.

'Gel Kayanos,'Sammy said, as if he was an expert in the shoe trade. 'Prints of a certain football team. Same as the lad here. The boy, Frankie, was in this van and if you're saying that he wasn't, then you had better come up with an explanation of how that got there, and who made the mark. I'll give you ten seconds to come up with something and if it doesn't sound right and you're bull-shittin' me, then....... '

Moose's large lips were now being licked by a tongue that in its furtive way was confessing guilt. It was interpreted as such.

'You know somethin',' Sammy said to the surrendering image in front of him, 'just think about it. If your father had stuck to John instead of Moose, we wouldn't have known where to start. And they say whit's in a name? Life's a right scunner at times, isn't it?'

***

Within half an hour they were sitting outside a house in a neighbourhood where they could hear the distant purr of lawnmowers mollycoddling the large lawns they had come amongst. The abrupt and dramatic conversion, from strenuously pleading his innocence, to a humbled almost snivelling wretch pleading for some understanding, was like watching the sudden collapse of a block of flats after the demolition experts had sited the right kind of explosives. The single footprint was the gelignite. Sammy had lit the fuse.

'If you don't co-operate,' he had explained to Moose, 'I will personally see you're dropped off in Gruinard, up the west coast there. Very scenic. And, tae pass the time you can watch dolphins happily playin' about up there. The rest of your stay would be spent trying to dodge the remaining anthrax spores, which they say could still be about there. It's up tae you.'

Moose began to talk. First a trickle, then a tsunami. He told them that he knew nothing about the strangers, didn't know which country some of them were from, and didn't care. They were paying him well to be on call to take them around the city, whenever they needed him, and had got in touch, initially, through his having driven for a firm which employed some workers from Eastern Europe. One or two spoke English but most did not. How many of them were there? Six at the last count, including the doctor. Which doctor? A woman who lives in a big house and who is treated like royalty. He knew that she had treated the lad for a head injury and that he had barricaded himself in an attic. At the announcement of that fact Sammy looked at Tam as if he was being asked to come to the aid of a loony. That moment passed quickly as Moose went on to explain that he was at their beck and call for the van, and had an appointment to take them to a club in Glasgow that night, for some relaxation and local hospitality.

'I'll arrange the hospitality, with pleasure,' Sammy said reaching for his phone. 'Make sure you recommend the *Latitude Club* for tonight. They'll have a really interestin' time there. Just you follow instructions.'

They moved off, Moose in his van, Sammy beside him, either on the phone, or talking into Moose's ear, obviously laying down instructions for what he had arranged in Glasgow later. Tam sat in a cramped position just behind, watching Moose nod his head so vigorously Tam thought it might fall off. The brothers followed in their car.

They parked no more than about fifty yards away from the house Moose had identified. Sammy put a finger in front of Moose's face and smiled with telling intensity. It was more eloquent than words. Then they both left the van and watched as it was driven slowly towards the house. It stood behind its own regal border of trees and large bushes. This was foreign territory to Tam. He could have been on the dark side of the moon, for all the familiarity he had of where he now was. He wondered if some of the neighbours peering from behind curtains, in this up-market area for nosey-parkers, would be having their first ever sighting of a Barca jacket.

It was a large two-storied residence whose stone facade had an almost pinkish tinge, reminding him of the colour of the stone in the substantial remains of the splendid medieval Bothwell Castle on the banks of the Clyde which he had visited, on a school field-study trip there once; or even reminiscent of the setting-sun washing Ayers Rock, as he had seen in books. He found himself counting the windows, eleven in all, in the front facade, which had two curved stone balconies at either end, above the ground-floor bay-windows. At one side a large conservatory had been added. A doctor's house? Could medicine pay that much? And what was a doctor doing consorting with a gang of bampots?

They watched Moose carefully as he drew the van smoothly into the driveway and parked it outside the portico entrance. They saw him alight and press a bell. He looked back very briefly, and almost nervously, in their direction, but they were sufficiently shielded by the trees and bushes to make their presence discreet, and since there were other cars parked in the street there was little chance of arousing suspicion.

Eventually the door opened. A large man came out and looked at Moose as if he was dirt. Great camaraderie, Tam thought. At that moment Tam felt everything could break down if Moose were just to whisper a warning into the man's ear. On the other hand, reassuringly, there was no sign of concern from Sammy standing now beside him with the brothers towering over both of them. There was not the slightest stir of uncertainty coming from the wee man. Then, after a few moments of discussion, out came the other three, chattering pleasantly to themselves as if they were welcoming a break from sentry duty. There was a lot of what sounded like joshing and joke-making as they piled into the van, their mood like those of a stag-night party, brimful with expectation. Oh, how little did they know of what lay in store for them, Tam thought. The van reversed out of the driveway and then swept past them; Moose, stern, and almost nobly upright, staring straight ahead.

They waited for what seemed an interminable time as Sammy waited for a call from the *Latitude Club* for verification that the merry band had entered the establishment. When, eventually, it came, all he said was, 'Bingo!'

They left the car and walked to the entrance of the driveway standing behind the stone pillars there. They had agreed that the four of them could handle the situation and that surprise was the most significant element. Once they got inside, nothing was to be ruled out, in releasing Frankie. Moose had talked them through the lay-out of the house. The light was gradually fading, helpfully. Lights were on in the downstairs rooms but they could detect none above that. Tam felt that lilt inside him as if his stomach was racing ahead of the rest of his body. It was like tension he often experienced at kick-off in crunch games. But it was never without that accompanying sense of exhilaration. They were getting places.

They chose to walk on the grass verge to avoid any crunching on the gravel driveway. The conservatory was dark. At one end of it was a door which obviously gave entry to the side-garden. One of the brothers opened it with an alacrity that suggested he had served an apprenticeship in keyless entry. There was sufficient light there to expose cane furniture and large leafy plants, of the kind Tam used to see when he was twelve, thumbing through the magazines, in his dentist's waiting room, while waiting for yet another examination of his brace. The door at the other end was partly open, and as soon as they passed through it they could smell cooking of some kind. Meat of some sort, Tam thought. The pungency of it suggested domestic normality, far removed from the nest of vipers he thought they had entered. There was a long hall stretching in front of them, brightly lit, with a deep-green carpet that mirrored the svelte lawns of the outside. There was a bust of what looked like one of those classical Roman sculptures on a plinth, near the front door which had a stained-glass design, green and red the predominant colours.

Sammy was at his side with the brothers a step behind. They heard a snatch of conversation coming from a room ahead of them, and to their right. A door was ajar there. Then, suddenly, there was the dog. A large dog, a malevolent spirit on four legs.

It was through the door and at them, like it had materialised out of thin air. And not a sound. No barking. There was only a snarl as it reached Sammy. It went for his chest. Taken completely unawares he fell back and crashed into a table with a red lamp on it, just behind him. The shattering sound echoed through the hall and Sammy let out a loud yell, 'For God's sake, get it off me!' which was like his trained coolness suddenly cracking. The Alsatian seemed to be snapping at his sweater, and although Sammy had managed to get a grip of its head, the suddenness of the attack had flummoxed him. The former European champion, who accurately claimed he had never been flat on his back once, in any canvas in Europe, was certainly now, flat-out on a suburban hall floor. One of the brothers lashed out at the dog with his foot and caught it on the side of the head. It released its grip on the sweater, but only for a second and was back into Sammy as if he was a rag-doll. The snarling of the dog, the increased yelling of Sammy and the bawling of the brothers, as they tried to grapple with the dog, and grab it round the neck, caused Tam to look around for something to hand that he could strike the dog with. The problem was he could see nothing which would help. With their focus on the struggle on the floor, they did not notice the entry into the scene of others, until a command was barked out. It was one sharp word. The dog instantly released Sammy and darted down the hall again where two figures had emerged. A man and a woman. The dog was rubbing against the woman who reached down and stroked it without taking her gaze from them. The man was holding something in his hand.

It took Tam a few seconds to realise what it was. A handgun. Black, and pointed directly at them.

The woman again said something to the dog which Tam could not make out, a name, or a command in another language. But it had the effect of calming it to a degree and it settled down nestling into her legs. Then the man spoke.

'Very discourteous of you to disturb our meal, gentlemen,' he said with a look of supreme confidence. 'If there is one thing I cannot stand and that is to be dragged away from the table when Beef Wellington is lying on my plate half-eaten. With all this fuss I might end up with indigestion. I could never forgive you for that. Now, I think you have been very foolish and it will be even more foolish if you try to resist me for I will use this without hesitation. I know how to maim people with this. And if I did it, I doubt if you would go squealing to the police. Burglary is taken very seriously in this city, although looking at the four of you I suspect you had more in mind than the family silver.'

'We're here to take Frankie home,' Tam blurted out.

'As I thought. Strange how you found this address though. Maybe we can get that from you later. I admit, it does surprise me, but then should I be surprised by anything in this city?'

'We found it because we're no' stupid, 'Sammy said, sitting up and smoothing his now ragged sweater down, at the same time giving the dog the look of a hanging judge. 'And another thing,' he added, 'I don't like guns. Guns are for cowards. People like you hide behind guns. And if you used that you wouldn't leave this city alive, in fact you wouldn't last until tomorrow morning because my people know we're here, and if I don't show up, when I said I would, this place will swarm with them, and their manners will do more than offend you. They won't be wiping their feet on the doormat when they come. So why don't you put that fucking contraption away, go back to your Beef Wellington, slap it between two bread rolls, plaster it with mustard and get the best out of our Aberdeen Angus, and give us the boy back?'

The man held out the gun with not a quiver of the arm. As he hesitated for a moment the woman spoke up.

'You speak as if you think you are like a warlord in Afghanistan,' she said in the kind of immaculately enunciated English, which seemed as if it had been acquired in a missionary school somewhere. 'How pathetic. We need some information from you, and the boy will not be returned until that is forthcoming. My colleague will shoot, if necessary, because he has done it before very accurately. For the time being we will have to hold you here until we get what we need. We have tried to treat the boy with some sensitivity but he appears to me to he would have preferred to have lived under the harsh conditions of ancient Sparta. I can't recall when he last ate or drank anything. But he is well guarded, that I can tell you.'

'You are on a foolish pursuit,' the man added, looking pointedly at Tam. 'None of us had anything to do with the attack in the lane, although we know all about it, of course. You are sadly and recklessly mistaken. There is no point in me deceiving you about that. Pity.'

Tam looked quickly at Sammy as if he needed reassurance that the man was spinning a lie. But the old boxer was now suddenly looking his age, although the indignity he had suffered was exacerbating the look. He gave him no response. Tam, though, leant down to give him a hand, and as he did so he saw something lying under the collapsed table. It was a lemony, yellowish thing. Then he knew what it was; a tennis ball. A tennis ball lying loose in this almost baronial setting? Odd. Suddenly it twigged. It was the dog's plaything. He had seen the exercise often enough in the parks, with dogs frolicking after balls like that, as if they were spectacular aerial gymnasts.

'I think your place will be the cellar,' the man said, this time using his gun to point back along the hall behind them. 'Let us not have any mishaps on our way there. Get him up.'

As he tried to pull Sammy up with one hand, Tam was able to lift the ball with the other and secrete it behind the champ's back. The texture of the ball in his hand did not feel like the quality that surely aided Andy Murray's cross-court forehand at Wimbledon, the very smoothness of such, turning it into a searing projectile. No, this was rough to the touch, serrated by the obvious teeth that had mauled it many a time. It was the product of playful brutality. He looked quickly across at Donald, who had seen his sleight of hand with the ball. It is not that Tam had ever considered the validity of telepathic communication, although he had heard claims about it. But, there and then, in an intense look into Donald's eyes he was praying that the muscular twin would be reading his mind as clearly as staring at a billboard advertising his favourite beer. The dog. The ball. Its plaything. Got it? This was no time to hesitate. Tam lifted the ball clear from behind him, holding it in such a way it was in full sight of the dog which started to stir slightly at its sudden presence. Then he held it in front of him, drew it back, and trusting on instinct to help out, launched the yellowy sphere high in the air just to the left of the man with the gun, who did seem surprised at the gesture, but obviously did not see such a playful act as threatening, his arm still rigid.

But the ball sparked the dog into life. It leapt across the man's body, upwards, bumping into the gun arm, and, at first missing the ball as it bounced high from the floor, leapt at it again in front of the gun. The man's arm bent for the first time, forcing him to lower the gun. It was a cue as obvious as a raised gate at a level crossing. Telepathy or not, it worked. Donald pushed with his back foot and leapt towards the man's legs, the dog now beginning to bark in uncontrollable excitement. The woman tried to punch at Donald, who rammed the man against the stained-glass windowed door, his head hitting the lower wood section with an echoing thud. Tam, head down charged towards him and landed squarely on top of the man as Donald wrestled with the gun arm. Then the place reverberated in a crashing noise as the trigger, almost inevitably, had been pulled in the struggle and suddenly large pieces of plaster from a fabulously ornate cornice rained on their heads as that single bullet to the ceiling seriously defaced the decor. Donald was now in command though. Craig disregarded the woman and went after the dog, which now, beside itself with anger, was snapping at Tam's backside as he held the man's legs. The kick Craig delivered would not have been to the taste of dog lovers. But enough of the niceties, Tam thought, as it flopped its way back the way it had come, almost drunkenly, then disappeared. The woman tried to join in the fracas by punching ineffectually at Donald's head, but by this time Sammy had strode across towards her and did nothing other than put his fist to her nose. She deferred, probably because as a doctor she guessed she might need plastic surgery if she did not play this right. Her arms hung limply by her side. Donald now had the gun in his hand, the man on the floor, lifting his head weakly near the door, in admission of defeat.

'Let's see that thing,' Sammy demanded and was handed the gun carefully like it was a time-bomb.

'I don't know anything about guns, except they kill people,' Sammy said looking down at it with obvious distaste.

'Frankie's in the attic. Remember?' Tam interrupted hurriedly.

Tam did not wait to debate the next issue but started to take the stairs behind him two or three at a time. Moose had described the geography of the upper floors. When he reached the next landing he had to go towards the back of the house, where there would be an additional narrow staircase leading to the attic. As he reached that, he heard the stamping of feet from above, and round a bend in the stairs he saw a gaunt-looking man coming downwards towards him with a knife in his hand. They stopped almost in unison. Tam looked at the long blade of the knife. Wicked. He knew about knives all right. He had witnessed the abuse of knives. He felt that this was worse than facing the gun, since it had been part of the reality of living, where he did, that there was always a never-too-distant threat of knives. But he was not going to retreat and he had to indicate that determination to the man.

'You've no chance,' Tam said to him. 'Your people downstairs have been done in. They're finished. The man and the woman. We've got them. That's why I've got this far. That thing is no use to you now.'

Nothing came from the man who gave the distinct impression he had understood not a single word of what had been said to him. That scared Tam. The man advanced a step downwards, the knife in the lead. Tam tried again this time, reduced to stresses on simple words and wagging a finger suggesting 'No! No!'

'Your....friends....we have them....they're our prisoners....'

This was met by a face of total incomprehension. It was then Tam felt that perhaps this man did not really want to use the knife, that it was only there to threaten. Was it worth the risk to push past him? He considered it. He would push up one side. Quickly or gradually? He was undecided. The man might be impervious to what had been said to him and he did look dour. But would he really stick that thing into him? Tam moved one step up. The knife was raised, pointing, the grip underhand, steady and firm. Tam wagged his finger again. He stopped though ready to try a quick leap, shaking slightly as he considered it. Then he heard the voice behind him.

'I'll put this right through your skull if you don't put down that butcher's knife.'

155

Tam turned to find Sammy, the man who knew nothing about guns and hated the sight of them, so he said, pointing the newly-acquired weapon towards the man's forehead.

'Sammy, I don't think he understands English,' Tam said warily.

'Oh, I think he gets ma point,' Sammy said, climbing up to beside Tam. The man looked at the gun steadily as if he was examining it closely, minutely. Then he seemed to become possessed and leapt at Sammy swinging the knife upwards. The former champion shimmied and ducked expertly, hoisting the body coming at him upwards, and thrusting him eventually over his shoulder and down the steep attic stairs. In trying to soften his fall the man seemed to twist and slam his back and neck against one of the steps letting out a throttled moan and went still, the knife clattering down the rest of the steps, like a loose skate.

'Not scared of guns, I'll say that about him,' Sammy said. 'Although I am. The boys put the safety catch on.'

Tam did not wait to deliberate on that, but hurtled up the rest of the stairs until he came to the door at the end of the short corridor. He tried the handle and shouted, 'Frankie. Are you there?' It was locked. He hammered it with his fist. 'Frankie. Are you all right?'

'Who's that?' came a weak voice from within.

'It's me!'

'Who?'

'Me. Tam. Who did you think it is? The postman? I'm gonnae kick this door in.'

'Tam, my mate! Heh! What kept ye?'

Tam tried to kick the door open and found it was stiff, solid, unyielding, like something was jamming it on the other side. He suddenly heard a great deal of heaving and pushing coming from the interior and the door began to respond to the heavy treatment with the foot. It gave. The lock smashed and a hand curled round from the inside to help pull it open. The face emerging was pale but smiling, in a sleepy sort of way.

'Are you all right?' Tam asked reaching out a hand towards his mate.

'Take me to a McDonald's. Quick.'

Chapter 11

They sat there in the restaurant eventually, watching Frankie devour his meal with the ravenous fervour of a lion shredding a wildebeest in the Serengeti. Tam could not bring himself to join in the mood of triumph. This was certainly not the end of the affair. The immediate aftermath had puzzled him. A large black van had arrived not long after the doctor and her two companions had been properly subdued and locked in a small hall cupboard where they pummelled the door and shouted mostly in their own language which they assumed was a stream of abuse that really needed no translation. The van crunched up the driveway and came to a rasping halt, and out of which stepped four very stern looking men. Police. They were in plain-clothes but Tam hadn't grown up in his neighbourhood without being able to identify police, even if they were dressed as Elvis look-alikes. The cupboard confederates were quickly shunted out into the van, still ranting, with the doctor deciding to do them a favour by lapsing into a single English sentence, 'You'll be hearing about this!' Tam did not feel any of his companions flinched at that.

One man, obviously the leader of the plain-clothed group, walked through the house without saying a word to them; dark-haired with a premature streak of grey running through the middle of it as if he had stood under a single drizzle of paint. Sammy and the leader obviously knew each other well and spent some time whispering together intermingled with purposeful looks in Tam's direction as if he was the subject of a debate. Clearly Sammy had been the lynch-pin of the entire evening. He had been on his phone incessantly since

158

the Silent One had been felled and the house had effectively come under his control. It had been operated his way. Now he had obviously called these men in. But it became even more puzzling when one of the policemen came down with the photographs of the men from the doctor's wall and Sammy and the leader went into another room for what seemed an eternity before emerging without a word, like they had just closed some sort of deal.

Although they had made an intensive search of the house they did not come near Tam nor Frankie. It was as if Sammy was shielding them, an informer and protector, and had been doing all the necessary talking. But it was becoming clearer to Tam that this wholly unacceptable abduction was not this group of men's priority at all, that it was a just a sideshow to them and that the man in the photograph was what they were really interested in. Tam wondered if they knew by then about the murder of the lawyer that morning. It certainly didn't surface. Either they hadn't heard or they hadn't linked it in any way. So this bunch had much more in mind that taking witness statements of what had occurred. Were they a law unto themselves? Without a single word directed to them, the men he took to be police, took off with their prisoners.

Tam was now firmly of the view that there looked to be a pact of sorts between special police operations and vigilantism that clearly was mutually beneficial. Proper? Legal? There's no doubt his father had accepted the principle of breaking the law to justify a cause when he took part in the miners' strike. He could quote that to anybody. But he felt uneasy about this particular event. He felt like he was in Sammy's fiefdom, and his stance against the gangs in the city, existed partly through blind eyes being conveniently turned on it, by a level of policing that benefitted from knowing constantly what was going on in the streets. On the one hand Sammy was key to all this, Tam supposed. On the other he was a practitioner of the kind of rough justice that many of the police perhaps envied. One day Tam would have to make judgement on the morality of all that. But not now.

Sammy informed them all, as he tucked in to a burger, that his tactics had worked out well elsewhere. The *Latitude Club* ploy had concluded perfectly, and several arrests had been made, after certain foreign nationals had become involved in a fracas with locals. Some of whom, Sammy admitted, had been drafted in to offer them a special welcome which included accusing the strangers of not joining in a singing of 'Flower of Scotland', even though they could not possibly have understood the political implications of the words, sending the English king 'home again'; thus, being interpreted as a slur on the national identity, retribution had taken place. All according to the script. And he admitted that sources had already informed him that deportations would take place quickly. Moose had played his part in leading them there, so had been awarded by being advised that moves would take place to seek a job for him, as an ice-trucker in the Canadian North-West territories.

'With a name like his, where else?' was all Sammy said about that. For there was no way Tam had got to the core of the matter, even though Frankie was now safe. Where were the Men in Black in all of this? Why did the smooth talker in the doctor's house and undoubtedly the director of operations, deny all involvement in the lane incident, but still knew all about it? And the girl at the moment could have been on the outer rim of the known universe, for all the information anyone seemed to have. So when they were dropped off at Gabby's, Tam and Frankie convened with the shopkeeper in his office.

Tam went through events again, if only to unburden himself of the aggravated isolation he felt by not speaking about his inner thoughts; then seemed to clarify nothing for anybody by telling them about the strange phone-call to Mrs MacPhail who lived nearby and who obviously had some connection with the girl in the lane, and even the bampots. That fact lay silently among them for a moment as Tam could see they were trying to make sense of that. Gabby admitted defeat for the three of them by breaking the silence in announcing that he had been at work on the Kingslie Industrial Estate where the girl had been dropped off. He had listed twenty-five different companies there of widely varying businesses. They poured over the neatly printed list.

'The Dreamsprung Beds Factory shop,' Frankie muttered. 'Think she sells beds or models in them?'

'Give me a break!' Tam muttered.

'Alright, how about the Fastnet Burglar Alarm Systems? She's certainly jangled your bells. How about that?'

'Wheesht!' Gabby said in the Scottish word he was probably fondest of. 'You'll drive yourselves mad. There is no way you can go through this list like that. It is a waste of time. Even if you walked through their offices one by one how long would it take? Maybe she doesn't even have a job anywhere there. Perhaps she was just calling in, a visitor like.'

They couldn't argue against that. They were staring at a dead-end again. Gabby, recognising a darkening of the mood, decided to move. He produced the photograph again but with a distinct sense of purpose. They gathered round it.

'Now look,' Gabby went on, 'it is clear from what Frankie explained about the other photographs he saw in the house that this young man was about to have a red sticker slapped on his face. In other words we could assume he was for the chop. Agreed?'

It was a lurid thought but seemed at the same time scarily logical given the series of events they had come through. They nodded.

'So what emerges from that assumption, from the very fact that they already have a photograph of this man?'

'They already know who he is,' Tam said.

'Of course, my young friend. He is not a mystery man. To you he is, of course. But not to them.'

'So?' Frankie said.

'So,' Tam went on without waiting for Gabby to say anything any further, 'it's not 'WHO he is.....'

'It's WHERE he is,' Frankie muttered quickly, clearly not wishing to be out-paced in reaching a conclusion that was now painfully obvious.

162

There was no more conversation until they had the photograph in front of them again. They widened their focus. There was a building in the background, but the snap had been taken at such a steep angle it displayed no special background identity. He was standing on cobblestones denoting something historical perhaps, although Tam had seen parts of his own city with newly-laid cobblestones in pedestrian areas, which were far from historical. It still all seemed peculiarly anonymous.

'The other thought is that they knew about the existence of this photograph but hadn't seen it, or else they might no' have gone to all the trouble to get hold of it,' Tam offered.

'Then again,' Gabby said, 'there might be something there we're missing about it. Ah, but I'm perplexed.'

He looked in slight despair. Tam changed the direction to unlock the jam they seemed to be in.

'I heard about the old woman today, a Mrs Rybak who had this in the first place. This fella's a relative. They might've known about the photograph that way. Where's that folder I left wi' you?'

Gabby went to the safe and produced it.

'I had a look through it when you were away,' he said. 'So many papers. So many words. And crazy words.'

'She played word games with people, the lawyer told me. It was her passion. That's why all these sheets are covered with all kinds of letters and words.'

'Was she going ga-ga?' Frankie asked.

'The very opposite, accordin' to the lawyer. She was bright as a button. I had a quick look at this one today, an anagram I think. MMTADRROY. I'm brain-dead after a' that's happened to me today. I cannae think straight. I'll go through all this in the mornin'. I need a sleep.'

'Oh, I will try this anagram, if you like,' Gabby said eagerly.

Frankie yawned, another sign that the night was over.

'Did you know there was one Russian sniper wi' a name I couldnae even attempt to pronounce, who killed 225 Germans in Stalingrad. Countin' them might put me tae sleep tonight.'

They left Gabby hunched over the table with a pencil and paper. Tired though he was, he enjoyed the walk back with Frankie and they parted with the promise that they would try to get a swim the next day. They badly needed to reconnect with normality.

***

The night was not good for Tam. He had nightmares. He re-ran that millisecond of murder over and over. He disliked that awful clamminess of sweat which suffused the bed sheets although he was in no readiness to get up. He lay long, finding it difficult to arouse himself. Lethargy was not what he needed at this juncture. But when it happens, it happens. It's difficult to shrug off.

His father aroused him. Thomas Brownlie opened Tam's bedroom door, stuck his head in and said, 'The Duchess has a touch o' bronchitis. Don't go near her for the next few days. By the way, I

164

thought I would let you know Joe Telfer was lettin' off steam about higher education the other night. His son got a degree in English at Glasgow. And do you know where he's ended up? Workin' in a call-centre. Cannae even get a job teachin'. Makes people think, is it all worth it? But you know me Tam. You know what I think.'

Every now and again his father would reflect on the growingly common sceptical view that going to uni was a waste of time. He did that simply to involve Tam. Once again he was able to take comfort from this short bulletin masterfully geared to reminding him of the support he would get if he still produced the goods at school or university. As for the Duchess, thank God for the bug that causes the tubes to clam up, he thought. Mark you, *Bishop to Knight3* wouldn't go out of his mind, bronchitis or no bronchitis, that was certain. He dodged having to face his mother at breakfast and made his way outside towards the library. He had a bottle of water and a bacon roll at an adjacent cafe and then calmed himself as he made his entrance. All the terminals shining bright, with web-addicts picking through the internet, were all occupied, so he went round the shelves and picked out an encyclopaedia and sat alongside some of the old-timers thumbing through the newspapers in the reading room. He looked up Belarus.

It was dense with information. Within it he noticed one particular section in which an American politician called Condaleeza Rice described the President of Belarus as a dictator. Not a happy place, Tam judged, given that it also indicated that there was a Belarusian government in exile, sworn to restore the country to democracy.

Then he saw the exiled group's little symbol which caused him to recall the eruption at the riverside. It was of a white knight, charging on a horse, sword in hand. It had been worn on the lapel of the murdered lawyer. On absorbing that, he shut the large encyclopaedia with such a bang that the librarian gave him one of those special, silent librarian looks which can turn blood to water. Frankie had news for him when they met, that would waylay them slightly on their way to the pool.

'I got some information about that Mrs MacPhail in Cochrane Terrace, you know the one you thought had somethin' to do with the bampots. Got it from old Mrs McGregor when I mentioned the name and address to her. You'll hardly believe it.'

'Why?'

'She's a psychic.'

***

They stood on the opposite side of the street and looked at Cochrane Terrace, which although as uniformly grey as the buildings around, had taken on a new mystic appearance to them.

'Will she know we're standin' outside looking up at her windae. Being a psychic and all that?' Frankie asked. 'Mrs McGregor says she actually helped out the police in an investigation once. It was in the papers some time ago. I don't read stuff like that.'

Tam did not reply, but was trying to fit her into the broader picture of the violence they had experienced. Had Frankie announced that she was a snake-charmer, he could not have been more puzzled. A girl is assaulted in a lane, a man is murdered in front of his very eyes, a friend is abducted, some bampots end up with a night in a Glasgow disco that they would never forget, and are about to be deported, a gun is pointed at him for the first time in his life, and now, enter the psychic. 'Do you think she does well on the lottery or at Aintree or Cheltenham or on the football pools? She might be able to give us a few tips,' Frankie added.

'I don't think it's all about crystal balls. I'm no expert on the subject but I think they talk about the dead and all that. Some of them think they even talk to the dead. Seances and the like. They talk about 'the Other Side'.

He solemnly intoned these last two words as if in mockery of such belief.

'Now when you come tae think of it she might be useful for me,' Frankie said. 'I would like tae know where my poor grandfather stashed the money he won on the Golden Pot at the bingo one night. Nobody's ever seen it. She would have tae speak up all the same, because he wore a deaf-aid. Or maybe you get your hearin' back on the Other Side.'

Now that they knew exactly where Mrs MacPhail was, and were trying to fit her into the frame of events, they decided it was time for the swim they had promised themselves. The Gorbals Swimming Pool, with the resplendent colours of progress, bore the distinction of distancing itself from the age when the neighbourhood was associated with deprivation and violence. They produced their cards, and inside they found the pool busy, packed with school-kids on holiday, and pensioners slogging up and down in two sectioned-off lanes.

After just indulging in the caressing of the water itself, and fooling around for some time, diving and swimming underwater, for as long as their lungs could hold out, they always had a two length race. Tam's crawl was the classic, mechanical chop-chop of arm and leg, propelling him through the water with a degree of elegance. Frankie's style was that of a man who has been told the pool is full of piranha fish which are particularly fond of the flesh of red-haired people. His arms would operate like a threshing machine, slapping the water frantically, as if scolding it out of his way, and sending spray on all sides, to the discomfiture of some pensioners whose expressions clearly stated, 'What is the world coming to?' It was always the same. Tam won that day though, and they sat at the deep-end their legs dangling, happily dripping, exhausted. For one brief, shining moment they had cleared their minds of all the pressures of the recent days. It did not last long.

As they were leaving they passed the front office where one of the supervisors came up to Frankie to tell him, in a friendly and jokey way, to be more considerate of other older swimmers when he was imitating a paddle-steamer in the pool. As Tam did not want to listen to Frankie's response to this, fearing that he would invoke the Court of Human Rights in Strasbourg, he got out of the way, by moving back towards where a young girl was sitting in a seat listening to a small radio, waiting for someone to leave the pool. She had the volume up. Suddenly the music that had been playing stopped, and a voice announced a news bulletin. He knew that voice right away; that slight transatlantic accent; that sweet lilt. He felt as if ants were running up and down and all over his skin, searching for his heart which was pumping even harder now than it had been in the pool. It was the girl from the lane.

'What station is that?' he snapped at the girl on the seat, who shrank back from him as if he were about to assault her.

'I dunno,' she said. 'What's it tae you?'

'Let me hear it to the end of that bulletin,' he demanded.

'Get lost! I listen to music,' she replied. 'I'm switching it over to somethin' else.'

Before she could lay a finger on any button he had it away from her, snatching it from her clutch and holding the speaker area to his ear.

'Hey, mister!' she screamed at the superintendent who was still with Frankie, 'That boy's pinched ma radio.'

Tam turned his back on them all, strode to the window, his ear jammed against the radio. He could hear her even more clearly now. That's where he had heard that voice in the past few months. He wouldn't have known which particular station, as he would browse through lots of them. Radio was all the same to him, one station merging into any other, in a seamless stream of repetitive music. He heard the superintendent shouting, and, in the reflection in the glass, saw the man striding towards him. The news she was talking about was of a fire at a distillery. But he couldn't have cared less what she

169

was on about. It was her. Just as the tall man reached him the voice said, 'The next bulletin is at half-past the hour.' Then, as a strong hand was laid on his shoulder, the jingle rang out from the speaker, in the form of a quartet of angelic voices, 'Radio Crystal 611'.

To Tam it was like listening to a choral satnav.

Chapter 12

Radio Crystal was housed in Kingslie industrial estate on the eastern edge of the city. He had waited overnight before going there, and that following morning he had listened carefully to her, several times, not only reading the bulletins but presenting a programme called 'PI' which stood for Personal Initiatives. He finally deduced, from the plugs for the programme, not having heard it before, that it was about the decisions individuals make to contribute to environmental enhancement of their communities in the context of global warming. In fact much of their programme was at the level of how to dispose of dog-shit.

But he was expecting too much probably. This was local radio. The voices on the phone-in seemed to relish this intimate, deeply local relationship, in which the melting of ice-caps was certainly less significant than fouling door-steps, as it were. The callers certainly had a great rapport with her affable, articulate presentation, handling them, as she did, with what appeared to be genuine warmth and interest. They called her Jilly. Jilly Grierson. The programme was announced as 'Jilly's PI'.

'Listen, Jilly,' one caller said. 'I have someone across the street, and I am no' goin' to name names, but he has three dugs, three no less. In the name of God it must be like Noah's Ark in his wee flat. Well, he lets them run wild. They do their thing all over the place. And he won't listen.'

The reply was cunning. Firstly formal, then personal and more human.

'You know of course that local authorities have the power to fine people who do not clean up after their pets and even dock their wages in some instances. But that's not the road we should go down in our neighbourhood. This man would listen you know, if you really took the trouble to explain all the circumstances. We just don't talk to each other often enough. We go into our shells and don't reach out. If we did make the effort it would surprise us all. Now, honestly, Mary, do you ever go out of your way to try to talk to this man? Ask yourself that.......'

It went on in that vein, throughout, which almost suggested she might have been currying favour to run for local office. He had also benefitted greatly from having listened to her programme. It was almost as if she had introduced herself to him through the medium of radio.

So it was, the next day, early afternoon, that he stood there in the reception area of Radio Crystal. Around him on the walls were plaques of the different Scottish clans displaying the wide variety of tartans. He had only ever worn a kilt once, at a wedding, but when a girl he fancied told him he had knobbly knees the kilt was banished for ever from his thinking.

'I'd like to see Jilly. The girl that presents the PI show,' he said to the receptionist sitting behind a broad desk. She looked at him with the slight petulance of a mother with no hankie to wipe away a child's snot. Before she could say no, which is what she looked like saying, he jumped in again.

172

'Tell her I'm the boy from the lane who saved her from the muggin'.'

She screwed up her face but reached for her phone and spoke softly into it, then turned to him.

'She's coming,' she said.

No more than two minutes later, Jilly appeared. She came through the door at the end of the reception area and walked breezily towards him, her lively eyes sweeping over him in a scrutiny that made his spine tingle. Having had the voice in his imagination for so long she seemed to be the holograph created from it; beautifully poised and confident in casual wear; her blue sweater and yellow trousers reflecting the comparatively exotic ethos of a radio station within a drab industrial estate. She reached at her blonde pony-tail and flicked at it, like it was something that charged her batteries.

'I'm Jill Grierson. They call me Jilly about here.'

'Thomas Brownlie. They call me Tam anywhere.'

She reached out and shook his hand; a positive, surprisingly strong handshake.

'Do you want Thomas or Tam?'

'Tam.'

'Good. We have much to talk over, have we not, Tam?'

'You could say so.'

'I have another bulletin to do before my shift finishes. Can you wait?'

'Until hell freezes over,' he said without blinking an eye.

She gave him a puzzled look and the suggestion of a tiny smile then turned away. He sat and eventually listened to her bulletin in the reception area's loudspeaker. She sounded crisp and confident. It was all local news this time, the sort he wasn't particularly interested in, but should have been. Then she reappeared.

'It's quiet at this time up in the little cafeteria. We can get peace there.'

It was certainly tiny, but cosy.

'To drink?' she asked, when they got there.

He almost let slip his favourite choice, but you don't drink Irn-Bru with a lady fair.

'Coffee,' he said, then stood as tall as he could, trying to suggest a kind of maturity that would be more in keeping with this new company. Already she was causing him to feel a rise in the temperature that definitely was not recording on any nearby radiator. He was several inches taller than her and he wanted to show that clearly, standing feet apart, the angle of head and shoulders aping a figure about to receive a laurel wreath. Then he felt stupid suddenly. What was coming over him? She was older. Well, not ridiculously older, he felt. Not hopelessly older. A bit like a young chemistry teacher he had fantasies about until she took part in a charity basketball game with the pupils and gave him a black-eye with an elegant but reckless elbow. Somehow it was a generational blow that he never recovered from as she suddenly aged before his eyes. He knew there was an arising of new fantasies now, that was for sure, but also wondered if there would be another black eye in the offing for him eventually.

The coffee pot was simmering. He was more used to instant. The brew tasted like it had been made of used Brillo pads, but he smiled politely as the first fieriness went down.

She put her hands carefully on the small table. She had long fingers with pink nails and a sort of emerald ring on her right hand. He felt he was under scrutiny, her eyes narrowing with a slight wrinkle of the brow occasionally that suggested more inquisitiveness than perplexity. She had a delicacy of feature but her whole frame reflected the great self-confidence of her broadcasting voice.

'The photograph......'

'It's not here at the moment,' Tam butted in quickly, and felt a sense of relief that he could get started now. 'All I've wanted to do from that morning I met you was to find you and give you the photograph back. I wanted it outta ma hands. But how can I do that now? It isn't just as easy as that? Do you know all the things that have happened to me and the others?'

'Others?'

Tam talked quickly through events, then summarised.

'A friend abducted, people goin' out of their way to help me find you and probably riskin' their lives, a gun produced, a sniper killin' a man just feet away.'

'Nicholas Carson, yes. Tragic! I read about it.'

'Witnessing it was, well, like it'll never be out of my mind,' Tam said solemnly. 'So I'm owed one big explanation. Badly. The name first of all. Who's the face in the photo?'

'His name is Andrej Matskevich.'

Andrej? The name clicked. The yellow folder name.

'From Belarus?'

'How did you know that?'

'Never mind But I want to talk about that lawyer. Shot, stone cold dead, right at my feet. Blood everywhere. Why?'

She held up her hands in despair.

'To scare you. To get rid of a man who was bothering them.'

'Them?'

'The people who came to search for Andrej Matskevich, of course.'

'Why did the bampots have to kill him?'

Before she replied she surveyed him as if she had to make a decision about what would follow. He wasn't quite sure afterwards how long that hiatus lasted but it made him squirm slightly. She took a deep breath.

'Look. You have been through the mill. I understand that. And you do deserve some transparency. I deal in facts but in doing so I have to make assumptions about certain factors. In short I don't know everything surrounding Andrej and I have to make calculated guesses about things. But there is so much that you do deserve to know that is unlikely to do you any harm. In fact it might be to your benefit. So in answer to that question I can only say they were wanting to scare you and get their hands on the photograph, for Mr Carson was becoming an increasing pest to them I believe. He had to go.'

'Jesus, you talk about murder like they were seein' off a relative to a week-end in Dunoon. I've just listened to you talkin' seriously about dog-shit on radio. You can change your tune all right.'

'I'm a journalist you know. One day it's dog shit. The next it's a Legionnaires Disease outbreak, next it could be a politician on the make. That's what we do, follow stories. Like the Andrej one. You understand?'

Yes and no, he thought. Yes to the journalism bit. But, no, to accepting that that was all there was to her. He would have to be content at that time with the simple narrative of what the daily grind of journalism was in reality.

'Carson was being watched by people from Belarus, we believe, in the interest of their state security. Nicholas Carson had been fully aware of that and had been central to disseminating dissident propaganda. A lot of Belarus protest documents passed through his hands. We've always known that.'

'Who are 'we'?'

'Oh, just friends, that's all.'

'So how did you get your hands on the photograph?'

'By chance you might say. It was not long after I had broadcast a programme on ethnic groups in the city and how well or otherwise they integrate. I received a very nice letter from a lady in a care home who pointed out that I had overlooked her own community

177

which although it wasn't big in numbers, still maintained its identity and harboured grievances which ought to be aired publicly, and that she had material which she would like to show me. I was intrigued. So I went along to meet her. A Mrs Rybak.'

'From Belarus?'

'Via her ain folk. She is Scottish but was married to an Eastern European diplomat. She didn't go completely native although she spent many years in that country. So she has great sympathy for the domiciles who can't return there for political reasons. She went on to tell me that Andrej was a distant relative who had come to Scotland on some specialist work. That was all she would say about him, as if she was wary of divulging much about family. Of course she was frail. But extremely bright. She actually chose to go into a care home, not just for the company, but to help others. Perhaps our generation can't really appreciate the anxieties of those who are in very advanced age. Dementia, Alzheimers.'

'Ay, it's always in the news now. But I can't say I've bothered much about it.'

'Do you know there is more concern nowadays about the wasting of the mind now than there is about cancer? Well, she regarded it as something of a crusade to fight against the threat, by keeping minds active. She started to play word games with the residents. As I understand it, she was regarded by some of the others as a pain in the butt at first. Then they did eventually latch on to what she was trying to achieve. They even began to look forward to her quizzes and anagrams. I thought of making a broadcast about that. She struck me as being......how can I put it.....significant.'

'Why did you become so interested in Andrej?'

'That grew. It was when she phoned me to let me know that another man had come to visit her a week after my visit, to find out if she could tell him where Andrej was in the country. She was suspicious, and warned me in the starkest and most surprising terms that his life might be in danger. Sadly, she passed away a month ago. The bampots, as you call them, had discovered where she was.'

'How?'

'I have myself to blame I believe. I had contacted the lawyer by phone after my first visit. She scribbled the only number she had for him on the back of the photograph. I should have been more careful. It was that call and the first message I left. I had to risk it. But it didn't pay off. It was hacked into in all probability.'

'Tell me about it. I think I got shafted that way as well,' Tam said ruefully, thinking of his telephone contact with Carson. 'But I have Mrs Rybak's folder with a lot of material in it.'

'Oh, you do?' she said perking up. 'I'd love to go through that again. Soon possibly?'

'You will. But then there's the men from the lane. The Men in Black. Where do they fit in?'

'I'm at the guessing game about them,' she replied. 'They could be freelance. Or even operating for the Belarus government. I'm just not sure. Who knows, one of them might be a skilled sniper. At this stage we can suppose anything. They're still out there, free and wandering.'

He wondered if she would have said as much to him if he had merely brought along the photograph and handed it to her. Almost certainly not. The retention of it in Gabby's shop was a tactic paying dividends. So he had hardly touched his coffee. When he did it was now lukewarm. She had ended on such a passionate note that it was almost as if she were a political animal herself, despite initial appearances. He was still feeling the repercussions of that firm touch of her hand though. It was certainly not making him think of politics.

'Why don't we just burn the photo and end the trail, if it means nobody will get their hands on him. Is that no' the safest way?' he found himself asking to cover his self-induced embarrassment.

'No. That would be utterly negative. I need to find him and talk to him and .....'

'Get a great radio programme out of it,' he suggested.

'Thank you for the career advice,' she replied, slightly taken aback. 'I am not engaged in a cynical exercise with this. Whatever the outcome, there will be no programme made about Andrej if it compromises his safety or his future. And talking about career, what do you do? Unemployed?'

'Still studying. I hope to get to university and do maths and physics. I get some part-time jobs in the summer just to keep me goin'. It's no' easy gettin' them though. I've been sweepin' up at a bakery recently. It only lasted three weeks though until the lad came back from holiday. But it put some cash into my pocket. I struggle by.'

The slight discomfort he had felt with his suggestion of radio exploitation dissipated quickly as she listened to that part. It was a self-evident sympathy ploy. So his confidence grew.

'How did you end up in that lane with the two goons?' he asked.

She sat back stretched herself and seemed to find some enjoyment in that query.

'As they would classically say, "thereby hangs a tale". It was this woman I had heard about, a Mrs MacPhail. A psychic. I was told by one of my colleagues here that this woman could help me in the search, if I showed her the photograph. All right, I admit it, it sounds a bit bizarre. But I verified from news cuttings she had helped the police with searches in her time, so she claimed. I had to try everything. I phoned her and got no answer. I then went twice in two days after still getting no reply. I was then informed by a neighbour who told me she had gone to Tenerife for a week. Now what I clearly did was excite some interest in that woman. Because it's obvious I was followed.

'One of the men who chased me had her number on his mobile.'

'Really? But he wasn't one of the two who waylaid me in the lane, was he?'

'No. I can vouch for that.'

'Nothing surprises me, I suppose. Well, I had to call her eventually, as I didn't want to waste any more time, to tell her what I was after. The Men in Black, as you call them, obviously picked up

181

that call and waylaid me when I came out of the taxi and dragged me up the lane. And I had thought by that time, my phone had been made secure.'

As she said that she turned away quickly as if something had slipped out she didn't mean to say and quickly asked, 'More coffee?'

A secure phone for someone who spent a lot of time explaining how to cope with dog-shit? It did seem odd. But before he could decline the coffee or offer any comment, she made it clear that she wanted closure on the matter.

'Oh, yes, it is such a mess,' she admitted looking slightly embarrassed about what she had planned. 'It was a long shot on my part. I have put it right out of my mind and so should you.'

'No way,' Tam replied. 'I have a mate who is workin' on that psychic angle even as we sit here.'

Chapter 13

'What prompted you to seek contact with your grandfather?' Mrs MacPhail asked. Frankie could see that she trusted him as much as he did her. She sat upright on a high-backed upholstered chair, looking, surprisingly, not much different from any ordinary woman he would see pushing a trolley in a supermarket. Admittedly she was decidedly heavy on the make-up, and had black eyebrows that looked to have been painted on her and looked like bat's wings, her large lips so red they could have been used as beacons on a misty coast. She looked through thick-lensed spectacles with eyes that seemed to penetrate under his skin. But he had expected a large fat woman, swathed in shawls, and surrounded by cats crawling all over the table and around his legs. Instead she wore a trim two- piece grey suit, like she might have been going to church, if psychics actually went to churches since they were supposed to know already all about the Other Side, he guessed. And she was not old and decrepit, but perhaps even a few years younger than his mother. The large round table was certainly what he had expected to find, although it was wooden and plain and shiny with no gadgets on it, which he thought might be used as transmitters to the Other Side. The room was certainly heavily-curtained and generally gloomy, with the exception of the lamp suspended from the ceiling over the table.

'Ma grandpa just left us. And that was that. No warnin'. Gone. I want to show a bit of respect and tae say sorry for a few things,' Frankie answered to her query.

He wouldn't have been able to arrange it at all had it not been for a near neighbour Mrs McGregor, whom he helped a great deal, even going shopping for her occasionally, because she suffered badly from arthritis. She was so grateful for what Frankie did for her that she had agreed to act as his go-between with the MacPhail woman, who regularly contacted her husband for her, on the Other Side. He had been in the merchant navy and had disappeared, apparently lost at sea. Frankie supposed Davy Jones's Locker was on the Other Side. 'It's never too late to speak to the deceased,' Mrs MacPhail said reassuringly. 'You brought something with you, as advised? And his first name?'

He felt inside his jacket pocket and pulled out the pipe. He kept the photograph securely in that pocket. That would come later, the real object of the exercise.

'Dick, was his first name. And this was his,' Frankie said. He placed it on the table. It was neither a Sherlock Holmes type pipe, nor a Gandalf pipe, but a simple brown pipe that had been so well smoked that the inside look irredeemably sooty-black. She put her hand on it without attempting to lift it, then stroked it.

'Cold,' she said.

'What is?'

'The pipe. And the atmosphere.'

That's a great start, he thought.

'I feel there is a barrier between us.'

Maybe she did have powers to read his mind, but he couldn't resist the feeling that this was just a variety act. He had to stick in there though. Then she picked up the pipe, closed her eyes and her lips moved soundlessly.

'Have you got there yet?' he asked.

'Where?'

'The Other Side.'

'Be patient.'

'When you get there ask him about whether he still needs a knee-replacement on the Other Side or do these things not matter there?'

'Please be quiet and concentrate. I want you to think of him and of a special memory you might share.'

Frankie felt that he had to push her a bit.

'If you get through to him on the Other Side, mention the Bingo Palace to him. He'll know what that means.'

'Would you please be quiet now!' she interrupted irritably. She was concentrating deeply now with a furrowed brow. Her hands were stroking the pipe like she would have classically done with a cat, had one been there. Again her lips were moving in a gentle slow chewing motion and he found himself trying to decipher what the silent words were. Psychics were obviously good for lip-readers. Then she opened her eyes which seemed to widen into a deep stare that sent shivers up his spine.

'Dick, can you hear me?' she hissed. 'Ah, I'm beginning to see him. He is coming clearer.'

Frankie looked into the gloom of the room around him. Nothing, only gloom. Her eyes were half-closed. He guessed she was looking at the Other Side.

'Tall man. Unbowed. Proud. Bald. He is talking. He has a slight speech impediment.'

True. He did have. The family thought nothing of it, being so natural to their ears that nobody really sniggered when 'Rambling Rose' coming out of his mouth, became 'Wambling Wose'. He was beginning to be impressed by her against his initial judgement. Then, without interrupting her mystifying stare, she stretched out her hands.

'Please,' she whispered. 'Hold my hands.'

He looked at her to determine what her intentions were, but could now see that her eyes were open, showing dark pupils with shiny white surrounds. This was a stare that looked as if it was there for the rest of the summer. He duly raised his hands and clasped hers. They felt like he was holding two ice-cubes. But, despite how cold they felt, her grip was firm and steady. Frankie did feel ill at ease.

'The last time I held hands like this was when I did the Military Two Step at our Christmas party when I was in primary school. Ma partner had been the Virgin Mary in the school nativity play but it went to her head and she did think she had certain powers and thought everybody was beneath her, especially me who was only one of the shepherds with a hat that was made out of an old tea cosy. So I tripped her up. The Virgin Mary fell flat on her back and swore at me. I never told a soul till now '

'Shhh!' she said. 'Concentrate. Can you hear anything?'

He listened.

'He is talking. Can't you hear him? He is saying that he is well and that he regrets many things that you were not able to do together eventually.'

He tried hard. Was that a whisper he heard?

'I went to the bingo with him. Is he sayin' anything about that yet?'

'He says he is enjoying the company of some of his old friends.'

'Is he playin' bingo with them?'

'Please. Pay attention. I don't want to lose him. He says that one day you will make your mother very proud of you by becoming a great success in life. He has every confidence in you.'

'Could you tell him he could be even more confident about that if he gave me a kick start in life by tellin' me where his bingo winnings went?'

'Shhh! He is saying something else but his voice is getting weaker......I'm losing him. Concentrate.'

'Bingo. The money. Ask him!'

'The voice is so thin. What is that? What are you saying? Ah, money in an old stocking......... under a bed ....at 44 Dunmore Street.'

'That was where he used to live....'

'He's going....I think we have lost him.'

'Keep him there...'

'It's now black, very black. He's gone.'

She whipped her hands away from him, her tongue licking her large lips as if she had just finished a dessert, and the tension, stretching from her taut gaze, right through her body, disappeared. The look she was giving him was that of someone who wished him out of the place as fast as she could manage. Frankie realised that all she had done was some homework on his grandfather, as Tam had suggested she would, and had probably quizzed Mrs Macfarlane cutely about background details. One mistake though.

'44 Dunmore Street doesn't exist any longer. It was demolished. He moved to a new address a year before he died. You would have got that old address from Mrs Macfarlane, wouldn't you?'

She looked at him as if she could not have cared less about being denounced as a swindler.

'He spoke. He then went away. That is nothing to do with me. It has all to do with the power of transfer from person to person. Yours, I have to say, was very weak.' Now was the time. The real reason for being there now that he had provided the camouflage.

'How about this?' he asked.

He reached behind him picked his jacket up which he had let fall on the floor behind him, took out the brown envelope which had been handed over to him ceremoniously by Gabby and Tam, and then held the photograph up to her like a trophy.

'I'll give you some thoughts all right. This man is in danger. Who is he? Where is he?' he asked.

At first she looked as if she was totally unconcerned about that challenge. Then he noticed the gradual shift of her gaze, from him to the photograph. He laid it on the table and slid it towards her. There was no reaction at first. All she did was look at it as if she was perusing a menu handed her by a waiter. Gradually, though, he noticed the slight changes of attention, the slight movement of eyebrows, the unclasping of her hands to place them on either side of the photograph, the pursing of the lips, the tiny movements of her shoulders as if the rate of breathing was increasing. Then she raised her head and placed one hand completely over the photograph and closed her eyes. This time Frankie kept his mouth tightly shut. Indeed, he lost track of time, sitting there, patiently watching her. The only movement was the increasing rising and falling of her ample chest and shoulders like she was trying to induce serenity. Then, after a long period, the eyes opened and she became very still, barely any movement, like she had still-framed herself.

'There is death there,' she said with one slow nod of her head towards him. 'A very cruel death. Death by burning. '

Her hand was still on the photograph. She closed her eyes and remained very still then opened them again to look down at the face.

'There !' she whispered.

'Hey, I'm no' daft, Mrs MacPhail?' Frankie blurted out. ' C'mon, what do you mean death by burnin'?

She remained in her own tiny bubble, absorbed by her own thinking.

'I see what I see. I feel what I feel,' she said placing her hand on the photograph and then just as quickly withdrawing it, as if she had touched a hot-plate on a stove, and emitted a snort of pain.

'I felt touched by heat there,' she wrung her hands together.

Very dramatic, he thought. Great performance.

She put her hand back on the photograph and started to screw her forehead and mumble. At least he could hear what was coming repeatedly from her lips.

'PH. PH. PH,' over and over again.

'PH? What do you mean?'

'PH,' she kept repeating and then stopped as if she was now intent on listening carefully to something. 'Terrible, terrible violence. That's what it brings me.'

'Fat help that is. What terrible violence? It doesnae make sense.'

'Sense? What is that? I have feelings. I have sights of things. I don't make sense to myself often. But what I see and feel is real to me, and you would be a fool not to try to make something of what I have just told you. I can say no more.'

She bowed her head and looked at her hands as if she wished to dismiss him. Frankie sat there wondering if he had just wasted valuable time on her. She pushed the photograph slowly back towards him like it was a huge burden on her.

'Thank you,' he said politely. 'I'll remember what you said.'

Frankie stood up to go and walked to the door. He turned round to give her a last look

But, what he saw shook him. There were tears running down her cheeks.

***

190

Just before he parted company with Jilly, Tam had decided that he would invite her to Gabby's the following day to meet Frankie and talk about how those two people had helped him in his hour of need. They were all in this together. It would be the ceremonial handover of the photograph and, perhaps sadly, all associations with the events of the past few days, and her, would come to an end. He had to be honest with himself and admit that the thought of simply walking away from it all, when they still had not solved matters to their personal satisfaction, was deeply bothering him.

A phone call from Sammy was to change matters considerably.

'How are you ma auld cock-sparra?' the jaunty voice said. 'We haven't deserted you. We're still in touch with Gabby about things. The polis tell me that that bunch of bampots have been deported, like right away, no messin' about, none of this appealin' to this person and that. Their feet never touched the ground. The doctor's trying to pull rank, and was tellin' folk apparently that if it weren't for people like her the NHS would probably go under. That's a big surprise, isn't it? She'll probably end up in the honours list at Christmas. It's called the power of respectability. That other two, the Men in Black you call them, will be dealt with if ever they go near you.'

Tam let the flow of words continue unabated.

'But that's not the main reason I'm callin'. I have a friend I would like you to meet. Well, to be absolutely honest it's been requested. Very professional he is. Hard, but fair. He's been trainin' in the gym here regularly over the past few days. Very fit man. He'd

191

like a few words in your ear. I'll be sending the brothers over to collect you. Where are you?'

'I'll be outside the Gorbals Library.'

The call ended. Twenty minutes later he was on his way back towards the east-end listening to the apparently inseparable brothers talking all the way to the gym, about their time in Iraq. Donald drove the car with great care, as if neither of the brothers had not yet made the full transition from the alleyways of Basra with their lurking LEDs, to the rolling traffic of their native city which had road- rage as a peril instead. They had imported their alertness. When they arrived there were young fighters in the ring again slapping away at each other. There was no sign of Sammy as the brothers took him straight into his office.

There were two men in work-out kits there, shorts and training vests, sipping on power-drink bottles.

'So this is the lad,' the older of the two men said, but although the welcome seemed pleasant enough, there was no outstretched hand, no smile.

'Close the door after you and don't let anybody interrupt us,' he said to the brothers who did as they were told. It was the man with the silver streak down the middle of his hair whom he had seen in the doctor's house in charge of what had appeared to be a select police group. Should he mention that or keep quiet? He chose the latter. The younger man remained silent, then walked over to the television set.

'You can call me Alex,' the first man said.

Friendly enough, but still no smiles. Tam looked back at the closed door, and even though he realised he was in a secure environment, run by a man who was now an acknowledged friend, he felt stirrings of discomfort.

'Who are you?' Tam felt entitled to ask.

'Friends of Sammy's,' Alex said, watching his companion inserting a disc into the DVD player under the television.

'What kind of friends?' Tam went on, intent on having specifics.

'Oh, I think we have to be clear about this,' Alex said as if he wanted to straighten the situation out with the younger man. 'We are police. And, let me assure you, this is not an official interview. It is intended as a friendly and informative chat. '

Tam's unease was hardly improved by that admission. Nor was the fact that he could tell they were not local, not by their accents anyway. English. Kind of *Eastenders* English.

'We've heard a lot about you from Sammy,' Alex said. 'All good. Of course we came upon you the other day as you know. It is all so complicated and Sammy wants to keep you clear of all the muck that everybody is wading through at the moment. '

The tension was easing slightly. Curiosity was intruding now.

'Indeed, from what we gather you have shown a lot of spunk. That's to be admired.'

It was getting even more relaxed.

'You're no' exactly traffic cops, are you?' Tam ventured.

'Correct,' Alex replied. 'But we have the same general purpose of keeping people on the straight and narrow. Same principle,'

'And you're from England?'

'Anything against that, Tam?'

'You stole Fergie.'

'And gave him a knighthood. We're tolerant people, Tam.'

He paused for effect. Tam suspected that the tolerance of which he spoke might shortly be put to the test.

'We are here with a warning, for your own good,' the man went on. 'Sammy has filled me in on a lot of details of what has been happening over the last few days even though we were not totally unaware of the presence of some really foul people coming into this city lately.'

'You don't sound like ordinary polis to me,' Tam said getting bolder. 'Folk round my area can tell your kind right away. You're Special Branch, right?'

'What's in a name?' Alex said. 'Let us just say that we get on famously with Sammy who has helped us through the years to try to keep trouble off the streets, in different ways. And he's much loved where I come from in Stepney, where we always thought the wee Scottish boxers were some of the most courageous men in the ring. And just to stay on that theme, you can sometimes get into real trouble when you try to punch above your weight, and that is exactly what you are trying to do now and if you keep at it, you could end up with a worse fate than lying on your back on the canvas. We want to show you something,' Alex went on. 'It's a video-tape we acquired some time ago. It's for your own good.'

His colleague pushed the start button and the screen sparked into life.

There is a smattering of patriotic-sounding music to start with and a symbol appears showing a white knight on a charging horse, silver sword in hand, which was now becoming almost a familiar sight to Tam. Then up comes a close-up picture of a statue of a man with a bald head and a little goatee beard and pans back until they see a crowd of people in the open air, in a square, listening to someone on a platform just in front of the statue, all of which is set against a brilliantly red stone structure. The statue, with an outstretched hand, is pointing to the heavens. A voice in English suddenly interrupts and says starkly,

'The Assassination of Taras Matskevich in Mazyr. May, two thousand and eight.' The English language narration stops as attention is focussed on an orator at a microphone who is speaking in that guttural language, full of passion, reminding Tam of some of the preachers in his mother's church that he had been forced to listen to. It is a harangue. But it is not that which arrests him. It is the recognition of a young man, sitting at the end of the platform, listening intently to what is being said, and applauding enthusiastically like the rest of the crowd, from time to time. It is, without doubt, the man from the cobblestones he had now become familiar with through constant examination of the photograph from the lane.

Perhaps a little younger, but not by much. The speech seems to be going on endlessly. Then there is a disturbance. Across the screen there is a flash like a strike of lightning, except it comes horizontally and diagonally from the back of the crowd, striking the platform just below the orator. There is an explosion, with a burst of flame and smoke mushrooming across the screen, accompanied by shrieks and screams. It takes a few moments for the smoke to dissolve and when it does they see the utter confusion as people are scattering in all directions and the platform party has broken up, with only three people remaining there, two of them crouching over the fallen figure of the orator, one of them the cobblestones man. Then the screen goes blank. No more follows.

Tam said nothing for a moment or two and neither did the two others. Alex broke the silence.

'We know about the photograph and we know about Andrej Matskevich, the son of the man you saw just being killed. We know that he left the country shortly after that and effectively went on the run with the hounds of hell after him. This was a demonstration in a Belarus town to protest against the statue you saw in the background. The statue is of a man called Lenin. The crowd, and principally the main speaker, wanted to remove it because it was a constant symbol and reminder of a political system they thought had been put behind them. But which it hasn't. It was a protest against increasing dictatorship. The end result, a disaster, and a young man now a target for assassination, like his father. But the plot thickens. Play it again, Sam,' Alex concluded in a peculiar, artificially light-hearted voice.

As the video was started again Alex became almost animated as he stepped forward and stood by the side of the television.

196

'I want you to pay attention to the right-hand side of the platform this time,' he said almost as if he were broadcasting himself. 'Forget the platform party. Concentrate on the group of people standing there, some of whom seem to have notebooks in their hands, in all probability journalists. What do you see?'

Tam concentrated. The obvious focus of attention had been the platform, but now, having been re-directed he could clearly see the group. They were a mixed bunch, men and women. But, even before the screen was to explode in the fatal climax, he sat bolt upright as a recognition hit him with stunning force. It was her. Clearly and distinctly. Out there holding something in her hand that could have been a microphone. Beyond any shadow of a doubt.

'Jilly,' he said. 'Jesus Christ!'

They turned the disc off and sat down on two chairs by the side of him, but did not say anything for a while, probably to allow him to digest what he had seen.

'She was there,' Alex said softly, as if to remove even a smidgeon of a doubt from Tam's mind.

'Why was she there? And you know of her?' Tam asked weakly.

'Of course. Know all about her. She was a freelance correspondent covering Eastern Europe. The public radio system in the USA hired her a lot. Hence that little bit of transatlantic diction of hers which surfaces from time to time. But she was obviously more than that. She had her fingers in other pies including the politics of the area. A kind of eyes and ears, we think. And it may be her instructions were coming out of the States too. Although we are not a hundred per cent sure......yet.'

All that cosmopolitan experience, all that involvement with politics, and yet he had heard her recently deal with the problem of dog-shit in a Glasgow street. The lady was versatile. Her image seemed to take on a different hue. Who was she really? And instructions from the States? Was she some kind of investigator? What was the word he was looking for? It came.

'Is she a spy?' he asked coolly.

'Oh, I don't want you to get carried away,' Alex went on. 'How do you define spying anyway? Just let it go. What we do know, just to make sure you realise you are dealing with more than somebody who reads weather forecasts, is that she trailed Andrej all the way to Paris where a great many European dissidents have settled in the past. Then, like all of us, she lost the scent, completely, until a certain Glasgow lawyer sent a message back to friends in Belarus saying Andrej had surfaced in Scotland. It was an act of naiveté on the lawyer's part, for which he suffered fatally, because the message was intercepted by virtually every party interested in this. The chase was on again, with a vengeance, and coincidentally a young lady with a great broadcasting CV turns up at a local radio station to volunteer to work free. For commercial radio, struggling to make ends meet in an advertising meltdown, this was like manna from heaven. Financed from another source, Jilly Grierson had got herself a base.'

'It doesn't sound real to me,' Tam said. 'So who is she really, and who pays her? You say she worked for American stations even though she's Scottish.'

'Mostly.'

'So the radio bit is just a cover?'

'You could say that,' Alex replied.

'And you really think this man Andrej is seriously under threat?'

'Many years ago Stalin in Moscow hired an assassin to put an ice-pick through the brain of one of his opponents. He thought he had been safe in Mexico City. He wasn't. Fanatics have long arms.'

Jilly with long arms? Surely not her. But how could he tell? From screen depictions of assassins, he knew they didn't wear labels. They could be aunties who favoured crocheting in between times.

'Why are you telling me all this?'

Alex started to wipe his armpits with a towel and then stood squarely in front of Tam his face stern. The adult-to-minor pose now.

'We know about the killing you witnessed. We slipped up there and we're still not sure who did it. You never know, you might have been killed yourself. Now we've been fair. We didn't need to explain all this to you. But we have. We're doing this now because even your friend Sammy knows what you have got yourself into is really dangerous and says, enough is enough. The folk that we know about could just squash you like a fly. We don't want that to happen. No more explanations. You're finished with this business. We don't want you to mess up your family and give them unnecessary heartbreaks. Don't go near that girl again. Don't even think about investigating anything to do with this. You might get in our way, and if so, you would definitely regret it. We could even arrest you for that. We have the powers. You're finished. Absolutely. Finito. Kaput. And one more thing. The photograph. We'd like to have it now.'

Alex's sudden, spiteful bearing got right up Tam's nose, just as suddenly.

'Sorry, we gave it back to Jilly,' he found himself saying. Alex hardly flinched but seemed to try to stand taller.

'I see,' he said. 'Jilly Grierson is one pain in the arse,' he went on, as if he actually knew her well. Strange, Tam felt.

'Don't forget what I said to you and don't let Jilly know we have met. That I insist on. Or else!' were Alex's final words.

Sammy was waiting for him outside, looking concerned, and for Tam it was like the old boxer had taken on a new appearance. Perhaps it was Tam's imagination but Sammy seemed to have a furtive look about him now, perceiving him as a friend of this man claiming to be police and who Tam now had taken an intense dislike to. Those last few minutes had been confirmation of that discreet dovetailing of Sammy with these people. Maybe that's how he's survived so long, Tam thought.

'You understand what that was about? It was about your own safety. We can't fool around with you now,' Sammy said to him, face to face, when they met at the front of the gym. 'It's for your own good. Go home, play your football. Have a bevy. Keep safe. This is out of your reach now. You've reached a height that's too dangerous. And at that level we cannae be there to lend you a parachute any time.'

Already, Tam was feeling in free-fall.

Chapter 14

Feeling flat, morose, bitter, fankled, confused, and wondering who the hell Jilly really was, he found little inspiration in seeing Frankie sitting at the foot of the steps leading from his own flats, looking flat, morose, bitter, fankled and confused. Back from the gym and the shock treatment, by the man he assumed was Special Branch, Tam felt like he was now merely a husk. And, for him to see his mate similarly like that, was like finding the remains of a firework lying in the street, the morning after a display; useless to anybody.

'Think twice about visitin' a psychic,' Frankie moaned. 'It does your brain in. Can you believe I came out and started to talk to my cat? Passin' the time of day with my cat, would you believe, askin' for its view on Scottish independence, and pissed off it couldn't give me a clear cut answer. There am I thinking, what use is a cat if it can't make up its mind? I need a break in Florida after that. If only I could afford it. Honest tae God, no more thinkin' about the Other Side. You feel as if you need somebody to screw your head on the right way again after you come out.'

'All right, spill it out. What went on?'

Frankie told him slowly, like he was an infant with his first reader, making sure every consonant and vowel added up to something.

'A waste of time. And I don't like bein' treated like an imbecile. Burning flesh and PH and tears. Stuffin' that down me like I was a wastebin.'

'PH. What's that? Means nothin' to me. To be honest I didnae expect much. '

'Oh, so now you tell me. I end up gettin' freaked out on a wild goose chase!'

'Well, you did say you wanted to find out about the bingo money. We had tae try.'

There was little Tam could add to consoling his mate. He couldn't bring himself at that moment to reveal what he now knew about Jilly. The embarrassment of having to admit that he couldn't explain why there seemed to be two Jillys and what it added up to, was almost more than he could bear. But he had to pull Frankie out of his depression. He told him what Jilly had explained about her interest in Andrej Matskevich, where he was from and that all this seemed to be centred on dissidents from Belarus. But he did not stray into the Special Branch territory.

'We're meeting at Gabby's. Jilly is coming to take the photograph. It's about time. I take it you've got it on you?' Tam asked.

They did not speak on their way to the shop, and Gabby could sense they were not in the mood for light-hearted banter when they got there. He received the photograph again and carefully put it back in his safe, like it was a family treasure; after which he listened patiently as Frankie recounted the details of the visit, this time speeding through it with little feeling.

'I could have got more out of talkin' to a haggis,' he concluded.

'Come, come!' Gabby put in. 'You have to think hard. There might be something in what she said.'

'Look,' Frankie said with more determination, and as if he wanted to now clear his chest of the matter. 'All right she looks at the photograph, a deep look, then she puts her hand on the photo. Right? She then starts to mutter this PH thing and then she tells me she smells burning flesh. Ok? She's not even lookin' at it, just feelin' it and says she almost got burned herself. Go on, where's the sense?'

They watched as Frankie slumped down on a seat, the depression seeming to hit him again and Tam decided to move away from the subject of the physic. All they had to do now was wait for Jilly. They had Gabby bring in his radio so they could listen to her on Radio Crystal. The shopkeeper kept popping in, on the verge of one of the news bulletins to listen to her, and then desert the counter altogether when eventually she was on her *Jilly's PI* programme. Again it was performed with aplomb and charm. Even Frankie shut up for a while and after due consideration announced, 'That voice could sell after-shave tae the Taliban.'

An hour later she arrived. Gabby brought her straight through to the office. In the closeness of the confined space she looked slightly taller, wearing jeans and a light-brown windcheater. Tam could faintly detect a subtle perfume insinuating its way through the exotic spicy aroma which normally dominated there. She had unloosed her blonde hair which nestled around her shoulders, and he could tell she had touched her face lightly with make-up, but only just, so that she seemed devoid of artifice, natural, glowing, her eyes appealing for attention. Tam gave them that. Frankie stood up abruptly and for one moment Tam thought he was about to come to attention and salute. Gabby fussed around her.

'A real-life celebrity come into my place,' he piped. 'They won't believe this back home.'

Tam smiled briskly. She approached him and to his slight embarrassment pecked a kiss on his cheek. The words, liar, cheat, manipulator, crook, twister that had gone through his mind since meeting the Special Branch, simply melted away in her presence. He didn't believe he could have felt like that but that deliberately ˙nced contact made him actually feel like he had been introduced ˙˙es he hadn't know existed. He quivered in a way that he ˙n't too obvious to her or the others. Of course he had been ˙˙˙. But he suddenly he felt naked, exposed and that she ˙recisely what was happening to him in an area sacred ˙ a few feet of Jilly, he now felt he was entering taboo ˙ing like that to someone who possessed a maturity that ˙ment beyond his reach. But as soon as she started to ˙serted himself and saw her, as he had to, as someone ˙onishing professional life of deception. As she started ˙d tell she was summing them up, looking at them in ˙t to dash off and write them into a report. He wanted ˙rything the Special Branch had told him, but he had to keep it to hˑelf. He had been warned.

'There is so mˑch I regret about this,' she said sitting sipping a coffee now. 'Now, about that psychic?'

Tam was about to recount Frankie's story about the psychic, but received a glaring stare from his friend that would have felled a bull.

'Nothin',' Tam slipped in. 'It was a waste of time.'

'Oh, you poor boy,' she said, and for one moment he thought his friend blushed. He felt that if she had asked Frankie then, to rush out and summon up an open landau with four white horses for her, he would have tried. At least he seemed to have thrown off his deep depression for the moment. Gabby, having got over his gushing welcome was more down to earth now, weighing up her words carefully and wanted more from her than small talk.

'Where were you from originally?' he asked.

'I was an Edinburgh girl you know,' she was telling them. 'Bo there. Went to the University but wanted to go into broadcast right from the start though, but even before that happened go opportunity to go to the States to Brown University for a year. I Ivy League one, no less.'

'Ivy? An agricultural college?' Frankie asked, still in th throes of awe.

'Well, I suppose you could say that, given some of th rites some of the poor students there had to put up with,' with a polite smile.

'What did you do at Brown's, apart from milkin' the interjected with a dig at his mate.

'Oh, this and that. I was always interested in Slavi dies. So I took up Russian there.'

206

They were looking at her anew, as if she was some quick-change artist, switching identities in front of their very eyes.

'But please I have not come here to speak about myself and I don't want to intrude any more into your lives. You will be better off with me out of it. So, now, at last, the photograph. You have it here I presume?'

There was an initial silence as if they had reached the epilogue.

'And the folder the lawyer had. Is it here?'

Gabby gave him a quick quizzical look as Tam shook his head, 'I don't have it here,' he said.

'Oh,' she responded as if she didn't really believe him.

'Perhaps later?' she asked, briskly balancing her tone of voice to make it clear she needed it badly but not wishing to sound desperate.

Tam nodded but felt strangely unsure in doing so. Gabby taking his cue, reached into the safe, where the folder lay but produced only the photograph. He presented it to her delicately. She took if from him and held it up in front of her face.

'Andrej. Oh, what a merry dance you have led us all. If only you could speak. If only.....' she said falteringly, and at the moment Tam knew that the photograph in itself, although at this time the only thing she could cling on to with its Scottish connection, would not change the fact that the trail was still icily cold for her; for all of them in fact.

'You know where to find me if anything crops up,' she said and Tam could tell there was almost a despairing tone to that statement. She pecked him on the cheek again, but this time he put his arm lightly round her waist, pulled gently and converted the peck into an embrace that would have embarrassed his none-too-prudish auntie if he had done that to her. Jilly, completely unconcerned, simply smiled so closely into his face that he noticed that her eyes were the colour of the blue that trimmed the edge of Messi's shirt.

'Thank you,' she said, turned, went through the curtain and was gone, so quickly that Gabby, who clearly wanted to escort her to the street, was left flat-footed. In and out. Its brevity was almost taken as insulting. Tam felt they were in unity about that without having to say anything. Gabby murmured about having to get on with his business and left them sitting there, aware that empty space had taken on a new meaning. They both felt deflated, without having to admit that to each other. Frankie broke the long silence. He had been pondering something.

'PH. There's something we might have overlooked,' he said. 'Maybe her eyesight was better than ours. She had these thick glasses on. I think she saw something we didn't when she looked at the photo. As simple as that. Then put on that act about burning and all that shit. What have we been doin'? Usin' our eyes. That's all. She had those thick lenses.'

'Forget about her. How could she be able to see something we didn't? I've got that photograph imprinted right here inside my skull.'

'That's the point. I wanna look again. Was there anythin at all you can think of that looked different?'

'Naw. There might have been a slight bit o' camera shake which cannae have helped. All we can see is a grey wall at the back ....and the cobblestones around him. I see them in my sleep.'

'What do we see?' Frankie asked pensively. 'What do we really see? Just cobblestones? Or when you think of it, they didn't all look the same, did they? They weren't all the same kinda greyness were they?'

Tam thought hard. He had looked so often at the photograph that not having it to hand was frustrating.

'I don't think that was of any importance,' he said, not wishing to go off at some weird and fruitless tangent. But he could see from the look on Frankie's face that was exactly what he was intending to do.

'Have you ever felt like you had an itch in a part of your back you just cannae reach unless you had arms on you like an octopus?' Frankie said. 'It drives you mad.'

'What's the point?'

'I've got something like that itch right now and it's not on my back. It's in my head and I think it needs scratched.'

'Ok. What's the joke?'

'The joke is on that psychic. I think there's a way of tellin' what she was gettin' at.'

'Explain.'

'Follow me,' was the retort, like his mate was beyond reasoning with.

Gabby did attempt to say something as they passed through the outer shop, as if escaping a fire, but everything was now a blur to

Tam as Frankie set the pace, which was like that of a 10k road-walker with the finishing tape in sight. Tam tried to attempt to quiz him, but Frankie was now buried deep within himself, even though the bustle of the city clamoured around them both. It was only when Frankie paused momentarily outside a shop in the long, busy Victoria Road that Tam grabbed at his arm and demanded an explanation.

'You'll see,' Frankie said. 'I have to see a man about his stamp-collecting.'

'Stamps? Tam blurted out. 'At a time like this you're thinkin' about stamps. And who collects stamps anyway nowadays?'

'I know bugger all about stamps but this man showed me the details of a Honduran 19th century issue when I was in gettin' some cat-food. Staggerin' it was. Just you wait.'

He made his way through the door of this pet-shop, leaving Tam to look at a window-full of pitiful, incarcerated hamsters. Five minutes later Frankie re-emerged. In his hand was a large magnifying glass which was about the size of a large dinner plate. His mate raised it to his eye. What Tam then beheld was not an eye, but the Blob From Twenty Thousand Fathoms, an image from a phantasmorgic world, the kind of CGI concoction that Hollywood would spend millions on, generating in 3D, and here was Frankie managing it with one hand. The magnification stunned Tam. But, not so much as to stop him from realising now what Frankie's sudden burst of enthusiasm was all about. What could he say? 'So the man in there is a stamp-collector? I see', was what he managed. Half an hour, and two crowded bus trips later, they sat inside the reception area of Crystal Radio with Frankie lending a philosophical appraisal of the digital age.

'The magnifying glass has been longer in existence than Apple, by centuries. It makes you think doesn't it? I suppose they might have an app like it, but not this powerful.'

He knew what his mate was getting at. He was meaning we are 'back to basics' without the help of Steve Jobs. Tam took the glass and turned it on the receptionist, and immediately the magnification turned her, the desk and the tartans on the back wall into a sort of melting Baked Alaska, the blurred colours seeming to nudge each other out of the way for prominence. Funny how a bit of glass could turn the world into an even bigger mess than it appeared to be for them at the moment. But closer to a subject it would hopefully reveal minute detail. They heard Jilly finish that bulletin, and five minutes later she was beside them. She could tell they were not there to pass the time of day. They meant business, real business.

'Come through,' she said politely.

They entered a long room with two rows of desks with monitors. Only three were in use, two girls and a man wearing earphones all tapping at keyboards. Beyond that they could see through a window into a studio with a microphone suspended above a young man in earphones who was busily chatting to his audience and swinging on a swivel chair, laughing, waving his arms, or playing with a large broadcasting deck in front of him. A disc-jockey if ever there were one. He was playing one of Adele's high-density songs. Could she sing that way because she was fat, Tam found himself suddenly thinking?

Jilly led them to a corner where there was a curved couch, in front of which was a table with a coffee pot on top, like it was a place of refuge for the staff from the daily grind of broadcasting. More intimate perhaps than a canteen.

'So? What's this about?' she asked and it was difficult to determine whether or not she was glad to see them.

'We'd like another look at Andrej, if you don't mind,' Tam explained.

'You haven't come all this way just to have a look at Andrej again. What's so special this time?'

Frankie raised the magnifying glass. Amidst all the modern technology of a custom-built radio station, Tam had to admit to himself that the glass had taken on the appearance a stage-coach would at a Grand Prix ; so basic, so out of its era. However, it was clear she was intrigued.

'We just want tae satisfy ourselves about something, if you don't mind?' Frankie said with a handsome smile that looked manufactured for the occasion.

'Are you two keeping something back from me, by any chance?'

'And are you keeping somethin' back from US...by any chance?' Tam responded and immediately regretted saying that, because he could tell immediately that he had put her on some kind of alert, as she looked at him for a few moments, as if sensing that, indeed, he knew more about her than she had supposed. 'There is nothing much

I can tell you, other than what you already know,' she said nonchalantly. 'The photograph was not in my possession for long, or else I would have put it to certain tests.' He was about to challenge her about that when she rose and walked to her work desk and returned with the photograph.

'Come on, what are we looking for?' she asked. Neither of them replied. Frankie pulled the photograph towards him then bent over it, the magnifying glass poised above it like a hovering spacecraft. He raised and lowered it, and at the same time seemed to swoop over it like he was following an imaginary grid, ensuring that nothing escaped the enlargement. Then he stopped, dead still. He raised his head and looked straight ahead of him and blinked as if he had a fly in his eye. Then he returned to that hunched posture like that of a craftsman engraving words on a trophy. He was like that for some time before he stood up to hand the glass to Tam.

'Top right-hand side,' was all he said.

Tam took it, and after playing around with it to get his visual bearings he focussed on that area. He held it there until he was sure, then passed the glass to Jilly.

'Top right-hand side,' he reiterated.

She swept a long glance at both of them, and took the glass with the uncertainty of someone who feels a prank is about to be pulled and that the glass will shatter into pieces on the touch. Then she repeated the actions of the other two.

'I see a symbol of some kind,' she said. 'I must say it looks like letters linked in a decorative style, set into the stone. Blunt letters;

213

simple and.........' She paused and held her head still. Not because she was straining for effort. There was something else in her reaction and it gradually grew on Tam what it was.

'Two letters, that's all,' she went on.

'What are the letters?' Frankie asked, his voice at such a low ebb it sounded as if he were suffering a trauma, and like a teacher of infants waiting for them to chorus the expected answer.

'P and H,' she said.

She paused, her body suddenly tightening like she had a spasm of some sort. Two isolated letters would hardly produce that response. But she knew, she definitely knew what they meant. He was sure of that; and of another thing. She now knew where Andrej was.

Chapter 15

'So?' she asked, shrugging her shoulders as if she had drawn a blank, and was demanding some sort of decoding from them.

Tam waited for more. He felt in his bones that she had been stirred.

'You got nothin' from that?' Tam asked.

'What was I supposed to get from it?' she replied.

'PH. Means nothin' to you?' Tam threw at her.

'You tell ME what they're supposed to mean.'

Tam could only recall his chemistry studies at that moment and threw it in for the sake of saying something.

'PH is a measure of acidity. But I doubt if it has any meaning here.

'I told you that con artist saw it with her own eyes,' Frankie said but with a degree of dubiety in his voice.

'The naked eye could not have seen those letters, Frankie boy,' Tam said, and then realised the mistake he had made, for the phrase 'Frankie boy,' was normally thrown at his friend as an expression of disparagement. The anticipated fusillade came.

'So, all right, professor. Are you trying to tell me that this woman could tell there were letters there just by puttin' her hand over them and feelin' them? That would take the biscuit, that would. She was wearing thick specs, the kind that make the half-blind see the far horizon.'

'What woman are you talking about?' Jilly asked.

'That psychic woman you were due to see,' Tam admitted.

'Oh! Really? You mean she.... '

'And I'm tellin' you that there is not a pair of specs in the entire system of the NHS that could have helped her see these letters,' Tam interrupted by turning to his mate.

'You're a man of science, so you tell me! Are you chuckin' all your theories out the windae now. Evidence. Give me evidence you keep tellin' folk, especially all those holy folk. I've given you the evidence, that this con artist tried to make out that she had some spooky way of givin' us information when she could see what it was with her own eyes. All that crap about burnin' and weepin' like she had heard bad news, that's part of the variety act. She wants to drum up business by hoping to get the likes of me, who she thought was some kind of dumplin', to go away and spread the gospel about her strange powers. So what's your explanation?'

'I don't have it at the moment. But I'm sure there is one.'

'Oh, big deal. The world awaits.'

'Ok, are you telling me she saw these letters thanks to Specsavers? I cannae swallow that. There had to be another reason.'

'You're arguing against yourself. You're saying that something unnatural happened in that room.'

'I'm saying nothin' o' the kind. I just want an explanation that's logical.'

Tam became aware that Jilly was sitting back in a relaxed position in her chair, with a hint of amusement on her face, as if she had come across two men fighting over a parking space outside a football stadium. He had no counter to Frankie at this time, feeling it was tactically sound to divert their focus on what they had learned, if anything.

'So what good does PH do us?' he asked looking directly at Jilly. She shrugged again.

He felt increasingly sure there had been recognition even in the tiniest whisper of her body language.

'Parking Here. Public Health. Power Hydrant. Power House. Purple Heather. ....' Frankie was beginning to reel of some suggestions that became increasingly bizarre including 'Paracetemol Here' which put a severe dent in his credibility as a solver of riddles. The only interpretation that Tam could put on it was that it was effectively a sign which stated simply, 'Dead End.'

'Cobblestones,' Tam said directly to Jilly, trying to feel her out.

'What do you mean?' she replied.

'Cobblestones are from the past. Maybe some historic place. Significant? No?'

'I suppose you could put any interpretation on it. But you could also spend from now till Christmas trying to work that out. I think we're back to scratch again. Sorry.'

'But if it is too difficult to work out, why was everybody puttin' so much effort intae findin' it? If you had already got the photo and looked at it and you couldn't see anythin' of value in it, why end up fightin' in the lane with two men, like your life depended on it.'

'They hadn't seen the photograph. That's why they were so desperate to get their hands on it. They had no idea what they could find there and I wanted to keep it that way. They weren't to know

217

what it would reveal. But they certainly had known of it since the days of Mrs Rybak in the home. At least that's the best I can think of. We were going to put it to some chemical tests, which we hadn't got round to, just in case there was something hidden underneath,' she replied. 'That's what we still await and what I'll be working on.'

'Who's 'we'?' Tam asked bluntly again, hoping for a better response this time. 'You seem to know a lot about all those bampots. Is that just from being a nosey reporter? Is that all?'

Just as he felt that he might have gone too far with that remark, she helped him.

'I was getting some help from friends, that's all. Nothing special.'

She said that with an air of finality. As if friends who gave chemical tests were like friends who helped her redecorate a room. It doesn't tally, Tam thought, but clearly there was no further angle he could pursue.

'I'll have to leave,' she said. 'I have another bulletin in half-an-hour. My last for the day and then I'm off home to sip a glass of white wine and collapse in front of the telly. I hope you understand?'

You bet he did. It was like she wanted rid of them now. This was the brush off, accentuated by what she said next.

'I am deeply grateful for everything that you and Frankie have done and I will think of something to show my appreciation eventually.'

She ushered them outside to the entrance like a kindly aunt, with the feeling within Tam she really did not want to have anything to do with them again. He was both angered and confused. He knew she was deceiving them. But Sammy and the Special Branch's warnings were having an effect. All he could do was fume within. It had to be the end.

'Right on,' was all Tam could weakly say as Frankie continued to challenge him to another bout of dispute about 'evidence'. Tam kept his mouth shut, which simply encouraged Frankie to create a whole string of new meanings for PH and was only shut up when Tam threatened to push him under the wheels of the bus when they got off, if he didn't belt up. But he had to keep Frankie on his side if he was going to pursue this which, despite his thoughts on leaving Jilly, he was already thinking of doing and he began to realise he would have to open up to his mate about the meeting with the men in the gym. A sense of embarrassment about having been duped by Jilly had held him back. He decided that when he saw his mate disappear into his close still muttering to himself as if two letters of the alphabet would be like nocturnal midges about to make his night a living hell.

When, the following early morning, he turned on the radio to hear her expected bulletin, it was another voice he heard. An announcement was made that Jilly was indisposed and that another broadcaster would take over her phone-in programme that morning, and for the rest of the week.

Indisposed? No, no, no! He didn't swallow that for a moment. He now knew she was on her way.

Frankie was lying in the sun doing rib-cage movement exercises. He was flat on his back on the roof of one of the lock-ups adjacent to his building, a favourite place of his, since at that time of the day most of the cars were out and young kids had the small play-park nearby to let off steam. He could climb up there with ease, using footholds in the chipped rough-casting, to engage in a sense of complete privacy. The material on the roof had a surprisingly soft texture to it like a non-stick putty. After being with the psychic, and experiencing his day-return ticket to the Other Side, he felt like an alien force had entered his body making him feel unclean. Then had come the matter of the PH which had dragged him even into meanings he wouldn't have mentioned in front of Jilly, although she was clearly a woman of experience who must have known a thing or two about men. He found it difficult to blank his mind to the letters. So relaxation was now the key. He would allow his chest to rise and swell as he breathed in such a way as to lift his rib-cage, like an air-filled balloon, up towards his chin, pushing the lungs to an extreme limit, then would let out his breath slowly, so that he could ultimately feel his muscles relaxing so much that he felt like he was floating. It was a technique he had read about in a magazine he had picked up in the doctor's surgery once. The fact that it was for pregnant women did not faze him in any way. It seemed to be working.

'C'mon. I'm no' havin' it. 'They're no just dumpin' us!'

It was Tam's voice, suddenly coming from beneath him. Frankie straightened up and in looking down he could see a disconsolate figure below.

'Dumpin' us? Who? What are you on about?' Frankie responded, lazily unwinding himself.

'Better get down here!'

As he did so, he saw Tam slouch against a wall with his knees almost up to his chin and his folded hands showing white knuckles. He had seen his friend like this before in a pre-ballistic mode. He sat a few feet away from him, curious, but at the same time reluctant to breach his mate's innermost thoughts. He knew when to leave well along. But after a minute or so Tam seemed to come round and exert visible self-control.

'I hadn't the heart to tell you this. But I cannae hold it back any longer, now that we don't have the photograph. I had a meetin' with some friends of Sammy's. They're polis.'

'Polis? What about?'

'I think they're Special Branch.'

'Are you havin' me on?'

'I can't tell you any more than that. It was a warnin'. Any more dealings with Jilly and this business with the photograph, and they'll get nasty with us.'

'Them? Why?'

'They think we're headin' for big trouble. It's for our own good they say. That gets ma goat when somebody says that. Makes me feel I could lash out at anybody if they said the wrong word.'

'The big boys, well, well. But what's their beef? I thought everythin' was wrapped up anyway.'

'The Men in Black still puzzle them. That's clear enough. They're out there somewhere and I must admit that gives me the creeps. Anyway they want us just to go home and be good boys and leave it to them. They said they would lift us, arrest us, just to get us out of the way and that would hurt our families. That's what it's come to. I could puke. '

'To be honest, up to this time my mother thinks the only adventures I get up to are helpin' out with Meals on Wheels sometimes. I'd want it to stay that way if I had the choice. Seriously, I want an easy life.'

'They could get us on any trumped-up charge if they wanted, I suppose. Out o' the kindness of their hearts. The thing is, Sammy is with them on this. He thinks we've done all we can do. There's more to him than just a wee Glasgae fella who runs a gym. A lot more. And as for her.......'

Tam's voice tailed away, his varied thoughts on her conflicting within him.

'We could go back and see what Jilly thinks,' Frankie said. 'She seems reasonable enough.'

'She's gone. Scarpered. Disappeared. Fucked off. Didnae show up for her broadcasts.'

'Meanin'?'

'Think of it. She knows where Andrej is now. That's for sure. I could see it in her face. Something clicked with her after using the magnifying glass. She's on to him. I know it. She's way ahead of us, mate. But we can still catch up.'

Frankie could feel the hurt in Tam's voice.

'Then why didn't she tell us?' he asked simply.

That sentence hung in the air for what seemed like an interminable time, without reply. Frankie had to answer it himself.

'Because she's not been straight wi' us? Is that what you're gettin' at? Right?'

Tam still did not reply but seemed to be in deeper thought now and Frankie realised he was going to get nothing more out of him at the moment.

'So that's it then,' Frankie said. 'Ok! You know something that I don't know. So what? Just as well it's finished. It was fun while it lasted. Except for that spooky trip to the Other Side. I'd rather go intae a cage with a hungry lion than try that again. Mind you, I didn't mind meeting up with the Silent One. More people should be like him. Nae talk. How do you think we'd get on without all the fanny you keep hearin'. It was an honour to meet somebody who didnae talk back to me and give me a slaggin'. And Jilly, what a bird! You wouldn't have missed her for the world, would you?'

Tam knew he was prompting him for some revelation about his feelings for her. No chance. Frankie just wouldn't get it. So he diverted the question.

'Where has she gone now?' he asked of himself aloud with a tinge of despair.

'Leave it out, Tam. We're done! It's all over! Time-up. The final whistle's gone! Head for the pavilion! So what? We've still got a life. Think o' the future.'

Then suddenly Tam heard his friend launch into a subject that he had never heard aired before, like they had come to a critical turning point at which they had to acknowledge that fate was not going to keep them conjoined forever.

'Ok, I might no' get intae a kitchen any time soon, but I know I've got to be patient. If it means stackin' shelves in Tesco's for the time bein' then that's what it has to be. And you! Think o' it. You've got a brain. Use it. It's takin' you places. We all know that. Me, I'm in a lottery, for God's sake. You, you're a cert. Think o' that. The Jilly thing is over.'

And then he realised what he just said. In looking at his mate he realised that it must have sounded like a betrayal. Tam, still deeply pensive, was visibly rejecting what Frankie had just uttered unwilling to accept this profound change in events. Frankie recognised that he had not made his mate's day with that diatribe. But it had to be said. Eventually Tam conceded the moment to his friend but with little sincerity.

'If you say so,' he said, but unable to disguise his pain.

He picked himself up from the ground and brushed down his trousers with his hands, almost absent-mindedly, and started to walk away from the lock-ups towards the opening which led towards the main road. Frankie sloped after him still eager to get another response. When it came it did not sound as if Tam was about to delete images of Jilly from his mind any time soon.

'The only thing we know about Jilly is that she worked at Crystal Radio, that's the only connection we've left to us. Except for one thing. The old lady's yellow folder.'

'A yellow folder? Of an old woman? That really excites me. Hallelujah, we've struck it rich! For God's sake have a life, man. I told you, forget it.'

Tam stopped abruptly. They had reached the corner of the building. He put his hand back and pushed Frankie away from the road.

'Don't take it out on me,' Frankie protested.

'Get back. Don't go out there.'

'What's up with you?'

'Listen. They're up there.'

'Who's up there?'

'The two from the lane. The Men in Black. Bloody sunglasses still on.'

'Where?'

'If we move down to the other end of the building they won't see us. We can slip behind the billboard there.'

Frankie followed on as Tam trotted to the spot he had recommended. They squeezed themselves behind the billboard which had a fret-work base, through which, when they bent down, they could see clearly, but still be hidden from view. They lay flat and looked upwards through the frames of the wood. In front, and above them, was a side road which curved down towards the main street. Tam always took that route down the short grassy slope, as a short-cut to Frankie's, as he had done that day. They must have tracked him. There was a short baffle wall at the top of the embankment, behind which he could see two figures standing, etched clearly against the sky. It was not just his eyesight but instinct, or this recently developed sensitivity to lurking threats, which had alerted him. He could also see the top of a black car obviously parked behind the wall. There was no movement there, and the longer he looked the more they resembled a couple of vultures waiting to scavenge.

'It's them, all right,' he said quietly to Frankie, as they crouched together at the base of the billboard peering up through the fretwork spaces. 'They just won't let up, will they?'

'Why no'?'

'Exactly. It means.....'

'I told you, forget it,' Frankie interjected and getting seriously pissed off.

'It means we're not out of this shit yet, for some reason, and if we're not out of the shit then it doesnae matter what Special Branch have been sayin' to me. We're still in this whether they like it or not.'

'I'll take your word for it,' Frankie replied with little conviction. 'So what's next?'

'They might have been waiting to jump me, but I don't think it's just that. If they knew where Jilly was, they wouldn't be up there,

226

they would be after her. They might think we could still be a link to her. But I think they just want to show me they're still around and that they can still do what they like, even though they must know what Sammy did to their friends.'

'Maybe you should call Sammy right now.'

'I messed these two bampots up and they don't want to let go. They think they can turn me into a nervous wreck just by showing up like this, spookin' me. Maybe that's what they want, more than just trying to find Jilly.'

'But you're no' part of it any longer. We're free of all that. So a big Ta to the Special Branch.'

'Some kind of freedom that is when you have thugs hangin' around starin' at you. Call that freedom?'

'Forget the yellow folder, forget Jilly, forget the PH, just get it out of your head now. You've accepted that. It's finished.'

Tam turned to look at him and Frankie could see that he was hurt and angered by that.

'So you wanna quit then? Absolutely fuckin' quit, eh?' Tam asked him.

Frankie peered upwards, from his flat position, at the two figures arrogantly making their presence felt, as if they had some kind of immunity from any reaction. Then he turned and looked at Tam closely. His mate was the right stuff. Come what may you don't let the right stuff down. You don't just turn your back on that. It's not that simple. He made up his mind. Then he felt a thought surging through him like it had lain in rest for ages awaiting the right moment to surface.

'Everythin's against us. We're being fucked around, bullied. That's what that is up there. And we don't like bullies, do we?' It was almost a recall of that day in class when together they recognised the intolerance of a teacher abusing her position. 'You've got tae stand up for yourself, haven't you? Did you ever see *Braveheart*?' he asked Tam, who was still looking up the slope at the rigid figures poised above.

'Ay I saw *Braveheart*, who hasnae?'

'Remember that scene when Mel Gibson, and his clansmen with all that blue paint on their faces lined up to face the enemy and they wanted to show that they weren't scared and that nothing could intimidate them? Remember how they showed what they felt about the scumbags? Remember?'

Tam nodded.

'That was about freedom, wasn't it?' Frankie suggested. 'There's a time and place for everything. Right now couldn't be better.'

'Are you suggestin' that.......'

'We want to show we're no' quittin'. Not you. Not me. Can you think of a better way?'

Tam looked up at the two black figures then without turning offered Frankie five knuckles and got a fist returning the compliments as if it were the call to action.

'So you're really up for it?' Tam asked without needing a reply.

The *Braveheart* moment it had to be. They stood up and straightened themselves before stepping out boldly in front of the billboards on to the pavement, standing there for a moment, looking up the slope to make sure that they were highly visible to the men. Then they turned their backs on them, slackened their belts and jeans and underwear, bent from the waist, and displayed bare bums of contempt, feeling with it, not only a welcoming draught around parts unused to full exposure, but a sense of liberation, like they had tapped a very deep well of frustration that had existed long before they had seen a man standing nonchalantly on certain cobblestones. At the top of the embankment they saw, through their legs, what appeared to be two men, in deep conversation, like they had just sighted a new planet swimming into view on a giant telescope and could hardly believe their eyes, but did seem to be focussing though, as if they were getting the message clearly. After a few moments, they vanished.

Tam and Frankie readjusted themselves, after hearing some car horns hooting at them; whether in support or outrage they were not sure. Nor did they care. They had done it. Their bums had conveyed a message that could not have been bettered by language and a loudspeaker. That was freedom. That was laying down a line in the sand. That was being scared of nobody or anything. For the time being.

Chapter 16

Several hours later after having eaten handsomely, although probably not all that healthily, at Gabby's, they retreated to Tam's flat and bedroom where he emptied the contents of the old lady's yellow folder on the duvet. He was delighted that Frankie was still interested, since he had felt that sifting through this material would have been a turn-off for him. They were only there some twenty minutes trying to sort out the bits and pieces when Frankie's phone pinged. He took it and sat with his feet up on a chair, his face transforming from indifference to appearing to be hearing of an earthquake occurring outside.

'Whit?' he blurted out. 'Are you at the jokin'? Are you sendin' me up? '

He put his phone on to loudspeaker.

'Listen to this, friend,' he said.

But all Tam could make out was an excited voice garbling on like one of those Latin football commentators who could make a goal seem like the Second Coming. It made an impression though, incoherent though it was.

'Did you get that?' he asked Tam with a smile on his face that showed his teeth like ramparts.

'Ay, sure,' Tam replied. 'Give me a break. Sounded garbage to me. What was all that about?'

Frankie had disconnected and was now to be a translator.

'They've done us!' he announced.

'Who's done what?'

'Those two bampots. The Men in Black. That was Gus McIntyre. He surfs all the time.'

'The internet?'

'Naw, Honolulo beach! Of course the internet. When he's no' doin' that he's sleepin', it seems to me. Those two bastards took shots of us in the street. Our bums have been on the internet. We're on YouTube. We've had over 50,000 hits so far. Is that no' what you would call goin' viral?'

Fame, or infamy, depending on how anybody would interpret their act, was not what Tam actually was seeking at that moment in time. He definitely savoured YouTube though. Whenever he had the chance at school, surreptitiously, or at Gabby's, under strict supervision, because the shopkeeper didn't want any 'hanky-panky' as he put it, he lapped it up. He especially liked viewing the famous in the acts of debunking themselves without realising it. Politicians, actors, singers. Watching a so-called star fall flat on his arse was worth all the other trash that they could watch. But he especially liked to see sports commentators in spectacular botches with their overweening egos brutally exposed. YouTube performed a worthwhile social act in that respect, he thought.

But this was different. Could he possibly watch himself, especially a part of his anatomy that nature had never intended him to see and in an act that few would understand? No way. It was all right at the time. The hackles had been up. Now the sound of an hysterical anonymous voice on the other end of a line caused a rethink. Would YouTube censor it eventually? He was beginning to feel so uncomfortable about it that it was like thinking he had let down a country which had given the world penicillin, television and Sean Connery.

'But how could they tell it was us?'

'Two things. He recognised the billboard and the road. Pinned it right away.'

'And what else?'

'Your Barca jacket. It was a right giveaway. He just added it all up and felt he was lucky because he just stumbled on it.'

'Jesus Christ.'

'He said he could send it to us on our mobiles to save us searchin'.'

'D'you think I want to look at my own bum. Do you think I'll get a right kick out o' that? No way, Jose. If it's there then I'll leave it to the rest of you. But at the moment forget it.'

'Hey, it was harmless,' Frankie intervened realising that Tam was now looking regretful. 'Look,' he went on, realising that Tam had been totally distracted from the main objective of examining the papers strewn out on the bed, 'we didn't riot. We didn't break intae a shop. We didn't loot. We didn't attack the polis. We didn't mug old women. We showed defiance. We showed we are not takin' the bullying. Do you no' think there are a lot of folk who would love to do what we just did? To walk into a bank and do the same to bankers? So what's wrong with addin' a bit of cheek to the world?'

Tam didn't feel comfortable but he steeled himself to stop being distracted. He knew his family wouldn't know what YouTube was anyway and never went near computers.

'Do what you want,' Tam said dismissively.

He could also tell that Frankie was now practically unhinged by this information and that no doubt he would have that image installed on his phone before the day was out. But to his credit he stopped talking about it in respect for Tam who was now looking over the fragments of papers strewn around the bed but with a deepening sense of futility setting in.

He watched his friend pick up a scrap of paper with letters, which he tried to pronounce, but gave up, when he sounded as if he were gargling with iron-filings. Frankie was definitely trying, even though his mind was now on other matters. Then, having failed to make sense of the word he spelled out the letters individually.

EMMSIHRUTA

'What does that mean?'

'Search me,' Tam replied. 'Except I was told she played word games with the residents. That looks like an anagram. Work it out for yourself.'

'I'm really trying to help out here my old mate, but you know, lookin' through an old wumman's scribblings, are you really being serious? And I'm no good at words anyway.'

'Try,' Tam replied, stretched out for a jotter, ripped a page out of it, and handed a pen to Frankie in a challenging flourish. Frankie bowed his head and stared at the letters. Tam picked up another sheet, back with a jolt to the reality of the task in hand. The sheets came in all shapes and sizes. There were written sheets with scrawled writing all over them, scraps of paper with single words printed on them, completed Sudoku puzzles and crosswords, obviously cut-out from newspapers and magazines. Her passion for anagrams was obvious as they lay on the pages, like they were examples from an exotic language; masses of them, with letters stroked out and rearranged, in her efforts to convert words into puzzles.

He had strewn around him a kind of eccentric memoir of a woman who wished to keep her mind active. It is little wonder Jilly had picked up the notion to publicise this. He tried to visualise a group of the elderly grouped around this woman, heads bent over pieces of paper trying to work out the puzzles under her scrutiny. The pair of them were like that now, silent, brooding, puzzled. Then Frankie erupted.

'Look, I'm no use to you with this. Let's face it I was never a great reader. It's doin' my mind in just trying to work this out. I want to catch up on YouTube . I'll try and find out if anybody else we know has picked this up. I know this is all special to you, but I have to admit I think you are up the fuckin' creek wi' this. Just look what you're tryin' to do. In fact, come to think of it, what is it you're really tryin' to get out o' this? For God's sake tell me!'

'I just don't know,' Tam admitted. 'I don't know if there is a solution to all o' this. I can face up to solving maths problems. I know if you apply reason and logic there'll be an answer. But with something like this, you're right, I could be up shit-creek, because I don't even have a starting point. You need something to build on. All this must have a purpose. I'll just have to stumble on.'

There was no point in trying to persuade him to stay any longer to help out. Frankie couldn't get out of the room quickly enough and in a sense Tam was glad of that. He had enough to compete with without having a completely negative mate beside him. As soon as he was gone Tam felt like he was wading through the detritus left by a receding tide, the mess looking more and more impenetrable and lacking any coherence. He looked at all the papers around him like he was about to examine the last will and testament of a total stranger. Then a sheet caught his eye for several reasons. Firstly, it was headed by a date, 4th April. Simply that. Scattered underneath, and all around this page were words she had obviously been toying with.

Some were scored out, as she obviously wrestled setting her anagram forms, others neatly printed, some which looked as if she had made several versions before settling on a final arrangement of letters. It was like looking down at a writhing mass of wires in one of these telecommunication boxes you could see open at the side of some roads, all seemingly connected with a power source, in this case the date. Doodles, scratchings, scribblings; all the product of an active mind intent on some sort of meaningful pattern. Then he noticed there was printing on the reverse side. He had seen that before. It was the one headed by MMTADRROY. Here there was a list that ran neatly down the page. It was as if they were the final products of all the experimentation with letters on the other side, and when he made the comparison it confirmed that view. He stared at them the way he would at an ancient script in a glass-cage in a museum. The first letters were RENJAD TEVIAKHMCS. The first group was a giveaway. ANDREJ. So the second had to be MATSKEVICH.

The rest followed.

PDEDTLOLU, HSIAOCHL DELYRI, GHHU MTARLIE, ITHDCERI NRBHFOEFED, RAKPTCI TMAIOHLHN, NRTMIA TLUHRE GKNI, CSRAO OOERRM, NOJH LABL, NJAO CRA, MSTHDA EROM.

It was the wrong technique just to sweep the eye over them all. It would make him dizzy. He had to have something to catch the eye. It did. The short one, two from the bottom, NJAO ARC. That was easy. JOAN OF ARC. All right she had missed out the 'of' but it was clear whom she meant. Then the third one down GHHU, that was HUGH obviously, although he would have to work longer on the second string of letters. So, the list was about jumbled names; Christian and surname.

PDEDTLOLU. He set to work on that one with pencil and paper, slashing out letters in different combinations and at the same time trying to make a sense of why it was there at all. Then it came. Not because of any familiarity with the word, but through the logic of nothing else seeming to fit. TOLPUDDLE.

It irked him to have apparently completed a mental task like that without grasping the meaning of it all. It wasn't like that with the algebraic equations that tasked him. Indeed he was now visibly tiring, his eyes watering with the effort of concentration. He looked across the bed at all the sheets of paper and noticed one which was folded up, like you would a letter inside an envelope. When he opened it out he saw anagrams spread out in such a way that they looked like they formed a long connected sequence. At the top there was another date. 20th April. He selected a few of the anagrams up and down that page, to try them out, but found them intractable. It was like battering himself against a brick-wall. He could make no sense of them.

He turned back to the previous sheet. But again he looked for anything that would catch the eye initially. NRTMIA TLUHRE GKNI did. Three names. The last one standing out as the giveaway. He sorted it out. MARTIN LUTHER KING.

The shortness of NOJH LABL could only work out as JOHN BALL, whoever he was. He looked at RAKPTCI TMAIOHLHN and worked at unravelling it. He got PATRICK HAMILTON out of that. He had already worked out a HUGH, so the following surname came quickly after that, not because he was familiar with it but because it seemed to solve itself, HUGH LATIMER. Then at the bottom of the list the EROM simply became MORE. Which meant that he had heard of this name, if only distantly, THOMAS MORE. There were schools named after him, he believed. He'd never come across most of these names before so it was difficult to work out the thread which connected them. What was it? By every account she wasn't a woman in her dotage but a sharp old biddy with her wits about her. So could he conclude that there was method and purpose in her apparent random scribblings? Was she consciously pointing to something or was she just one of those history freaks who try to live permanently in the past. Whatever it was he needed some starting base. The last thing he wanted was to leave a scattering of scribbles strewn chaotically over the mattress. It would reflect his own incoherent thinking. He was feeling the tentacles of frustration gripping him in a vice.

Suddenly the bedroom door opened and his sister surged in. Sarah was not given to formalities.

'Do me a favour!' she barked.

Big mistake, Sarah, he thought, as he recoiled. Big, big mistake. Wrong time, Sarah. Wrong fucking time to pick, Sarah. He knew what he had to do. But coolly. Calm down. It's penalty shoot-out time, Sarah. He spoke softly.

'Remind me, what charm school did you go to again?'

'I'm having a party at the weekend for some of my friends. I don't want you or the red-haired loony anywhere near this place. My friends have taste.'

'In their backsides.'

'So make yourselves scarce. What's this litter here?'

She lifted one of the sheets from the bed and looked at it briefly then let it flutter down again with her practised look of distaste and as if there were danger of contamination.

'Have you met that bird again?' she asked, reminding him of their stair-head meeting and her fertile imagination. 'What's to report? Or has she given you the heave? Or is it all show on your part? I must confess, 'Our Tam wi' a bird.' It just doesnae sound right somehow.'

'You'd better sit down,' he said almost cheerily.

'No time. I was just in to warn you about the weekend.'

'I think you'll have to take time. I've somethin' to tell you.'

'Spare me the riddles, what are you on about?'

'That last boyfriend you had a couple o' months ago. Did he ever say anything about losing his mobile?'

'Don't get you.'

'A mobile. Did he ever tell you he lost it one night?'

'So what. Folk lose mobiles a' the time. What's so special about that?'

'Him. He's special.'

'Right on. I know that.'

'Not the way I see it.'

'And where, if you don't mind me asking, is this leadin'?'

'To you. Straight to you.'

'This had better be good.'

'It's better than good.'

'No wonder I lose my patience wi' you all the time. What's that supposed to mean?'

'So he never told you about the lost phone. The phone that took the video.'

'Video? Whit video?' she said her lowered voice signifying that he had made positive contact.

'That he took of you and him.'

She lowered herself on to the bed and crossed her legs firmly like she was bracing herself.

'What do you know about any video?' she snapped.

'Plenty,' Tam replied, very coolly. 'Mucho plenty.'

'What's it got to do wi' you?'

'Despite what you think o' me, I look after your welfare. Or perhaps I should say Frankie and I do.'

'Enough of that fanny. Spill it out, get to the point?'

'I'm talking about a video taken on your boyfriend's phone. You and him. It's all the rage these selfies. I cannae understand why, but there's no accountin' for taste. And for you he went a step further and made a wee movie.'

'Me and him?' she said her eyebrows tying to meet each other in a display of affronted innocence.

'A video selfie, you might call it. Correct? What is it you would call him, a voyeur? He likes to record his scores and then keep it for his own pervy satisfaction. Well, the long and short of it is that you and him had steam comin' out your ears.'

'Bastard!' she snapped and he wasn't sure whether she was referring to him, or the Casanova with the pixels.

'He got well and truly pissed one night down at the *Town Tavern,*' Tam went on. 'He was braggin' about his exploits and was showin' folk what he had recorded on the phone. There was only one person there that night who recognised the girl on the phone.'

'Who?'

'Frankie.'

'Sweet Jesus. Him!'

'The eejit as you call him did you a very big favour. When Casanova stumbled off to the loo Frankie just got up, lifted the fella's phone he'd left on the barstool and snuck out. He deleted everythin' on it, but not before he had transferred the humpin' to his own phone since he wanted to let me see how talented my big sister was. Next day he went back and told the barman that he had found the phone outside in the car-park. Your boyfriend was so pissed he didn't know up from down that night. So deed done.'

She tapped fingers on the tight lips then managed to speak.

'I knew nothin' about this. Nothin'. I didn't know he had his phone set-up for that.'

'Set-up? You would have thought Steven Spielberg had directed the bloody scene. You must have known. And if that's your personal kink then so what? If you get a kick out of watchin' yourself in action then so be it. Who am I to be objectin' to a bit o' slap and tickle, although it was more like Sumo wrestlin', to be honest, as you well know.'

'Look I have a personal and private life that is nobody's business. And I'm bloody sure you're not going to interfere wi' it,' she hissed at him.

'If there's a mobile about anywhere you can forget the life that used to be called private,' he said as flashing through his mind came an image of hordes from Patagonia to Vladivostok mulling over four bare buttocks in a Glasgow street on YouTube.

'But it's just that I would like you to show Frankie and me a bit more respect. I don't want you to cuddle me every time we meet. Bugger that! But stay out o' my business, stop carpin' on about me stayin' on to get to university and puttin' the strain on the household and all that crap you keep churnin' out. Or else.'

'Or else what?'

'Or else the Duchess and Ma and Pa would like tae see how a girl they thought was pure enough to play castanets in a Salvation Army band has another interestin' side tae her.'

'You wouldn't let them see that!' she said almost in a whisper but utterly convinced now he would.

'Up to you. As you can see I'm busy. Got a lot to do. Do you mind?'

She said nothing but stared past him at the Messi poster on the wall. Then she rose from the bed, beaten but unbowed, her chin jutting out, her lips pursed in a show of contempt. She gripped the door-handle.

'Oh,' Tam added as the door opened. 'Another thing. Because of what Frankie did for you, next time you see him I want you to kiss him like you were havin' a date wi' George Clooney for the first time.'

She turned and stared at him but all she saw was a look of 'Or else' on his face. He felt as if he had turned a corner. It wouldn't be the last of her, of course. She was his sister after all. His own flesh and blood. She'd still be around plenty. But he suspected it would be the last he'd see of Cruella de Vil.

His phone rang again. Gabby spoke.

'Worked out that word at the top of that page.'

'And?'

'MMTADRROY remember?' he spelled out.

Tam looked straight at it on the page.

'It's MARTYRDOM,' Gabby said.

***

The two men in the car beside Jilly did not speak much during the journey. She didn't mind that as she was not in the mood for chat. She had told them the journey would take up to two hours. They had a satnav and had pinpointed a destination, but Jilly spurned the mechanical instructions and directed them down the scenic route. They showed little interest in the landmarks she pointed out, except one which she told them had a connection with Robinson Crusoe and with the man who wrote of the city they had left behind, 'the dear green place.' It elicited from one of them, the big one, the gruff sentiment that he wished he could abscond to a desert island and that it would offer more pleasures in life than the crowded island he lived on. The other one kept playing with his phone, sending and receiving texts that came and went in streams.

At one point though, her head drooped and she almost succumbed to sleep. Perhaps it was the well-upholstered car and the smoothness of its drive that weakened her defences, but she literally had to bite her lip as her relationship with her two companions had to be based on fully conscious alertness. This was her dilemma.

Companionship, yet caution. Caution every step of the way. She had been well-briefed and was fully aware that her pursuit had a clear objective, but with so many side issues that she could still easily end up trapped in a snare. When they had met earlier they were courteous and very knowledgeable about their business and of the agency's ubiquitous patronage which could lend all three the impression of invulnerability. That did not settle her. It all sounded too pat, like everything was out of the text book. But she had learned in Eastern Europe that text book procedure in this business did not exclude improvisation. That was necessary for survival. So, basically, she had to prevent her mental faculties dulling. And that meant not ignoring her own sensibilities, like the guilt she definitely felt in having left without a single word of explanation to Tam.

It had been the only way. It was better that the two lads were now out of this. As soon as Tam had turned up at the radio station there was little she didn't know about their whereabouts and their motivation. Of course, at first, she had been surprised by their initiatives. And deeply thankful for them. Then she had begun to realise this sprung from a resilient Glasgow culture which she was fully aware sometimes displayed itself in ugly ways but which also contained a spirit of defiance in times of adversity that brought people together in bonds of improvised self-help. The place was renowned for that. It tickled her to think of two teenagers being guardians of that tradition. Certainly Tam had the looks of a potential patrician; tall, with aquiline features that could have been stamped on an old Roman coin, and of which he was probably unaware. She the harsh fact. Then something stirred him after midnight when he knew he could not sleep. Not names. One name. He wondered about it. It started as a glimmer then blossomed into such a display in his mind that he had to get out of his bed and scatter the pile of papers back across the duvet.

He fumbled his way through them until he reached the page he wanted. Down the list he went, scanning quickly to see if anything registered on the optic nerve. He stopped over one. A mundane name. Except for something that began to stand out.

PATRICK HAMILTON

It was almost as if he heard a whispering. P and H, the initials. P and H. Over and over again it whispered at him and then almost shouted.

A coincidence? He stared long and hard at the initials. Alright, but where do I move next, he thought? Simple. He picked up the phone and rang Gabby. After five rings, which he counted impatiently, it was answered.

'Gabby, do me a favour, please, if you can. Google the name Patrick Hamilton for me. You can take it he is probably Scottish, or something to do with Scotland.' Gabby was used to these requests from the boys and generally complied.

'Will do. I will get back to you. I have a salesman with me at the moment.'

The towsy background conversation about khaki entering the Brownlie family was still going on. Tam rubbed his eyes and

could sense leadership in men and he looked like a candidate for that if only through his determination to beat the odds and get his degree when so many others in his environment clearly fell by the wayside. Yes, it was possible he had a crush on her. She could sense that as well, slightly. Anyway, it would pass, now that she was out of sight, possibly for ever. She did not regret though, having held so much back from them. It was unavoidable.

'Left or right?' the driver asked when they came to fork in the road.

'Left,' she said.

'Sure you know what you're doing?' came from the other man, almost cynically, lifting his head from the phone.

'Do you doubt me?'

Better to sling one back at them like that, assertion being the better part of valour in this bizarre partnership. Of course she wasn't absolutely sure she was on the right path since there was a lot of thinking to do when they reached their destination. But she was sure they were getting much closer to Andrej. Based on what Mrs Rybak had said they were in the home stretch. Of loose ends there were plenty yet. She certainly knew precisely what Andrej was working on. There wouldn't have been this degree of searching if it had been purely political. It had started out that way then grew another dimension which is why so many were interested in him. But under which roof was he? They did not have much time left to pin point his location exactly. That was still the puzzle.

'This car-park do?' the driver asked when they reached their destination.

'For the time being,' she replied and then when they came to a halt stepped eagerly out from the artificial atmosphere of an overly-powerful air-freshener which had started out as pine-wood but after two hours smelled like tar. So she breathed in deeply, the strong smell of the sea lifting her spirits.

**

Tam spent an uncomfortable couple of days trying to make sense of events. He had come to a dead stop though. Mrs Rybak's papers he had gathered neatly together and they formed a tidy pile on top of the small bookcase in the corner of his room. He couldn't bring himself to put them back in the yellow folder as he felt that would be the ultimate sign of defeat. He would look at them from time to time, edge close to them, then turn back. He was resenting them now because they had opened up nothing to him that would deliver him from this gloomy sense of failure. He tried the bakery to find out if they had any more work for him. But they were at their full complement now. This was certainly no consolation. The Duchess still had bronchitis and didn't want to see anyone. He was definitely at a damnable loose end.

Frankie had phoned and texted him several times to talk about the YouTube extravaganza, worrying on his behalf that his parents might now have heard. He assured his friend that they and their social

circle were as much aware of the existence of YouTube as they were of Fermat's Last Theorem. Frankie was not into Fermat either and wanted an explanation. He didn't get one, as Tam, good as he was at maths, only used the phrase to conjure up the complexities of the subject he was pursuing. Frankie was getting ready for a job interview and the last thing that Tam wanted was to distract him. So he felt isolated for these two days, not even visiting Gabby's; sullen, eating with the family reluctantly and noticing a strangely subdued Sarah, who oddly cut off her mother when she asked Tam about this girl she had heard about, and changed the subject abruptly by saying she was thinking of applying to join the army. He was glad of that because that set the cat among the pigeons with his father delivering an emotional pacifist speech and his mother putting her hand to her mouth and only muttering one word from time to time. 'Afghanistan.'

He had made what he hoped to be a constructive contribution to that discussion by suggesting that Sarah with a Bren gun might hasten the downfall of the Taliban. Since it didn't go down all that well, he retired to his bed early to read some of his maths book. That was the intention. He couldn't concentrate. Any mental step took in any direction was thwarted by the letters which continu danced in front of his eyes like a confused Dashing White Serge He had even to think hard again about *Bishop to Knight3* as if h now unsure of that move. But he did resolve that one. It was c Surely. All that was with an effort though and he was nagged failure to find any idea of a key to it all. There wasn't one. T

246

247

suffered the usual torment of waiting for someone to call him back. Eventually it came.

'Got him,' Gabby said.

'Well?' Tam asked impatiently.

'He's a gentleman from the 16th century no less.'

'And?'

'He died on the 29th February 1528. In Scotland, as you suggested. And......'

'And what?' Tam asked impatiently.

'He was burnt at the stake.'

'Burnt? Where?'

'In front of St Salvator's Chapel. They've got a memorial to him there.

'What kind of memorial?'

There was silence.

'In the name of my ancient father I can hardly believe it,' Gabby said almost whispering. 'It's on the cobblestones. His initials.'

'PH?'

'My God, yes!'

'But St Salvator's College, where the hell is that?'

'St Andrews.'

It didn't take him long to conclude that Jilly had gone there, but not to play golf.

Chapter 17

In the morning he gathered the material into the folder and made for Gabby's. The shopkeeper was at the bank but his wife simply nodded Tam through to the backroom, like he was part of the family. He sat at the computer there and became engulfed by the material he raised on the two names, Patrick Hamilton and St. Andrews. One fact clinched it for him. They had eventually embedded his initials into the cobblestones to commemorate his martyrdom and to remind the walking public that the urbanity of their world sometimes stemmed from horrendous deeds in the past. He sat there for a while pouring over the information and was so engrossed that he did not become aware of Gabby entering and standing behind him, until he felt this tap on his shoulder.

'Looks like you are still involved in all of this,' Gabby said pensively. Tam could tell right away that Gabby knew about the warning and the scolding he had received from Special Branch. That really didn't surprise him. Indeed, as he stared back at the genial face in front of him now, he wondered if Gabby had special links to the Special Branch himself, given his closeness to Sammy and his awareness of potential threats from certain communities, in these days of potential terrorism. Gabby also an informer? It takes all kinds, he thought.

'Put it down to historical research, that's all,' Tam said.

'I hope you just restrict yourself to that,' Gabby said with a paternal smile, although at the same time there seemed to be a suggestion in his voice that he couldn't really believe that was possible any longer.

'I worked out the word Martyrdom and you found your martyr.' Gabby said. 'Enough is enough. Maybe that will settle the issue for you, no?'

Of course Gabby knew Tam was now selectively deaf. Then he changed his attitude and gave Tam a hearty slap on the back and walked out with a light-hearted comment.

'Next time you are on YouTube, use the other end of your anatomy. A song would be preferable.'

The remark was so casually indifferent to what he and Frankie had done that Tam felt a sense of relief. He did not care how Gabby had got to know about this, although it did confirm his opinion that the shopkeeper missed nothing; the perfect characteristic of an informant. He phoned Frankie, after thinking carefully how to spell out to him what he now knew.

'We've had over a million hits and I think You Tube have let it go as a bit of fun,' came the reply. 'I can't believe it. I don't think anybody will recognise us outside our pals. Ok, they might all spill the beans on us like admittin' they know these two YouTube celebrities. You can't blame them for that. But the roof hasn't fallen in on us so far. We're Braveheart freedom fighters, can you believe that?'

There was no point in trying to contest that lurid imagination.

'Where are you?' he demanded.

251

'I'm just comin' out of that job interview at the Crescent Hotel,' his mate replied.

'How'd it go?'

'I told them I had heard their service in the restaurant was too slow and they had to do something about it.'

'You could have told them you suspected salmonella was present in their fucking kitchen as well. Are you takin' all this seriously? Do you really want a job?'

'I believe in tellin' it straight.'

'Try grovelling sometime.'

'I've worn out the knees in my jeans tryin' that, and look where it's got me.'

'Remember what Robert the Bruce said about tryin', tryin', tryin'. He saw the spider in the cave trying to make its web, over and over......'

'It's tarantulas I'd need to take to some of these job interviews.'

'Tell you something I'm not kidding about. I think I know where Jilly's gone. I need to see you. Ever looked at a murder scene before? Time you did. I'm on my way.'

***

He sat waiting for his mate on a bench looking across the river to where the fatal shot had probably been fired at Carson. This was as good a place as any to transmit to Frankie how a believable phenomenon could be a worse experience than something inexplicable, as had disturbed his mate in the aftermath of the visit to

252

the psychic. Or so he would try to suggest. He saw his mate bounding towards him with a white paper-bag in his hand.

'Saluti,' he chirped at Tam, in his Italian-waiter mode. 'Made these m'self'. He proffered the bag to Tam who took out a heavily sugar-coated doughnut and thrust it into his mouth in the spirit of adventure.

'7 out of 10,' he adjudicated after he had devoured it. It was actually better than that, but he wanted at that moment to keep a tight rein on his mate, and before Frankie could open his mouth in response, Tam stood and pointed to the path in front of them.

'That is where the lawyer was shot,' Tam said pointing downwards. 'You'll never know how fucking horrible it was. It's something that'll spook me for years. I can still smell the blood, let alone see it spreadin' out around him, his head lookin' like it had turned into a beetroot. I can still see him lyin' there. You cannae suffer more than that.'

'I'll be in tears in a minute,' Frankie said. 'I understand your pain. Is that it?'

'No. There's something else. I know where Andrej is. And I can tell you how I found out.'

Frankie presented the bag again but Tam declined, stood up, turned to the river and then back to his mate and, with a deliberate deep breath, began.

'The old lady Mrs Rybak is visited by Andrej. You've seen her stuff. She gets inspired by Andrej's visit for some reason and devises anagrams of names which have something in common.'

'Like what?'

'I'm comin' to that. It's her passion. But what she doesn't know is that accidentally she's given us all a clue as to where the photograph was taken, because she refers to a particular name, a name buried among others. Andrej probably sparked her off on that thinking. And he had gone to that spot for a special reason. All of the people on the list were martyrs of one sort or the other. Why was she obviously placing Andrej among those who died for their own beliefs? That I just cannae tell. And why did he go to that spot? My guess is he got some kick out of being there. But only because he is in St Andrews up to somethin'. He's no tourist, that's for sure. All right, it's a bit of a gamble, but as he was visiting that Mrs Rybak from somewhere in Scotland, I think he's still in St Andrews. That name definitely meant something special to him anyway.'

'What name?'

'Patrick Hamilton. PH. The initials. Got it?'

He examined Frankie's face which revealed only puzzlement, then a slight realisation of where Tam was heading, but only slight.

'No, I havenae got it. Who was Patrick Hamilton?'

'The martyr. PH was the spot where he lost his life. On the 29th February 1528. The very spot.'

Frankie looked away, his eyes narrowing as he was slowly trying to grasp where Tam was leading him to.

'The spot where he lost his life? How?'

Tam took another deep breath.

'He was burnt at the stake. They say it took six hours before they could say he was dead.'

'Burnt at the stake?' Frankie repeated quietly. Then he stood up and walked down to the railing on the river bank and propped his arm up there looking down at the waters. 'Burnt at the stake,' Tam heard him mumbling. He turned back and sat down beside Tam on the bench with a thump.

'Burnin',' he said. 'Are you thinkin' what I'm thinkin'?'

He did not need a reply.

'How could Mrs MacPhail smell burnin'? From 1528? What's the catch?'

'I know how badly you felt after that visit,' Tam replied. 'Let's just say we've both suffered. I watched a man die right here in less time than it takes to sneeze. You think you sampled the Other Side. We've got tae put these things outta our minds and get on and try to finish what we started.'

'In other words you cannae explain it, can you? You especially don't believe in all that supernatural crap, do you? Well, go ahead and explain this. She smelled burning, she said. No mistake. If she knew all about this why didn't she just come out and tell us about it.'

'Maybe there was only so much she could work out. Or else that's just the way of psychics. They dangle you, leave you guessin', wantin' more. If it gives you peace of mind we'll deal with that later. I've got other things in mind, urgent things, because I know that Jilly is heading for St Andrews right now looking for Andrej and I'm not sure in my mind what she wants to do when she gets her hands on him. I have to go there.'

Frankie seemed to shake himself out of the almost catatonic state he had gone into on hearing about the burning at the stake.

'You say it took six hours for the fire to kill him,' he said softly. 'Would it take us that long to get to St Andrews?'

***

There was no Plan B. Plan A was simply to get up and go. They would cover themselves by telling the respective families that they were staying with one another. The families rarely met to chatter. They would get away with that. It happened often. It was a gamble though. If they had thought rationally about the prospect they would not have reached the end of their respective streets. They were skint, had no idea where they could stay overnight, apart from sleeping rough, didn't know where Jilly or Andrej would be, if they were there at all, and could only think of hitching lifts. But the impulse was too strong to resist. As they studied a contour map of Fife later, in an old atlas, with St Andrews looking like a carbuncle on the head of a little dog sniffing the waters of the North Sea, the ancient town seemed as distant to them as the north col on Everest; which simply increased their desire to get there. Then Frankie spotted a name on the map. Pittenweem, the tiny fishing village on the other side of the Fife coast.

'Albert, the fishmonger, brings fish from Pittenweem round our way every week. Sells a lot. I wonder?' he ruminated. Tam could almost hear the whirring of a disc drive as Frankie was clearly devising something. He departed the scene in haste, trying to finger his phone at the same time. About one hour later came the call to Tam.

'We've got a lift,' Frankie announced, sounding jubilant through the phone. 'Albert is going to take us to St Andrews and drop us off. All he wants from us is to put some pamphlets through some doors next week to advertise to customers in a new round he's organising. That's if you don't mind travellin' in a fish van. He'll be here the day after the morrow.'

So that gave her four or five days ahead of them. He had to swallow that. There was nothing he could do about it. It was the only way. He spent these days pretending to be studying and keeping away from the rest of the family, taking his meals through to his bedroom as if he was a dutiful son dedicating himself to study. The family were not on speaking terms because of Sarah's sudden attraction to khaki and she stomped about the house like she was preparing to be a squaddie. All he did was pore over Mrs Rybak's papers and still could not crack that particular sheet which looked like anagrams, but were not.

Then the day came. Before he was picked up he decided to try Jilly's phone. He had been doing this repeatedly with no reply. Again there was no response. Eventually he prepared to leave a message, wanting it to be brief and terse. He tried to sound clinical.

'Thanks for the phone number you gave me. I know where you are. St Andrews. I've seen the DVD of you in Belarus. You know a helluva lot more about Andrej than you've admitted. Strange, eh? You're no' what you pretend to be. I don't care who you work for, but if you don't answer this I'll go to the *Daily Record* and let them know that a local radio personality is living a double life. They're interested in these kind of stories about show-biz people and all that. You could gamble that they'll just laugh at a teenager comin' with that stuff to them. That would be a risky gamble I think. Just read the pages and you'll know they sniff around for things like that. I don't know what you're covering up, but they'll blow it for you. You can get back to me any time.'

He felt he had struck the right tone as he made preparations to head north-east.

Albert, the fishmonger, turned out to be a small tubby man with a musical Fife accent that went up and down the scales in pleasant arpeggios. They sat at the back of his reeking fish van the following afternoon, after his neighbourhood delivery, and immediately realised that when they made their exit in St Andrews they would smell to the heavens. The yellow folder lay where, shortly before, there had been piles of haddock, sea-bass, salmon and crabs, all now about to go down the gullets of Glaswegians. The arrangements they had made for this trip into the unknown were few. They had scraped together a few pounds. Tam had dug deep into a drawer for a thick black sweater to wear under the Barca jacket, recalling what his mother habitually said about the east coast, 'always a nip in the wind'. He brought a plastic cover for the yellow folder. Frankie had acquired a white snap-back cap with 'Blackpool' emblazoned on the front, accompanied by a brown jacket he had never seen him wear before. It had many pockets, like people on grouse-moors wear. He decided not to ask him where it had come from. Indeed they did not talk much, until the phone call came.

It was when they were crossing the Forth Road Bridge. The looming presence of the famous rail-bridge to his right, in its new muted-red coat, set against a sky of serrated white clouds stretching towards the North Sea, seemed to herald the entrance into a new hemisphere. He had first seen the bridge in an old movie called *The Thirty Nine Steps,* but his mathematically inclined mind always perceived its girded structure, thereafter, as the practical strength and strange beauty of triangles. When he was considering that, his phone rang. It was her.

'Tam?' she said. 'You hear me?'

'Clearly,' he replied.

'I'm so sorry about this....'

'Where have I heard that before?'

'No, I mean it. Sorry about you not understanding. And why should you? Not understanding that this is all too big for you to carry on any further with me.'

'Don't give me that. Get to the point. Will you meet me in St Andrews?'

'Are you sure about this?'

'The Special Branch are after you and I can tell you the tabloids would love a story like yours. They would blow your identity, like using dynamite. Would whoever you work for like that?'

The silence convinced Tam he had made his point effectively enough.

'The Special Branch, you say. How would you know something like that?'

Tam did not reply to that.

'When do you intend coming?' she asked after that pause.

'We are on our way,' he said boldly.

'Really?' she said, then paused again, as if taking a deep breath of self-control. 'Phone me when you get into the town and I promise I'll meet you. I want you to look for a place called Grannie Clark's Wynd. Anybody in the area knows that. When you get there, phone me and I'll give you directions. And listen.'

'Yes.'

'I have nothing against you. In fact I really do like you. I mean that.'

The sucker punch, beautifully delivered. Don't fall for that, he thought, as the call went dead. But that immediate negative response was quickly challenged by that other percentage of him which desperately did not want to fall out with her. It had been stuck at about 23% but was now heading back to 49% on the back of her last remark. It could be tipped one way or the other, very easily.

'Who is she workin' for?' Frankie asked roused by the phone conversation. 'Have you even the remotest fucking idea?'

'It's something to do with the Americans. I think that's what Sammy's friends think.'

'Americans?'

'I can't say too much, but readin' between the lines, I think they believe she could be helpin' their government in some way. That's what it sounded like to me.'

'A lassie from a radio station in Glesca workin' for the American government? Give us a life.'

Then he paused, his face screwed up as he tried to come to terms with disbelief sluicing through him.

'Wait a minute,' he said. 'You're not goin' to tell me.....'

'Tell you what?' Tam asked as his mate paused in puzzlement.

'You're not suggestin' that......Jilly, our Jilly, is secretly workin' for the Americans and into chasin' after foreigners. Which could mean...very possibly could mean...'

Again he paused, this time with an almost anticipatory smile creasing his face.

'Mean what?' Tam prompted, getting slightly impatient.

'That she's CIA,' Frankie said with relish.

Tam was silenced. A joke of course. Purely a joke. How could that be? On the other hand....

'You've got some fucking imagination,' Tam said, but couldn't rid himself of the notion that anything was now possible about this woman. It was preposterous but intriguing, all in the one. He also knew that once a seemingly outrageous idea had fermented in

Frankie's head, leading to a heady brew of wild imaginings, not even a tranquillising dart could counteract the fever.

He watched Frankie pace about even the limited confines of the rear of the van like a new train of thought had seized him. Tam began to regret having even mentioned anything about the States.

'You'd think the hardest thing she could do would be crackin' an egg for an omelette,' Frankie said. 'What a cover she has when you come to think of it. Would you believe it? And you said she fought well in the lane. It figures. They'd teach her that at Langley.'

'Where?'

'Langley. The centre of their operations. It all figures.'

What figured for Tam was that Frankie was now beyond restraint. Better to leave him make his own way down that fantasising path.

'This is a new ball game now,' Frankie said rubbing his hands together in glee, like he was just being offered a favourite dessert. 'Never thought I would meet a real live CIA person, in the very flesh. She'll be tracked by satellite and all that, won't she, all the way from Langley? Maybe somebody's listenin' to us right now. The CIA, would you believe! She'll be into cyanide tablets slipped into drinks and exploding cigars like they tried with Castro, and guns with silencers. I don't know what she's up to, but I'm definitely on her side.'

If that was what was going to enliven his mate and bolster his enthusiasm then he would let him believe what he liked; even that she was licensed to kill. Tam wanted to keep him that way. For he realised they had only the barest information to cling on to without really knowing what to do next except shadow or pressurise Jilly. But, even that meant he had now committed himself to a rocky road, with possible landslides imminent.

Chapter 18

An hour after leaving the bridge, they were within sight of the ancient town of St Andrews. They drove into it from the west along a long flat road. The town itself rose undramatically on the horizon, like it had attained a cosy compromise between the waters of the North Sea on the north and the woods and bluffs to the south. Being so flat they could only assume where the sea was, as there was barely a glimpse of it as they approached a roundabout on the edge of the town. It was there Albert cursed at a car which had driven so close behind they almost collided.

'I dinnae drive Jap cars,' he shouted. 'My grandfaither was in the Changi concentration camp during the last war. His atrocity stories stuck wi' me. I don't care how good the fuckin' Lexus is.'

Tam looked quickly at Frankie who tried to lean forward to get a view from the front window. He nodded back to Tam.

'I saw it in the wing-mirror,' he whispered. 'But one Lexus is the same as any other. I suppose. No?'

Tam raised his hand in a calming gesture, relegating the incident to merely a coincidence. But he wasn't sure if he believed that himself. Albert, still cursing, in that sing-song voice of his, dropped them off where they had requested, and offered some advice. 'If you're interested in finding somebody, then go into *Northpoint*, it's a cafe. Everybody goes there. The waitresses know everybody in the town and if they dinnae, then they can soon find out for you. Try it. And above all, dinnae trust anybody who doesnae speak with a Fife accent.'

They were outside St Salvator's College. The peaked bell-tower rose above them, as a kind of sedately superior watch-tower for the surrounding lower grey-terraced houses. The pavements were crowded with strolling tourists and the line of traffic in this street was moving only by inches. This congestion seemed to disappear when they saw what was at their feet, the cobbled PH.

The initials could not have been clearer now. They were riveted by the sight of the cleverly conjoined letters. In awe of them, they stood there, stubbornly, as others with almost sacrilegious indifference, strolled by without so much as a glance. Tam wanted to stop folk and tell them that that very tiny spot was where a stake had been put up to destroy a brave man and he had learned from his brief research that students avoided walking over it, superstitiously believing that to do so would mean failure to pass their finals. People probably wouldn't understand martyrdom nowadays, Tam thought. Frankie sat down, on all fours, on the cobblestones, and placed his hand on the stone letters, just like the psychic had laid hers on the photograph, Tam unable to tell if his mate was now in awe of the woman's apparent powers or whether he was affording it protection from insensitive feet. Frankie sat there, head down as if in meditation or like he was part of the homeless.

Suddenly he heard a loud American voice saying, 'Oh, Phil, just look at that poor boy.' Then he saw a large woman in a garish orange sweater, fumble in a large blue bag, and with admirable, but certainly misplaced sincerity, lob two coins towards Frankie, straight into his lap. 'There, honey. Have one on me.' And then walked on her way.

The accidental beggar rose to his feet examining two fifty-pence pieces like a miracle had taken place.

'Do you think our luck is turnin'?' he asked. Tam did not reply, because when you are laughing hysterically, it is not so easy to do. Frankie was less amused, but by the time they had reached Grannie Clark's Wynd, after assorted foreigners dolled up in multi-coloured golf gear, had directed them there, they discovered it was a gap between two rows of terraces, leading on to a concrete path bisecting the fairways of the golf course. They could see swards of green grass, and beyond that, a hint of beach and sea, the aroma of which came straight to their nostrils in heady wafts.

He did not have to wait long for a reply to his call to Jilly. She had obviously been waiting, poised.

'You've arrived. Good,' she said calmly. 'Now you are in Grannie Clark's Wynd. If you look down the lane you will be looking at the most famous golf course in the world. The Old Course. I want you to go down to the edge of the fairway, where you will see a path leading right across the two fairways there, the 1st and the 18th. You are allowed to pass over, when it's clear. Go across to the sands on the other side. You will see a path almost immediately to your right. That takes you down on to the West Sands. You won't miss me. I'll be there. I have to tell you I have two companions with me. They have been with me for some weeks, but have lain low in Glasgow, for many reasons. Thought I would let you know that. Take care.'

She sounded almost eager by the time she had finished speaking, which lifted his spirits a little. At the edge of the fairway they joined a group of people waiting for the right interval in the golf foursome to cross over, and by the looks on the surrounding faces, it was as if they were about to enter some holy shrine. They were so infected by the hushed reverence of all around that Tam wondered if he would have to take off his shoes, respectfully, before crossing the hallowed turf. The stately buildings at the end of the course, stood sternly like sentinels, holding the world at bay from this treasured tradition. One golfer, just in front of them struck a shot towards these buildings, aiming for a flag they could see fluttering in the distance.

'He's short,' came from the mouth of one of the on-lookers. 'Could be tricky. He's in the Valley of Sin.'

'Valley of Sin?' Frankie muttered. 'So golf has a sin-bin as well?' Then there was a mini-stampede to cross the course before the next golfers marched down the fairway. They could see the broad sweep of sands in front of them now, stretching away in a brown spread that seemed to go on endlessly. The tide was so far out it was difficult to see where sea and sky separated, and people frolicking, far out there, bore the resemblance of corn-flies hovering over cow-dung. Tam's eyes, accustomed to buildings and traffic and crowds of people, were dazzled by the clarity and vastness of the scene. But the last thing he wanted was to be distracted by nature. So, when he saw her, it was with a sense of relief.

She was sitting with her back to the long stretch of reed-topped dunes, in what appeared to be a grey jogging suit, her hair loose and swinging gently around her in the breeze coming from the sea, athletic-looking, even in repose. They trudged through the sand towards her, and though she did not turn towards them, he felt she was aware of their every step.

'So you found me,' she said and then turned and looked up at both of them like they had just been playing hide and seek. 'I must give you credit for the way you have hung in and kept to your task. I can't take that away from you. Have you two been out fishing by any chance?' she asked, sniffing, thus revealing that even by the sea and in the open, they both stank, as if they had been in the search for *Nemo*. As she said that they heard a shout.

'Hi!'A tall lanky man in jeans came sliding down the dunes from just behind them.

'This is Hank. From the Bronx. NYC,' Jilly said without any great enthusiasm. 'Tam and Frankie. From that dear green place, Glasgow.'

'The Likely Lads. Heard all about you,' Hank said without even a suggestion of offering them a handshake. He was tanned, with a full head of straggly brown hair, which hung down over a white shirt and a bulging yellow life-jacket, accentuating what looked like a solid body.

'Fancy a trip round the bay?' Hank said, beaming.

'We have a motor-boat out there, in the bay,' Jilly said, by way of explanation. 'And a dinghy at the edge of the water to take us out.'

Tam could see the white, sleek shape of the launch and the yellow dinghy lying on the beach like it was sunbathing.

'If we find the time,' Tam replied politely.

'We'll make time. You must come out and see us and maybe have a bit of chow. We got some of your great Aberdeen-Angus meat out there just waiting to be incinerated,' Hank said.

'Give the boys time to take pause,' Jilly said. She didn't like Hank. That was clear. Tam was glad of that because at first he had to admit to himself he had felt a slight pang of jealousy when he saw the tanned figure sliding down the dune.

Then she noticed the folder Tam was carrying.

'So you've brought that with you.'

'It's something for Andrej, if ever we get to meet him,' Tam said. 'He deserves it. All her scribbles and jottings that you said fascinated you in the home. I don't suppose you'll be doing a broadcast about her after all.'

'She was an extraordinary lady,' she said 'and if things had worked out differently I would certainly have produced something about her mental games and how she tried to fight against decline. But why would she want to send it all to Andrej? What possible good could it do him?'

Those questions did not sound genuine to Tam.

'More to the point where is he?' Tam asked brusquely. 'You've traced him here. What next?'

'Hey,' Hank butted in. 'We can talk this all over out there on the water. What a pleasant day to be in a boat.'

By the look on her face Tam could sense that Jilly was not enthused by this idea. So he jumped in with the obvious question.

'You knew as soon as you saw the PH, didn't you? And that psychic knew as well, for some reason, which kinda spooks me. But you're no psychic. So how come?'

'History. Pure and simple. I don't know what they do now but they used to teach Scottish history well in my day, and since I specialised in it at one stage, I knew something about mediaeval Scotland and the Reformation. PH, it just clicked and I recalled actually walking over those very cobblestones when I was a student on a visit up here. Patrick Hamilton. The man burned at the stake for defying the church.'

'Can I get one thing out of the way?' Frankie butted in before Tam could add anything. 'Do you support water-boarding?'

'Do I what?'

'You know, the CIA stuff.'

'As it so happens, no I don't. But I'm not sure what relevance it has at the moment.'

'And rendition, is that what you call it?'

'Frankie,' Hank said in a tone of admonishment, 'you are not by any chance wishing to conduct a debate on the Geneva Convention on prisoners of war, are you? I'm perfectly prepared to state a case, but could you please tell me what it has to do with why we are here?'

'Who is Andrej?' Tam snapped in, just as he felt Frankie was about to expound on the rights of man. 'Why have you trailed after him all over Europe? Can he be that important?'

'Oh, he is,' Hank said, but as he did so there was no disguising the distaste that spread over Jilly's face. He was starting to wonder why there could be a relationship at all, based on his first impression that somehow they were at odds with one another.

'Never been on a boat like that before,' Frankie said, looking out to sea, with the obvious hint that he would jump at this opportunity.

They looked towards the placid bay. Tam felt sure there were other moods lying out there on the waters, but at the moment the phrase that came to his mind, and heard before in a classroom, was 'painted ocean'. It did look tempting.

'Come on,' Hank said. 'Follow me.'

The tall American had seized the initiative. They were sucked in, as he began his long, loping stride towards the dinghy by the water's edge. Jilly clutched at Tam's arm behind the man's back and tried to say something, but Hank turned almost as if he didn't want any private conversations, always smiling, but Tam was beginning to feel it was forced.

'Are you back-up?' Frankie asked Hank as the four of them climbed into the small dinghy.

'Back-up?' Hank echoed. 'I'm up-front in everything I do, isn't that right, Jilly?'

Jilly, sitting just in front of the man with the oars, shrugged her shoulders in deliberate indifference, as the dinghy edged away from the beach. Then, as they felt the sway of the pull of the oars, she spoke.

'The first and practical fact I can tell you about Andrej, is that he is a passionate sailor. He came from a landlocked country certainly, but there are over 11,000 lakes in Belarus. He learned everything about boats on Lake Naroch, the biggest of them all. And he sailed in France as we know when he was in exile there. He couldn't possibly have come to this coast without getting a boat of some kind for himself. So we got ourselves a small cruiser. We thought we could live in it and at the same time call into the various little harbours up and down the coast, just in case somebody had come across Andrej. We have the photograph with us. So that's our plan. Although there are many places around the coasts here where you can berth. But like the needle in the haystack we might just sit on it by chance. We have to try.'

'Wait a minute,' Tam said, 'before we do anything else I have to tell you we might have been followed all the way up here.'

'Sure,' Hank replied. 'That fits.'

'Fits?'

'It was expected,' Jilly said. 'As soon as I listened to your message I knew they would have tracked the call, and be right on your trail. We knew what would happen. The fact is we want to flush out anybody who might be after Andrej. We're prepared for that. It's like having a boil, there comes a time when you have to lance it and get all the suppuration out. Time's up for just hanging around waiting.'

It was hard to credit this was the same woman who had been talking to the public on radio, so recently, about such serious matters as canine hygiene.

***

The name on the side of the motor launch they reached was *Angelina,* out of Portsmouth. It towered above them. They climbed on to the low deck at the rear. Above that was the cockpit with the controls of navigation. Underneath was the cabin entrance. The living area was more spacious than they had anticipated. There was a dazzling white-leather cushioned interior, which in the sudden transition from travelling in a fishmonger's van, to being in a James Bond boat, the likes of which could not belong to ordinary mortals, bewildered them.

'Come inside,' Hank said pointing to the interior, 'We can have a chat.'

They sank into the soft, soothing leather seats, which made Tam feel almost immediately relaxed, to the point of feeling like closing his eyes. The small table in the middle looked like marble, with a laptop computer sitting ready for use. Jilly sat opposite them as Hank fiddled with the computer. Then they saw another figure walking round the edge of the boat with a bucket in his hand, as if he had been swabbing. He was a towering figure who made the cabin feel smaller when eventually he entered and stood at the end of the table.

'This is Gregory,' Jilly said. Again a suggestion of distaste in her limpid voice.

Gregory nodded, then sat beside Jilly folding his arms across the chest of his large polo-necked Aran sweater. He looked grizzled compared to Hank, the grey hair and the stubble on his face denoting captaincy perhaps.

'If you are interested in boats,' he said, 'then I can tell you this is 18 metres long and can do up to 33 knots and it's so manoeuvrable I could put it through the eye of a needle.'

Brief, but believable, Tam thought, although even in its listless rest at anchor, he could still sense the latent power; it seemed a luxurious beast of a thing. Gregory's immediate purpose was to impress.

'I know what you have come through,' Jilly began, 'and I do understand your frustration. Perhaps together we can get to Andrej though.'

'Why do you think he's here in St Andrews? Who is he? Why is he so important?' Tam asked.

The slight movement of the boat was sending tiny reminders of where they were, through their legs and up into their reclined bodies. This sensation seemed to vindicate his use of the newspaper threat to expose her. Would they have got this far if he hadn't flourished it? And how much further would they be allowed to get? Perhaps they had no more answers. He had to try.

'Why is he here in St Andrews?' Hank echoed laconically. 'Because he is working with somebody. And being a university town it's safe to assume that we are talking about the combining of skills and expertise, the harvesting of knowledge. That is what we assume. And we've got to find the source.'

'And then?' Frankie asked.

'We take him where he can work in great safety, for the good of mankind, even if that sounds a bit high-falutin' to you,' Hank said.

'Andrej is a physicist of the highest order,' Jill went on, trying to sound more amenable and separate herself from the more rugged approach of the other two. 'He came here for specialised assistance. The academic world works on different levels from us and their connections are global. St Andrews we believe had something which met his needs to further his work. It's that we're trying to trace.'

Tam could hold back no further. It had been bottled up too long, and despite the Special Branch warnings, it came out.

'You saw his father being assassinated, didn't you? You were there. And you followed Andrej all the way through Europe. And your job with the radio station was a bit of a phoney, wasn't it? And you are not even Jilly Grierson, I suppose.'

Hank and Gregory registered no reaction to this. Frankie's slowly opening mouth could have caught a swarm of flies, as bemusement set in, hearing all this for the first time.

'Oh, I'm Jilly Grierson all right. And as for how I have conducted my life that's an entirely personal matter. We don't all fit into simple categories of life, you know. I go places and I do things, just like one of Miss Jean Brodie's girls. And people seem to think I do a good job for them, wherever I go. That is my only criteria. So, think what you like. I am here for Andrej's good.'

As she said that she looked at Tam, and as she could see the two men were engrossed in something on the computer, gave tiny nods in their direction, then shook her head, as if hinting at a disapproval of them that would have to remain wordless. For whatever reason this was not a happy trio.

'Your world is different from ours,' Tam said. 'I just don't get it. How can I take your word for anythin'?'

'That is entirely up to you.'

It was clear she was going to reveal nothing more of herself.

'Now, if you're going to be with us, I'd really relish having a look at Mrs Rybak's file,' Gregory said. 'All that stuff she worked on, all the bits and pieces and word games. It will be like reading a diary, I suppose.'

Tam could see Frankie trying to puzzle his way through this recent revelation about Jilly in Europe.

'Sometimes folk like to keep their diaries secret,' Tam answered taking it in his stride again.

'But you've gone through the folder yourself,' Hank persisted.

'It's just about an old lady passing her time. That's all.'

'Then why bring it all the way up here to give to Andrej, if ever you get to meet him?'

'Sentimental reasons,' Frankie suggested, snapping out of his puzzlement in an effort not to be completely sidelined. 'You know what old people are like. I've got a grandfather who was like that. Left everythin' to us. Except his bingo winnings.'

'We will treat it with proper respect of course,' Hank went on, and Tam knew that it would be foolish to be obdurate about it, out here in the bay on a powerful launch, over the side of which they could be dumped, if this cordial meeting took a sour turn.

'Please, help yourself,' he said and handed the file over to Jilly, who took it like she wished she didn't need to. She handed it over to Gregory with a blank expression on her face.

'Jilly will help us, won't you Jilly?' Gregory said. 'She met the old lady, didn't you Jilly?'

This was almost like a command and far from cordial. Jilly said nothing but followed them out to the rear deck and sat beside them as they placed the folder on a small canvas table and proceeded to pour over and pick at the bits and pieces of papers with relish. They would exchange scraps with each other and mumble one or two things, then pass on to another item. This wasn't an appreciation society. They were searching for something specifically. Jilly was showing little enthusiasm.

Tam walked out from the cabin and stood over them, as if exerting his right of ultimate ownership of what he had brought. Jilly, then, quickly sensed that Tam was aware that this was not just a casual perusal of the recreational habits of an old lady but something more focussed than that.

'She certainly knew how to fill her time,' Hank said looking up at him.

277

'What are you lookin' for?' Tam asked coldly.

He took a moment to think about that.

'Anything. There might be some thought, some idea, some hint about where Andrej is. She played word games with people according to Jilly. It was her thing. Did she do it with Andrej during his visits? That's about as open as I can get.'

Then he went back again to looking at a scrap of paper.

Hank had a notebook and pencil and was engrossed in some anagrams. Gregory was now smoking a large cigar and looking like he was sorting out the scraps into categories. As he watched, Tam found himself forced by this spectacle into re-evaluating Mrs Rybak. An old lady simply worried about dementia, both on her own part and for the others around her? Would they really be beavering away, on what she had left behind, simply on that basis? Who was this Mrs Rybak who had returned to her native country effectively to die amongst her own people? Just your average old lady in her dotage? No, no. She was special. For some reason.

When the steaks were cremated for dinner and they sat around the table in the small cabin, the intimacy of such not appealing to Tam, he was nevertheless too hungry to quibble. Frankie advised them that some time they should try mixing whisky-saturated haggis with a fillet, topped with black-pudding. They listened dutifully, but Tam could tell from their expressions they would rather eat shoe-leather than try that. His mate then went into a long spiel about how he would take any job in a kitchen to start with and that being a chef was nowadays as important to society as a brain surgeon. Nobody was prepared to contest that. Jilly said hardly anything. He had wanted to talk to her privately but there hadn't been a single moment when the men were not breathing down their necks. There was no privacy to be had in these confines.

'So what did you find?' Tam asked, eventually, when they were on large mugs of coffee.

'Find where?' Gregory asked. Out of respect to others he had discarded his cigar.

'In the cuttings.'

'Oh, that,' he replied. 'I would hazard a guess that Mrs Rybak had a very fertile mind and liked word games. That's about all I can deduce......at the moment.'

'I doubt if anything much will be found,' Jilly said.

Again there was that tiny hint of disapproval in her voice.

'Hey, you two,' Hank said, almost taking his cue from what she had just said. 'Where are you putting up tonight?'

The fact that they were preparing to sleep rough somewhere was not what Tam wanted to admit, at this stage, so he parried that one.

'We've one or two ideas,' he said which amounted to an admission that he didn't really know.

'Then why don't you put up here,' Hank went on. 'We're a bit tight in the berths but we have sleeping bags. The weather is not going to be bad. You could stay out there in the rear deck if you so wished.'

Tam realised that it was an option that was too good to refuse, even though he felt uneasy about the two men he had just met. Jilly was certainly still a mystery woman, accentuated by the fact that it was staring him in the face that she certainly didn't enjoy the company of the two men. So he still didn't feel greatly threatened by her.

'Stayin' here for the night would be fine, but I'd like to look at the material in the folder myself again anyway,' Tam stated. 'I'll keep it in order.'

He could sense Jilly relaxing a little on hearing that and wasn't sure whether it was because they were staying or it was on hearing he would look at the papers again.

'Of course,' she said pleasantly, as the two men remained poker-faced about the suggestion.

The sun had almost gone down by the time they put out the sleeping bags. Jilly hovered near them, but either Hank or Gregory was always at their elbows. Crazy though it may have seemed, he felt that they were watching her, as if they didn't trust her to be on her own with them.

When eventually they were separated, preparing to bunk down for the night, Frankie rushed out the question that he had obviously dammed up earlier.

'Why did you no' tell me all this about Jilly before?'

'I hadn't the heart. I was kinda ashamed that I'd got you intae this mess. I mean I was stupid and thick about it all. I didnae like to admit all that.'

'Wonder Woman can do anythin', I think. Naw, I don't blame you. You know that. I just think you're a big saftie. There's nothin' wrong with that.'

'What do you make of them?' Tam asked softly, lying snugly enough now in his sleeping bag.

'Gregory looks like he eats iron-filings, and Hank is slick. He could probably sell a Celtic jersey to a Rangers fan.'

'Nobody's that bloody slick. But I see what you mean. I'll tell you what I think. This is no team. I've been watching and listening to Jilly. She's just not part of them, even though she's here. It would be like watching Messi wearing a white jersey and playing for Real Madrid. It's phoney. Everythin' seems like they're supposed to be together and yet they're not. I think she was trying to indicate something to us without being able to speak up. I think if she had been on her own she would tell a different story. She's still involved. That's for sure. But something is no' right.'

'Wonder Woman will have somethin' up her sleeve. You can bet on that. And why did she no' give you a hint about these two when you were on the phone?'

'Can anybody we've met, so far, trust sayin' anythin' through a phone, eh? Listen. Tomorrow I want you to do me a favour. I want to take the dinghy and get ashore somewhere and get to that *Northpoint* place the fishmonger was talking about. I think it's a wild shot, but you never know. I just want to talk to somebody who knows the town and the university well. I don't think it's goin' to be as easy as

281

all that, but I just don't want us to be cooped up here under their gaze all the time.'

'And the favour?'

'Row the dinghy back to them. Keep your eye on the folder. And on them. Tell them I'm off to see the town. I've never been here before. Either you or them can come back for me. I'll have the phone. Any funny business, contact me.'

'Mate, this is the CIA we're talkin' about here. Not the boy scouts. Are they goin' to buy that?'

'Forget the CIA bit. We don't know who these folk are. But I'm going to try that place.'

The night seemed to be shorter than usual, because daylight eventually seeped through his closed eyelids in a manner he was unaccustomed to. Nor had he ever awakened with a bed moving underneath him, as if it was on caster wheels. A wind had got up and some spume swept across his face. Instinctively his tongue reached out to his upper-lip and for the first time in his life he tasted the sea. It didn't repel him. Indeed he felt it almost as if it were part of an initiation rite. He struggled out of his sleeping bag with a renewed belief that he was well and truly fit for purpose now, fit for that eccentric mode of life which Jilly and her kind seemed accustomed to.

He shook the shape beside him vigorously, as he was now impatient to move on.

Frankie pushed his head from under the cover and clearly did not know where he was. He sat up and looked around him obviously trying hard to imagine how he had got there. When his groggy face had determined that, all he could say was, 'I take it an extra hour is out of the question? '

'Move it,' Tam said urgently. 'I'm goin' ashore.'

'You're soundin' now as if you've sailed the seven seas.'

'Belt up. Move. You're going to help me with the dinghy.'

They both looked at the tender, tied neatly at the back, and bobbing up and down as the bay waters were now less congenial. The dinghy had now attained a new significance.

They stepped into it, awkwardly, but with a minimum of noise. The light was coming from the east, behind him. The coast, and the town behind it, looked bleak, dark, and unappetising. Tam pointed to a headland, with what seemed a broad path winding its way up beside the craggy outline of the remains of an ancient castle. Frankie guided him as he pulled strongly on the oars after slipping into a rhythm. Tam found he was enjoying the exercise, and Frankie had to tell him to slow down as they reached the first rocks. Tam rested the dinghy against the side of one rock, then stepped out and splashed through a few feet of water onto the shore. He looked up. The dark, proud remnants of the castle which must have been magnificent and strategically significant at some stage in history, formed a jagged shape at the edge of the promontory like the prow of a battered ship, a sight that would have dominated the waters for miles around in its prime.

When he turned back Frankie was struggling to get into his rowing position and looking like he was trying to disguise a panic attack, but not with much success.

'Just to let you know,' he said, 'I've never rowed a boat in my life. I hope the local coast guard are no' on strike.'

Tam pushed the boat away and watched his mate try to come to terms with the oars. It looked like somebody playing blind-man's buff on water, with the dinghy swinging one way then the other as if it were demanding to know where it was supposed to go. He did not need such a painful sight this early and on a strange shore. He would have to leave him to it, come what may. There was indeed a concrete path which curved around the base of the crag and led upwards to the town. But it was only six-thirty according to his watch. And he was hungry and cold, the bay waters reminding him that swimming in there would not be for the faint-hearted. He huddled in against the foot of the crag between two large rocks, and in taking comfort from that, he began to doze. He did not know how long for, but when he snapped out of that and looked seaward towards the launch, it was clear that Frankie had succeeded. The dinghy was there. And then he became aware of a presence. There to his right sitting nonchalantly on the rocks was one of the Men in Black, smoking.

As he rose slowly to his feet, restraining the surge of panic, the other one hove into view, simply throwing skimmers into the water in the tiny bay. It was all so casual that Tam actually found himself counting up to six skims for one throw. Not that their casual postures were making it easier for him to comprehend. They, in fact, looked more menacing than had they come at him in a rush. Were they toying with him again? He turned to make his way up the concrete path but the one skimming stopped, then walked across and barred his way. It was the only exit.

The other one threw his cigarette into the sea and walked towards him. The pincer movement was obvious. There was no way out, except the sea itself, but, swim as much as he did in the Gorbals pool, he knew going back into those cold waters, with the launch so far out, might be suicidal. That option was taken out of his consideration when the one who had been smoking walked quickly to the water's edge, cutting off any route there. There was no way out. The two Men in Black converged on him. One of them spoke, as Tam simply stared past them towards the sea, refusing eye contact.

'You had a small sleep, yes?'

It was polite and non-aggressive.

'Will you come with us please? Up the hill. Yes?'

Tam turned away from them and could see cars parked in the street, just at the edge of the entrance to the castle. There might be people up there he thought and, anyway, if they really had wanted to do him harm it would have been easy enough in the shelter of the bay. They walked behind him as he climbed the steep, curving path. It was near the top, tucked into a little rocky alcove, that he noticed someone sitting, propped against a wall, reading a newspaper. It was lowered as Tam neared.

'Good rest?' the face appearing above it asked, displaying a broad expanse of very white teeth in a welcoming smile.

It was the man he had come to know as Andrej Matskevich.

Chapter 19

By the time he had reached the launch, Frankie felt as if he had rowed via the Seychelles. His arms were numb and his raw hands felt like he had been caressing a porcupine. He had seen exercise rowing machines in a gym before and thought they were really for old maids. He would look at them now with renewed respect, before giving them a wide berth. In the last few yards he was urged on by Jilly and the two men, who had now come on deck to encourage him and were greatly amused by his efforts. They had to lean over and haul him into the launch with great care, as if they really did need him.

'Where did Tam go?' Jilly asked in a way that suggested that she was genuinely concerned about him. Frankie could tell that she was not entirely approving of what they had done. But they had got their dinghy back.

'He just wanted to stretch his legs and get around the town a bit. He's always wanted to come to St Andrews,' Frankie said, although it did sound a bit weak, even to himself. Jilly was not satisfied with that.

'When are we due to meet up with him again?' she asked.

'He said he would phone,' Frankie answered. 'Could be he'll want lunch, he doesn't have much money with him. Or else he might be goin' to an internet cafe to see himself on YouTube. He hasn't seen that yet, I don't think.'

'What's this about YouTube?' Gregory asked.

'Oh, it was just a joke. I think we were getting towards a million hits for showing our bums to the world.'

'Your what? This we must see,' Hank said moving into the cabin. 'Tell us all about it.'

The laptop computer was opened and after Gregory had used what looked like a satellite phone and linked it up, they were able to access the internet. Frankie told them of the circumstances, the place, the action. They searched and found it, then sat around and watched the clip. The two men chortled. Jilly simply looked at him like he had been auditioning for some freakish talent contest. And, he thought, how do you look a lady straight in the eye after having revealed part of an anatomy that she probably thinks was far from alluring. Did it make him any less of a person in her eyes? He bowed his head slightly. Jilly changed the tone and the subject.

'We'll have to go ashore and get some supplies and maybe bump into your friend,' she said. Then she turned and sat down opposite him, their knees almost touching, as the two men hovered near her.

'Have we been absolutely frank with each other about Andrej's whereabouts here?' she asked. 'So far, so good, you might say. But I don't think you would have come this far without knowing a lot more than you're admitting. I realise you stumbled into all of this, but that doesn't detract from the fact that you might have information that could be useful.'

As she said that she kicked his foot slightly and Frankie was sure he saw her slightly, very slightly, shaking her head, as if she was hinting, 'Say nothing.' Odd. The question and that clear movement of warning made him realise it was as if she had been expected to make that assertion and the two men just behind her became very still as if they were anticipating a reply of merit. Tam was right. This was no team. And Jilly was playing a part that was now slightly scaring him because it made little sense. Whose side was she really on? He simply parried her advance.

'I can tell you it took six hours to burn Patrick Hamilton. That's all I've learned so far, except that there is a place called the Valley of Sin on the Old Course. Golfers are strange folk.'

He could then see the slightest smile of gratification passing over her lips. The answer had suited her down to the ground.

'I see,' she said, 'Make sure you get something to eat. We won't be long.'

Frankie rose and watched them pulling away from the launch. Off to chase after Tam, he wondered? But, when he looked in the cupboards inside, he knew that they did really have to replenish their food supplies, if they were on an extended stay. He whipped up an omelette for himself, slapped marmalade on almost burnt-through slices of toast and felt his stomach rumbling in acclamation. Then he went back on deck and surveyed the scene. He could see no sign of the dinghy now. People were beginning to stroll along the West Sands and joggers were testing their own strengths by running up and down the dunes. They would certainly sweat over there, for the wind had died considerably from the night before and the sun was dipping in and out of clouds, like it was toying with its admirers, but inexorably the temperature was rising.

Because of his red-hair, and the fairness of the skin associated with it, he had always been warned about too much exposure to sun. It was tempting though to think Glasgow could be a safe haven for those imperilled by sunlight. He disliked sunburn anyway, so he moved back into the cabin. But he took his trainers off as they were damp from his short trip and accidental splashing. He thumbed through some DVDs lying on a small cupboard. One caught his eye. On its cover was a knight on a white horse, charging with spear in hand. Now then, the last time he had seen that was in the doctor's house. It increased his curiosity. He moved to the laptop which had been left in sleep mode, requiring no sign-in, then slipped the disc in. Within seconds a face appeared, in still frame. He knew it instantly, having been obsessed by that other photograph of Andrej. In the middle of the face was the arrow sign to operate the video. He placed the cursor on it and clicked.

He was now looking at Andrej in a white lab coat, at a blackboard, scratching up what looks like complicated equations. Then Andrej turns to camera. His voice starts. He is speaking in that harsh language again. He points to the board and changes a figure on it and then returns to his laptop computer on a long desk with various microscopes arraigned along its length. He points to the laptop and turns back to the board, as if he is explaining its relevance. Then he lifts the laptop and moves to a window, the camera trailing after him. It is dark outside and there is an array of lights on buildings in the distance behind him. He sits there and starts to operate the laptop, at the same time inclining his head towards the window as if to draw attention there. The camera then tracks back with him until he is standing beside a door. He points back to the blackboard again and then suddenly the lights in the room go out. It is all black for a few seconds. Then they go back on again. Andrej is playing with the light switch. He keeps doing that on and off, occasionally turning to say something about what has been written on the blackboard. Suddenly Frankie recognised a phrase amidst the full spate of the other language. It flashed past him, so he stopped the disc, ran it back and played it again to make sure he wasn't mistaken. He wasn't. It stood out clearly. 'Cyber attack.'

Andrej then talks solemnly to camera for a minute or so, three times repeating that phrase, in the last barrage of words, so that there is no dubiety. Then the pictures end.

Frankie played the disc three times. He had, on the one hand, gained the impression of a man talking solemnly, concerned, trying to impress. Then on the other, was a man childishly playing with a light switch. And cyber attack? Where did that fit in? So the DVD was essentially a disappointment for him but it did increase his curiosity. Andrej's identity was still a puzzle.

He lifted his phone and tried to contact Tam. There was no reply. There was no valid reason for him not to reply, except if he was in a bad area for reception, but it didn't seem like that, as it was ringing as normal and he was getting the answer service. He sent him a text. 'Where are you?' Then he went back on to the deck and looked around the bay. He could see the dinghy on the shore with Gregory sitting there on his own. The other two had gone. He looked towards the old castle and the tiny bay where he had dumped Tam. There was no sign of him. He tried several times before he concluded that his mate had some kind of problem.

***

Andrej was smaller than he had imagined. Dark-haired, very white of face, either by nature, or not, having been exposed to the sun for some time. Well, it was Saint Andrews after all, not Saint Tropez. He had large kindly eyes which looked like he was a man not difficult to please about anything. He was also one of those men who had a shadowed chin, like he would have to shave several times a day. He wore a brown track suit and black and white trainers. The Men in Black seemed as if they never took off either their suits or dark sunglasses. Did they sleep with them on? They were paying no attention, separate and staring out to sea, as Andrej and Tam sat at the top of the hill on the grass, looking out across the bay towards the launch.

'Scotland's coastline is remarkable,' he was saying. 'I have travelled all over. On the west, especially in the north-west, you have these marvellous mountains running into the sea with great sea-lochs. On this side, you have the gentle lapsing of land into sea, which gives you the impression the horizon out there is the very edge of the world.'

The distinct accent did not mar his easy and obvious command of the English language, which was spoken with a care to vowels and

292

consonants like they had been weighed by scales, within his larynx, for maximum clarity.

'Unfortunately my time here is running out. I will miss Scotland,' he went on. Then he changed tack. 'My friends here,' Andrej went on, 'met you in the lane and they have been watching you closely ever since.'

'Met me? They whacked me. Lucky I survived,' Tam replied.

'As I understand it,' Andrej said pleasantly, 'you attacked them first.'

'But they were attacking a girl.'

'Ah, Jilly! Yes, you could say that there was some rough stuff, unfortunately. I am told you were very brave, and they came away from that experience thinking that you could look after yourself well. They were impressed.'

'Big deal. That doesnae explain why two grown men would attack a single woman. A woman you know well, as I understand it.'

'Oh, she and I go back a bit. But they simply approached her without thought of malice. She had something which we believe she had stolen from someone we once knew. A Mrs Rybak, who would not have released that photograph to anyone. And certainly not to Jilly Grierson. In the lane she would not negotiate with my two friends.'

'What right had you to it?'

'It was a family photograph. It was ours, simply ours. Now, my friends have seen you with a yellow folder. They could have intervened before now but they suspected, like me, you were being

293

followed and watched by others and had they approached you they would have been in danger themselves. It was a pleasant surprise to them, and to me, that you suddenly headed this way. I have to congratulate you on your initiative. Now you obviously know of Mrs Rybak. I have to stress that the photograph and the folder was hers and is now mine.'

'Ay, of course. Her name keeps croppin' up. And you know somethin', I'm findin' it difficult to believe in her somehow. She just doesnae sound real. It's as if she's just been made up to cover something else.'

'Oh, she was real, very real. Without her I would not be here. Without her I would not have progressed my work. Without her I would not have been able to keep under cover and still communicate with people. '

'An old lady in a rest-home?'

'But a supremely intelligent old lady. And who commanded great respect throughout certain circles in Europe.'

'Which circles?'

'Let us just say, in certain diplomatic circles. When her husband died, rather than come back here to live on her own she wanted people around her. And she liked to organise. That was her nature, that was her profession. Her name was renowned. For in her heyday behind the old Iron Curtain, she was a woman who pulled strings. I think the term is, controller. Her expertise was in arranging passages of safety for political refugees. A kind of Scarlet Pimpernel. When the Berlin Wall came down and this tremendous upheaval in the east took place, she was one of the first to realise that she would not be made redundant, because despots still existed in many countries which were supposed to have thrown off the shackles. I was one to suffer from the dictatorship in my native Belarus. And since her husband was related to my family, she took an interest in me. In my work as a physicist, I knew of research going on within university circles here that would help me. She arranged the rest. Very secretly.'

'Not surprisin', considerin' they wanted to kill you.'

'I am not sure they did. I believe the group that we observed putting you through a hard time was sent to grab me and take me back. They failed of course, thanks to you, and I may say, MI5 or 6, whichever, for I have never been able to tell the difference. My information from my two friends there, is that they were last seen being put on a Polish fish-factory ship at Plockton in the north–west to be taken back to Lithuania, where several of them are wanted for crimes against humanity.'

The two Men in Back suddenly turned towards them and, in unison, nodded.

'I am sure you thought these two guardians of mine were tied up with the doctor and her cronies,' Andrej went on. 'That is not surprising. They were only seconds behind the snatch of your friend, and they stayed down there in Glasgow because we knew the photograph was with you. As long as we kept it from the other monsters who came from Belarus, that was all right by my two friends there. They kept their eyes on you, even when you would not have suspected. And they knew you had support from your own people who obviously can't be messed about very easily. My two friends were being vigilant on your behalf. They saw who killed the lawyer.'

Tam squirmed uneasily, that crushed-face image floating in front of him again.

'Who did it?' he asked faintly.

'From what we have been able to pick up he goes by the name of Gregory.'

Tam looked out to sea. He could now see the launch sitting there like a tiny white ornament in an immensity of blue sea and sky; innocuous, easy on the eye, the emblem of the good life. There was no sign of activity there. Tam felt the dampness rising from his feet taking a grip of him again, making him shiver. First, he had felt a sense of clarity emerging on the whole rigmarole, listening to Andrej. Now the thought of a murderer on the launch clouded his mind again. He had to plough on to try to regain his footing again.

'If you were in danger all the time, why did you give Mrs Rybak that photograph of you standing near the PH? It was a clue to where you were.'

'It was largely sentimental. And to remind her I was within reach of her in emergencies. She was in danger too. And she certainly respected the historical connection. She was always a supporter of the underdog, the outcast, the rebel, the reformer. So she liked the reminder I had chosen for her. I was hounded out of my own country and Patrick Hamilton of his. Although his departure was in a most horrendous manner. So far I have been more fortunate. I thought it was a neutral photograph, unless you knew the context and the background, and Mrs Rybak was the only one who did. Even the assistant who took it for me from the top of an open-decked tourist bus that was parked there at the time didn't know the true significance. I felt it was all I could do to remind her of me. I owed her that. It was eventually taken out of the home, and so began the hunt.'

'You mention the hunt,' Tam said. 'You know that Jilly Grierson is out there on that launch?'

'Of course. But I know when to duck and dive. I am an expert on that. I've known Jilly since the days she began her career reporting around Eastern Europe. She was brilliant at languages. But I never knew who she really was attached to.'

'The Americans?'

'I don't think you would be far wrong. Difficult to pin it down. I do know that there is great rivalry between them and the British, even though they are supposedly on the same side.'

Tam thought of Alex in the gym and his mention of Jilly as if he knew her personally.

'So Jilly was and probably still is, a wanderer,' Andrej went on. 'We find it difficult to put a label on her.'

'Which side is she on out there?' Tam asked. 'She doesn't fancy that pair, I could tell that.'

'Perhaps she is working to orders. We shall see.'

Tam stirred himself even though the thought that he had taken dinner the previous evening with a killer who had sent a bullet through a man's head only feet from him, was bringing the squeamishness on again. It wasn't the time to indulge in personal anguish though. He thought back to the last evening and Jilly's dislike of the two men, her obvious reluctance to work in unison with them, and yet still accepted the need to be with them. Did she know what Gregory had done?

'They've been going through that yellow folder I brought from the home,' Tam explained. 'It's full of Mrs Rybak's word games as you know. We brought it for you. I thought she would have wanted that. But the two men are definitely more interested in it than I thought they would be. It's on the boat right now.'

Andrej's eyes wandered to the bay. He didn't seem alarmed. If anything he looked saddened by that news.

'Perhaps my good fortune is ebbing away. Who knows? But I had to break cover to find you and the folder. Perhaps too late.'

Tam offered a minor encouragement.

'So far all they've done is study the papers. I haven't seen anything that's excited them. Maybe they haven't found anything worthwhile.'

'Certainly they have skills in these matters. But so had Mrs Rybak.'

'But why this way. Bits of papers, word games. It's kinda ancient.'

298

'We played it this way because Mrs Rybak would not trust electronic communication. She was a little old fashioned in some of her ways certainly, and probably thought, very perceptively I have to say, that a smart phone was simply an invitation to invade someone's privacy. No phones, no computers. That was to be the rule. She would send me information by letter to an address over the water there in the city of Dundee. I would travel there every week to pick up any relevant information, especially about the people I could link up with, through her. It was, what they call in her own trade, the 'dead drop'. I needed a piece of information from her which would enable me to complete my project. It didn't come. She had died. But I knew it still might exist. Indeed it had to exist. It was the final fit, the invaluable bit. I thought of the folder. That is why I am here.'

Tam thought of all he had tried to interpret in the folder.

'I'm good at anagrams, well, reasonably good. But there was a page I couldn't get. I just couldn't make sense of it. So if these weren't anagrams then..........?'

Andrej looked at him as if he didn't need to complete the thought.

'Word games always fascinated her,' he answered. 'She couldn't kick the habit in her old age. But it seemed a natural extension of the secret work she did professionally. Anagrams she could do in several languages. But, of course, there was something else. That particular page you were talking about, can you recall if there were any marks on it, apart from the letters of the alphabet? Anything unusual?'

Try as he may he could picture nothing more than the implausible letters that defied unscrambling. He shook his head.

'Can't think of anythin',' he said. 'Why would that be important?'

'There was another habit she couldn't throw off. It was ingrained in her, even though I did not think it was necessary. But she was the boss. So she sometimes used code.'

'Like on that page?'

'Of course. I have been expecting it. It was what I have been waiting for. I needed it.'

Tam looked back at the boat again and shivered realising the proximity of Frankie to a ruthless monster. Andrej by comparison seemed composed.

'Mrs Rybak had a favourite method. It was simple but it required attention and concentration. She sometimes used a process called Caesar's Shift. It was named after the Roman Emperor who first used it to communicate secretly with his generals. It means that the letter you see on the page is only a substitute for the actual letter in the sentence. The real letter is a number of places further back on the alphabet. 6 or 7 or 4 places. Whatever. If the key was 7 then an H on the coded message would really be an A. You are counting back seven letters. If the number is 4, you come to D. And so on. But you need to know the key, the number of places to count. Mrs Rybak amused herself with that. She did it regularly, obviously thinking she needed to keep me up to speed on matters of decoding. That is a possibility. Not so sophisticated that you would need the Enigma

300

machine to break it down. But damned infuriating to those who wouldn't know the key.'

The talk was interrupted by a shout from one of the Men in Black.

'Andrej, they return!'

They began to walk back towards the edge of the castle. Tam stood up and just over the tops of the rocks to his left he could see the miniature shape of the dinghy with three figures in it, heading back towards the launch. He didn't know whether it was that sight or the dampness and cold getting to him but he began to shiver noticeably.

'You must get something to eat and drink to heat you up. You're suffering,' Andrej said solicitously.

'I'm all right,' he replied. But he wasn't. He was cold and bewildered and in an internal ferment that felt as if it would never settle. He had to be positive though.

'Just a thought,' Tam said as the Men in Black passed him like two benign beach attendants. 'I could phone Frankie, my mate. He'll still be on board. The folder will still be there I'm sure. I can phone him. If he gets it we could talk him through what he had to do. Mind you, if they knew he was trying to hide something they might get nasty. He's had enough problems over this. I don't want him to make them any more suspicious of us or they might get bloody nasty. At the same time I don't want to scare him out of his tiny mind. If I told him Gregory was a killer, he'd jump into the sea, phone and all.

Somehow I've got to sound concerned but not panicky. He could phone us the details. '

Andrej quickly assessed that suggestion.

'I know it's a big risk to talk on phones with these people about but we have to take the chance and if we just stay ahead of them we should be all right. It's a gamble and I know it demands a lot of your friend to go through this process. Is he reliable?'

Tam didn't quite know how to answer that.

Chapter 20

Frankie could see the rowing boat setting out from the shore heading back to the launch. He was still pondering what he would say to them, if anything, about the video. What he had just watched, without the English language, was what it must have been like to watch a silent movie without captions. The pictures could lead to all kinds of interpretations. All right, there was the blackboard and equations. There was the white lab coat. There was the accompanying laptop. So, he could forget plumber, joiner, electrician; Andrej was a scientist, or a researcher or a teacher. That much was obvious. But the turning-off-the-lights spectacle wasn't so easy to tackle. A trick? A demonstration? A happening? An experiment? Whatever Andrej was saying was not meant to be a bundle of fun for the viewer. Of that Frankie was not in much doubt. He didn't know the language but he could tell the tone was deliberately grave. He had experienced more light-hearted orations at funerals. And chilling, in a kind of way, after watching it for the third time. But in a peculiar way it had scared him, something he hated to admit to himself.

Frankie prowled inside the cabin and gently pushed open the door of one of the back berths. Inside he could see an assortment of electronic equipment, opposite bunk-beds. There was an array of dials and headphones and tiny screens, like he had seen once in a television outside broadcast unit which had braved entry into his school once. He was about to investigate further when his phone rang.

Frankie grabbed at it so eagerly it flew in the air and he had to catch it like a slip-fielder, juggling with if for a few second before hugging it to his ear.

'Where are you?' Tam's voice came.

'Where are YOU, more like it? I've been trying to phone you for the last couple of hours.'

'I'll explain later. They're goin' to take me to *Northpoint* . I need somethin' inside me.'

'Who's they?'

'Never mind that just now. Do you see them rowing back?'

Frankie looked towards the shore.

'Clearly.'

'I want you to do something before they get back, like pronto.'

'Calm down.'

'Just do as I say. Get your hands on the yellow folder and talk to us when you get it.'

'Us?'

'Just get it.'

Frankie went inside and saw it lying on the back of one of the couches. He took it and opened it up.

'Right,' he said.

'Just spill out the papers and I want you to look for one which has a date at the top right hand corner. There were lotsa dates but I think it was the 24th April on the sheet I'm talkin' about. Top right hand side. Have you got it?'

'Don't be so fucking impatient,' Frankie said.

'I want you to get that sheet out of there and do something for us before they get back, now have you got that?'

Frankie fumbled among the papers mumbling 'Us' under his breath, as if to show his confusion.

He found himself snatching at the papers, in his own impatience, which was not going to aid the cause. He took a deep breath and tried to be more controlled. There were lots of dates among the bits and pieces. He stood up and looked through the open door. The boat was getting nearer.

'This is impossible, 'he said to himself, but Tam heard it.

'Don't let us down,' Tam replied, his tone becoming graver. Frankie flipped through the papers keeping his eye on the top right hand side.

'I've got something,' he said eventually. '24th April.'

'That's it, I think,' Tam replied. 'Now what do you see on that page?'

'Looks like anagrams, spread down the page.....'

'They're not anagrams. Listen carefully. Are there any other marks on the paper?'

'What kind of mark?'

'Anythin'. Somethin'. Just look, up, down, sideways, any which-fucking-way. Just look for marks for us.'

'You'll piss me off with that tone. The paper is clean. There are no marks. Just jumbled letters.'

'We're looking for a key, a number, something that links to the letters. This is code you're looking at.'

'You mean like micro-dots and things like that.'

'No. There's a clue in there about a number, an important number.'

'There is nothin' I can see that tells us anything about any number. Have you got that? Nothin'!'

Frankie heard a muffled conversation in the background.

'Who are you with?' he asked.

'Never mind who it is. It'll take too long to explain. Look at the letters closely. There has to be something there.'

Frankie looked back towards the course of the rowing-boat. He thought they would reach the launch in about five minutes. The letters on the page seemed to dance in front of his eyes now, taunting him. They were just letters, after all. But as his eyes crept along each word he did see something that would have been difficult to spot on a casual reading. There was something different about some of the words.

'Tam, this might be nothing but I can count, one, two, three words which seem to be fainter than the rest, just slightly. No' italics, just fainter. Maybe it's nothing. That's all I can spot.'

'How many did you say?'

'Three.'

There was a pause. He heard a muffled conferring.

'That might be it. It's possible. If that's all you can see we'll have to go with it. That's the number. 3. Got it?'

Frankie shook his bemused head wondering who else was there.

'So what do I do with this 3?' he asked.

'Now look. What is the first letter at the top of the page?' Tam this time asked.

'First letter is S. So?'

'That's only a substitute letter. If you count three letters back from that, you get ....P. That is the real letter. You are looking at a code. We're going to use 3 as the key. It's possible that's what the different printing of the letters is telling us. It means that the real letters are 3 back in the alphabet.'

Frankie looked into the bay and saw the dinghy only about twenty yards away.

'This is gettin' to me,' he said over the tightly-held phone, 'But I'll have a go.'

He heard a muffled conference going on in the background before Tam came back to him.

'As soon as you've worked it out phone us. We need this badly. We're goin' to *Northpoint* right now. I'm dyin' o' hunger. Contact me as soon as you've done this. I can't tell you how important this is.'

Then as Frankie thought that was the last of it, another voice came on the phone again, but speaking calmly and with determination.

'Time is of the essence,' it said. 'We must stay a step ahead of them.'

Then the phone was turned off. Frankie could have phoned back to ask who the mystery voice was and ask what kind of essence time actually was. Vanilla? But that might have sent Tam right over the top. He had never heard his mate so snappy like that before. So he arranged himself with a pen and paper and started on his wordy quest, ticking off the places carefully with the tip of the pen then substituting the letters as accurately as he could just above the originals. Then he heard the dinghy making its presence felt with a slight bump against the side of the launch. Jilly was off first, walking towards the cabin carrying brown paper bags. Hank was just behind her. She still looked glum.

'Been relaxing?' she asked. She did not look towards the folder but walked straight through to the little galley area and started to dump articles out of the bags. Out came jam, butter, bread, fruit, eggs and packs of what looked like pre-packaged food from a supermarket.

'There we go,' she said looking back at him. 'That should keep us going.'

Then she turned and walked past him, as if he was now an irrelevance. Hank picked up the folder and went back on deck again. Gregory was already there. He certainly looked the more genial of the three now, sitting back with a relaxed smile on his face as if he was about to tell stories to kids. He now seemed a nice considerate kind of guy. He even picked up Frankie's trainers and wiped at them, before putting them neatly on a shelf. How considerate. Was St Andrews air suiting him? Frankie turned away and squeezed himself into the small galley. Food was the furthest from his mind but nevertheless he placed the shopping articles neatly into different segments of the cupboards there. Then he looked back to the others and saw they were discussing Mrs Rybak's papers, passing them around and swapping opinions. They certainly did not know at that stage that a single sheet was missing. He took it out and started to work on that April 24th sheet. All he thought of was the number 3, and with no great confidence in this whole process, looked at what was in front of him.

SLFNXS EHKLQG UDJGDOH KRXVH
RQH PLOH GRZQ WUDFN
LQ ROG IDUPVKHG
LJRU KDV OHIW QRWB
HOHYHQ LV WKH KRXU
JRRG OXFN JRG EOHVV

That old biddy certainly had odd ways with her. Couldn't she just have written normally? He clenched his teeth and started.

The first thing he did was to write out the alphabet in a straight line at the top of the page. And immediately underneath printed 3. That was the lynch-pin number, they hoped. The words started to recompose themselves quickly after that, although the words emerging meant nothing to him. He hoped he was getting it right printing each one carefully, distinctly. He checked and double checked his decoding until he was sure that he could not have made any errors. However, how could he really tell, since the message that had been unfolded just read like a riddle? He realised he was shaking now.

'What have you got there?'

It was Gregory's voice behind him.

'Oh, just some recipes I was thinkin' about.....now that you've got all that grub in,' he answered as naturally as he could, and at the same time folding up the sheet and slipping it into the top pocket of his jacket. He could see Gregory was not convinced. But Frankie, turning away, now knew he was vulnerable.

Then he heard his phone going again. It was Gus McIntyre, the web-surfing addict to tell him that the hits were still coming in to their *Braveheart* moment on YouTube. It couldn't have come at a worse time but Frankie listened patiently to the ramblings as the other three looked on.

'Is that Tam?' Jilly asked politely.

Frankie put his hand over the mouthpiece with the web-surfer still shouting excitedly at the other end.

'Naw, it's a madman who thinks we might get more hits on YouTube than these Twins talkin' gibberish in their nappies. Personally I think he's goin' a bit over the top about that.'

As this seemed normal enough he kept the conversation going to suggest that he had nothing in his mind other than having his ego stoked by somebody in Glasgow who thought he was some kind of hero. He did not know how long this had lasted until reality intervened again. It came in the form of an abrupt silence at the other end. He looked at his phone.

Battery gone. Jesus Christ. Not now. The impulse was to throw the thing into the sea in anger. Bloody batteries. They're all the bloody same. He couldn't recall when he had last charged the phone. He felt weak. Was Tam and the mysterious voice he had heard really relying on him all that much? Of course they bloody were. He could tell that in Tam's tone. He would like to have bawled across St Andrews Bay. 'Houston, we have a problem!' He would never have believed he could actually be in as desperate situation as that moment of emergency in outer space, but that is exactly how it felt there and then.

It would only be a matter of time before they missed something from the folder given the scrutiny they had put it under. Gregory went back to the others and he could see him talking closely into Jilly's ear. She looked back into the cabin. Frankie was now sure he was on borrowed time. The men had made their minds up about him. He couldn't be trusted. The one thing he would now have to trust was his own memory because there was no way he could get off that boat with that piece of paper on him. He looked hard at the words and tried to sear them into his mind.

The words stared back at him menacingly. He had to get rid of them. He stuck the sheet back into his pocket, and nonchalantly stepped out on deck.

'Hi, folks. Don't get weather like this back in Glasgow,' he said as he emerged on the deck. 'Mind if I have a look at your boat? Havenae been up front yet.'

The two men gave him blank looks of 'Do what you like.' Jilly didn't lift her head. He held the rail and swung himself round the side of the boat and edged his way to the front. They were paying no attention. Then he took out the sheet, crumpled it into a ball, and threw it as far out as he could. He saw it bob about a bit. Then, agonisingly, it seemed to be moving. Frankie's urban upbringing leaving him with little appreciation of tidal movement and currents was now having that lapse in his education filled for him. For the ball of paper was now heading back towards the boat. It bobbed about, swirled, then tantalisingly seemed to move towards the rear of the boat where the others could have a grandstand view, especially as it was the only object in sight on that large blue expanse of water. He knew they were alert people he was with. The sort that would never missed a trick. Curious people probably trained at Langley in spotting the unusual. This blob of paper now looked bloody unusual to Frankie.

It was Hank who spotted.

'Trash,' he said. 'Have people got no respect for the sea?'

Jilly gave Frankie the strangest of looks. Was his look of innocence just too artificial? She looked over the side of the boat at the ball of paper, then back at Frankie. He turned away from her. She couldn't know. Surely not. It was his nervousness that was confusing him. One of those steamy looks of her and he was beginning to think he might have to use his Gorbals pool threshing machine action to get to the shore. Would it be cold in there?

He watched Hank fetching a long pole with a pike on the end of it, from the back end of the boat, and then starting to reach out, poked at the white ball. It seemed to toy with him; first it looked as if he could pull it back, then it would slip away. Frankie edged nearer. He thought that he could take Hank into the water with him. One leap and they both would be in the drink, accidental-like. Hank was now stretching, really stretching, as the paper ball seemed to be gathering pace in the wind.

'I'll end up in the drink, if I carry on like this,' Hank shouted in exasperation. 'Too bad. It's not my mess after all. '

He threw the pole back, on the deck, in disgust, as the white shape moved further away from the boat now, the capricious current seemingly playing tig with them. Frankie's sense of relief could have been discerned even by some of the seagulls who were now attacking the paper, mistaking it for food. One of them got to it. Another dived in to snatch it as well. Two more entered the fray, until there was a battle royal, producing loud screeches of rage. The ball had become shreds now; Mrs Rybak's machinations were sinking into St Andrews Bay like a large disintegrating jelly-fish. It was a sight which gave Frankie the confidence to step towards them again.

'Jilly, I wouldn't mind goin' ashore. Tam might have got lost.'

She pondered that for a moment.

'Hank,' she said eventually. 'Frankie needs a lift.'

'Sorry, my friend,' Gregory put in. 'We're very fussy about who comes and goes in this boat and what they take with them. No offence meant but could I see what you have in your pockets before we agree to take you anywhere?'

He surveyed the multi-pocketed coat up and down. Hank looked quizzical. Jilly looked slightly concerned. Frankie, unperturbed now, acted. He pulled at the wooden buttons quickly, took the coat over to Gregory and looking as if he was handing a donation to a collector of jumble for charity he said, with a barely concealed expression of relief, 'There we are. Feel free. There might be a moth or two in there but don't let that put you off.'

As he said that he could hear the seagulls giving vent to their frustration at having been denied the prospect of a tit-bit in the waters. It sounded like 'Hallelujah' in his ears. He was clean.

Gregory went through every pocket with no apology and as if he were breaking cover and not caring that he was showing another grimmer side to his personality. And Frankie had thought there was something appealing about him. When he had finished Frankie noticed that Jilly was looking disapprovingly at the searcher. But at that moment she said nothing. She's definitely on our side, he thought. They're not. So why were they partnering? Gregory gave up the task without a comment and Hank escorted him to the dinghy.

Hank climbed in first, but before they could move off, Jilly whispered, 'Your shoes. You've left them.' Embarrassed he turned back for them. As he passed her to get to the boat she looked at his feet pointedly and simply said, 'Take care.' It left him thinking, that if they mistrusted him so much, why was it so easy to get off the boat? Hank was a powerful rower. They moved quickly into the shallow waters near the short promenade leading up towards the town and carefully, with astonishing precision, made sure that he did not get his feet wet, by almost lifting him bodily on to a rock, from which he could step on to dry sand. Why were they so attentive? They're actually shunting him out of their own grasp. Is this for real?

He began to murmur those strange words to himself that he had worked out from the cryptic sheet, and repeated them over and over until he got strange looks from an elderly couple sitting on a bench overlooking the sands.

'Mornin'' he said politely to them. 'I'm looking for *Northpoint.*'

Chapter 21

The first thing that could not escape his attention, as he approached the cafe, was the declaration printed below the cafe's name. *Where Kate met Wills, (for a coffee).* He had to pause for a moment to grasp the meaning. When it sunk in he felt that this might be the nearest to royalty he would ever get. Where, precisely, did they park their royal bums, when they were both students in town, he wondered, as he entered and looked round the crowded interior, which felt as accommodating as a sauna, packed and humid as it was. 'Take me to the royal table,' he felt like asking one of the waitresses, as she almost skipped past him holding a tray-full of assorted drinks with the skill of a juggler. But when he saw a hand being waved from a corner and recognised Tam, sitting there with two other men, he barged past a small queue waiting for a vacant table, to accompanying protests. The two men were identically dressed in black with sunglasses that looked to Frankie as if they could withstand a direct laser beam. Surely not? Couldn't be! The two figures were still, straight, lifeless, but even from a few yards away he could tell if somebody touched them without permission they would probably break their arms. Tam was sitting in front of what looked like a large mug of steaming hot chocolate with something swimming inside it that looked like a melting marshmallow. It seemingly hadn't had a curative effect on Tam's anxiety.

'What the fuck happened?' Tam snapped, but clearly relieved to see him. 'We expected a call, for God's sake.'

'Battery's buggered,' he replied.

'So we're buggered as well then?' Tam asked aggressively, obviously shaken. 'We kept phonin'. We thought you would be takin' your time. That's all.'

'And time is of the bloody essence. Don't keep on about that.'

'We needed the decode, for God's sake.'

'You've got it.'

'Where?'

'Here,' Frankie replied touching his temple.

'Where exactly?'

'Inside the cranium.'

Frankie could barely take his eyes off the pair with the sunglasses.

'The what? Am I hearing right?' Tam shouted above the din of the cafe and betraying a slight lack of trust in what his friend's cranium, a favoured niche for many a fantasy, could deal with.

'Ay, I've memorised it.'

'Memorised it? You! You sing 'Flower of Scotland' every day of the week and you still haven't got the words right. What chance have we got? All right. Out with it.'

'Not here. Who could you trust in here? I'll tell it to Andrej. Only him.'

He was deliberately taking poll position on this and Tam was in no mood now to argue any further. Tiredness or exasperation or both was weakening his resolve to be assertive. Then Frankie lent forward and whispered.

'Are these two...the...you know who?'

'Ay, our YouTube cameramen.'

'So you think *I've* got explainin' to do,' Frankie said, 'I walk into this cafe and find you sittin' beside two men who've been hounding us for days, and who put us into YouTube without our permission and watch you slurpin' into that horrible mess of hot chocolate and marshmallows, and you believe I've fucked things up.'

Tam began an effort to get a grip of himself.

'All right. We'd better talk. Calmly.'

'You go ahead before I start on them,' Frankie said.

The Men in Black sat there sipping their tea like old maids watching first Frankie, then Tam, unburdening themselves to each other, with Tam explaining that he had been dead on his feet until they had brought him there for food and that Andrej had important preparations to make just in case things were to work out and in any case he didn't like to be seen in such a public place as *Northpoint,* and Frankie would be taken to meet him. Eventually Frankie turned to the tea-sippers.

'Do you two speak English?' he asked them. They both nodded together.

'Last time I checked we had over one million hits on YouTube because of you two. Big ratings these. How would you two like us to do you the same favour? Nothin' on except your sunglasses.'

The Men in Black turned towards Tam as if he could prompt them for a reply.

'Their English is not all that good,' Tam replied, and was thankful for that fact. 'Andrej is waiting for us. He is desperate for good news.'

Frankie looked around nonchalantly now at the royal mating nest.

'You know it wouldn't have sounded the same, would it?' he said.

'What wouldn't?'

'Kate met Wills...for a hot chocolate with marshmallows in it.'

'Move. Andrej says....'

'......time is of the essence, I know,' Frankie replied. 'And now, I think you are about to tell me we're goin' to be travellin' in a black Lexus, right?'

There was no need to answer that. It was outside. Suddenly it had changed its appearance. At that moment it carried no menace. Fear had been replaced by puzzlement. Sitting in the back seats, as the car purred away, they did not feel the sense of privilege the soft leather under their bums might normally have induced. Without communicating Tam knew that his mate with the fertile cranium would be asking himself the same question, 'What next?'

Sit tight. That was the first and only prerogative as they swept up a hill, away from the centre of the town eventually, driving between an avenue of trees, then turning sharply into a driveway at the end of which was a large greystone house which looked as if had been there before golf had been invented.

The Men in Black led them into a hallway whose walls were covered with portraits of solemn men wearing wigs, and in some cases holding what looked like scientific instruments. The floorboards creaked under their feet, as if the historic figures on the wall had actually trod the very same boards. There was a humming sound in the background like somebody had struck a note on an organ, and it had got stuck. Old though the house seemed, Tam sensed a freshness in the air. And as soon as they were taken into a large room with bay windows, overlooking the roofs of St Andrews, he realised that this ancient building had been gutted inside and that they were now in a modern air-conditioned lab. There were four men sitting there wearing white lab-coats. There were large widescreen desktops, glaring at them vividly, on the long desks in front of them. Set against a wall were an array of microscopes and small electronic boxes with various dials on them. That slight hum was still in their ears, as if a generator was at work. One of the men rose and came towards them.

'So, this is Frankie,' he said and stretched out his hand.

'It's you then,' was all Frankie could say to counter the unforced geniality of the approaching Andrej.

'Oh, I hope you are not too disappointed,' Andrej replied. 'And these are my associates without whom I could have done nothing.'

Frankie was almost in awe of this fugitive figure now, and felt strangely tongue-tied. The other three men simply nodded recognition in their direction.

'Welcome to our research lab. It is an off-shoot of the university. There has been scientific research here stretching back through the centuries. Before he wrote his *Origin of the Species* Darwin took some inspiration from the work around here, long before he wrote his famous treatise on evolution. You are on hallowed ground.'

Then he changed tack.

'You have it?' he asked.

'Eh, we have to explain something to you,' Tam said and squirmed..

'The fact is,' Frankie coolly joined in, 'I had to memorise it. I have it up here in my napper. Word for word.'

Andrej did not seem unduly disturbed. Was he the kind of man who could trust people quickly through instinct? He had to be, on this occasion.

'Come over to the window,' he said and led the way, as if he did not want the assistants in the lab to hear what was about to be said. They followed on to the large bay windows which gave them a panoramic view of the whole bay, stretching into the North Sea and towards the far green and brown Angus coast.

'First let me hear what you have,' he asked.

Tam was holding his breath. Frankie was closing his eyes. The wind was rattling the window panes. There was that hum in the background. There was a long pause as Frankie, still with his eyes closed, could be seen silently mouthing words. Then he spoke.

'Pickup behind Ragdale House. One mile down track in old farm-shed. Igor has left note. Eleven is the hour. Good Luck. God bless.'

He opened his eyes. Tam, looking at Andrej for some visible sign of reaction, was seeing a man who looked as if nothing could disturb his self-control. Not a muscle was twitching in him. The three of them stood there for some moments before Frankie spoke.

'That was it......I think.' he said, and then slowly repeated it so that they would realise he really had planted it fertilely in his head. Then he waited for the verdict.

It came gently. It came in the form of Andrej reaching out and holding Frankie's hand and simply squeezing it, once, then standing back almost in admiration of his lanky, gawky, flat-footed friend.

'It makes sense,' Andrej said simply. 'It fits. I now know what is to be done. I owe you so much, you two, so much.'

'Andrej, please,' Tam began in an imploring tone. 'What's this all about?'

He contemplated them for a moment then spoke.

'Look out there, towards the sea. There's going to be a deluge,' he said pointing to the east, over the darkening expanse of sea, and at a battalion of dark clouds assembling for its blitzkreig on the bay.

'I mentioned to you the origin of the universe and the evolution of our species. Just using your eyes now brings it to mind. Look at that coast line,' he added nodding towards the West Sands. 'Flat. Under threat. They are worried already about erosion down there. If sea levels continue to rise, and if we continue to think parochially, that putting up local netting will solve a problem that really has to be tackled globally, then who knows what it will be like in twenty, thirty years time. Would part of the famous Old Course disappear? It is very possible.'

'Fish in the Valley of Sin? They couldn't talk about birdies then,' Frankie said, almost to himself.

'Now look to the heavens,' Andrej went on. 'Think of space, of communication and how we are truly a global village. Sit at a computer and nothing is distant. So around us is a different kind of threat, passing through us unseen, but as threatening as that thunder approaching us now. It is a silent thunder. The thunder of a cyber world that threatens us all in ways that could drench us in such dislocation that our mundane ways of life could be turned upside down. Few of us are alert to the dangers. But, perhaps I sound too.......too hectoring about that to young people like yourselves. Sorry.'

He stopped and sighed. It was clear Andrej had not really lost the first bloom of youth himself, but he was obviously poised to make a further point, in the mould of a man of some experience. But Frankie's initial reserve, at meeting the man they had so desperately sought, suddenly reversed and he let fly.

'I ran a DVD in the computer on the boat. You were at a blackboard chalking up equations. Then you switched off the lights in the room. Then you switched them on again and went back to the blackboard. It looked a bit daft to me. Then you wrote something.'

There was a bench seat around the curve of the window. Andrej sat down obviously measuring his reply.

'I know about that tape of course. It fell into many hands. So let me put it firstly, this way,' Andrej went on. 'I am a physicist basically. Above all, I am a practical man. I ask people questions

323

like, "How would you feel if you could not boil an egg in the morning or heat your shivering body because of a sudden failure of power? How would you feel if you were on a jumbo-jet and could not land, even though you were running out of fuel because the radar and beacon systems were failing? How would anyone feel if all their personal details were transferred, without their knowledge, to someone else who could effectively obtain and exploit their personal identity? Take them over, in effect. I like to remind people of the humdrum acceptance of the internet, and also the catastrophic nature of cyber attacks. Coastal erosion will be but nothing if we cannot come to understand what the internet may do to all of us, long before the sea invades.'

'All that sounds a bit far-fetched,' Frankie interrupted.

'Pay heed, my friend. In 2007 the entire social and professional fabric of Estonia was invaded invisibly, through the internet, causing chaos. The state was put into limbo from which all kinds of problems ensued. Their computers had been flooded by what they call botnets. But let us not dwell on technical terms at the moment. The fact is, that the attack almost brought the professional life of that country to a standstill.'

There were good teachers, there were awful teachers, and you could tell that within minutes of them opening their mouths. Tam knew from experience. Even within a few sentences Tam had decided that Andrej was the kind he could sit and listen to for hours in a classroom.

'Individuals have to be concerned as well. In another case we know about, a man receiving treatment in hospital had his medical record hacked into. It was deliberately changed so that the new ward shift administered the wrong drug. He died. The hackers then changed the record back to the original, so that the nurse would be blamed for negligence. It was assassination by internet. Far-fetched? Yes, you are right. Perhaps it is better to realise that we do live in a far-fetched world which can be reached by simply tapping on a keyboard.'

The quality of his sentiments covered the fact that he hadn't answered Frankie directly, and in a darker mood he added only a minimal amount.

'These pictures you saw, were for some of my students. I was explaining something of my work to them, and of its purpose. It is not that I revealed crucial information. But I told them enough. Unfortunately, as I said, the tape wandered.'

'Jilly and her friends?' Tam said.

'I am assuming it was taken to a country which has an interest in these things. After that came the order to hunt me, perhaps not like pursuing a whale with a harpoon but more like trailing a wild animal who has to be tranquillised with a dart and then transported to a scientific zoo. German rocket scientists were sought after, on the conclusion of the Second World War. The big powers put on their safari jackets and went hunting.'

'So who is Jilly working for?' Tam asked.

'America,' Frankie said almost indignantly, as it seemed so obvious. 'They're CIA. It's sticking out a mile.'

'I think if you cannot tell for sure who is behind plotting of one kind or the other you tend to blame CIA or Mossad, the Israeli secret service,' Andrej said calmly. 'But I am not so sure in this case. There are other big players in this business. I am now thinking that Jilly is criss-crossing between loyalties, and I am not sure who she would work for now. In that sense it does not matter to me who they represent. I must keep myself clear of them all. No, I am preparing for another demonstration which I hope will awaken many people to the dangers of this new world.'

'We've had a fair share of danger in our own wee world,' Frankie put in.

'Oh, indeed! I have thought very carefully about you two. I suspect it would not be easy for me to tell you just to go off home now back to Glasgow. You have come a long way in more senses than one. And I clearly understand the interest you have taken in all of this and the bruises, probably mental as well as physical, that both of you have suffered. You certainly deserve more than just a sweet goodbye. I have to admit that I would not have been here, at this crucial moment, but for you two. So I have an offer. You can of course return to Glasgow right now, with my thanks and my blessing. But perhaps you would like to be in on a little bit of history. It very possibly might not be without its risks, but I have an uncanny feeling that I need you, above all, as my talismans. I believe in talismans. What say you?'

There was no need to consult Frankie on this.

'Where are we going?' Tam asked.

'The Isle of May,' Andrej replied. 'It is there I have to part with this world.'

* * *

Tam did not travel well on the back of that last remark. He did not have the heart in the first place to ask Andrej what he meant by it. To him it sounded like one of these ornate phrases that are meant to sound less scary than the real thing, like using 'kicking the bucket' to soften the meaning . Basically, if you snuff it, you snuff it, whatever you call it. On the other hand it might just have been loose language. By 'world' he could have meant the professional world he was involved in. Was he thinking of a career change? Did scientists have career changes? Whatever they did, they remained scientists. But like any others they probably got pissed off with their lot and needed like others to get out of the rut. That probably was it. Whatever, he could see this new trip had an expeditionary look to it. For Andrej had put on a thick Fair Isle sweater, the kind you might see in an old photograph of an aged fisherman, and he talked much more excitedly than he had in the lab, as if he was experiencing a rush of adrenalin, of the kind Tam's PE teacher had always said was an essential prelude to reaching maximum athletic performance. This was no game they were playing now. At the back of his mind there was another thought. Why had Jilly not tried to make contact by

327

phone? And why had Frankie, as he had related, managed to get away from them with such apparent ease given the heightened sense of suspicion which hung around that boat?

They were with Andrej in a large Mitsubishi 4X4. The Men in Black were behind them in the Lexus. They had no satnav, but they had obviously consulted local books before they left and had worked out where Ragdale House was. They turned inland, judging that they had travelled something like half an hour away from the coast. The only annoyance was the sudden presence of tractors which would suddenly swing out from fields without warning and command the narrow roads like the invasion of mechanical beasts. It slowed them down and agitated Tam and Frankie who were now on edge, keen to know what was to come next and would it upstage anything they had already experienced? Andrej though, never even tapped his fingers on the steering wheel, frustrated though he certainly ought to have been, stuck behind unthinking farmers who couldn't have realised that the Men in Black could take umbrage at lack of courtesy. Then they saw it. They could hardly miss the landmark; a large house with green shutters, in desperate need of coats of paint and re-plastering. Certainly, in contrast with other farmhouses they had seen around them, it didn't look as if it ever had anything to do with agriculture. Then they turned off the main road and drove for another mile down a rough track, towards a farm-shed which looked to be in the terminal stage of dilapidation. When they stopped, just behind it, they watched the Men in Black come from their car and kick at what looked like a padlock on the corrugated iron doors. The doors fell apart. They moved inside boldly then staggered out together, carrying what looked like a large, light-brown sack which was bigger than the average potato sack they had often seen being delivered at Gabby's. They followed that with a second, placing them both carefully in the boot of the Lexus.

Then they handed Andrej some notepapers that had come from the interior of the shed. He scrutinised them carefully before nodding his head in a sense of both relief and understanding.

'Igor is a reliable man,' Andrej said simply. 'So far so good.'

The light-brown coverings suggested that the bags contained either sand or concrete. It was all Tam could think of as they went on their way.

'There it is,' Andrej said as they reached the brow of a hill, shortly after, and looked down on the long stretch of the Firth of Forth. 'The Isle of May.'

He was referring to what looked like, from a distance, a tiny wedge of earth, out there in the middle of the wide estuary. As they drew nearer, it began to remind Tam of a large landing craft that might have decided to anchor itself there during the last war, its blunt nose of cliffs facing up-river towards the ring of hills, cuddling Scotland's capital Edinburgh, on the horizon, to the west.

'There was martyrdom on that island as well,' Andrej said. 'Adrian, a Hungarian missionary, was murdered there by the Vikings many centuries ago. They founded a monastery on it as a result. Now puffins and seals and all kinds of wild life rule there. Since arriving here it has been my sanctuary. A tiny island, dominated by the

329

temperament of the weather and the tides. Nature controls it, nothing else. Yet, on it, you can understand what the word 'freedom' actually means.'

He shut up after that, and lapsed into a deliberate silence as they glided down into Anstruther harbour. The seafront there comprised of a long street of sedate shops and houses, with a small marina inside a broad harbour, whose two long arms of jetties clutched a wide assortment of boats to its bosom. The forest of masts spearing the air were bobbing around like sensors, recording the capriciousness of the wind. Tourists were crowding the narrow single pavement and some had formed a long queue outside a fish and chip shop, the people standing there as if they were pilgrims about to visit a shrine, rather than to gorge themselves. On the far side of the harbour Tam could hear the sounds of a small carnival, as soon as he stepped out of the car. Children were screaming on the roundabouts in both dread and enjoyment. The Men in Black and Andrej paid scant heed to this, and busied themselves carting their gear towards a long ramp which separated two lines of boats. When Tam and Frankie offered to help, they were almost brusquely shooed away by Andrej's companions.

The boat was named *Marmion*. Without any word of explanation they began to board. It was of a different character from the launch they had left behind in St Andrews bay, with the covered controls having two swivel seats, behind which there were short stairs leading down to what looked like a very tiny cabin area. It clearly was an older boat though, and certainly not as sleek-looking or as plush inside as the *Angelina*. Andrej busied himself setting up two computers side by side on a small table in the middle of the living area. Tam watched the Men in Black stacking the large sacks near the bow of the boat, where, after covering them with a large tarpaulin, they secured them with a thick web of ropes to the railings. He could see them fussing over the sacks like men putting luggage on a car roof-rack, and then nodded their satisfaction.

Tam and Frankie went up on the small deck again as the Men in Black walked back towards their Lexus to collect something. Andrej was now engrossed in his computers.

'Well?' Frankie asked. 'What do you make of all this?'

'As if you think I've worked it all out,' Tam replied. 'He's only tellin' us so much. So far I'm puzzled about these sacks. Is that what they term ballast? Wish I knew more about boats. Keep your eye on the Men in Black. I'm going to have a look.'

Tam edged his way round to the bow with the help of a railing. Beneath him the tide was well out and he could see the bottom of the harbour as a brown scum. He looked back towards the car park but the two of them had gone inside their Lexus. It was evident that the sacks were tightly secure. But he was able to slip his hand under to lift the tarpaulin slightly in places. He circled the area, lifting and looking, but all he could see was the brown heavy-duty sacking covering the contents. Except at one corner he noticed small black print on one of the sacks which simply stated, CAN. He gave up and went back to Frankie. Not much to go on there.

Frankie was scrutinising the fish and chip queue with growing relish but, just as Tam felt a suggestion was about to be made by him about eating, Andrej's head emerged from the cabin, inviting them to join him. He had been looking at the map of the island.

'This is where we are heading,' he said. It was flat on the table. He reversed it so that they could see it clearly.

'We will land where the little pleasure ferry the *May Princess* lands. It is a tiny little inlet which can only take one boat at a time. The ferry will not be in operation tomorrow because the weather forecast is not favourable for them to berth with so many passengers on board. We are not as strapped as that. I will be setting to work as soon as we arrive. You are going to be invaluable. My two friends are going to be busy with another piece of work at the other side of the island. This is your part to play. I would like you to cover the two landing areas for me and to alert me to anything unusual you spot, either on the sea or on the island itself. I cannot be interrupted.'

'Doin' what?' Frankie blurted out. 'Feedin' the birds?'

'I wish it was a simple as that. I will be feeding into something to be more widely seen by many more people.'

'On that wee island? It just a piece of turf from here,' Tam went on.

'You'll be surprised. It doesn't really reveal itself until you get closer. Now let me show you,' Andrej said.

He opened the lid of the computer and already there was something on the screen. It was a picture of a small sandy bay with cliffs around. They were pictures from a web-camera. It was panning slowly along cliffs, then it would stop abruptly, focus on a bird, then move again.

'This is a recording I took some time ago. These pictures go out live on the internet 24/7. The camera out there is being operated remotely by a member of the public from the Scottish Seabird Centre in North Berwick, just over the water. You can just book a time, walk in off the street and be your own David Attenborough pointing to your heart's content at all that nature has in store out there These cameras are going to make a very considerable point for me.'

'What point?' Frankie asked.

'Let us say, a demonstration.' Andrej replied. 'It should capture an audience. But enough of that. I want to give you something.'

He reached behind him on the small couch and produced two white envelopes.

'This will pay any expenses for your return to Glasgow. It's very modest because I have been existing on hand-outs myself to complete my work. But you are due it. It'll get you back. I cannot thank you enough. Your staying power has been remarkable. You are credit to your country. But I have to admit something. The *Marmion* will not be returning. You will have to stay on the island overnight with my two friends and go back on the small ferry next day. I think the conditions will be fair by then. We have taken care of your passage. Now that I have told you that, once again I have to remind you that you are free to leave and go home right now. It is up to you.'

It was an offer he knew they would refuse, but at least it had been offered, maintaining Andrej's persona of decency.

'You just tell us what you want us to do now, 'Tam replied.

'I will tomorrow. I wonder if you could leave me here for an hour or so. I have some preparations to make. Please?'

They walked on to the wooden-spine walkway and strolled down to its end which put them at the epicentre of the small marina. The rank smell of seaweed dominated. It would cling forever, Tam thought. They opened their envelopes and found fifty pounds each there.

'The *Marmion* is not comin' back,' Tam muttered. 'Then where is Andrej Matskevich headin'?

In his mind was that haunting phrase, '...it is there I have to part with this world.' Perhaps he should have come right out and asked what that meant, back in the lab. But its very strangeness was off-putting. He couldn't have framed a question that would have made any sense.

'We could put the cash together and hire a taxi back down to Glasgow. End this all in style. How about it?' Frankie asked and probably meant it.

'A demonstration?' Tam mused, as if he hadn't heard Frankie. 'I wonder? What's in his mind?'

'Nothing would surprise me now,' Frankie replied. 'What isn't so surprising is the state of my stomach. I'm joining that queue.'

They both did. They ate their fish and chips eventually, out of small boxes, spearing the contents with tiny wooden stakes, fighting off impudent, garrulous seagulls who did not have the temperament to wait for the remnants, but were intent on mugging them. They could see the Men in Black sitting on a small bench, at the other side of the harbour, watching them, as they had obviously been doing for days, but for the first time they seemed a comforting line of defence. It was when they were strolling back to the boat that Tam's phone delivered its calypso ring. He knew instinctively it was her. But what he didn't expect was the sudden question.

'I suppose it would be a waste of my time to ask you two to turn round and go home, like right now?' Jilly asked.

'What?'

'You heard. We know where you are. Exactly.'

Tam found himself looking around as if she was standing at his back.

'You know?' he asked incredulously, sweeping his eyes round the holiday scene of passers-by crowding the narrow pavements along the harbour front and the throng sitting munching their fish and chips nearby. Where was she?

'You were tracked. We have a very sophisticated GPS tracking method to hand now. Gregory put a small adhesive pod on the sole of Frankie's trainers when they were on the boat. He would have felt nothing. An intermittent signal did the rest. Please, don't tell him. It may hurt his feelings.'

He looked at Frankie, then at his feet. They were once large feet. Now forever after Tam would see them as duped feet. He thought it would be better not to say anything, at that moment, since his mate was still in his fish supper bliss.

'Where are you?' he asked a slight shiver running up and down his back.

'Close-by, but out of sight.'

'You used us. Just like that. What kind of woman are you?'

'I didn't use you. They did. I had to find Andrej as well, you know, and in case you don't believe me, I am here to help him not to harm him.'

'We're finished. How could anybody trust you any longer? Piss off.'

'Wait. Hear me out, for God's sake.'

'Why? To listen to another load o' shit. '

'Gregory and Hank are not working for us any longer.'

'Us?'

'I was charged with finding out who they were really working for. That's why I was with them, snooping, listening, picking up everything I could about them. Well, I had a breakthrough in St Andrews. Everybody makes mistakes, even the best in this business, and they made one. They left an e-mail on their computer, forgot to delete it. It had a sound attachment. The voice was speaking Mandarin.'

'Mandarin? Chinese? How would you know mandarin?

'I know enough to identify it from Swahili, that's for sure. The Chinese are over everything now. Economic strength, technical know-how, ambition. It all goes together. I sent the e-mail to my friends for translation. It was enough. That pair had sold out. Probably they own a penthouse in Shanghai by now, for they certainly didn't do it for air-miles. Treachery can be a lucrative business and they are now in it big time. We had our suspicions about them for some time, and I had to play my part as po-faced as I could. Now I've slipped away. We berthed in a small harbour a couple of miles away in Cellardyke. When they were on their computers, I slipped ashore. I'm on my own now in a small hotel and there's nothing much I can do at the moment until I get some help.'

'And you want me to swallow all that?'

'I'm at the stage when I can only cross my fingers and hope that you take me seriously. That's why I'd like to see you get the hell outta there now. You've had your thrills.'

'Andrej is a friend now. We're not deserting him.'

After he had said that Tam felt that it might have sounded artificially noble and sentimental to her. But she didn't knock him.

'Sure he's a great guy. I know him only too well. And I want to help him.'

'You mean you want to get your hands on him. Are you any better than the Chinese? Really? If what you say is true?'

'The fact is he's a hunted man and for some time he's been up for grabs because of his talent. But I don't want to see him get hurt. That, believe you me, is the bottom line. Are you with me on that at least?'

'How could it be anythin' else? We've been helpin' him and we intend to stay and do exactly that.'

'In which case could you pray tell me what he's got stacked in the front of his boat?'

'How do you know that?'

'We had a quick look at the harbour an hour ago. We could see you inspecting it?'

Tam felt that shiver again.

'Nothing of much interest,' he replied.

'You looked interested.'

Tam felt no anxiety about describing what he found.

'Don't get too excited,' he said. 'They were bags of sand.'

'Sand?'

'You heard. Sorry to disappoint.'

'How do you know that?'

'Because I looked under the tarpaulin and felt the bags. Felt like sand when I pressed them.'

'Really,' she muttered as if in another train of thought and as if she didn't really believe that carrying bags of sand on a boat was meant to enhance beaches anywhere around as there were some glorious ones nearby. She was decidedly sceptical.

'Sand,' she muttered again. 'Tell me,' she went on,' any marks on the bags by any chance?'

So what? Tam thought.

'Only three letters stamped on. CAN.'

There was a silence that prevailed for so long he worried that the connection had lapsed. Then she spoke.

'CAN? Like C-A-N,' she said spelling it slowly.

338

'That's it.'

'CAN! Do you know what CAN most likely is?'

He found himself stupidly shaking his head.

'CAN stands for Calcium Ammonium Nitrate. In other words, fertiliser!'

'So what?'

When she spoke again her voice sounded placid enough but with a deliberation that added tension to the tone.

'You might have forgotten by now the Oklahoma City explosion back in 1995 and the bombings they suffered in Delhi in the past. That fertiliser was the basis for the making of those bombs. MI5 foiled a terrorist attack in London, a couple of years ago after they traced the plotters to the purchase of exactly that fertiliser. Its properties are well known. It can be gold dust for terrorists. If that has been deliberately primed you could all be sitting on a time-bomb. Does that merit your attention?'

'Tell me another,' Tam rebutted. 'I just won't swallow that. He's no terrorist. I'm not that naive!'

'Those two despicable rats I've been with won't go near him until they get to know where he's heading and what he's up to. And my friends won't be around until tomorrow. So I can't do much right now to establish that. I'm stuck. But he's not going far, that's certain. And in that respect he's not going to get away now that's he's been tracked here. So you have time to get your arses out of there and catch the next bus home. Got it!'

'No chance,' Tam replied. 'And you know that. Good try.'

There was silence again as if she was in a rethink.

'Something comes to mind. I want you to walk towards the harbour until you can get a clear view of the other side of the Firth. Please, do as I say.'

There was nothing for it but to obey. The Men in Black rose and started to walk towards him about a hundred yards away, as if they could not let him out of their sight. He moved round one of the clutching arms of the harbour until, beyond the Isle of May, he had a distinct view of the Lothian coast.

'Well?' he asked. 'What now?'

'You see that white building on the other side? It's tiny from that distance but it's pretty distinctive, isn't it? I've seen it so often from the Fife coast.'

'Sure. I see it.'

'That is Torness Nuclear Power Station.'

Then she clicked off. From that distance the nuclear plant looked like nothing more than a sugar lump waiting to be dropped into a cup of tea.

Chapter 22

There was no going back. If he had said anything about the impending pursuit as suggested by Jilly, Andrej might have ditched them for their own safety. Tam wasn't having that. He would even have stowed away, if it were possible in such a small boat, to see this through now. He and Frankie had come this far and deserved to be at least witnesses of the outcome, however dangerous that was likely to be. So he held fire. But there was another factor which came into play. Not for one moment had he felt threatened personally by Andrej, neither in his presence, nor in trying to fathom what may lie in store. Indeed even now, despite all the recent revelations, he felt comfortable in the physicist's presence. What's more, Jilly was now twisting his relationship with Andrej into knots with her own revelations. He was feeling far less comfortable with her now. So, she was split from the two on the boat now? All on the basis of stumbling across an e-mail? And she admits she was spying on spies, to boot. This is for the fucking loonies, he thought. And what was she trying to feed him, by bringing up the presence of the nuclear power station sitting on the other side of the estuary? If she was linking fertiliser containers stacked on a boat, with an inviting channel of water leading to a nuclear installation, it was pure fantasy stuff. Is that what she very cutely wanted him to think, without actually having to state it? In a short time, he had come to realise that if you want to stop people thinking clearly, feed their imaginations. He breathed not a word to them about Jilly's last phone-call.

As the *Marmion* edged out of Anstruther harbour just before lunch-time, on the tide, the following day, Tam was in no mood for idle banter, even though Frankie tried hard to amuse him by feigning sea-sickness, only a hundred yards out into the waters. Or was he feigning? The boat's bow was certainly responding to a lively sea, leaping up and down like it was clearing hurdle jumps and he had to admit he was occasionally feeling little squirms in his own stomach. The Men in Black sat impassively on the tiny rear deck. They could have been in the Clyde Tunnel for all the reactions they were showing to the speed, the spray, the coming and going of the sun, and the island increasingly inviting attention. Tam sat at the accompanying bucket seat while Frankie was behind him on a bench. Andrej sat at the steering wheel and was now talkative. The previous evening he had said little, other than a pleasant, 'Sleep well', to the pair of them and bedding down himself on a bench, just behind where he was now piloting. They had bunked in tiny beds downstairs. The Men in Black had stayed in their Lexus, like men in a television commercial, crazily beholden to a particular car.

'Good solid boat this,' Andrej was saying. 'Exactly what I needed. I have to be careful taking it into the island, because we go through a narrow passage towards the small jetty. That's the tricky bit. It's where the *May Princess* the ferry berths. It's called Fairhaven. The helpful confirmation is that it won't be sailing today because it is rough around the island. They never take chances in these conditions. Landing can be hazardous. We can't afford to be fussy. We have to chance it. Normally there is a warden on the island

342

but we know that he is on a visit to his head office in Edinburgh over the next couple of days. The island is clear.'

Tam was imagining Frankie was going white around the gills, as they splashed further on. The transformation of the island as they got nearer was astonishing. They suddenly became aware that it was bigger, longer, and higher than how it appeared five miles away in Anstruther. The cliffs suddenly emerged like they had simply sprouted up in the time since they had left the marina.

'I'm going to go right round the May before I berth. I want to make sure nothing else is tied up anywhere. Have a good look around. At this time of the year there are no puffins, they've gone and the nesting is over. But there's still plenty birdlife around,' Andrej shouted at them over the din of engine and wave splash.

Something was gripping at Tam, pulling him away from thoughts of fertiliser, nuclear plant, Men in Black, Jilly and the two men, Mrs Rybak's notes, Andrej's mission. It was simply what he was now beholding. What had been, from the distance, a morsel, was now taking grandiose shape. He could see sharp-edged cliffs that looked as if they would be impossible to scale, rock formations of such variety he could have believed that some giant had wrestled with the island and squeezed it into submission, leaving it with the legacy of wildly varied structures, such as those standing as thin spears pointing sharply to the skies, or one which looked like a giant totem pole that would stand there till the end of time, or others with such twisted deformities that they reminded him of the creatures Luke Skywalker had come across in the bar in *Star Wars*; and, in stark contrast, tiny sheltered bays which surely would have attracted privateers on the run from the customs in days gone by; and, all around it, its birds, speckling the air with their swoops and dives; below all that, seals, surreptitiously emerging from the sea on to rocks, then sliding back again to disappear under the water with the kind of ease that incurs envy in human swimmers. It brought to mind a traffic intersection, a Spaghetti junction of wild life.

'This is where we come in,' Andrej shouted and slowed the engine after skilfully taming the buffeting they were receiving and eluding the nastiest of rocks. There was a long avenue of them forming the inlet they had to slip through. One large, fat seal lay so close to them as they neared the jetty that Tam could have reached out and touched it. 'Do you know that some people believe that seals are really the souls of drowned sailors?' Andrej said softly and with an obvious respect for that odd belief.

The fat one simply stared immovably back at him, with a 'Get Lost' look on its whiskered face, although he would never look at another one again without thinking of shipwrecks. Then, slowly, carefully, Andrej eased the boat over the last few yards until it bumped gently against the concrete jetty. The Men in Black had leapt over the side and secured the boat to its mooring position.

'We have to go uphill,' Andrej indicated, as they stepped off.

There was a well-worn path in front of them, and as they passed a small wooden tourist office which seemed closed for the day, they began to see a building emerging above them, at what looked like the highest point in the island. He had been so distracted by the sights of nature that he had not really noticed it from the sea. At first glance he thought it was a town-hall that had been lifted from some main street, but then the tiny turrets at one of its wings even suggested a mini-replication of a Scottish baronial castle. It had a walled approach, and from its large square base, a castellated tower emerged, on top of which sat a huge, caged glass bowl, like an unattended boil.

'This is the old lighthouse,' Andrej said when they reached it. 'It's defunct now. An extraordinary building. It doesn't function any longer because they have two smaller ones at either end of the May. I wanted to bring you here because you can see most of the coastline from here. Help yourselves. Have a look.'

Tam and Frankie started to wander. They walked round the base of the building, all the time looking out to the vast expanse of sea, which was starting to look like it was getting nasty, the scalloped edges of the white horses displaying the mad ferment that the wind was whipping up.

As they took all this in, they could hear Andrej beginning to shout into a phone, the wind carrying his voice round the side of the old lighthouse, as if they were standing in a wind tunnel. Obviously the elements were making it difficult for him to be heard, by whoever he was in contact with. But they did hear one word distinctly, interspersed as it was with indistinct chatter, 'Torness'. Tam pulled Frankie away as he was about to walk back towards the other three.

'Stay a minute,' he said, 'I have something to tell you.'

It was then Tam had to come clean with Frankie. He described in detail all that Jilly had said to him the previous evening, down to her maddening conclusion and mention of Torness, and which, now that he had heard it again, coming from Andrej's lips, added to his confusion. He even had the courage now to tell Frankie about the tracking from the sole of his shoe. Frankie whipped the trainers off, and after examining the sole of his left one, poked out a tiny almost transparently thin little pod which he held with a grimace, as if he had just discovered the kind of dog shit discussed on *Jilly's PI*.

'That's why they almost threw me into the dinghy,' Frankie said woefully. 'They just sat there and watched me all the way. I feel unclean,' he added, shuddering. 'Ach,' he went on, 'Stanley would have found Livingston a bloody sight sooner if they had one of these things back then. I suppose this is progress,' he said, trying to be charitable to technological advance, even as he hurled the pod into the air like it was indeed filth.

'Never mind that,' Tam said. 'You've heard what I've had to say. Who do you believe? Her, with that line about ditching the other two men. Or Andrej and the Men in Black, here with us. We're in no man's land.'

'Then how about staying there,' Frankie replied, putting the trainers back on. 'Maybe we should make ourselves scarce, find somewhere to hide.'

'With a boat down there that might be carrying explosives? We'll have to come up with something better than that. Imagine ducking out of it all now. No way. We have to come down on one side or the other. First thing though, is to be up front with Andrej.'

When they walked back to the other side Andrej was in deep discussion with the Men in Black. 'I have something to say,' Tam said, butting right into the middle of their conversation. 'Like, right now!'

They were taken aback by this abruptness, but broke up their huddle and stood listening.

'I spoke to Jilly last night. On the phone. She thinks you have fertiliser on the boat which could be turned into explosives and I think they will come after us because it hasn't taken too much for them to work out where we are heading. Another thing. I'm very sorry. I've been so fucking selfish. I didn't want to tell you about something else I learned on the mainland,' Tam said nervously.

'What?'

'That they put a tracking device on the sole of Frankie's shoe.'

They all looked at Frankie's feet. He did a kind of sliding movement of embarrassment that looked a bit like Michael Jackson's 'moonwalk'. Andrej soaked in what had been said, but did not appear as edgy as he should have been, merely muttering at first, 'I see.'

Tam was about attempt to explain his motive for that but instead Andrej took over.

'I think you might have believed I would have ditched two stowaways on the harbour-side on learning that. Correct? You wanted to see the end, the finale. It's me who encouraged that. So without knowing it I was complicit in you holding your silence on that. And in any case, knowing it yesterday would have made no difference. It was too late. By that time they would have followed me anywhere on the sea. I did think we would have a good day and night's start on them, after breaking cover, and everything would be over before they even saw a single rock on this lovely place. That is not to be, so we must prepare for them coming, for they will certainly come now.'

Andrej had read his thinking brilliantly. If the scientific mind of which Tam was in the embryonic stage could lead to unemotional reasoning like that, then Andrej was now a model for him. But he still had to speak up.

'The explosives,' he blurted out.

'The fertiliser? Oh, yes, many things can be done with such a substance. Trust me it is being put to good use. You will not be harmed. Nobody will be harmed. I assure you of that. It will bring not so much as a blush to your cheeks. I can explain just a little bit. You are owed that much. My plans have to be carried out in three stages. Three specific stages. Stage one is simply arriving here safely. So bear with me and above all trust me.'

Perhaps it was the setting on this wind-swept island. But his words did carry a kind of dignity that quelled most of their doubts. But only so far as determining not to be a passive spectator to what might ensue. He was on red alert. Andrej waited for a response. Tam simply nodded genially at him. Frankie squirmed on his duped feet. They were with him, up to a point.

'The map please,' Andrej said.

One of the Men in Black produced it from one of the bags.

'This is the island,' he said pointing to it spread out on the grass. 'There are two recognised landing areas. The one we're at now, and this one on the other side facing down towards Edinburgh. They call that one the Altarstones. That's a landing where you have to climb a steep ladder to get on the island proper, depending on the tide. But it's do-able, with a bit of risk, even on a choppy day like today. Then there's the cove further down the cliffs on the same side. That's possible for a landing, but maybe unlikely. So I want the pair of you to keep to the high ground to make sure you can see around the island for any traffic heading our way. If you see anything then we've got to know. Right away. Because, for sure, they will come now. In fact, in some way it would be just as well they came. But it's the timing that matters.'

Tam felt a little tremor passing through him at the thought of some kind of confrontation. He sensed it would not consist of a diplomatic pow-wow. He thought again of the dead lawyer by the Clyde, and with Mrs Rybak's persistent presence superimposed on that, it set him off thinking about how to make an anagram out of the word, 'Mayhem'.

'What's part two and three of this plan of yours?' Frankie asked. 'If that's not too much of a strain on you to explain.'

'Parts two and three will be non-existent unless we handle part one properly. We intend to do exactly that before any further explanations. Here,' Andrej added reaching into the bag. 'A pair of binoculars each. We have work to do.'

They moved uphill then split up, Frankie heading for the landing place on the other side of the island and Tam straight down the middle toward the cliffs. When he got to a high spot he surveyed the sea, firstly with the naked eye. There was a tanker churning up towards Edinburgh and small boats dotted around, showing little interest in heading for the island. Over on the Lothian coast, towards the nuclear station, he could see two naval vessels which looked as if they were criss-crossing each other's path, like engaging in some exercise. Then he raised the binoculars to his eyes, identifying the ensigns clearly and men on deck in various duties. He turned in the opposite direction. It was then he saw it. At first it was like spotting white-horses charging at a cluster of rocks. Then he focussed properly. It was the *Abigail* from St Andrews Bay.

Except it was static. There was no movement. Nor could he see any figures on board. It seemed to be drifting aimlessly. The magnification got him so close he could almost see some cracks in the paint-work. But it seemed deserted. It was making no movement towards the island and it certainly did not seem to represent a threat of any kind. That mystified him. But it was nevertheless in the vicinity. He needed to get back to the boat to warn them.

As he walked down towards Fairhaven the heads of two seals glided through the inlet towards the boat, gracefully, smoothly. If only he could develop that ease in the Gorbals pool. Their movement seemed effortless and he wondered what provided the dynamic for such elegance, as they neared the landing. Except that, scandalously bereft of much knowledge of wild life as he had, he did know that seals did not have the capacity to climb from water and begin to walk on two legs, as they were now doing at the side of the *Marmion*. The seals had become human.

Garbed completely in black wet-suits, two figures were now on the jetty, their pace clearly dictated by caution. Tam stopped for a moment, still finding it difficult to digest this. Nature had given the figures camouflage and now they were only a few yards from the boat.

One of the Men in Black came out of the cabin and proceeded to edge towards the heap at the front where the tarpaulin had been taken off. He didn't reach it. He toppled forward as if he had been tripped, slipping and slithering into the water, as if an invisible hand had pushed him. It was a hand more visible though. It belonged to the leading figure. In it was a gun, which had just disposed of one of Andrej's stalwarts. Tam could not move now. Even if there had been a point in rushing down there, his body was refusing to budge, his legs immobilised. He was so scared he was fighting against peeing himself. He heard a bellow coming from the *Marmion*. It seemed to tilt and rock violently from side to side. The other Man in Black came rushing out like an enraged bull, but he got no further than the edge of the boat's deck before he was felled in exactly the same manner, his body twitching at first, then becoming incredibly still, like it had just formed a bridge between the boat and the jetty. The two figures moved forward and stood like sentries over that body, but both pointing guns towards the cabin, from which Andrej slowly emerged. He looked astonishingly calm. He stared down at the body in front of him, making the transition from the eager scientist with a mission, to that of a man cornered, humbled and having to submit. There was no movement in that tableau, for what seemed like minutes, until Andrej slowly sat down on the tiny bench, crossed his legs, looked despairingly at the two corpses, then sat back, as if his fate was sealed and the next move was up to his attackers. Both of their head coverings came off.

Hank and Gregory now looked different to Tam; like strange creatures from the seabed initiating a take-over of humanity. He crouched against a dyke that run upwards towards the middle of the island, then peered round it to see that the two men were still standing over Andrej. They were talking. If he hadn't witnessed the horrific deaths of the two men who kick-started this whole affair, he might have thought he was looking at three friends relaxing and swapping stories about the day's fishing. The turmoil was scouring Tam's inside. Nausea, deep within, had taken possession. He started his deep breathing as advised by Frankie, to see if that helped. He got over the initial phase of shock and began to feel calmer.

He couldn't just sit there. The compulsion to move towards the boat, rather than away from it, was almost overwhelming though. They were talking and he wanted to hear. Was Andrej in league with them after all? He had to know. He saw that he would be able to crawl down behind rocks on the side opposite to where the *Marmion* was berthed, and had to take a gamble that he wouldn't be seen. It was a risk, of course. He left the binoculars propped against the wall and moved. The grass was dry at that hour. The rocks he aimed for were varied in size and height and he scrambled between them without losing sight of the boat. But they were definite cover. He reached a clump of sizeable rocks level with the *Marmion*, then without any great effort and, uncomfortable and hard on the knees though it was, he propped himself up against two rocks which formed a kind of U shape together, with another in front, which could have pleased a secretary as a desk, and, pressing himself into a wedge between them, he settled in.

Although the sea still murmured and whispered and splashed around him the voices were borne comfortably over the narrow-spaced inlet, as if they were in a tunnel that amplified the sound. He ventured a quick look over the 'desk' and saw they had done nothing with the bodies. One was floating like a large water-plant, face down, bumping gently against the side of the boat in unison with the dictates of the tide which seemed now to be going out. The other was strewn across the edge of the boat to the jetty.

'Frankly,' was the first word which Tam picked up. It sounded like Hank. 'Frankly, you've been a very lucky man so far. A lot of time and trouble and expense has been spent on looking for you. How you were able to last so long I just don't know. That Mrs Rybak must be some smart cookie if she was the one pulling your strings all those years, even from her death bed, Jilly tells us.'

'Where is Jilly?' Andrej asked.

'Ah, now there's a tale,' Hank answered. 'You might be better asking "Who is Jilly?" There was never ever going to be a last leg for Jilly with us. We knew she had been put in to check us out. And she knew we knew. She played along and so did we because it suited us. She was working for others but if it meant shortening the search, then so be it. We used her, she used us. Even to the extent of having to accept those two lads butting in. Shrek and Homer, we called them.'

Which one of us was supposed to be Shrek? Tam wondered, in added discomfort.

'That's the way it goes,' Hank went on. 'She's obviously skilled in those things but when push comes to shove, you have to act. We ditched her. She ditched us. We could have blown her head off if we had wanted to but in this business when you are still in the bargaining business you have to keep all your options open. Until we get bucks in our hand, she is still an opening to others. The parting of the ways wouldn't get in the way of what we intended to do anyway.'

'You are all insane,' Andrej said with a sharper edge to the comment. 'Don't you understand? I am no magician. I don't have a trick up my sleeve. I am a scientist working hard putting certain theories into practice, that's all. I have no quick fix like these crazed scientists you see in a Bond movie. It is perspiration not inspiration that drives me.'

'We don't care if they want you to run a hamburger stall,' Hank replied. 'If they think you're worth a few bucks, and they're prepared to pay, then we are at their beck and call.'

'Who's prepared to pay?'

'They will tell you when you eventually meet up, so next step is, we get you out of here.'

A large bird came and settled down on a rock only a few feet away from Tam. He guessed it was a seagull, but bigger than he had ever seen before. Maybe it was of a different species but it seemed it didn't like Tam's presence, looking at him like the intruder into this sanctuary that he certainly was. He had heard of seagulls becoming more belligerent with the public, and the huge size of the beak nature had provided it with reminded Tam of the biology class catch-phrase that kept surfacing, 'the survival of the fittest.' Such unprecedented closeness made it look as if it was fit to pierce armour-plating with such a beak. The bird's body was quivering, and it looked at him threateningly.

'Not that it matters any longer, but what crazy scheme had you cooked up for this little paradise?'

It was Gregory's voice this time.

'Nothing that you would understand,' Andrej replied. 'And may I say that I work for no one against my will, and I think it is very foolish of your backers to think I would.'

'Wait till you hear their terms before you get so high and mighty about all of this. I suspect they will give you whatever you want to carry on your work.'

'They will not be able to give me my friends' lives back again, will they? Unless they have technology, of which I am unaware.'

The bird inched forward. At least that is what Tam thought it did. Weren't birds like this supposed to be scared of humans? Behind it, the sea was getting rougher as the wind strengthened. It was time he did something with his feathered companion. He reached out with his hand and waved a silent 'Shoo' at him. It squawked and leapt like a rocket and swung away over his head towards the jetty. The sharp noise jolted Tam and he slipped, causing some loose rocks beside him to cannon off each other and splash into a small rock-pool. They couldn't possibly have missed that sound. Tam contrived a quick glance above the 'desk' and saw all three looking in his direction. Gregory moved first, slowly, as if assessing carefully what action to take, then jumped from the boat onto the jetty, gun in hand.

Tam turned. He had few options as he positioned his feet ready to flee. Now that they knew where he was, to return up the hill would put him into an area where there was no real cover except the buildings at the top, and as they had guns and wanted to use them, then opting for that route, he had no chance. It was the rocks on the beach he headed for again. His first leap caused him to stumble because the receding tide had left most of the rocks slimy, and sheathed in a green residue they had become treacherous. He leapt from rock to rock though, with an agility he thought might be to his advantage, against the bigger heavier figure just behind him. All that training he indulged in weekly might pay off for him now. These were only fleeting thoughts of consolation though. He had to remain optimistic as he reached an even narrower inlet than Fairhaven with what seemed deeper water though and which in effect was like a large, deep, rock-pool. On this side of it there was a small overhang, jutting out to sea, almost like nature had provided a diving-board for the rock-pool.

He turned quickly and his prediction was right. Gregory was finding it difficult keeping his feet and even had he wanted to use his gun, which clearly and thankfully he seemed constrained to do at that moment, it would have been difficult to effect a balance for accuracy. Killers maybe didn't need much of a footing though. But he had to shake him off somehow. He edged round the rock-pool and when he reached the other side, saw how dark it was down there in the water. Then there was the overhanging ledge which intensified the opaqueness. Time to take a risk. He took breath and jumped.

He had never before entered water fully clothed, his Barca jacket seeming to bloom and bubble outwards, like it was ungratefully desperate to separate from him. After the initial shock the water did not seem as cold as he thought it would be. Or was it the sheer excitement of the moment that was insulating him? He pulled himself under the ledge, only his head above water, although he could feel the churning bottom of shingle and sand at his feet. He waited. The sea was chattering at the rocks further out from the pool, as the tide was definitely pulling away. It was hard to sift out a trace of Gregory from the bickering of waves and birds and wind around him. But then he heard the uncertain feet, immediately above on the ledge. The murderer of the lawyer had reached it. Tam could also tell he was taking stock. And unless he was an absolute idiot, and he doubted that, he would take an interest in the pool. So he had to remain still. Anyone trying to see under the ledge would have to risk leaning over. And that is exactly what he felt Gregory would do.

He heard shuffling. With the angle of the sun occasionally breaking out, in spasms, from the ink-dark clouds above, he was offered glimpses of reflections of above. In one instance he could see the large shape mirrored in the water like a liquid statue, legs apart, gun held about hip level. It was a shape of suspicion, or indecision. But, for the moment, it seemed reluctant to move any further. You cannot really sweat underwater, especially not within waters edging the North Sea, but he felt like he was sweating now. The way he had acted in the lane in the first place had astonished some. They could not understand the power of impulse. He couldn't understand it either. It just took over. That was the sort of thing that could shorten your life, seemed to be the view of Sammy and Gabby.

Too bad, he thought, as the vision of his Barca jacket being ruined by salt water flashed through his mind, and impulse, in its reckless way took command. He pushed himself out from the ledge, and with Gregory looking outwards and around, Tam grabbed at a leg and pulled like he was the anchor in a tug o'war team. Gregory did not fall in. He fell back. Unprepared as he was there was something like a snort, then Tam heard a soft thud and a choked, gargling noise, from above. Tam dragged himself upwards, using the ledge as a grip, now well beyond caring what was in store for him. He could hardly believe this bampot had been laid so low. Gregory was in obvious agony, holding the side of his head with blood streaming down his face, his eyes closed tightly, his mouth buckled, his body in repetitive shivers, like he was succumbing quickly and about to lose consciousness. The rock just behind him looked like it had been splashed with dark-red paint. To his side, lying there like a harmless piece of singed driftwood, was the gun.

He still looked down at Gregory, who was bleeding profusely and irregularly convulsing. Had he been a friend, Tam would have been concerned with what he was seeing. As it was he felt nothing. It was time for calculation. There was a long pause as he looked back to where the jetty was. He could see the top of *Marmion*, but nothing else. Then he looked down at the gun. He took a step forward and lifted it. He held it, at first, like he was scared it might give him an electric shock. There was no way he could tell what kind of pistol it was and held it between his thumb and index finger with a feeling of distaste. It had been used to kill people after all. But it was irresistible. It fitted into the palm of his hand surprisingly snugly, almost as if it had willed him to do so. Tam then noticed one of Gregory's legs shaking like it wanted release from the rest of his frame. He was in a really bad way. It was time to indicate to Hank that events were not working out as they had thought. The gun is now yours, he thought to himself, with a sense of unexpected power lending him renewed confidence.

Tam started to move back towards the boat, stepping over the now inert body and getting eventually into a position where he could clearly see Hank standing over Andrej. He stood legs apart, and the incidental tuition of how to use a gun he had accumulated, in the many movies he had seen, was all he had to go on. Hank was busy ramming some point home to Andrej. All Tam had in mind was to shoot and hit the rocks behind the jetty. He felt the rippling vibrations of his pulses as he raised the gun, holding it in both hands, like he supposed was the ideal stance, his finger gently on the trigger. Then he fired. Twice. In quick succession. And the sharp crack was echoed by ricochets in amongst the rocks on the far side and both shoulders felt jerks, like after-shocks. His body reverberated, not with the power of the shot, as much as the tension being released in a flood. He saw Hank ducking, then raising his head again, until Tam knew he had been spotted. Then he turned back amongst the rocks and sped past Gregory's body still lying near the pool. He heard something whining past his head and the crack of something hitting a rock just behind him. He turned away from the sea, and on better grass footing, pounded the earth as he headed up towards the wall where he had left the binoculars.

He calculated that Hank would find Gregory and make an effort to revive him. That would give him time to take breath and work out what to do next. He was shivering. The clothes he wore now had a chilling clamminess around him. He waited a few minutes then raised his head to look down towards the boat with the binoculars. Neither Hank nor Andrej were there. The deck was clear. He edged closer and then could see the head of Hank kneeling near the pool, obviously tending to Gregory. But the boat seemed to be rocking slightly and as he looked at one of the portholes he saw Andrej's face. It looked like he had been locked into the cabin under the deck. Keeping his eye on the area of the rock pool, Tam bent and ran, holding the gun-butt tightly in his palm, but his hand well away from the trigger. When he reached the boat all thought of his own safety dissolved as he pushed himself towards the small door which led to the cabin.

'Andrej,' he hissed. 'You there? Andrej?'

'Be careful. Look after yourself,' came the reply. Again unhurried, unruffled.

'Stand clear,' Tam said. 'I'm going to kick at this.'

He slammed his trainer, in open studs, red-card-tackle style, against the door. Three times he struck it until there was a splintering sound and it burst open. Andrej calmly looked at him before pulling himself out. His eyes fell on the gun in Tam's hand which he was holding away from his body in obvious distaste.

'What happened?' Andrej asked.

Tam described the events at the rock-pool. Andrej looked over the rocks. They could just see Hank's head in the distance.

'All I did was fire to scare the shit out of him. I had to. I'm still shakin'. Jesus! Me with a gun. I still cannae believe it.'

His hand gave him this odd sensation that he had just pulled it out of a pan of boiling fat.

'Give me the gun, please,' Andrej asked, with extraordinary politeness. He took it, clambered over the body of his colleague, which still had not been touched, and walked calmly to the rocks which he negotiated tentatively, but with a sure foot. Tam saw him make his way slowly to where Hank seemed deeply involved with Gregory. Then he dipped out of sight. Tam listened. There was nothing in his ear but the wind and the cackle of some birds. Then he heard two sharp cracks. One quickly after the other, followed by a long screech, that could have come from a bird, or from a man in pain. Then he saw Andrej re-emerge from among the rocks, walking calmly away from that spot, his back to the rock-pool, and any imminent danger, like a matador turning his back insolently on the bull. When he reached the boat again he seemed no different from the man who had left a few minutes before.

'Will you help me with the bodies of my colleagues?' he asked politely as he put the gun down on the floor of the deck.

Tam was about to respond, and bend down to assist, when his attention was distracted. On the hill coming down towards them, yelling like he had the hounds of Baskerville after him was Frankie. Tam could tell he was not the bearer of glad tidings.

Chapter 23

Frankie had been won over by the birds as he had moved towards the Altarstones landing. The binoculars were giving him close-ups of contentment. No wonder men had always wanted to fly. He watched fascinated as they swooped and circled and rested and pecked and then started the whole process over again, using the rocks like they were refuelling stations. He had often wondered why people would spend hours gazing at them just as he was now. Now he understood. This was like being offered a view of a restless and fascinating world to which he was denied entry. The cliffs proclaimed that most of all. Birds used them as easy resting places, while he shuddered at the thought of the sheer cliff-face he was looking at. Then he spied the plunges into the sea. Birds like spears diving straight under water. He saw so many indulging in such acrobatics, that he almost felt like a judge at a diving contest, awarding points for execution and entry. What was it they called them again? He wasn't sure. He was certainly not a walking encyclopaedia and the island, at that moment, was Google free.

Then he saw it. It was orange in colour. At first it was just a speck. Then it grew in size. It was a very fast-moving boat. There were five people on it. He trained his binoculars on them as the boat swung round to make an entry into Altarstones landing. It slowed down as it slid in towards the concrete jetty from which a path led up between a cleft in the cliffs, towards the lighthouse. He didn't wait to see them berth, but took off like a youngster of old running to report a sighting of the Vikings, who had once vanquished the island. He

363

moved closer to the lighthouse and from that vantage point used his binoculars to look down at Fairhaven. What he noticed firstly were two bodies. One was lying across the side of the *Marmion*. The other was floating beside it. Tam was crouched on the deck. Then Andrej came into vision, clambering over the side of the boat, but with a gun in his hand. All this was difficult to take in. He certainly wasn't hallucinating. What had happened in such a short space of time? He was floundering for an understanding. Oh, to be a bird! But at least he had legs. Just before he started to run, he turned to look back, and saw, behind him, the first head rising into view from the Altarstones landing.

***

'They've come,' Frankie shouted.

'Who's come?' Tam answered.

'Five of them. The boat they were in was like a tornado. You should have seen the speed.'

'Never mind the speed. Who are they? Where are they?'

'They landed at Altarstones and they're making their way here. I'm positive about that.'

Andrej became active.

'If we can get the two bodies on to the deck, I could just about manage to sail out of here before the tide goes fully out. Help me.'

Touching corpses was not an experience they would have volunteered for. And, in lifting them and positioning them on the deck, they were discovering the awesome power of inertness, as they struggled to manhandle the dead weight and at the same time fight against nausea. It was also taking them longer that they had imagined. Andrej fussed about in the cabin for some time, then came back on the deck, as if he was about to say a farewell. He did not get the chance. They heard the megaphone, clearly and distinctly.

'Please, stop what you're doing,' the voice rasped. 'We are police. Come off the boat, please.'

Five figures were moving towards them. They could see Andrej making a calculation about getting the engine started and getting out of there. But they could also tell that he was not really prepared for such an abrupt departure. It was not a surrender he was offering. It was more a simple acceptance of his fate. No hands were raised. He simply put them in his pockets as the figures descended quickly on them. One of them looked distinctly out of sorts in a wrap-around orange life-jacket. It did not suit Jilly.

She was beside the man with the megaphone. That face stimulated a quick series of images. The doctor's house. The man with the grey streak in his hair. Sammy's gym. The harsh talking there. Special Branch. Bullish type. It was Alex. They were all wearing life-jackets.

'So you couldn't take a telling!' Alex roared at Tam as they neared the *Marmion*. 'Now look what you've got yourself into. What a fucking mess! Could you not keep your noses out of this?'

'Alex,' Jilly interrupted,' give them time to take breath, for God's sake man.'

At that moment Tam felt flummoxed. Who was Jilly now? She knew somebody in the Special Branch by his first name? He thought he had been prepared for anything about her. He could not have been more disorientated if he was discovering she was really a hit-woman from the Mafia. Andrej was first to respond to their appearance on the jetty.

'There are two men out on the rocks over there,' he said. 'One of them has a head injury. Very serious. The other has injuries to both knees. They will need assistance. One of them will still be armed but is going nowhere, given what has happened to his knees. And......you might take into consideration the fact that they murdered the two men you can see here.'

'Andrej Matskevich?' Alex demanded sternly.

'Yes, of course, that is me,' Andrej said pleasantly.

'I have to detain you. You are in this country illegally and you will have to answer.....

'Just you wait a minute,' Jilly interrupted. 'We have an agreement. There has got to be a lot of talking with Andrej before you initiate something like that, or else there is going to be a diplomatic storm, believe you me. Now stand by the agreement.'

So, that's what it's like being on the same side? It was clear that Jilly had some leverage, of some sort, over the Special Branch man. A coalition of unequals. Alex did not contest the point with Jilly, but rerouted his anger to the other two men with them.

'Get over to the rocks and see to that pair,' he snapped. 'I'll join you in a minute.'

Then he himself stepped into the boat and looked at the bodies and at the pistol.

'That's a Sig Sauer P226,' he said, impressed, or wishing to impress. 'That's one of the guns the Seals used to take out Osama Bin Laden.'

And Tam had used it. He suddenly felt very mature, an illicit feeling he was sure, but it was there.

'We'll have to get that body out of the water,' Alex went on. 'But leave them be, until we get back,' he said, then edged round the boat to the bow to look at the large carbuncle shape there. He pulled at the canvas and snapped again at Jilly.

'This is it?'

She nodded.

'I'll be back,' he said vaulting on to the rocks in pursuit of his colleagues.

'Go inside,' Andrej said noticing Tam's increased shivering. 'There's a small cupboard at the back. You'll find an old track-suit of mine there. Dry yourself and change. I know you must hate parting with your Barca identity, but there is a time and place for such a transformation.'

Tam was glad of the offer, and moved into the cabin, stripped, and grabbed eagerly at a towel, then pulled at the cupboard. Various items fell out including a large flashlight and maps. Then he noticed a large sports-bag lying at the very back of the cabin, half open. He looked in for the track-suit, but what he found was sub-aqua gear. The suit, the oxygen cylinder, the flippers. All in pristine condition.

And clearly not there for decoration. The track-suit had been pulled out and was jammed between the bag and the wall. He put it on and felt the warmth relaxing him. He went back up and noticed Jilly poking around the hump at the bow herself, lifting up the tarpaulin sheet and peering under it. Frankie edged forward.

'Well,' he whispered to Andrej and Tam, 'that's it. All over then? Finito?'

'Have faith,' Andrej whispered back to them. 'There will be a way out. There always has been for me.'

Chapter 24

Tam kept his eyes on Jilly as they walked up the hill towards the lighthouse. She had said to him briefly, on the jetty, 'We need to talk.' You bet, he thought. They had left the three officers, whom they now took to be Special Branch, busying themselves at the crime scene, having escorted a crippled Hank and carried a barely conscious Gregory, back to the boat; Hank in no mood to offer any resistance and Gregory fit only for the ministrations of a brain surgeon, it seemed. The boat was high and dry, the tide having gone right out. So they were making for the lighthouse, Jilly having apparently gained permission for entry. It was obvious she had pulled many strings almost overnight.

'I knew it would rain tonight and would be a bit wild,' she explained as they approached and used the key for a door at the side of the complex. 'We can stay the night here and get going in the morning when the tide comes in. You certainly don't want to be near the corpses any longer.'

Tam carried his wet gear with him, but the Special Branch men had taken the binoculars away. He would be glad of shelter for the night. As for the disused building, it was almost a shock to come upon something that looked sparklingly clean and fresh. From its base, inside, a spiral staircase rose towards the redundant lamp at the top. But no ordinary staircase. Its bright elegance, with surrounding walls of subtly-hued pastel colours, and the contrasting rich brown steps leading upwards, reflected the clear impression, gained from its castellations outside, that whoever had built this had offered the

369

accidental impression that this small isle was a kind of colonial possession. Tam felt dwarfed by it all.

'It's like a staircase to the heavens,' Frankie said, his voice hushed in respect.

'There's a door here,' Jilly said, disregarding the sense of awe Tam and Frankie were displaying, and pushing her way through it. They passed through a long, wide hall.

'In the past this entire building could house a couple of families with ease,' Andrej went on, having clearly done his local homework, and been in there before. 'This was the living room.'

'Make yourselves comfortable,' Jilly said.

Tam was now bothered about that plan which Andrej had first outlined for them. Stages two and three, as he had stated, whatever they were, now seemed still-born. He was cornered. All right to talk about having faith. But at that moment he could see no way out of the impasse. Andrej though seemed surprisingly jaunty and spoke first.

'So, Jilly Grierson, who do you work for? Spill it out. Frankly.'

'I think Tam and Frankie should go back to the staircase,' she replied. 'We have things to talk over.'

'They stay here. They saved my life. They are up to their necks in this, and now is not the time to shut them out. So let me repeat. Whom do you represent?'

'People who want you to work for the values you cherish, and who will provide the means by which you can continue your work, and in circumstances which will enable you to live an extremely comfortable life,' she replied a bit pompously. 'They will be in Anstruther soon, tomorrow at the latest, and will be able to put you beyond anyone else's reach.'

'I value choice. So do I have any choice in the matter?'

'You will have the choice of lab, or assistants, or finance, or any kind of resource you deem necessary. Isn't that what any scientist would want?'

'People built atomic bombs under these same circumstances and came to regret it. Who are these people?'

'You will meet them.'

He chuckled.

'You know, Jilly, I knew exactly what would happen over the last couple of days. I knew you would come. That didn't bother me. However I didn't take into account your two former colleagues from the boat. They caught us unawares. That was the only blind spot. Tragically. I will always blame myself for that lapse.'

'More than you were fooled. They were freelance. Working for us, as we supposed. And we all believed we were singing off the same hymn sheet, until they made a stupid mistake with an e-mail. There were big bucks being offered. It had to be bucks. They wouldn't have accepted yuans.'

'Ah,' he said. 'Them. The Chinese plunder the web. I know that. I'd like to see the Great Wall of China, but on my own terms. Perhaps I should thank you for closing that off.'

'I'd guess where you are likely to end up, you'll be into hot-dogs and burgers and cokes and Haagen Dazs and watchin' baseball on the telly, eh Jilly?' Frankie asked, as if his proposition was beyond dispute.

'Actually, Scotland is a nice place to live in. Grass isn't always greener on that other side, as they say,' she replied.

She was never going to admit anything of any significance, Tam knew. But she couldn't be allowed to get off scot-free. He got philosophical.

'Is lying a part of your business or is it just in your nature? Or do you have to go to classes for it?' he asked.

She was genuinely taken aback by that.

'Where I've had to work, nothing is sacred. Alas, not even the truth.'

With that she turned towards the door, then, as if she had remembered something, turned back to them.

'My Special Branch colleagues tell me they hope to get a helicopter in here at first light to get Hank and Gregory and the corpses off. The rest of us will follow by boat when the tide turns. I would recommend you all get some rest. And, lads,' she said pointedly addressing Tam and Frankie, her voice lowered like somebody about to tell you something intimate, 'I have something of interest to tell you. At least I hope it will be. I did some investigation into that MacPhail lady, the psychic. Apparently, she was secretary of a spiritualist organisation that holds biennial meetings. Two years ago they met in St Andrews. They apparently did the whole tourist bit, with special interest on those who have shuffled off the mortal coil. That group even claim there is a likeness of Patrick Hamilton's profile etched on one of the college walls that strangely appeared after his execution. Can you believe? So she was no stranger to the place. She knew about the PH. Does that help in any way?'

She didn't wait for a reply, but swivelled and was gone.

Tam and Frankie looked at each other wondering which of them was the more gratified on hearing that.

'Told you. A fraud, if ever there was one!' Frankie said with undisguised pleasure. 'And to think she had me holding a conversation with my cat.'

'She helped, though,' Tam admitted, 'in her own strange way. She wanted to leave us dangling. Not say too much, just enough to be mystified by her so-called powers. It's technique. Part of the act. I suppose psychics need that just to keep the pretence going.'

For a brief moment Andrej seemed to be a bystander.

'Something is distracting you,' he said.

'No,' Tam answered emphatically. 'It's just something we've settled between us. Forget it. I just want to know what it's been like for you being chased, hunted.'

'Lonely,' Andrej said, then paused, as if he knew he wasn't sure if they would understand what he meant. 'My mission is to serve science for the good of us all. That is why I am here on the Isle of May. It has its very specific purpose. But I need my phone. It is in the boat, tucked away in a safe spot just waiting to be put into operation. It is the only computer I need to complete my work.'

'The second and third parts?' Frankie asked.

'Precisely,' he replied. 'If you want to warn people about the potential dangers they face, the best way to do so is to give them a rude awakening.'

'And your phone is as important as all that?'

'It is the fulcrum of a whole network of support for what I am doing. Listen, I grew up in a small village in Belarus. I used to watch old women gossiping together. They could comfort themselves with their chat, but I know they could also spread poison and turn people against each other. It seemed to be their role in life. Computers are like that. They talk to one another. They chatter just like the old women. And like them they can be harmless, but they can also spread poison, in the shape of confusion, chaos, not to say disaster. When I touch a computer and bring it to life I am looking at my village street and hearing whisperings of the old women. So people got interested in me because I demonstrated, in great detail, how Estonia could have avoided the cyber attack on their institutions in 2007 which almost brought the country to its knees. I was working to perfect algorithms to build firewalls around any country's defences. But there has to be a warning.'

'What kind of warning?' Tam asked.

'You will see, hopefully. Nothing is absolutely certain, although we are confident we can make an impression on the complacency of the authorities. But I need the boat and I need my phone. Or perhaps you are now tired of all this uncertainty. I could hardly blame you.'

'Uncertain? Us? How could you think such a thing?' Tam said facetiously.

'Come with me,' Andrej answered. They followed him out of the room and entered the entrance hall with the spiral staircase inviting them upwards. He led the way. The climb was like turning inside a large canister which made them almost dizzy. There was a small door at the top which Andrej approached with such confidence that he must have been there before, not surprisingly. When they passed through that they were out in the open, on a balustrade that suggested the battlements of a castle. The huge glass lamp-case loomed above them. The Isle of May was now spread out at their feet. The inspiring spectacle of a small island contained within a vast besieging sea, the audacity of its cliffs taking on the elements, the wild life using it as a home, or a resting place, only brought to mind Andrej's belief that nothing was now permanent in the global crisis of climate change. Could this island be another inevitable victim of the advance of the seas?

There was still plenty of light, although the sun had succumbed to the clouds. But the indentations and the twisted contours of inlets and cliffs were still clearly discernable. They could see the two landing jetties on either side of the island, with the boats now stranded by the low tide. There was much movement round the figures near the *Marmion*. He could make out Jilly in deep conversation with Alex. Oh, how he would like to be eavesdropping that one. No love lost between two folk who were supposed to be on the same side. Or were they? Then he noticed right below them, near the front entrance, one of the Special Branch men, smoking a cigarette and leaning against the wall as if he was on sentry duty and pissed-off to boot.

'We're twenty-four metres up here,' Andrej said. 'The cliffs down there are double that height. Now, look over towards the end of the cliffs. They call that Pilgrims Haven. That's where the cameras are. They're solar powered and connected to the mainland at North Berwick by dishes, and transmitting pictures every day, live into the internet. A godsend for bird lovers....... and for me. By mid-morning I must have my boat near that same cove.'

He left that last comment dangling as if he awaited a response from one of them but Tam found it so odd, just like the comment back in the lab when he mentioned ' leaving this world', that he let it be.

'Excuse me,' the voice said. It was one of the officers, his face peering through the small door. 'Would you come with me, Mr Matskevich?'

Andrej smiled at them.

'I will see you later, I hope.'

They watched from the top as he was escorted downhill towards the first of three squat buildings which lay in a hollow beside what looked like a small sea-loch, reflecting the darkening clouds overhead. The two figures disappeared into the middle of the three.

'Stages two and three,' Tam muttered, watching the elegant and dignified figure walking as if he were taking his constitutional. 'I suppose he meant what he said about that. Trouble is you can listen to folk talking about UFOs and they sound believable at times. Is his mind the same? Is he hoodwinkin' himself? That would be the worse bloody outcome of all.'

Undeniably that impression was beginning to infiltrate into Tam's mind. He felt Andrej was certainly a decent man. But a fantasy is a fantasy no matter how well you get on with folk. No. He tried to nudge that thought out of the way. He was a scientist above all else. Superstition was out. He knew for Andrej it was the moment for hard facts.

'Do our people do torture?' Frankie asked.

Sinister though it looked, Tam could not bring himself to entertain the notion.

'I think they might want to interrogate, that's all.'

'Do you trust anybody in this business?' Frankie asked.

'Mrs MacPhail,' he said trying to lighten the conversation.

'Don't even start on that again.'

'Some of the things Andrej says, ring a bell with me. Just that.'

'Cameras? A godsend for him? Doesn't add up.'

'I'd like to have a look at these cameras. In fact that's just what I'm going to do. By the way, these two bampots Gregory and Hank called us Shrek and Homer.'

'Which one of us was Homer?'

'It's a toss-up. So how do Shrek and Homer get out of this? That guy below is not going to wave us through, is he? He's there to keep an eye on us, not just Andrej, knowing Alex.'

'There are lotsa windows on the level just below this,' Frankie pointed out. 'The ones at the side would be the best bet. We could maybe get out that way. I know it's high up, but I'm willing to have a go. You know, I think birds have the best of this world.'

***

They spiralled down to the second level, then opened a door into an entirely empty room with a large window looking out over another balcony. It was shut and latched securely, but they released that and it opened easily. They climbed through and looked down from behind a turret, which faced away from the island, towards the Fife Coast. They didn't admit it to each other, until afterwards, but this began to look like an abyss to them. It was impossible to tell how high it was. Below them was a grassed courtyard. Beyond that there was a wall and what looked like steep incline just outside it. From there they could turn any direction without the 'guard' seeing them. There was no other option. Tam jumped, his eyes on the ground below, which sped up until, almost involuntarily, he fell forward into a roll, which seemed to soak in much of the impact. He almost felt a sense of exhilaration in that achievement. Frankie, however, let out a small, stifled moan as he landed, then rolled over on his back, one leg in the air. He kept his oath muffled, although it was genuine enough, then gamely got to his feet quickly and started to limp towards the wall of the large courtyard they had entered. The crossing of the wall was easy, and they eased themselves down the next incline gently to keep the noise to a minimum. Frankie was still cursing under his breath and limping heavily as they moved away behind the lighthouse, unseen from the other side. Tam knew from his assessment of the island's contours that if they kept away from Fairhaven, where the *Marmion* was, it would be impossible for the man outside to see them. Frankie led the way to the Altarstones landing where the Special Branch's long, orange-coloured outboard motor-boat was lying. It was covered entirely with a matching orange tarpaulin. Then they kept close to that side of the island and although Frankie was limping badly they made good progress until they came to the cliffs. Slight vertigo was what Tam felt when he ventured a look downwards to the sea, breaking against the base in long, persistent waves. Frankie was sitting on the grass, shoe and stocking off, nursing his ankle.

'Fuck! It's swelling up already,' he informed.

Tam walked along the edge, then towards Pilgrims Cove, which emerged as the cliffs tailed away slightly, then looked down into an enticing, tiny pebble and rock shore. There were two cameras there. One mounted on a pole attached into a rock; the other lower down and close to the beach on a bracket fitted to another rock. And, even as he scrutinised them, he could see a movement as if somebody was focussing on him. When he moved from one to the other, the higher one turned and followed him. It was uncanny. He felt like waving at the lens, like a football supporter might, when he spots himself on the giant screen at a ground. But the mood passed quickly, as he thought of why on earth Andrej seemed to be fascinated by them. When he returned, Frankie had got to his feet and was walking gingerly around testing himself.

'It'll be a few days before I can bash these old feet about,' he said.

Tam ignored that. Sympathy seemed inappropriate.

'We're not goin' back to the lighthouse,' he intimated. 'We'll spend the night somewhere else. I want to keep out of the way of these people until we can come up with somethin' to help Andrej.'

'Is that so?' Frankie replied. 'And where do you suggest we go? It's goin' to rain heavily tonight according to Jilly and you can expect them all to pile into the lighthouse. Haven't you had enough soakins?'

'We're not going back. There might be a cave someplace. An island like this must have a cave somewhere.'

'With a spider in it telling us to try, try and try again, no doubt. Come on! That's a fairytale. Think again. And if we don't appear up there, they'll be searching all over for us.'

The word 'search' promoted a thought.

'Where's the last place they would look?'

'Amongst the seals?'

'No. Their own boat. It's possible it wouldn't occur to them. I'd bet on it. It's covered with that tarpaulin. We could get under that. And if they have that accommodation in the lighthouse, they won't be going near Altarstones in the rain. '

'I like that,' Frankie said. 'Their own boat. How about that?'

They did not immediately go directly to the jetty but waited until the light was failing, then, gingerly moved towards Altarstones. They could see a light in one of the rooms in the lighthouse and the twinkling lights of the Lothian coast, stretching all the way down towards Edinburgh; other than that the darkness was intensifying. They could barely see in front of them, but Frankie knew exactly what was there, and since the tide was well out, helped guide their way along the concrete path, winding all the way down to the jetty. They carefully eased themselves into the long slim boat, which was now lying high and dry. There being no light, they stumbled around for a bit until they were able to prise themselves under the tarpaulin which was unpleasantly cold to the touch, but, once under it, they felt both relieved and snug.

'I'm starvin',' Frankie said. 'I feel as if my throat's been cut.'

'We'll just have to stick it out. There's nothing else.'

'You know,' Frankie went on. 'I just don't get this. Why is Andrej interested in these cameras? With Wonder Woman and Special Branch all over the place, and on top of him, he's talking about cameras and having to get off his mark by tomorrow. No, I give up. I just want home now, quicker the better.'

During the night Tam thought he heard loud voices and heavy rain, and that lights were beaming near them from torches probably. But he wasn't sure. Perhaps it was his imagination, he thought, as he eventually became conscious of dawn seeping through the tarpaulin. He was feeling cramped and stiff, from lying on the ribbed bottom of the boat, as he cautiously pushed his head above the cover. The rain had stopped, although as he threw back the tarpaulin, the rainwater it had gathered, splashed over his arms. It took him several shakes to arouse Frankie. He put his finger to his lips to suggest the next few minutes would be silent.

When they climbed the ladder, and looked around, the island seemed to have been refreshed by the rain, with birds engaged in floating, spiralling, aerial ballets, that same sight of which probably had engaged the minds of the original settlers, the monks, all those centuries before. The lighthouse looked quiet but when they walked further along the coast line they could see down to the *Marmion* and four figures there, crouched and busy on the deck. No Jilly though.

'The ankle has ballooned,' Frankie complained, limping badly. They neared the cliffs. Tam could see little traffic on the sea around the island although there were tiny specks of single fishermen hauling out lobster-creels just off Anstruther. But then he was distracted by the sight of Frankie edging towards the edge of the cliff with an intent stare as if he had spotted something.

'Watch it, don't go too close. The edge might crumble,' Tam warned, although he felt the ground around was firm enough.

Frankie, clearly, was ignoring this reminder, edging even further forward. Then he lay down on his stomach and put his head firmly over the edge.

'Come and see this,' he commanded. Tam lay flat alongside him.

'See that crevice down there. I could slide down and jam myself in there. It's only about eight or so feet down.'

'You've got to be fucking joking. That's impossible.'

'Hear me out.'

'This had better be bloody good. I know you've been fascinated by the birds, but they've a wee bit of an advantage over you in these situations.'

'If I can get down there, then you can see there's really no way back up. Right?'

'So far, so logical, and so fucking mad. What gives?

'If anybody came along here they could see that I would need, well,.... rescued.'

'Get to the point.'

'This ankle is doin' me in. I'll be limpin' for the next week or so. I know that from bitter experience. And here we are hopin' to help Andrej get to his boat and get out of this place and here am I feelin' bloody useless. Maybe it was the bad ankle that made me think of somethin'. Remember what our coach keeps saying about decoy runs, about deceiving defences, about pretending to do one thing and then springing a surprise. Get them to take.......'

'....their eyes off the ball,' Tam, interrupted, echoing the coach's oft-repeated tactic.

'It's about distraction, right? Keep them looking in one direction and then before they know it they've been conned. We need them to take their eyes off the ball. We need something to distract them all. They say there's a helicopter comin' this morning. Supposin', just supposin', we could get them all interested in saving the possible future winner of *Master Chef,* from almost certain death. Are they going to keep their eyes on Andrej and the boat with me clinging on for dear life? Distraction, that's what I'm looking at down there. Unless you can come up with some other brilliant idea.'

Tam stared at the crevice which was about forty metres above the waves. The drop below was sheer, which meant that manoeuvring towards the crevice would be hazardous, but certainly not impossible. But there was no grip for a return journey. Frankie would be taking a one-way ticket.

'No fucking way,' Tam said emphatically.

'I'm down there, they all get involved, they've got to help out and that gives you the chance to get to Andrej, wherever he is, and get him on to his boat. At the moment we're outnumbered. Wonder Woman and the Special Branch are too much for us. We've got to get them to take their eyes off the ball. What else is there, tell me? Distraction. It's a possibility. Anyway, I've got a head for heights.'

These last words were lies, noble lies, Tam thought, as he doubted if Frankie had ever been higher than a second-floor landing in his flats. What he did appreciate now, was that his mate was deadly serious. He also realised that having come all this way they had reached an impasse. His presence on the Isle of May was coming to nothing. They themselves were about to become nothing more than waste produce. That thought kept his lips sealed as he tried to find words to dissuade Frankie from such a perilous venture. The words wouldn't come though. The silence was his concurrence. Although he shivered as he realised that. He had discovered from the fight in the lane until now that his body had developed a great propensity to shivering at the least turn of events.

'Agreed?' Frankie asked without turning his head and still staring at the crevice below. His mate remained silent. It was on. 'The hardest part will be gettin' Andrej to the boat. You might have to do a bit of fightin', certainly runnin'. You never know,' Frankie added.

'We'll wait,' Tam said, now committed, but nervily. 'We want to see a sign of the helicopter before we do anything. They'll all be focussed on that.'

They looked out to sea and at the sky which had lightened considerably. The sun was striving to come through thin cloud. Tam sat there with mixed feelings; the tranquillity induced by the hissing of the sea, the shrieks of birds, the murmuring of the wind alternating with his sense of dread. Of all the twists and turns of the past days this was the moment when they realised, almost finally, that they didn't really know what they had let themselves in for. It was Frankie who eventually spoke.

'There it is,' he said.

Chapter 25

It was only a speck at first but it was unmistakeably a helicopter. It was coming from the direction of Edinburgh. Low and fast. Frankie rose and stretched himself, put the sore-ankle foot gently on the ground and tested it by pressing it carefully into the turf.

'Ligaments. Won't be able to kick a ball again for about a month,' he said. 'They say bathin' an injury in salt water is great for recovery. Well, there's plenty salt water down there.'

The remark was foolhardy, of course, but what else could have been said? He walked to the edge. Tam followed and Frankie recoiled slightly.

'I know you want to help me, but don't touch. No hand asked for. Just let me go about this my own way. I can see where I'm goin'. I know what to do. As long as I keep pressin' my back into the rock-face and don't look down, that's the way. Easy. Well, maybe not that easy. Now for it.'

Tam felt his body was weakening at the sight of his mate gently sliding downwards, angling himself towards that cleft in the rock, which he now reckoned was at least ten feet below. He couldn't afford even the slightest slip. In such a situation he found himself believing that a slip would be fatal but that he had to believe it could not happen to such as Frankie. Guilt he felt, to a degree, but they were now too far committed for it to stop him in his tracks, especially as he had no idea how this whole improbable ploy would play out. The helicopter was eating up the distance, and now he could see some markings on it. It was beginning to bank towards the

Fife coast, and he imagined there would be a recognised landing area on the middle of the island. Frankie was moving as slowly as a snail on a bed of treacle, but he was getting there. The odd thing is that as soon as he had embarked on it he was already at the point of no return. There was no way anybody other than a skilled rock-climber, with the full regalia, could have got himself back up. Frankie stopped. Tam listened. He wasn't sure if he had reached the tiny crevice since his mate's body was covering that area.

'Got it,' he heard floating up to him on the breeze.

'Now, just concentrate,' Tam shouted. 'Jam yourself in. Things are going to happen and happen fast. I'm going to make sure of that.'

His mate, clinging to a cliff-face, was not an image he would pride himself on, at any time in the future. He knew that at the very least Frankie would be slammed for being a daft boy, basically unstable. Yet, he wasn't. He was a romantic. That's what he was. He had read and been taught about romantics. They were all basically daft. But how could you have progress without them, he had been told. There was no time left for mulling over that.

The helicopter had turned sharply and seemed to be heading for an area just between the lighthouse and the closed tourist office. It was Jilly he had to target. He was pinning his faith on the fact that despite the deviousness of her basic profession, she still had something of a heart underneath it all, and that even if she could have used that evil-looking Sig Sauer, as part of her trade, she still had some humanity left in her. He saw the group making its way up from the *Marmion*, with Gregory, his head lolling to one side, being almost carried up by two of the officers, and Hank, hands cuffed behind him walking slowly and arthritically, as if his knees would need replacing. Jilly and Alex were just behind. Tam ran towards her, his arms waving, so that despite the clatter the chopper was making, it would catch her attention. She was engaged in deep conversation with Alex and it wasn't until he saw the chopper making a landing just in front of the lighthouse that she became aware of the frantic figure running towards her.

'Jilly,' he screamed, above the noise. 'Frankie's in trouble on the cliff. He's in real danger. '

She cupped her hand to her ear indicating that his voice was not penetrating. He bawled again and run towards her and when he was only a few yards away, she bawled back at him.

'In the name of God,' she screamed, 'where did you two get to last night? We searched all over the island for you in the dark. We thought you had tried to swim back to Fife, or something insane like that. What were you up to?'

Alex looked at him with contempt.

'We wanted to spend a night on our own, in the open. All right? Now for God's sake will you come and help me or else Frankie is about to fall over the edge of a cliff.'

'Let him,' Alex barked. 'Jilly, we're taking these two killers back on the chopper and we've to get the corpses back up here as well. That's top priority. Those boys have got right up my nose and I'm not going to be waylaid by them. Get lost, son!'

Jilly hesitated. Then she moved.

'I'll be back', she yelled at Alex. 'Now, Tam, where exactly?'

When they reached the edge of the cliff, Tam bawled down, 'How are you?' They could see the top of Frankie's red mop. It could have been taken for a russet-coloured bird's nest if it weren't delivering delicate human sounds from underneath.

'Are you goin' to move your arses and get me up outta here!'

'How in the name of all that is holy did you get down there in the first place,' Jilly screamed at him almost indignantly.

'I got too near the edge. I slipped.'

Jilly flapped her arms in exasperation but reading the situation clearly.

'If anybody tries to get near you they might slip as well. We're bad enough as it is. We'll have to get a rope. Maybe there's one in one of the boats,' she said.

'How is he going to grab a rope if he's using both hands to grip the edge of that crevice?' Tam asked being very practical now, and not devious.

Jilly was getting even more flustered, as if this was all coming on the back of her internal feud with Alex. Even though the helicopter was making a din, in the background they could hear the birds screaming a fusillade of piercing rebukes at the humans and their utter follies.

'We'll have to confer,' she gasped and took off in the direction of the chopper.

Tam followed at a pace, but with Jilly well in front of him he saw her starting to argue with Alex and point to the cliff edge. Another two men had stepped out of the chopper and bundled the two prisoners into the hold; Gregory and Hank looking like broken men. When that was done the whole group, less the pilot, started to move towards the cliffs. Tam counted the numbers carefully. Jilly, Alex, the two from the chopper, and the other two from the original Special Branch group. That meant only one unaccounted for. Guarding Andrej, he assumed.

Alex, on seeing Frankie's precarious position, could not restrain himself.

'You fucking idiot. You bloody clueless nutcase. You brainless twat............'

'Make up your mind. Which fucking is it?' came the voice from beneath the bird's nest hair.

It was probably not the most judicious statement for Frankie to make under the circumstances,for Alex began to splutter.

'You think I'm going to waste any of my men's time on this ......this.....'

'You ARE going to spend time,' Jilly interrupted. 'This boy is in danger. Are you just going to let him drop off, into that below? Is that what you want? I would be witness to it, I can tell you.'

Tam remembered the cameras and wondered if somebody operating them remotely, over in the Scottish Bird Centre in North Berwick was getting more than they had bargained for. Indiana Jones instead of ornithology.

'I could get a rope, just in case,' Tam volunteered, realising he had to give himself an excuse to leave the group.

'It'll take more than a rope,' one of the men from the chopper said. 'We'll have to use the winch. I think that's the only way. But get a rope just in case, son.'

'I think there's one in the boat,' Tam said.

Alex was still fuming, but again Jilly was proving she had some sort of hold on him; perhaps even superiority.

'Go, son,' the man from the chopper said, before turning and making his way, with his colleague, back up the hill to where its blades were still rotating.

'We'll stay here,' Jilly said facing down Alex's attempt at stern authority, then focussing on Frankie, with genuine concern. Tam backed away from them. His first move was in the Fairhaven direction, but then he made a quick diversion, when they were all staring at the red-hair on the cliff, heading for the building he had seen Andrej disappear into. To do so he had to cross a small dam-like bridge, over the small loch there. He could see an officer standing outside the low, white building, staring at the helicopter and the activity around it. It gave him encouragement, in sensing that there was indeed some potential in the tactic of distraction. He moved to the rear of the building. No lights were on and the dusty windows suggested disuse. They were tiny. He tried two at the back, but there was no movement and they were probably jammed by ageing, if nothing else. If ever there was a time to gamble it was this. There was a brown boulder, about the size of cannonball, lying on a slope behind him. He picked it up and with no great delicacy launched it at one of the windows. It crashed through. He waited.

There was so much clatter from the helicopter that he hoped nothing had been heard by the man on the other side of the building. There was no reaction. He stood in front of the window and with another smaller stone smashed at the remnants of glass on the surrounds. Then he ran and jumped at the window, gripped the surrounding frame then levered himself forwards and downwards into a room, lit only by the window he had come through. He landed on a stone floor, which jolted and slightly winded him. Glass was strewn around, and he felt his right palm nicked by a piece. He put it to his mouth and tasted blood. But he had little time to reflect on that as his eyes were suddenly consumed by the sight of huge pieces of machinery that looked like three massive turbines and strewn all around spanners of different sizes as if this was a power-house that had been vacated at short notice for some reason. But rust tinged all the apparatus, so how long had it all lain there? It all seemed in stark contrast to nature in rampant form all around it.

He passed through it, in an uncanny silence, the sea no longer in evidence, the birds silenced, moved into a dark corridor and listened. He heard somebody humming, pleasantly, with the odd word thrown in. Words he didn't understand, but certainly identified. The door it came from had a light shining underneath. He tried the handle. It opened with surprising ease. In front of him was Andrej, cup of tea in hand, reading some notes from a sheet in front of him. He looked up at Tam with only mild surprise.

'Oh,' he said, then looked down at the paper again. 'This is an offer they are making already,' he went on, without raising his voice and lifting the paper in his hand to show Tam. At that moment he wished Andrej could summon up at least a smidgeon of urgency. 'Good of them to put it on paper. Somebody once said, I believe, that a verbal contract is not worth the paper it's written on. You get that?'

Tam didn't. There was no time to get a grip of much at the moment, with only flight in mind.

'I think we might be able to get to the *Marmion* if we can slip the man at the front,' he said.

Andrej put down the paper.

'You think?'

'They are all round the cliffs and the helicopter. If we can get out the back, I'm sure we can slip round to the jetty.'

'You're sure?'

'No. I'm not sure. But I don't think you want to just sit here, do you?'

'Of course not. Which is an opportune time to give them my answer to their proposition and hope that you are right.'

At that he stood, and with a great flourish of contempt, ripped up the piece of paper in his hands into shreds which fluttered helplessly to the floor. Tam led the way back to the disused, rusted turbine room which as he passed through reminded again him that only nature was permanent.

When he went through the window he firstly checked that the officer at the front was still engrossed in activities further up the island, and then waved Andrej on. They were in a gulley, which provided them protection from a sighting from the cliffs. They skirted round the last of the three buildings and made for the rocks on the beach, well below the sight of the officer. The helicopter was taking off again, as they made their way directly towards the shore. Tam kept his eyes on it as he led the way along the rocks. They kept close to the beach again, hidden by the dip in the ground. But when they got closer to the boat, Tam realised his count of people had been wrong. There was somebody on the *Marmion* after all.

The figure was bent over the fertiliser bags at the bow. The only explanation was that he had not seen someone else coming out of the helicopter. And indeed this man seemed to be wearing a helmet, with a visor over his face. This was no bird-lover come to indulge in this paradise. This was bomb-squad. He was encased in suit that probably doubled his actual bulk.

Tam stopped behind the wall near the boat and both of them crouched.

'What's going on there?' he asked Andrej bluntly.

'Oh, I think they are doing the obvious and checking things out. But, if I can get down there, they are not likely to influence events anyway,' Andrej replied.

'What events?'

' I think if he is expert, as I am sure he is, he won't take too long to figure out what we intend.

'What do you intend?'

'Something I can't quite explain. I am sorry.'

Tam was feeling quite weak now.

'What am I doing here?' he asked, mainly of himself, but got his reply whether he wanted it or not.

'Following your instinct. You have not really put a foot wrong in all you have done for me. I'm being perfectly honest with you about it now. Is honesty to be an obstacle between us? I need to get on the boat and go. I have timings to keep to.'

'Sorry,' Tam replied. 'I can't take this in any longer I'm crouched behind a wall looking at a boat that could be just a massive bomb. I missed my five-a-sides and a needle chess-game with my hottest rival because of you. Can I sacrifice any more than that, I ask myself? '

'You are perfectly entitled to alert them to me, if you so wish. I would not obstruct you in any way. But it has to be one thing or the other, don't you think? Go ahead. Now's your chance. You can hand me over. You deserve the right to choose.'

There was little breathing space left in such a tight situation like this. But Andrej's openness could not be pushed aside easily. He thought for a moment the fairest thing would be to leave him now to his own devices, but that thought died a death quickly, for one over-riding reason.

'You know what kept me goin' on all this time? Curiosity,' he whispered. 'Pure and simple. And curiosity killed the cat, so they say.'

'But cats have nine lives....... so they say,' Andrej replied quickly. 'Curiosity is also what makes a great scientist. And I think you have the makings of one.'

'I'll have to start counting the lives I'm using,' Tam replied, not entirely convinced he was doing the right thing. Above them he could hear the helicopter revving again, and saw it rising high above the cliffs, with the hatch door clearly open and two men staring down, as at a target.

'We have to get that man off the boat,' Andrej said.

'Stay here,' Tam replied.

He moved to the other side of the dyke and started to run. It was a sprint this time. He had to make himself breathless by the time he reached the jetty. His lungs were screeching when he set foot on it and made for the boat. The man rose and turned towards him as he panted up to the bow.

'Alex sent me,' he gasped. 'I think he's your gaffer, isn't he? They found a package up at the side of the lighthouse. He thinks they want to blow it up and that that is what they've been here for all along. He thinks this is just a decoy. They've had to move the helicopter because of that. You can see it now getting out of the way. He says you've to get your arse up there as fast as you can. You know what he's like.'

'Why did he send you?' the large figure swathed in padding that made him look like a grizzly bear. He had slid up his visor.

'Have you had a look at your mates lately? I would be quicker than any of them.'

'Why not the mobile?' the man persisted.

'Couldn't get a signal. You've got to move I was told.'

He did at last, but with the reluctance of someone who was technically engrossed in an interesting challenge. He lumbered off the boat, and slowly made his way up hill, like he had the weight of the world on his shoulders. It was when he was clear of the dyke that Andrej moved. He bounded from the jetty on to the boat like a mountain goat and then came to a sudden halt as he looked at the back deck. The two bodies of the two Men in Black were there, with some scrappy material covering their faces, obviously in preparation for the return journey by helicopter. Tam, suddenly made aware of them, felt a queer emotion that he didn't quite grasp. These were the men who had started his involvement in this whole whirl of events, and somehow he felt this strange bond with them. It was as if he owed them a kind of gratitude, for having turned his ordinary life upside down and opened a vista onto a strange world. Andrej went below and came back quickly with the phone in his hand.

'My computer,' he said almost in triumph. 'Now to get this boat started,' Andrej said. 'And for you to get back to the others.'

'This is part two?'

Andrej nodded as he climbed into the cockpit.

'Part two.'

'Where are you heading?' Tam asked.

'Not far.'

'You said a funny thing to us back in St Andrews . You said you were taking your leave of this world? What was that about?'

'What it says. We can do that in all sorts of ways. My work has to be seen to be finished by others, all those chasing after me. The hunt for me will be over soon. Believe me when I say that although things did not go quite to plan, it is an added benefit having them all on the island at this moment, as witnesses. Soon I will be left alone in what they will think is perpetual darkness. That will be the third stage.'

Standing there in the wind, with the aromas of the sea in his nostrils and the sounds of the island providing a chaotic but natural background, these last words felt to Tam like he had just heard a benediction delivered to him in a strange language that was beyond his immediate understanding. The *Marmion* was about to move off shrouded again in a mystery. Andrej stepped to the edge and grabbed Tam's hand, shaking it with real warmth.

'You know it was Mrs Rybak who wanted the boat to be called the *Marmion*. Maybe because of her days dealing with the nasty and shady world of spying; lines from that poem she would quote over and over to me in the times I knew her. *Oh, what a tangled web we weave/ When first we practise to deceive.* You could hardly argue with that now, could you? Thank you.'

Then Andrej stepped back to the controls and started the engine.

Chapter 26

Frankie kept his eye focussed on the distant Bass Rock. That large carbuncle on the Firth was his spirit level. If he kept it firmly in his sight, without budging his head; it meant he had stability. If it moved, in any way, and the Rock started to shoot upwards in his vision, it would mean he was on his way down. Not desirable. So he looked neither up nor down, but kept his neck stiff, to a degree which almost balanced the pain he was feeling at the other extremity, in his ankle. At least he didn't feel cold. Fear? Yes. First step towards insanity? Very probably. Faith in others? Receding. He tried to keep his mind a blank but found his imagination was a stubborn sprite, conjuring up all kinds of ways he would hit the rocks below. He had wedged himself into the crevice and felt secure to a degree, so long as there was not much movement. He was also glad of the information that Andrej had given him, that had they been there in the spring, the birds would have ganged up on him, and he wouldn't have survived their defence of their nesting territory on the face of the cliffs. Then he heard the enormous clatter of the chopper.

When the winching began and one of the officers came down to establish the safety harness and grabbed him in a less than amorous embrace, Frankie muttered in his ear, in a fit of relief and gratitude, and tried to lighten the situation by using a line from his disco patter, 'Do you come here often?' The man, replied with a short word which his mother would not liked to have heard. Then upwards they swung. Frankie was swept away in another sense, by the view, of one area in particular. Underneath him, he could see the *Marmion* slipping out of the inlet and then churning up the water as it headed out to sea with Andrej clearly at the helm. But then he noticed there was a scatter of people beneath him. The Special Branch officers had sighted this as well and were rushing towards their own boat at Altarstones. Frankie felt his feet gently touching the grass, but the sense of relief was marred by the sight of Jilly waiting for him. Wonder Woman was now a raging bull.

***

As soon as the *Marmion* had edged out of the jetty, Tam turned to see how much progress the grizzly bear had made going up the hill, so that he could make himself scarce to avoid the man's wrath, when inevitably he would discover he had been deceived. Instead he saw a figure with binoculars standing on a ridge waving frantically to others. They had been spotted. Tam turned to the sea again. The *Marmion* was making good progress, but he couldn't be sure what speed it could attain and where exactly Andrej was taking it. He assumed the Special Branch boat would be fast. And they had the helicopter. He started to run again, straight up the hill towards the middle of the island where he saw the chopper lowering a twosome to the ground from a cabled harness. Alex was leading a charge towards his boat obviously, accompanied by the rest of his squad. Jilly was there, her arms folded ominously, and staring at Frankie, as he stepped out of the harness, like he was about to spread bubonic plague. Tam slowed down to a casual walk, as if nothing was amiss and strolled towards them.

'What's the fuss?' he asked as the chopper was settling down again and Frankie's saviour was hauling himself back into it. She replied, saying something, then bawling at Frankie, her arms semaphoring livid anger, her voice drowned in the welter of noise coming from the blades as it took off again, banking away across their heads, obviously having been alerted to what had occurred at the inlet. It was in pursuit. When the noise abated she came across towards him.

'Nice one, eh?' she said. 'You have a future in this business. That's certainly one for the book. As soon as I heard you were down seeing Andrej off, I knew we'd been fooled. I fell for it hook, line and sinker. '

'Put it in your CV. It'll show you're a normal human bein',' Tam replied, still desperate to see the best of Jilly emerging.

'Waste of time, really,' she replied. 'He won't get away. And now it makes it even worse for him when they get him. And as for you two, you might be clapped in irons now. Alex, as you have gathered, isn't one of nature's gentlemen and thinks they should bring back hanging for ignoring Twenty's Plenty. So there might not be much I can do for you after that game you've just played. I can promise you they are in no mood to mess about. Andrej has no chance. I'm returning to the lighthouse. We'll watch the capture from up there.'

She made off and offered no objections as they trooped after her, covering the ground quickly with Frankie limping gamely behind them. They did see the grizzly bear making his way down back towards the jetty at Fairhaven again, probably wishing to strangle the lad who had told him about an unidentified object. The lighthouse guard had left and was probably on the orange boat with the others. When they finally climbed to the top turret, beside the huge lamp, they could see the *Marmion* had made good progress in the general direction of the open waters of the North Sea. But, curiously, it had slowed down and looked as if it was stalling for some reason. There was a vivid orange slash across the waters as the Special Branch sped outwards in that direction from the Altarstones inlet.

The *Marmion* had now turned in a long arc and was pointing at a spot roughly between Pilgrim's Cove and the sheer cliffs. Then, it came to a complete halt, way out, in line directly to the island, almost like a bull pawing the ground before the charge to the sword. It was static. Then they saw it revving again, churning the water as it headed back.

'Looks like he's giving in,' she said almost smugly.

Not a chance, Tam thought, although this move did seem odd. The two boats, although they were still far apart, were bound to meet if they stayed on track. The *Marmion* kept coming, making no concession whatever to the increasing presence of the orange boat. Above them the chopper was keeping a discreet height above the *Marmion*, occasionally banking over, as if to inspect it.

'What's he doing?' Jilly asked as the two boats appeared to be only yards from each other. The orange boat tried to cut across its path. But there was no flinching. The *Marmion* kept ploughing towards Pilgrim's Cove, bouncing up and down as if the engine was at maximum drive. The orange boat was now trying to manoeuvre alongside it. They could not see into the cockpit because Andrej had drawn the protective covers to avoid a drenching. They heard a shot. It was a warning. It came from the orange boat. The helicopter increased its height. The cliffs were looming. The *Marmion* was making no detour. If anything it seemed to be picking up speed. Tam could sense Jilly tensing up beside him.

'Merciful God,' she uttered. 'He's insane. What's he got in mind?'

'The cameras, that's what he has in mind,' Tam muttered although he wasn't sure if Jilly heard him or not.

The *Marmion* hit the first series of rocks just to the side of Pilgrims Cove and seemed to leap in the air like a salmon heading for the spawning grounds. As its bow jutted into the air and smashed against the succeeding massive pillars of rocks, they saw, firstly, a billowing of red, orange and white clouds, bursting out of that bay, like a small volcanic eruption; then, after a few seconds, felt the reverberations; the displaced air swelling and exerting an invisible muscle with a fury that seemed intent on sweeping them off the balcony. The lighthouse shook as the delayed sound smote their ears, making them stagger, their faces bearing the brunt of a feeling that a blow torch had been applied to them. The flames and smoke rose, billowing outwards, and buffeted by the wind it was not long before they there was an acrid stench in their nostrils. The chopper had backed off. The orange boat had held its position about fifty yards from the shore but was bouncing up and down, buffeted by the chain reaction of waves, slapping firstly against the cliff, then rebounding seawards. The burning was continuing and it was difficult to see through the density of smoke which was rising in torrents of black, and spilling out over the sea. Birds were swooping frantically and screaming.

He turned to Jilly. She was ashen. She seemed steady enough, but there was a bewildered expression on her face. Frankie, holding his nose, spoke.

'Poor bugger. Why?'

Jilly left them there, gently easing herself through the door and back to the stairs, like someone with a hangover.

'He seemed a level-headed bloke,' Frankie went on. 'He didn't give the impression he would do somethin' like that. I thought he was up for the fight. And all that talk about plannin' everything carefully. I feel sick.'

Tam was not suffering that way. He was more entwined in a puzzle. Why, with such a violent and vivid explosion rocking him to the core, almost feeling as if his eyes had been irremediably scarred, did he keep feeling that he had not witnessed a finale yet?

Chapter 27

They saw the first pictures of the explosion on the television news programme at six o'clock that same evening in a tiny hotel lounge in Anstruther. The newsreader spoke over the explosive scenes of the *Marmion* crashing into the rocks, and attributed the pictures to the cameras installed for bird lovers on the island. It had gone out on the Internet, around the world, it reported. It could have been watched live anywhere on the globe. Tam, sitting with his large coffee, watching Frankie demolishing a full Scottish breakfast, including black-puddings the size of cartwheels, despite the evening hour, took no satisfaction in having had a deluxe grandstand view of it all. It is not something he would ever want to boast about. He had developed a strange uneasiness about what he had seen. Perhaps it was the sense of injustice about it all that had swept over him like the blast waves from the explosion. And with it had come a queer sensation of having been left in the lurch at Andrej's incomplete explanation of the three stages of the operation. What was the whole story? It bothered him.

In the news report they did not give out any details about who might have been aboard the boat, except to say that the police would be giving a press conference the following morning. Although, in explaining the power of the explosives, which apparently had been used, they did mention the gruesome information that body parts had been found in various spots on the Isle of May. What they did not say, and what he had seen with his own eyes, was the sight of some scavenging birds, fighting each other for what was certainly not

405

worms. Some of the Special Branch had to intervene strongly to stop it; Alex being a very humane sort, of course. The Isle of May had fallen into the possession of a small army of different officials, flown in by another couple of helicopters. These included some military uniforms and men with brief cases. After a couple of hours Tam and Frankie were allowed to go near Pilgrims Cove. Another launch had towed away the deserted *Marigold*. All they could see were some small pieces, fragments of whatever was left of the *Marmion*. You might have thought that it hadn't existed in the first place, although the power of the explosives accounted for that. Small fragments of wood were still smouldering, even hours later.

They had been taken back to the mainland in another police launch. To avoid the invasion of the press and television cameras which had assembled at Anstruther harbour, they dropped them off at the tiny mediaeval harbour of Cellardyke, where the *Abigail* had been berthed, only a couple of miles away. Then an unmarked car, with the clear intention of keeping them entirely anonymous, took them to their hotel. That suited both of them. For Tam felt they were now inductees into the exclusive world of treachery, deception, connivance and the chameleon-like existence of the under-cover agent. Thus, anonymity would conspire to strengthen that feeling. Tam even felt a slight tug of the emotions when he saw an empty Lexus car being taken away by a breakdown lorry.

As he looked around the crowded lounge, he could see how absorbed the locals were, and indeed heard some of them claiming that they had seen, heard and felt the explosion in the harbour from five miles away. Maybe myth was edging into the event already. He got the feeling that this ogling meant that the locals were getting some kind of kick out of it, that in its tragic and bizarre way it was putting the area on the map; that in the age of the internet you were not worth a damn if nobody took any notice of you, of what you did, and where you lived. Or how you displayed your bum.

Alex, bristling with urgent authority, had been so immersed in the investigation that he had virtually ignored them, although they felt their comeuppance might still only be delayed. Jilly had made arrangements for them to stay that night in a small harbour-side hotel.

'Do you think the government is paying for this,' Frankie asked, munching and looking around at the comforting cosiness of the place. 'Or the CIA?'

'Just think of the money spent on Trident and eat up,' Tam said, echoing his father. He had no appetite left himself. They were waiting for Jilly to appear. She was now the fulcrum of what was left to do. And what was left to do was to make it possible to return home to family with assurances that the Special Branch would be sent packing and get off their backs; that family would be kept in the dark and they would feel no sense of loss in not being able to boast about the historical charm of St Andrews or the walking on the sacred turf of a famous golf course which had a sin-bin. They would learn nothing. Gabby and Sammy would know where they had been, that was certain. So they would have to treat Jilly cautiously about giving them any backup if that were required. Tam had tried to keep an eye on her for that reason. She had been busy herself, mostly on the phone. It had been welded to her ear as she stomped about the grounds around the lighthouse, alternating between fulminating and sweet-talking. But then, that was her down to a T, he supposed. She parted with them after making sure they had found their lodgings. She had meetings to attend she said. The usual brush-off he felt, when, several hours later, she still had not come to talk to them.

Both of their phones were going off at regular intervals. About YouTube. Frankie did most of the communication though.

'Over a million and a half hits on You Tube now,' Frankie informed him as they stepped outside and walked towards the harbour for better reception, since the hotel owner had admitted that phoning from certain parts of the town was harder than it had taken ET to phone home. Also, the lounge in the hotel had become crowded, with the only topic of conversation the explosion on the island. It was getting too hot for them and they didn't want to hear another word spoken about the Isle of May. They had needed air. Outside there was still a queue at that fish-shop, making Tam wonder if there really were that much fish left in the sea. They wandered down to the harbour's edge and sat on one of the benches overlooking the marina.

'What kind of people does that make us, having our bums watched by millions, now that you come to think of it?' Tam asked sourly. 'Are we any better for it? Or are we just suckers for the voyeurs?'

'What's eatin' you, my old mate?' Frankie replied, and seeing himself in the role of stress counsellor. 'What gives? I know it was frightening to watch a guy we met, and liked, ending up in a blazin' inferno, not countin' the other two poor fellas. But what can we do about it? What's done is done. You'll get over it.'

Tam looked across the water to the Lothian coast at the lights where the Torness power station stood. Night was closing in. They sat there silent, their own batteries run down. Out there, on this moonless night, the Isle of May had been swallowed up in the darkness. There were occasional blinks from one of the lighthouses to alert the world it had not moved though. There was no wind for the first time that day. Then, as he continued to look across to Torness, the clarification took place.

One moment there was nothing but ceaseless uncertainty hanging over him, then there was clarity. It was rational. That's what it was. It was the constant and unavoidable images running though his mind on that last day which now formed an inescapable logic. Not a Eureka moment. More like the gentle satisfaction of bending over a maths paper and solving a problem. But it was not without a degree of exhilaration. Because he knew exactly what was going to happen next. Stage Three.

'There was a full sub-aqua outfit on the *Marmion*,' he said abruptly to Frankie.

'So?'

'If he was making the kind of trip that he had in mind, if he was going to end up on the rocks blown into bits, why did he have that on board?'

'Sub-aqua gear on a boat a surprise? Are you kiddin' me? Now a parachute, that might puzzle you. So get real.'

'No. It was something he brought with him. I saw the bag. He'd packed it. Why?'

'Maybe he thought he'd do a bit of diving off the island just to pass the time.'

'You really think that he was out there to pass the time? No. And think of that phone of his. He kept telling us that it computed a lot for him. Why would he be concerned about that if he was going to snuff it?'

'What is this adding up to?'

'Andrej's part three.'

'Part three? Are you jokin'? He's gone, up in smoke. His phone with him. Even the smartest phone in the world couldn't survive that kind of blast.'

'Maybe it wasn't in the blast.'

Frankie was about to say something but stopped short, confounded, trying to work out Tam's inner meaning. When he had, he shook his head.

'No. Impossible. We saw it with our own eyes. We watched the chase. We saw the line it took. It was deliberate.'

'Of course it was deliberate! Cannae argue with that. Do you remember when it turned towards the island and seemed stalled?

That was before the helicopter got near it. And the orange boat was still a distance away at that stage. Could he have gone overboard, in the sub-aqua gear and given everybody the slip?'

'My take on that is, no. He was a martyr,' Frankie said. 'Just like Patrick Hamilton. He must have known he was going to end up the same way. That's why he wanted to visit the PH spot. Buggered about in his own land, chased around the continent. Enough is enough. Martyrdom, that's what he was after all the time.'

'Or to make people think he had martyred himself,' Tam said, thinking of Mrs Rybak and the lines from the poem *Marmion* that had been quoted to him about deception. 'It was all deliberate. He even knew the cameras would be trained on the cove. Without any question he would have had a helper on the cameras at the time at the bird centre, that Igor man probably, just to make sure that they weren't trained on some other part of the island. Remember they can swivel 360 degrees. It was all timed. He kept using the word timing. It went global.'

'I don't buy into that,' Frankie replied. 'How could the boat have driven itself into the rocks?'

'He was an expert sailor. He knew his boat and how to control it even if he wasn't steering. They can have autopilot on these boats. He set the course and let it rip. He'd organised it to control the speed. All that makes sense.'

'There's no way that could have happened. Stage three was just made up to keep us goin'. And why would he want to pull a stunt like that anyway?'

411

'To get all the bampots off his back for good and just get on with his life and work. His identity was gone but he wasn't. He saw it as freedom.'

'I see it as shite.'

'That disc you looked at of Andrej. What was he doing again?' Tam asked.

'Talkin'. In that language of his. How was I supposed to make anything of it?'

'Yes, but you said he did something else.'

'Oh, that. I think he must have been playin' games. He stood at the side of this lab he was in and just kept turnin' on and off the lights at the switch. Except he wasn't laughin'. I didn't get it. It looked kind of childish to me.'

'He was lecturin'. Or maybe warnin'? But what about? Lights? There's a thought. Mrs Rybak gave him the go-ahead for something he had planned way ahead. Recall the mention of eleven being the hour? Was that a time?'

'She had lost her marbles,' Frankie said snorting. 'All these stupid word games and having codes and all that palaver. Leave her out.'

'Stage three is next.'

'Where? How? I don't get it.'

Before Frankie could add to that, the sound of brakes and a coming to rest of a vehicle just behind them made them turn away from the harbour's edge. It was a police car. Jilly emerged from it. She had obviously freshened herself up. The ashen look had gone and the dabs of make-up and the dynamic blonde pony tail gave her a rejuvenation that almost took Tam's breath away.

'Well?' she said. 'Got your feet back on terra firma then?'

The car turned away from them and sped off. She was obviously joining them. Tam was not sure if he was in the mood for any interrogation, but she launched into sympathy.

'This has all been horrible, disastrous, sad, tragic. You name it,' she said. 'Andrej was a well-meaning man and a brilliant scientist. His nagging obsession was with cyber terrorism of course. He had come up with computer techniques and accompanying software which apparently was ground-breaking. He made the mistake of demonstrating the potential to too many people and the word got around, and especially since he was a fugitive from his own country, he was apparently up for grabs. They were all after him, including us.'

'Langley?' Frankie asked drily.

'Not that again,' she replied, putting her hand to her forehead like the subject gave her a headache.

'Go on,' Frankie interrupted. 'Tell us. You must make a fortune out o' them.'

'Frankie, please, stick to the kitchen. We knew he was planning something or other,' she went on, 'and we worried about Torness when we heard about what he had stacked the boat with. But we can't understand why he would want to lay down that red herring. What we couldn't have bargained for is that he would use it against

413

himself. He chose oblivion rather than live out the rest of his life as an exile or a scientific prisoner. I find that all tragic.'

'And Torness is still there,' Tam fed her, feeling now, overwhelmingly, that it was not a red herring. Torness Nuclear Power Station was the target after all. A different kind of target. Something none of them had imagined. Specially not Jilly. Or did she? How could he tell now what she really knew? Was she genuine in blandly accepting the outcome?

'The plant is invulnerable, I'll have you know. And we had two frigates out there patrolling, just in case. Now, as for you two I've had discussions with Alex who is a bit of a bampot, as you would say. If you keep your noses clean for the next year or so nobody will know anything about any of your involvement, especially contriving a cliff-rescue, for which you could have been for the high-jump...... if Frankie can forgive that expression.'

The light from a nearby street lamp was revealing her as relaxed, like a girl ready for a bit of dancing. She looked in party mood. A trial was over for her.

'You know something, that poor little island over there was violated by us humans,' she said. 'The best thing to conclude is that it will still be there long after we've gone. For the birds, for the....'

She stopped. There was an acute silence. She put her hand to her lips. She was just looking, squinting in some surprise.

'Odd,' she said. 'Over there behind you. Look, the lights have all gone out. Isn't that all so unusual. I can't see the Torness lights. Everything is black.'

They turned slowly and looked into the inky darkness of the Firth of Forth where seconds ago they had seen necklaces of light adorning the Lothian coast, all the way down towards the Bass Rock and Edinburgh. Now it was a black sheet. Then, with that same suddenness, every light in the harbour and around Anstruther town, spread out in front of them, went out. Sudden darkness can be as stunning as an explosion, as they were now experiencing. Jilly was merely a suggested presence now. They could barely be assured either of them was still there.

'My God,' Tam muttered to himself. 'He made it. He's turned them off.'

Up on that black sheet in front of him, Tam was drawing mental pictures. The sub-aqua suit, the stalled boat, the valued phone, computers chattering to each other like old women, the lecture in the lab with the light-switch, the co-ordination he stressed, his expertise, the end of pursuit, and freedom. Frankie was looking at the luminous dial of his watch.

'Four minutes past eleven,' he said quietly. Then there was a long pause before the two words came that sounded to Tam like an acclamation.

'Stage three,' Frankie said, in soft assent.

'Not bad for a man who's parted with the world,' Tam whispered back.

He felt Frankie's hand reaching out to touch his arm and then gripping him with a handshake that was confirmation that all doubts had flown.

'Hey, you two still there?' Jilly's voice came at them. 'This is spooky. It certainly is one big power-cut. And in summer. Anyway I can't see a damn thing in front of me. I hope you two gentlemen can be gallant enough to escort me back to the hotel. I don't want to fall into the damned harbour.'

They moved forward until she was able to grip both their arms. She hooked hers through theirs. Tam took great satisfaction that Jilly Grierson, broadcaster, spook, quick-change artist, Wonder Woman, call her what they may, was now under their command, as they walked into the darkness, and like in so many previous days, did not really know where they were heading.

***

It was two days later, when they had returned to Glasgow in an unmarked police car, that Gabby read out to him a statement printed in full in the *Herald* newspaper and apparently sent throughout the internet. It came from a group calling itself *The Marmions,* claiming credit for the biggest power failure ever in Scotland which had affected large swathes of the east coast. Gabby read it in a voice which was very proper, like he was investing it with the gravitas it warranted.

'It was our intention to demonstrate the appalling laxity of the authorities in their handling of potential cyber attack. By the installation of software, secretly injected into their computer systems, and with the use of a flood of other computers, a single smart phone was all that was required to co-ordinate this attack on that part of the National Grid in and around and beyond Torness. It confused the domestic interface of computing and sent the wrong signals to sub-stations. The resultant breakdown of power produced the black-out. Keeping to our plan it lasted only thirty minutes. We make no apology for any inconvenience. A full explanation of the system we used has been sent out to various parties. This must create a new awareness of continuing threats and the absolute necessity to build defences, firewalls which ought to be set up to protect our infrastructures. We are a wake-up group. That is the first step. We will now campaign to shock and alert others throughout the world while at the same time looking at potential solutions. Computers must not talk to each other with forked tongues.'

Gabby looked over the edge of the newspaper at Tam.

'Can a computer have a forked tongue?' he asked wryly.

'They can chatter like old women, somebody told me not so long ago. Spreading poison.'

'Talking about chattering, what's happened to Jilly?' Gabby asked.

'Gone. She left us in St. Andrews. Took a photograph of us standing with PH at our feet, for her own record she said. A bus load of tourists came pouring out of this bus to go into the college grounds. They were pushin' and shovin' like they got a prize for snapping the first photo. Well, we got all mixed up with them. When we had untangled ourselves she had gone. Just disappeared. Again.

Couldn't see her anywhere. We searched up and down the streets, then gave up.'

'Maybe she couldn't face saying the farewells,' Gabby replied charitably. 'Clearly she has emotions.'

'I had just asked her if she would miss Andrej, having known him so long and pursued him so much? Never got that reply and I'm left wonderin' why not? Could it have been too near the bone? Could it be she didn't want to tell me any more lies? Could she have outsmarted everybody? Jesus! What I'm I sayin'?'

'You'll never know, will you?' Gabby said with an annoyingly knowing look on his face.

'I think my imagination is playin' tricks with me. Anyway, I don't think we'll be hearin' her advice to the public on dog-shit any time soon.'

Tam was determined to say no more. He preferred to retain the memory of that walk in the dark back to the hotel when she had clung to his arm like her life depended on it. He had hoped she had bruised it, as an impromptu tattoo reminding him of their strange encounter and of his own elusive feelings about her. But in the light of day there was just his familiar arm with familiar veins and nothing else. She had left no trace and that made it seem like she had just vanished through that door in the lane again to her own wonderland.

He did admit to his family that the fishmonger had taken them to Fife out of the goodness of his heart and they had accepted Tam's explanation of wanting to see the university there with the prospect of his applying soon for admission. That appealed to them. An acquaintance of the fishmonger had put them up, he said. It fitted neatly. Jilly would have admired his dissimulating aplomb now, his apprenticeship well and truly having been served.

He hadn't needed to spell details out to Gabby who probably knew a great deal, through the Sammy-Special Branch grapevine. But not everything, not the real conclusion. Only two people knew that. And they were two of Gabby's best customers. To everyone else a man had gone to his death in a terrible boat accident on that little spot called the Isle of May, just off the Fife coast. There would be no mention of Frankie and him ever having set foot on it. Frankie was bound by that.

'By the way,' Tam said. 'Where is Frankie? He was supposed to meet me here.'

'You missed him by half an hour. He tells me was very taken aback by the greeting he got from your sister, Sarah. She embraced him with great enthusiasm. A big hug and kiss. He hadn't expected that. And he learned that Brad Pitt is in town. They're making a movie in the city, converting the centre of Glasgow into the middle of Philadelphia. They're casting for extras. He's gone in to see about it. It's about an invasion of zombies and the fight against them. He says he could make a strong bid because he knows at firsthand how the CIA operates. He wouldn't tell me how. And, in any case, he claims he's an expert in zombies since he's done studies of how people behave with their Ipod earplugs in. He thinks he might be type-cast either way.'

Tam left, wondering if Brad Pitt knew that he was probably going to get a script consultant as well, if Frankie was taken on. He made his way to the Duchess's and deliberately chose to walk down the ill-fated lane. It reverberated with memories. But he could not afford to linger. He had to put himself on competitive edge, heading for the showdown, his mind concentrating on *Bishop to Knight 3*.

The Duchess had recovered from the bronchitis. The word had come that she was now fully fit and had astonishingly endorsed Sarah's desire to join the army, which made Tam feel like he had won the lottery. He entered her flat with the key he always kept. He hung his Barca jacket up dutifully in the hall. It hadn't shrunk much, but Tam could still smell the Isle of May on it. He walked into the living room where she was sitting at the chessboard, waiting patiently. He kissed her on the forehead.

'Good to see you,' he said, although she remained silent.

The positions of the pieces were exactly as they had been left those many days before, seared into his mind. He made his move.

Bishop to Knight 3

She paused for only a second before reaching out and taking his bishop with a castle.

'Checkmate,' she said.

E N D.

A Subtle Sadness by **Sandy Jamieson** is a rigorous exploration of Scottish Identity and the impact on it of the key Scottish obsessions of politics, football, religion, sex and alcohol. It deserves to be read by everyone seeking to understand the Scottish character.

A Subtle Sadness focuses on the family and personal history of Frank Hunter, a sad Scotsman with a self-destruct streak enormous even by normal West of Scotland male standards. Frank Hunter is a product of Scotland's unique contribution to mixed marriage, with a Protestant father and Catholic mother. A man of considerable talents, in both football and politics, he brings a peculiarly Scottish approach to the application of those talents.

A Subtle Sadness is the story of a 100 year fight for Scottish Home Rule, from 1890 to 1990,

A Subtle Sadness is also the story of the emotional and political impact of Scotland's quest for the World Cup, with 5 consecutive qualifications in the crucial years from 1973 to 1989 covered by the book.

A Subtle Sadness covers a century of Scottish social, political and football highlights, with disasters and triumphs aplenty, culminating in Glasgow's emergence in 1990 as European City of Culture.

A Subtle Sadness is also a reflection on sadness, depression and mental health as affected by that Scottish identity and those key obsessions. And a searing scrutiny of the Scottish male capacity for self-destruction. Illustrating that capacity to the full, Frank Hunter's story is a memorable and haunting one.

A Subtle Sadness can be purchased in any of the following ways.

From the Ringwood website www.ringwoodpublishing.com for £9.99 excluding p&p, or ordered by post or e-mail for the same price. All copies signed by the author.

From www.amazon.co.uk either from Ringwood(a signed copy) or from Amazon (unsigned copy).From any good bookstore or online bookseller

The e-book version is available for £7.20 from the Kindle Book Store or Amazon.co.uk

Calling Cards by **Gordon Johnston** is a fresh and exciting addition to the ranks of Tartan Noir. It is a novel exploration of the impact of stress and trauma on individuals, encompassing their resort to addiction, recovery, and denial. It highlights the influence of the equally corrupting desires for success or revenge. Linking the small Scottish worlds of journalism and politics, it has been favourably compared to State of Play in its creation of an intricate network of linked strands, as it builds to a compelling climax that leaves many people changed forever.

"An anonymous email leads West End Journalist Frank Gallen on a quest to unravel the links between a campaign against a housing development proposal in Kelvingrove Park; personal and political corruption at the highest level in Glasgow City Council; and the increasingly frenzied activities of a Glasgow serial killer.

Gallen and DI Adam Ralston engage in a desperate chase to identify the serial killer from the clues he is sending them, in time to stop him from implementing the climax of his campaign of killing."

"Calling Cards is a fascinating examination of people under stress. Extremely well-written in a fluid style very easy to read, it is both the story of an increasingly desperate hunt for a Glasgow serial killer, and an examination of how people cope under intense pressure. It marks the arrival of a new and very welcome addition, Gordon Johnston, to the ranks of distinguished Scottish crime writers."

"Calling Cards is a psychological thriller worthy of a place in the top rank. It is well-written, and easy to read with a fast flowing style."

Calling Cards can be purchased in any of the following ways.

From the Ringwood website   www.ringwoodpublishing.com for £9.99 excluding p&p, or ordered by post or e-mail for the same price. All copies signed by the author.

From www.amazon.co.uk either from Ringwood(a signed copy) or from Amazon (unsigned copy).From any good bookstore or online bookseller.

The e-book version is available for £7.20 from the Kindle Book Store or Amazon.co.uk

Torn Edges by Brian McHugh is a riveting mystery story linking modern day Glasgow with 1920's Ireland.

When a gold coin very similar to a family heirloom is found at the scene of a Glasgow murder, a search is begun that takes the McKenna family, assisted by their Librarian friend Liam, through their own family history right back to the tumultuous days of the Irish Civil War. The search is greatly helped by the discovery of an old family photograph of their Great-Uncle Pat in a soldier's uniform.

The McKennas quickly realise that despite their pride in their Irish origins they know remarkably little about this particular period of recent Irish history. With Liam's expert help, they soon learn that many more Irishman were killed, murdered, assassinated or hung during the very short Civil War than in the much longer and better known War of Independence. And they learn that gruesome atrocities were committed by both sides, atrocities in which the evidence begins to suggest their own relatives might have been involved. Parallel to this unravelling of the family involvement of this period, Torn Edges author Brian McHugh has interwoven the remarkable story of the actual participation of two of the McKenna family, Charlie and Pat, across both sides of the conflict in the desperate days of 1922 Ireland.

"Torn Edges is both entertaining and well-written, and will be of considerable interest to all in both Scottish and Irish communities, many of whom will realise that their knowledge and understanding of events in Ireland in 1922 has been woefully incomplete. Torn Edges will also appeal more widely to all who appreciate a good story well told."

TORN EDGES can be purchased on www.ringwoodpublishing.com for £9.99 excluding p&p or ordered by post or e-mail. It is also available online from Amazon.co.uk and from all good booksellers.

The e-book version is available for £4.99 from the Kindle Book Store or Amazon.co.uk.

Paradise Road by **Stephen O'Donnell** is the story of Kevin McGarry a young man from the West of Scotland, who as a youngster was one of the most talented footballers of his generation in Scotland. Through a combination of injury and disillusionment, Kevin is forced to abandon any thoughts of playing the game he loves, professionally. Instead he settles for following his favourite team, Glasgow Celtic, as a spectator, while at the same time resignedly and with a characteristically wry Scottish sense of humour, trying to eke out a living as a joiner.

It is a story of hopes and dreams, idealism and disillusionment, of growth in the face of adversity and disappointment. Paradise Road examines some of the major themes affecting football today, such as the power and role of the media, standards in the Scottish game and the sectarianism which pervades not only football in Glasgow but also the wider community. More than simply a novel about football or football fandom, the book offers a portrait of the character and experiences of a section of the Irish Catholic community of the West of Scotland, and considers the role of young working-class men in our modern, post-industrial society.

The road Kevin travels towards self discovery, fulfilment and maturity leads him to Prague, enabling a more detached view of the Scotland that formed him and the Europe that beckons him.

"Written in a thoughtful, provocative yet engaging style, Paradise Road is a book that will enthral, challenge and reward in equal measure. It will be a powerful addition to the growing debate on some of the key issues facing contemporary Scotland"

Paradise Road can be purchased on www.ringwoodpublishing.com for £9.99 excluding p&p, or ordered by post or e-mail for the same price. It is also available online from Amazon.co.uk and from all good booksellers.

The e-book version is available for £4.99 from the Kindle Book Store or Amazon.co.uk

School Daze by **Elaine McGeachy** is a hugely enjoyable romp through the social, sexual and professional dilemmas facing three recently qualified young teachers as they try to cope with the increased stresses in the modern day education world."

Caitlyn, Jamie and Jennifer all share an infectious enthusiasm for and deep love of their chosen profession. Qualifying on the same course, then based in the same Glasgow Secondary School, they work hard at becoming good teachers. Facing temptations including a highly attractive male pupil, a charismatic Head Teacher and a tall, dark and handsome mysterious stranger, they try to steer an acceptable course between their professional responsibilities and their desire for a fulfilling social life.

With great sensitivity and a refreshing absence of sensationalism, **School Daze** tackles the vexed issue of why smart, attractive young teachers risk reputation and career by romantic involvement with pupils.

"The dazzling tale that is **School Daze** will be loved by all young teachers, and by all those ever taught by a young teacher who wondered what passions might lie behind the prim face properly presented in the classroom. It is ideal school holiday reading material for both groups, highly recommended."

School Daze can be purchased in any of the following ways.
 From the Ringwood website www.ringwoodpublishing.com for £9.99 excluding p&p, or ordered by post or e-mail for the same price. All copies signed by the author.
From www.amazon.co.uk either from Ringwood (a signed copy) or from Amazon (unsigned copy).From any good bookstore or online bookseller
The e-book version is available for £7.20 from the Kindle Book Store or Amazon.co.uk